DEEPER, OLDER, DARKER

P. J. Richards

To Neil, Robin, Miranda and Rosalind,
all the magic I will ever need,
all my wishes granted.
Thank you.

Proudly published by Snowbooks Ltd
ISBN 978-1-913525-16-3

Illustrations by P. J. Richards
Typeset by Emma Barnes in LaTeX

British Library Cataloguing in Publication Data.
A catalogue record for this book is available from the British Library.

DEEPER, OLDER, DARKER

P. J. Richards

snowbooks

Chapter One

Inter canem et lupum – between dog and wolf.

The abandoned church of St Agnes was held in the pause of twilight. It sat in silence, locked with rust, its broken windows brimming with glass tears for the congregation of graves.

Peter Oldfield: archivist, botanist, and First of Ninestones, watched the topmost branches of an ancient yew tree steal the last golden benedictions of sunset from the church. He jotted observations in a notebook already crammed with sketches and citations, seemingly self-assured, just an academic on a field-trip – but question marks curled behind all of his theories.

Peter sighed, tucked the book into his jacket, and shook out his cramped writing hand. He wanted to pace the pathways to help him think, but had to contain his nervous energy for the sake of secrecy. He scrutinised the tumbled boundary walls and the thorns that formed a ragged hedge over them; the ranks of graves nestled in spindly oxeye daisies or swathed in ivy; the wooden gate hanging off its hinges, and the track leading through the grass to the rutted lane he'd trudged to reach the chapel. This was the terrain of his currently shrunken world and he knew it off by heart.

As Peter ticked off the list of unchanging details, he took recompense for his vigilance from the graveyard itself. He found it fascinating and frustrating, like a book of half-told tales with the most intriguing pages defaced or missing, and it was testing his talent to a degree he'd never experienced before. The only fact Peter felt sure of anymore was that he needed more time – and the irony of that notion wasn't lost on him, as he watched the sunset through more than two thousand years' worth of yew branches, twined into a net of wood and shadow.

Time was so abundant here it lost its linear nature and hung suspended in the air with the dust motes and dandelion seeds. Peter could see beyond the peaceful facade, though, and instead perceived the scene as a freeze-frame in a duel. The evidence was all around him. A damaged bough, crippled by the axes of the faithful long ago, had grown back high and hooked, to score its tally through the church's ridge in obsessive red lines; another had gouged one of the windows to reach inside, and lay snarled in lead, ring-barked by the stone mullions.

Peter wouldn't live long enough to witness the outcome of this battle, but he knew the wounds inflicted by the yew would be fatal for the church if it remained derelict. Without worshippers it had lost its heart. Its oak skeleton was sagging, its roof tiles crumbling like old grey teeth, and the walls were blistered by frost damage where winter stalked the building each year, taking bites where it could.

The yew had staked its claim to Hatiston's holy ground long before the church was built to usurp it, but its demotion was coming to an end. The tree had spent years throwing down buttress branches, advancing in century steps, and soon its sapper roots would undermine the foundations of its rival.

For a breath or two the scent of crushed grass and warm bark was overlaid with frankincense, as if the church had heaved a sigh. Peter was transported to a childhood memory of splintered colours on a stone floor, of singing, yawning, and staring at a petrified medieval knight lying on a tomb, its praying fingers snapped off, a loyal curly-coated dog frozen at its chainmailed feet.

A surge of nostalgia bore Peter down. He reflected how half his own life was probably already gone, and that all the preceding, and possible years to come, would be easily measured in the rings of the thin staves sprouting from the ground-sweeping boughs of the yew. He touched his fingertips to its red bark, seeking reassurance, reaching for the soul of the tree, but it was unresponsive, cold as rock, and a small doubt grew seed-like in the pit of his stomach. He took his hand away and brushed it off – he couldn't allow himself to see omens in everything, the plan was portentous enough.

Peter turned his face up to the deepening sky. A contrail drawn by the soundless silver arrowhead of a plane was being cut and shuffled by high unfelt winds, and he wished he possessed the talent to read the stark modern runes before they dispersed. He imagined the scream of the engines, the howl of the air as it was ripped apart by blades of fuselage, and the empathy it invoked worried him.

He leaned against the tree, needing something solid and protective at his back. He had been forbidden to bring his longbow and was missing its reassurance. Instead he filled his empty hand with his notebook and thumbed through its densely written pages.

Scrabbling talons on the church roof made him flinch and look up. A crow announced the death of the sun in its stony voice, and flapped away.

A Dog and a Wolf are in this place.

The excerpts of alchemical allegory copied into his book were stalking him, repeatedly catching his eye amongst the other paragraphs and diagrams, rising into his consciousness like lyrics to a song he couldn't shake. They kept triggering the primal part of his mind into seeing the headstones as prowling animals, but it was too risky to use the brash light of his phone to lay the ghosts. It was becoming too dark to read, and hard to concentrate on anything other than the lines of cryptic alchemy. Peter gave up trying, tucked his pen under the elastic around the notebook, put them in his pocket, and faced towards the oncoming night in the constant arms of the yew.

The West affords a Dog familiar to Man.

A wren shuttled back and forth, chasing moths through the weft of branches until it sensed his gaze and flew away. He shifted his feet. The ground was too full.

Pressure from the crowded earth had tumbled most of the graves, casting them like runestones, though any knowledge that might have been divined from them was long gone. Lichens fanned over their inscriptions; the condensed breath of time, tracing then eroding all the dates, deeds, beloveds and promises of resurrection. The air ate memories as the earth consumed bodies – yet a dark consolation grew beneath.

Folklore claimed that churchyard yews would stretch a root to the mouth of each corpse, making a hidden green-man of every buried body. Their essence would be drawn in with the sap. The tree would remember them.

And yews, he knew, were practically immortal.

A most fierce Wolf comes from the East.

An unnatural stillness was settling with the dusk. One by one the songbirds fell silent. Then, breezes suggesting movement of more than just air began to fret around the graves, tousling the nettles and ivy and bringing an intermittent, distinct reek of sulphur. Peter willed himself invisible, unreadable, cold as the mottled stones. He lowered his head so that his eyes couldn't be seen, and observed the progress of the disturbance from under half-closed lids.

The shreds of sky between the yew twigs darkened, distilling the last light into the glitter and paradigms of stars. Ahead, the full moon was rising from the thorns, eclipsed and blood red.

The Dog may appear with the form or kind of a Wolf.

Currents of air moved along the wall of the church, rattling the doors, leaping up at the windows, until the yew branch that had smashed one of the gothic frames offered a way in.

The smallest of sounds came from inside the building: the click of falling plaster, the scuttle of dry leaves snatched by draughts – easy enough to dismiss – but Peter knew what paced the nave, and he stayed hidden, thankful it was distracted for a time.

Though it has become Tame through the many generations.

Focussing too much on what was manifesting risked drawing its attention; he needed a diversion of his own. He dug into his coat's deepest pocket and pulled out a roll of photocopies and filter-papers. Reading the text was impossible, so he sorted through them until he found the bold black print of a 17th century woodcut, showing in primitive perspective, the church and yew of Saint Agnes. In the centre of the picture, surrounded by figures wielding spears and nets, was a wolf. Despite the naive style of the art it was easy to see the savagery of what it depicted. The animal was being pinned down by men with leering, gargoyle faces that were far more disturbing than the exaggerated ferocity of their enemy.

The scene was static and cartoonish, but the mute agony of the wolf twisted from the lines, the torture all too vivid, as it was cut open and flayed alive.

The hunger and voracity of the Wolf is known to be very great.

The instructions that Peter followed were ambiguous, deliberately so he assumed, but ignorance helped to mitigate his guilt, part of him even welcomed the danger as a form of penance – as the price of lying to his company. He considered how he was going to break it to them: the ends justifying the means would certainly not be enough.

As his thoughts wandered, the woodcut illustration seemed to lose its form, becoming claw marks torn through the page. Alarmed, he realised the picture was too evocative, so quickly swapped it for the filter-papers. Their undertone was more refined, harmonising with the alchemy. He concentrated on the grey and brown stalagmite patterns on the pages, tidemarks left by metallic solutions seeping into the paper then drawn towards the influence of their affiliated planets. It was an arcane and beautiful method of tracking conjunctions – art for science's sake – and had a resonance that was positive yet undefined. He held the sheets like a flick-book and watched the formations melting to mud, over and over, becoming part of the process and hiding himself in their dissolution.

When his prey is wanting he will feed even upon the earth.

Back when Peter had first sifted through the parish records for testimonies, it became evident that the accounts had been rewritten many times, with crucial information edited out. But he had persisted with his research, becoming more absorbed – and more secretive – as the weeks grew into months, until finally, he was able to see though the layers of folklore to the generative event.

With a start, Peter noticed how the breeze chasing around the outside of the church was converging on the yew. Isolated branches were being struck by the wind, one after another – a methodical hunt moving down from the canopy, each blow bringing down a whirl of needle-leaves. He slowly backed himself against the massive tree, slid the papers into his coat, and closed down, reflecting the texture, colour and cold of the bark.

As soon as they meet, they fall upon one another.

The rising moon was emerging from the shadow of the Earth as a disc of hammered silver, and in conjunction Mars and Saturn shone like red and white gems in the black branches of the yew, seemingly close enough for Peter to pluck them and hold up before his dazzled eyes.

With a smile, he felt that he truly understood his part in the alignment. Despite his forebodings he believed what had been promised – finally trusted his role as the catalyst.

They are full of jealousy, fury, rage and madness.

The questing wind died away. The graveyard held its breath.

On the furthest side of the yew from Peter, under its branches and within a ring of collapsed graves, a hollow in the ground began to glow. At first it was on the very edge of visibility, only clarifying when Peter altered his line of sight a fraction to the side. But as he peered, leaning forward, anxious not to lose its location, it flared into a lion's mane of emerald light, casting a spiked crown of shadows.

The unexpected beauty captivated him.

A gust of wind snatched and spun the weathervane on the tower, and whined through the louvres of the belfry windows. The bell tolled softly, once.

The chime broke Peter's thrall. He emerged from cover and ran for the light, ducking under the low branches of the yew, tripping over broken graves; hoping the noise he was making would be lost in the seashore hiss of the rising wind in the leaves. He reached it without falling, dropped to his knees before the light – then faltered, repelled.

Precious seconds slipped through his fingers.

The glare gave his hands a deathly pallor: the skin seeming taut and thin, the bones showing through, revealing the cadaver he would become. Peter shoved the fear of his own death aside and reached into the light, but it shrank from his touch and began to dwindle. He chased it to its source, frantically ripping grass and cords of ivy away from the shimmering earth; bracing himself in anticipation of a violent recognition. To his surprise, the radiance itself gave off no hint of its origin: no heat, cold, or pain.

He had at least expected pain.

Peter pulled a blunt trowel from his belt – an archaeologist's weapon – its blade worn from use. He held it high in both fists like a dagger, and stabbed down into what was left of the light, then started digging with a rhythm as rapid as his heartbeat. Flicked dirt blew into his eyes, he blinked and rubbed his sleeve impatiently across them, lines of cold sweat ran down his back like the stroking of dead fingers.

The wisps grew fainter and shorter until only a smear of luminous green lined the rough hole – still Peter hacked into the ground, while the wind pounded him from above and blasted around the flanks of the yew.

His arm jarred painfully as the trowel struck a hard surface. Recognition shot through him and he shuddered. Forcing his hands into the soil he felt for the edges of the stone, and leaned all his weight into working it free from the packed earth.

The resistance broke suddenly with the pungent scent of riven wood.

He hesitated.

One will kill the other.

The stories spoke of a trap set within the roots of the yew. Told how a monster attacking the parish had been tricked into swallowing a stone, how that weight in its belly condemned it to lie forever ensnared by the guardian tree. Over time the tale had lost its place to the fresher fable of the Hatiston wolf, but Peter had found both legends entangled in their death throes, and dragged them apart.

Only one relic of the original battle remained: on a wooden rood screen, carved when the church was new but the story already past living memory, was a panel depicting the first creature in age-blackened oak, flanked by demons and cut over with precautionary crosses.

And here, under his clenched hands, lay the literal manifestation of that legend.

Peter knew he reserved the choice to press the earth back into place and leave, this duty was to be undertaken willingly, or not at all. Risks and rewards accepted according to the codes of the Bowlore.

So he made his decision, and in that instant his meticulous study and cautious interpretation was reduced to crumpled paper in his pocket – there was no place left in the graveyard for condescending rationality. Peter felt completely vindicated, completely in control as he prised the stone, newborn damp, from its socket in the root.

He was neither.

And from them comes a great poison.

Immediately the wind died down, gust by gust, indrawn breaths sucked into a brooding storm's eye.

He hugged the stone to his chest in expectation.

The Wish Stone... Wisht Stowne... Wulf Stan...

With each step back in time, an insulating layer of story was sloughed off and the packaged imagery became more sharp-edged. Less fairytale, more nightmare.

For though the Dog lies prostrate, he is not yet overcome.

Peter's elation evaporated. Like the wren in the yew branches, he felt eyes upon him. He caught his breath, tried to stifle his panic. It had seen him.

He was marked.

And even in his death the Dog will overthrow his enemy.

Terror laid him open. Without his longbow he had no defence, and the shock of that calculated betrayal finally killed his lofty and aspirational trust. Left with nothing else, he held up the stone like a shield against the advancing evil – silently praying for pity.

But the wish granted was not his.

Without warning, the burden of centuries of hopeless imprisonment felled him – stone first, face down – into the grave-robbed hollow. The crumbling sides gripped his shoulders, and he sucked in soil with breaths that stretched his lungs to tearing. Granite distended his gut; a lead heart hammered his ribs. Peter fought to push against the stone, but his hands spasmed, clawing it tight to his chest.

Primal horror crushed out every thought except survival. He twisted and thrashed, gagging on grit and splinters of root that crammed his mouth, leaving no room for the air he struggled to reach. Peter screamed out the dregs of his breath into the suffocating earth – even as the wind picked up again, tugging at his hair and clothes, mocking his arched back.

A blackness pooled at the base of the ancient yew, darker than the night, unreflective of the moon, unrelated to the shapes around it. Watchful. It split into thick braided roots, questing over the ground to the place where Peter lay, and then reared up, clotting into long shaggy limbs, broad body, wide jaws, dagger teeth. Blood-red eyes opened. Ignited.

And in a sudden silent rush, it was upon him.

Chapter Two

Catrin Fitzgerald sat down on a chilly metal chair, by an outside café table encircled with cigarette butts. Without looking she used the tips of her nails to push a saucer, doubling as an ashtray, as far from her as possible; lips pursing as it juddered across the sticky tabletop.

Opposite her, David Horsman leant on the table, dew darkening the elbows of his coat. A haze of cigarette smoke marked the air around them as his. He took a long draw, then positioned the saucer back in the centre of the table.

His demeanour betrayed a confidence that he could charm his way out of trouble.

Not this time.

Catrin allowed the silence between them to build. A car drove past, close to the pavement, adding to the fumes. As she waved them away exasperatedly, David used the inadvertent break in eye contact to swap his attention to the café window, wanting a couple of seconds thinking time without her glare. 'Why do you even need my version of what happened?' He addressed his reflection, ruffling a hand through his hair. Abruptly he focussed back on her. 'I know you've placed a watch on my company.'

Catrin blinked, hating herself for the tell, then sidestepped the disclosure. 'How the hell did the thief break your claim?'

David yawned, apparently bored.

There was a moment of astonished silence.

'You didn't even put a claim on it?'

'Look, let's face it, what was the point?' He flicked ash onto the saucer. 'Only you were interested in it.'

'Really? Someone else was *interested* enough to risk stealing it! Was there any protection on it?' David shook his head and Catrin leaned across the table, her composure gone. 'You're playing me off against another company aren't you?'

'Now, what could I possibly gain from doing that? And by the way,' he pointed at the open café door, 'you might want to take it down a decibel or two?'

Undermined by the rebuke, she hissed, 'Why the hell did you arrange for us to meet *here* then?'

'You sounded like you needed a good strong cup of tea.'

David could feel the heat of her fury even without an arrow levelled at him.

They fell into a constrained silence when the café owner shuffled out to clear the table next to them; hooking mug handles onto his thick fingers and circling a wet cloth over the coffee stains. Catrin noticed the owner sneak a nod of fraternal sympathy to David, who winked in response.

She silently beseeched the cold sky, exhaling her frustration.

When they were alone again David smiled. 'Come on, it's just part of the game – don't take it so personally.'

'The game?' Catrin shook her head in disbelief and stood up, shoving her chair. It caught on a paving stone and overturned with a clatter, but anger had liberated her from her usual reserve, and she made no attempt to pick it up. 'Are you seriously expecting me to treat losing the Wolfstone as a *game*?'

'Well, I was talking about putting an outsider off the scent,' David shrugged, 'but yeah, why not?'

'Because…' Catrin struggled to keep her voice low and even. 'Because even if you don't take our pact seriously, I do. And so will everyone else when they find out what you've done.'

'Are you sure about that Catrin? Do you really think you'll get any other company to give a fuck about our deal and your little obsession?' He took a long drag on the cigarette, rubbing his forehead as if he had a headache. 'I was just doing you a favour and it didn't work out. No more, no less.'

'It's my path, *not* my obsession!' She stepped up to him and he leaned back on his chair, grinning.

'You say potato…'

She took a deep breath, then resumed an even tone. 'You owe me – and you know it – so if I can't trust you to pay your debts, I need to ensure I'm in a position to take them instead.'

David sighed resignedly. 'And?'

'As of now, the truce between our companies is over.'

He didn't react.

Catrin stifled her need for a reply, and marched away.

David watched her to the far end of the road before she was swallowed by the street's morning bustle.

She didn't look back.

With a yawn he turned to face the window, intending to confront any stares: the couple of glances he did catch quickly dropped away. The owner had his back to the door, and the handful of customers concentrated their attention on their food and phones. It would take more than an argument – even one laced with strange references – to pierce the armour of routine. Satisfied, he hauled himself from his chair, righted Catrin's, balanced his roll-up on the saucer, strolled into the café and up to the counter. 'Just the one tea, thanks.'

The owner smirked as he fetched a mug. 'Reckon you're out of your league there, mate.'

David's casual manner dissolved. 'Wrong, *mate*. She's out of hers.'

He turned from the startled man, made for the door and slammed it behind him.

Outside, the cool air sobered his mood, he knew he was overreacting and quickly closed himself down to maintain anonymity. He picked up his cigarette from the table, sucked the taste from it, threw it down, and took out his tin to roll another. He started walking.

The truth – which he had been denying even to himself – was that he felt humiliated by the misstep with the Wolfstone. He had never allowed his confidence to degenerate into complacency before, and now it had wrecked the truce with Silbury. Keeping such a prominent company on-side using talismans he didn't want had been convenient and profitable, plus their affiliation leant an air of legitimacy to his less reputable dealings – but he had thrown it all away. *Time to change tactics.*

Attempting to win back Catrin's trust would be a waste of effort; even she had her limits. The path of least resistance would be to take it in his stride and move on, but his curiosity had been provoked. Whoever had considered the seemingly unremarkable and folksy find worth the risk of stealing, had also managed to remain under the radar, and that took skill. If Catrin presumed he was behind the plot, all well and good, but the fact that he wasn't infuriated him.

Evidently the stone was valuable after all, and the effort of tracking down the thief would pay off, in one form or another. At least it wouldn't look so defeatist when he told his company what had happened at Hatiston. An excuse for a raid would soften the blow. He resolved to recover the talisman, claim it, and then offer the Wolfstone to the highest bidder.

Or get Catrin Fitzgerald, First of Silbury Hill, to beg him for it.

§

Catrin walked off the worst of her anger and neutralised her expression before she headed into work. The last thing she needed was a concerned interrogation from any of the regulars at the shop.

She reached the door a few minutes late after grabbing a coffee on the way – she couldn't stomach tea with David's jibe still ringing in her head – but luckily only one customer was waiting to get in, and it wasn't anyone she knew. Catrin smiled apologetically without making eye contact, fumbled the key into the lock, shoved the heavy door open, flipped the sign to open, then sought refuge behind the counter where she set her cup down and busied herself with the till. It seemed to do the trick, the man gave a cursory glance at the shelves of bric-a-brac, and then went to browse a bookcase of paperbacks at the far end of the room.

Catrin switched on the electric bar heater beside her chair, and took off her coat. There was a to-do list on the counter, written in purple biro; a stream of consciousness babble that Catrin skim read. Less than a quarter of it was needed, and the rest would inevitably be superseded by the next missive slipped into her hand along with her pay, when Winifred (*never Winnie, I'm not a bear)* popped in at the end of the week. But three crates of jumble, fresh from the local auction, needed sorting, and since it was the least taxing – and most distracting – chore available, Catrin set to, willing herself into the working day.

She stacked willow-pattern plates according to age, watercolours by skill, frame and subject, glassware by condition; dropping the rejects into a recycling box. And then her hand touched a small silver spoon amongst the tarnished cutlery and crumpled yellowed newspaper.

Recognition.

Catrin looked up. The man was still slouched over the books, thumbing through the scuffed orange Penguins. He didn't look ready to leave any time soon.

Fuck.

She held her hand over the spoon, careful not to touch it again. It was delicate, unlike any of the other pieces lying in the crate: its bowl crafted to resemble a scallop shell, its stem like a twisted frond of seaweed, its finial a tiny natural trident of polished red coral. It glittered like a seashore treasure at the bottom of a rock pool.

Catrin felt for the silver bracelet around her wrist. Found a charm in the form of a wolf's head .

Get out.

The man shifted his weight from one foot to the other.

Get.

Out!

He raised his head from the book he was reading as if he'd heard something.

Catrin envisaged a shadow falling over the bookshelf, the ink from the printed words spreading, soaking the pages like black blood, oozing through the paper onto the man's hands, over his skin–

There was a small thump as the book hit the floor. Before Catrin had straightened up from where she was crouched by the crates, the shop door was swinging and the customer had gone. She let go of the wolf.

Light. Light. Light: a warm summer breeze blowing the blackness away, lifting the protection. She went over to the door and closed it. The silver spoon drew her back. She went down on one knee to stroke the smooth metal. Winced.

It was so full of salt tears. Made and given as a final gift, it had never touched warm lips or stirred sweetness into a drink. It was a talisman of drowning sorrow. Catrin sighed, and then with a frown she scooped it up along with the mundane knives and forks, sugar-tongs and jam-spoons, and tipped them all, chinking, into a basket labelled £2 for 5. It would disappear under the waves of oblivion again.

Some things shouldn't be raised.

The taint of its misery lingered, fuelling her regret. She shifted the second crate, glanced over its muddled contents but couldn't motivate herself to go through it. Instead Catrin settled on her chair behind the counter, taking sips of cold coffee whilst she replayed the encounter with David, adding all the things she wished she'd said.

The illusion of control gained from finally cutting the ties with David's company was evaporating. Disgusted at her own naivety, Catrin realised that she would certainly still be losing out to him in some form: there was no such thing as a clean break in the Bowlore.

During their uneasy alliance David had used his undeniable talent to find wolf-related artefacts, and initially she was grateful for anything, regardless of its quality. But then it became obvious that David, anticipating the end of that honeymoon period, had been deliberately keeping back finds she couldn't resist, ensuring that any disillusionment with their bargain would be countered by her craving for what he had to offer.

And just over a week ago, he had promised her the Wolfstone.

Catrin's subsequent research had revealed that it was more often called the Wish Stone, an incongruously cosy-sounding corruption of 'wisht': the old English word for uncanny. Yet in the short time she had been aware of its existence, it had filled her with unaccustomed hope.

She was well aware of her susceptibility to wolf talismans, and that her Silbury companions saw it as a dangerous weakness. But she refused to curb her passion, sustained by the knowledge that everything within the Bowlore was defined and ruled by intuition.

She finished her coffee and threw the cardboard cup in the bin. Another customer walked in; one she knew by sight but not name, requiring only a cursory greeting before Catrin could get back to sorting stock – and creating consoling scenarios in which the crisis of the Wolfstone wasn't insurmountable.

She knew the identity of the thieves would be exposed soon enough, and that getting the Wolfstone back from whichever company it was – even if it was another Fort – would still be better than being beholden to David. Regardless of the outcome with the stone, she had been presented with a legitimate reason to end the truce without her company having to back down. A significant advantage within a culture that preyed on vulnerability.

Abruptly, a pair of Victorian cranberry-glass vases; an ironically dog-eared dictionary of cat breeds; a pottery cottage, and an onyx ashtray were pushed across the counter towards Catrin. She straightened up with a smile, served the customer, watched them leave, then returned to introspection.

Something David had mentioned kept niggling: that there might be a related find, affiliation unknown, something that he might be willing to deliver along with the Wolfstone – at a price of course. At the time she'd dismissed the offer as an enhancement to draw her into the deal, but if it turned out to be more than just bait, it could potentially be used to locate the stone, or be vital to any restoration.

Chasing after two finds would split her focus, but there was no choice. Real or not, claimed or not – she needed to plot a way to take it as well as the Wolfstone. Since the end of their truce had effectively shut the door on any form of bloodless negotiation, there was only one manoeuvre left. Challenge Badbury Rings.

Catrin's phone rang, startling her from her reverie. She fished it from her bag, but at the sight of the caller's identity, put it back down. It rang till the answerphone message kicked in, cut off, then started again.

With a deep sigh she relented and picked up. 'Hello, Patrick.'

'You okay to talk?' He sounded nervous.

She checked that no one was heading towards the shop door. 'What's wrong?'

'I think Badbury are going after the Wolfstone.'

Catrin fell silent.

'Did you hear me?' He waited a moment. 'Catrin?'

'I heard you.'

'What's made him suddenly want it? He didn't give a damn about it yesterday – have you spoken to him?'

'Yes.'

Patrick paused. 'So… what happened?'

'The truce is off.'

'Off! When the hell were you going to let me know?'

She ignored his question. 'When did they set out?'

'They've just left.'

'Do you know where they're headed?'

'No… wait, don't let him bait you, Catrin. Breaking the truce is the best move you could've made, don't let him draw you back in.'

'I can't let him have the Wolfstone.'

'I don't believe this!' Patrick's voice was harsh. 'It's nothing, let it go!'

'You don't understand.'

'You're right, Catrin, I *don't* understand!' His angry words faded as she took the phone away from her ear to cut the connection, but before she tapped the screen she heard: 'Christ! I *knew* I shouldn't have told you–'

Catrin turned off her mobile and laid it neatly on the counter.

She hated conflict within her company, hated arguing with Patrick most of all. He was usually her most loyal support, the one who would explain her behaviour to the rest of Silbury; healing rifts, holding everyone together. If her Second's patience had run out she must have gone too far. To her surprise even that knowledge didn't change anything.

The gauntlet had been thrown down, and she was more than willing to pick it up.

Chapter Three

The Ninestones company: Peter Oldfield, Lawrence and Jed.

The night had taken its toll on them all.

Lawrence, compelled by an unresponsive mobile and a nameless apprehension, had been on the road since midnight, initially to fetch Jed – who complained and yawned in equal measure – and then to go in search of Peter.

They had woken a handful of Peter's close friends and relatives by phone, questioned them fruitlessly, and then pacified them with the usual lies. Having exhausted all conventional options, they had resorted to dowsing a ream of maps for his possible location. Jed's hematite pendulum, drooping in sympathy with his eyelids, had abruptly tightened its orbit to point at the icon of a steeple on one of the maps.

Lawrence drove like they were being hunted.

The clouded sunrise and the headlights of the car had finally revealed the place where their First lay. He was crumpled awkwardly, face down in a scraped out hollow lined with exposed roots. Terrified, they had turned him over to find him alive – just – his clothes and gaunt face smeared with earth and sap, and the blood seeping from a multitude of scratches. Black mud drooled from his gaping mouth, and his half open eyes were flecked with dirt and blind to the sullen dawn light.

His body was as cold as the stone he still gripped.

Despite the confusion and fear, they had adhered to the codes and cleaned up the site as best they could, brushing soil back into the hole and scattering leaves to disguise it. Vigilant to the threat of snipers they had carried Peter to the car, his dead weight slung between them, before they even attempted to remove the stone from his hands. There were rumours that some companies would bait traps with the felled, gaining easy shots from unwary rescuers, and so they scanned around nervously at every crack and rustle in the trees.

Jed had loosened the arrows in the quiver slung at his hip, so they could be drawn more quickly, and had laid his longbow carefully across Peter's body as they carried him, ready to snatch it up in case they were attacked. But the churchyard had remained peaceful and vacant, haunted only by the birds, by the shadows from the church, and by the boundless memories of the yew; and they left without incident.

Now Jed was driving Lawrence's battered Land Rover along the narrow country roads, firing agitated questions over his shoulder.

'If he was shot for that stone, how come he still had it when we found him? It must've been a sniper.'

'Look, this isn't the time or the place lad.' Lawrence rubbed his eyes. 'Let's just concentrate on the matter in hand. We'll have all the explanations as soon as Peter's awake.'

'Why didn't he just tell us what he was going to do? We could've taken our bows – made sure he got away.'

'I know, but just leave it for the moment would you?' He noticed Jed's frustrated shake of the head and added,

'I'll take a look at his notebook as soon as I can. See if I can deduce anything from it.'

Jed accelerated angrily in a series of bumps and crashing gears, and Lawrence had to brace hard to stop himself and Peter from being thrown against the bodywork.

'Steady on!'

'I'm trying to get us there quickly! *You* said there's no way of knowing how much time he's got left.'

'Fair enough lad, but remember it's a tree not a casualty department. We need to arrive in one piece.'

Lawrence looked down at Peter, at his sallow skin and sunken eyes. He lay as if dead, cocooned in a moth-eaten army blanket scavenged from under the seats, with his head pillowed on the paisley silk lining of Lawrence's carefully folded jacket.

The stone had been worked from Peter's grasp; from fingers that felt like they would snap before ever giving up their hold, then wrapped in the papers that had fallen from Peter's pocket, and left on the floor between Jed's quiver, bow, and a bucket of clagged digging tools. Away from the arcane setting of the graveyard it seemed a disappointing trophy.

There was no way of telling how long Peter had been lying under the yew at Hatiston. They hadn't spoken since the day before yesterday and that had only been a mundane conversation, certainly nothing to imply he was after a talisman or about to risk his life. In all his time within the Bowlore, Lawrence had never witnessed anyone this close to death before – the Covenant violated so dangerously. Jed was almost certainly right, the situation did bare the hallmarks of a sniper attack, but the sheer coincidence of Peter ending up as a random target whilst on a clandestine mission was too much for Lawrence to accept. There was more to this, he knew it. Despite his show of confidence, the realisation was closing over him that they might never find out the truth.

He felt once again for his First's fading pulse, plucked a loose thread from the blanket and held it close to Peter's slack mouth: it hardly moved, only shallow wisps of breath remained. If they couldn't locate a hollow yew before he stopped breathing altogether, he was a dead man, and no conventional option: no hospital or resuscitation or medical treatment of any kind would make a difference. The nature of Peter's injuries meant his life was being prolonged by its bond with the yews. The price of that pact was that nothing else would save him.

Lawrence tucked the blanket neat and tight, in a gesture more for his own comfort than for Peter's. *Hold on my friend.* He shook his head in sad remonstration. *Why didn't you trust me?*

Jed drove the winding roads with a fervour that far outstripped his skill; swinging up to the hedges on both sides to make turns at speed, hardly slowing when he passed occasional cars, mirror-smackingly close; he noticed Lawrence waving apologies out of the back window. But none of it mattered, Peter was dying, he could tell that much from Lawrence's unguarded expressions caught in the rear-view mirror.

It was all up to him. Life and death. He felt terrified – and exhilarated.

Since joining Ninestones he had learned about his site and Hallow from Peter, had been taught the occult discipline of how to aim by Lawrence, discovered and developed untapped talents, been as conscientious, dependable and studious as they wanted him to be – and had treasured every moment. But sometimes, when he heard them condemning the Forts for their sniping and raiding, for the money they were rumoured to make from selling finds to outsiders, and the risks they took by pushing the system to its limit; it made him wonder if he'd made a mistake in joining a Stone company. At the time, the choice offered him was whether to accept a place in the Bowlore: the alternatives within that world had only become apparent later.

Because he had been introduced by Lawrence, Second of Ninestones, he had become Third of that company.

And he was happy. Mostly.

They were approaching a crossroads and Jed slowed to select a route. He didn't have a map or directions, he didn't need them. He put his hand to his neck and pulled up a leather thong on which he wore a metal and bone charm, the first talisman he had found and still his favourite. It was a tiny, lodestone-filled skull of a swallow, the fine beak gilded, two polished silver orbs shining from its eye sockets.

He held it momentarily, concentrating on the image of a hollow yew. In the cup of his palm the skull twitched, bird-quick, to the right. He kissed it, tucked it away, then heaved on the steering wheel, accelerating back up to the limit of the straining engine.

He sensed that they were close to their destination. He hoped they were close enough.

A church steeple came in sight, rising over a cumulus of trees, ghostly and mournful in the filtered light of the overcast morning. Jed scrutinised the leafy outlines looking for the darkest, widest spread. With a jolt of relief, he saw it.

At the furthest edge of the church enclosure, sculpted by the prevailing winds so that it seemed to be leaning away from its host, a yew tree straddled a low stone wall, like a massive animal caught in the act of escaping.

'I've got it!'

'Thank God.' Lawrence forced positivity into his tone. 'Pull up anywhere lad. If we incur the wrath of the locals, we'll just pretend to be Yanks!'

Jed winced. Even a deaf and blind man wouldn't mistake Lawrence for an American tourist, they'd smell the tweed.

The lay-by they parked in was narrow and overgrown, nestled in the lea of the church wall and mercifully undisturbed. Only the clucks of the jackdaws circling the steeple broke the silence. The church itself appeared to be well maintained, the graveyard grass and shrubs trimmed, the paths swept, and here and there, bunches of flowers laid against the marble or granite headstones: good for the parishioners but bad for the companies, neglect meant safety. At least it was situated on the edge of the village, ringed with open fields, and the yew itself was far from the road and prospective passers-by. They had no choice but to make the best of it.

Jed and Lawrence carried their First over to the yew, avoiding the pathways and keeping close to the perimeter walls for cover, then laid him gently on the bare ground by the tree while they searched for a way inside its broad trunk. They found an opening facing towards the empty farmland, where the roots flared up and over the stones of the wall. It was a tapered split corniced with rumpled bark and fringed with sprays of twigs, just wide enough at its base to allow entry.

Lawrence patted the flank of the tree unselfconsciously. *We need your help old man.*

They were completely surrounded by the wider canopy of layered and drooping boughs giving them the privacy they needed, and creating a strange indoor-outdoor feel, as if they were in a broad, dark green tent, fragranced with resin and damp earth.

The air was still, they didn't speak. Their silence was part reverential, part a symptom of fearful denial.

Moving Peter into the heart of the yew was slow and difficult. They managed it, without words, without mention of the waxy chill of his skin and the strange emptiness of his body, as if he was as hollow as the tree. Neither of them wanted to bring the reality of death upon them by speaking of it.

The yew was lit within by a fissure far above, where the trunk divided to form the canopy. Once their eyes had adjusted, the dim light it gave was sufficient for their needs.

The floor of the hollow was soft with dry leaves and sloughed bark, the walls were made up of a sinuous tangle of red heartwood buttresses, flowing upwards and around navel knots pressed in swells and curves of the pale exposed sapwood, or draped across deep slits in the grain. A living cave, in a primeval, infinitely slow dance.

Lawrence and Jed laid him out, and crawled out backwards from the tree. There was nothing more they could do.

§

Nothing.

And then.

Blood moves again, drawn on by the sap-tide. Capillary lines strained thin but caught just before breaking. Air filters back into tiny hidden branches of stilled lungs.

Fluttering beats.

Between.

Long, stifled pauses. Sprouting back from a deep winter decline. Thump by thump. Heart within heartwood. Red as life.

And then.

The Dreams begin.

Drawn up from the Land, pulled in by the roots. Given as an unremembered gift.

But these have been savaged.

Mauled to shreds.

§

Peter's scream brought them running.

They had been walking around the perimeter of the graveyard, keeping a lookout whilst pretending to read gravestones and admire the church's architecture. Lawrence had broken off from that pretence to return to the car for the notes; the tension of waiting was more than he could endure, he needed a more substantial distraction, and he wanted to be alone.

Jed, sprinting, reached the tree first and clambered his way in.

Peter's eyes were wide, gleaming in the dimness, his jaw stretched in a straining animal howl that tailed off only when his lungs had given up the last of their air. Split skin at the corners of his mouth bled lines of red through his pale stubble, and his arms were crooked as if still holding the stone out in front of him.

Tentatively, Jed reached out to calm and hush Peter, but as their eyes met he jerked his hand away in shock; there was nothing left of the man he knew, what cowered before him was a void. He yelled out in panic, 'Lawrence! Something's wrong!' *Is this what happens if you're left too long?* No-one had warned him of this possibility, he felt deceived, horrified.

Peter slumped forwards, moaning a fragmented sound like a diminishing echo.

'Mind out of the way!' Lawrence barged Jed aside, who, grateful for the excuse to get away, backed out of the tree to make room. Huffing, Lawrence crawled inside. There was silence as he assessed Peter's condition and composed himself, then words of encouragement, spoken evenly, repetitively, could be heard coming from the heart of the tree.

Jed ran his fingers through his hair and kicked at the ground. *That's not enough! Can't you see his face?* He stepped up to the top of the opening and put his mouth right to the split. 'What the hell's happened to him?' There was no answer, so he reluctantly put his head and shoulders back through the entrance, squinting in expectation of what he would see.

Lawrence was dabbing the blood from Peter's cheeks with a white handkerchief, folding it after each wipe to tuck away the dirty red stains and provide a clean surface for the next. His jaw was set, his eyes bright with tears, and he had to clear his throat several times before voicing the obvious. 'This isn't right.'

'What do we do? How can we help him?'

Lawrence rubbed his eyes with a trembling hand, then reached into his breast-pocket and brought out a small silver hip-flask, tracing his thumb over the engraved cartouche of three arrows bound together with a sprig of yew. He began unscrewing the cap.

'What good is that?' Jed's voice rose in frustration. 'Look at him, he can't drink anything!'

'It's not for him.' Lawrence tipped it twice to his lips, taking a good mouthful each time, then offered it up to Jed. *You're a good-hearted lad but for God's sake shut up, and let me think.*

He watched Jed hesitate, then accept the flask. As he raised it to drink, Lawrence noticed how grimy the tattoo on Jed's forearm was; the Celtic-knotwork hares scratched over, the moon at their centre eclipsed with dirt from struggling to lay Peter in the yew. And just for an instant it took Lawrence right back to their first stilted conversation, two years previously, when they had met – by chance – at the Ninestones circle; he sketching, Jed dowsing. Back then, they had chatted about his tattoo, newly inked and outlined with reddened skin, rather than mention the profound recognition they were both experiencing.

The brandy warmed Lawrence's gut, chilled by fright, and steadied his mind. *Must keep calm and carry on.* An appropriately grim maxim intended as a rearguard spur.

'Deduction is merely a process of elimination.' He teased the fabric of Peter's dark blue shirt away from his chest, and then carefully leaned him forward to do the same at his back, all the while supporting Peter's lolling head with his shoulder. 'So, we'll start with the basics.' Although it was stiff with blood and dirt, the shirt was whole, missing the telltale cut of a broadhead arrow. Just to be certain Lawrence lifted it up, but the grazed and bruised skin of Peter's torso only bore two thin white puncture scars, both long healed.

'Well, we can be sure he wasn't shot.'

'What?'

'There's no sign of it.' He smoothed Peter's shirt back down, then cupped his cramped hands, trying to warm them between his own. He spoke to Jed without taking his eyes off his First. 'It's got to be something to do with that blasted stone.'

'But I don't get it—' Jed passed back the flask, nearly dropping it in his haste to withdraw his arm from the claustrophobia of the tree. He closed down to protect himself. 'A talisman can't do that to no matter how dodgy or wild it is – it's just a battery isn't it?'

Lawrence grimaced as he freed up one hand to deftly unscrew the flask and take another sip of brandy. 'Well that's not exactly right, they—'

'They don't do *that!*' Jed stabbed a finger towards Peter. 'He's been drained.'

Lawrence leaned close to the entrance and fixed him with a glare. 'Listen lad, I took the opportunity to check his notebook. One thread he was investigating said the last wolf in England was killed at Hatiston, its pelt wrapped around a stone and then buried in some sort of vernacular banishing ritual.' Lawrence lowered his voice to an earnest whisper. 'Since everything points to Peter having found the actual stone – and God knows what kind of essence it's been imbued with – we have to face the possibility that he's inadvertently released…' He searched for a descriptive. Failed. 'Something.'

'Wait! There's nothing in him, I know what I felt – what I fucking saw – he's empty!'

'Look I can't categorically state that you're wrong, but just think about it, no sniper shot has been declared – we certainly would've heard by now – and even the basest of the Forts wouldn't just leave someone to die.'

There was a pause as Jed accepted the undeniable fact. 'Okay then, if we go along with your idea it means he's not protected and the yew isn't healing him – so what the fuck are we still doing here?'

Ever the pragmatist. 'I agree lad, we must make a decision. For his sake I think we're going to have to shelve our pride and ask for help.' Lawrence was already pulling Peter towards the opening. 'Grab his arms would you?'

'Who can we go to?' Jed avoided looking directly at Peter's ghastly face as he helped heave him free of the trunk. He felt sick and defeated.

'We'll need the big guns for this.' Lawrence emerged on his knees, rubbing his back. 'One of the Sanctuaries.'

'Which one?'

Lawrence stood up and hooked his arms under Peter's, indicating for Jed to take his legs. He spoke quietly and solemnly. 'The closest.'

They made certain their route back to the Land Rover was clear before they broke cover. There could be no convincing explanations if they were seen by outsiders, but luckily the village was a second-home and commuter ghost town, holding its working-hours breath. They heard the sound of a distant car, the gossip of the jackdaws, a blackbird's chittering alarm call, and their own footsteps, nothing more. Reassured, they moved out from the shelter of the yew and retraced their path beside the wall, panting with effort. They were as closed down and careful as they could be.

But they were being watched.

Jed shivered convulsively and dropped to a crouch, still supporting Peter's legs, yanking them all to a halt. He looked behind, staring past the churchyard and into the fields.

Lawrence automatically ducked down, as far as he was able, following Jed's line of sight. 'What is it?'

He flinched as if stung, sucking air through his gritted teeth, eyes wide with shock. 'Someone's taking aim at me!'

Lawrence reacted with a speed that belied his age, grabbing Jed by the arms to heave him against the base of the stone wall. In the same second an arrow clattered off the topmost rocks and cartwheeled into the grass.

Jed pressed himself harder into the shelter of the wall, mumbling thanks.

Flat on his belly, Lawrence endeavoured to drag Peter closer to them. 'Save your gratitude for the drive home lad, we've rather a long gauntlet to run first.' He eyed the open space between their position and the car. 'The wall will keep us safe until it curves around to meet the gate.' He paused for emphasis. 'Then it's a case of getting through it before the sniper can loose. That's as much as we can hope for, I'm afraid. The bugger will have more than enough time to take aim.'

Jed nodded mutely. His back still burned at the place he would have taken the arrow.

'Come on lad, up and at 'em!'

They hugged close to the wall and moved quickly, stooping almost double to stay within its protection and hauling Peter unceremoniously through the grass at its base.

Two arrows hissed overhead and shattered to splinters on a gravestone directly in front of them, forcing them to a halt.

'Shit!' Jed covered his face with the crook of his arm.

'It would appear,' Lawrence brushed the slivers of wasp-coloured wood from his hair, 'that we have more than one assailant.'

'The bastard could've shot two arrows off the same string, they weren't aimed – he's trying to flush us out!' He risked the briefest glimpse above the wall but saw nothing.

'I'm well aware of the tricks employed by snipers, but look at the branding.' He pointed at the feathers attached to the broken shafts. 'That's black, this one's barred and

– as I'm sure you noticed – the first was a cheery canary yellow.'

Jed gave a noncommittal shrug.

'And that, unfortunately, puts us in rather more of a predicament.'

'D'you reckon it's a whole company on a raid?'

'On us!' Lawrence managed a smile. 'I don't think so. We're hardly more than tiddlers in this particular pond. Most likely they were just passing through and found us by accident.' He ducked as another arrow crested the wall.

Jed stared at him. *Why are you avoiding the fucking obvious?* 'What about Peter taking that stone? Don't you think it might have something to do with that?'

'Peter would never knowingly endanger his company.' Lawrence looked away as if the matter was settled.

'He didn't know what the fuck he was doing, even I can see that!' Another three arrows fell close by, the last one buried in the turf right up to its yellow feathers. 'Look at the angle, they're getting closer! They know we don't have bows, they're coming to pick us off!'

An arrow zipped between them as if to emphasise his point, narrowly missing Peter's outstretched legs, close enough for them to feel the air being cut, and the thud as it hit the ground. 'We can't do this! If we're shot, who'll save Peter? If he gets shot, he's dead! We've got to surrender!'

'Listen!' Lawrence leaned across and took him by the shoulders. 'Listen to me, lad. We have to trust our First's judgement. If Peter thought that stone's worth claiming, then it's also worth defending. Whatever happens, we *must* keep hold of it.'

'How the fuck can we defend anything if we're unarmed?' He flinched as an arrow shattered noisily against the wall. 'Even if the stone's valuable, is it worth dying for?'

Instead of answering him, Lawrence turned his impotent rage on their unseen attackers; at the wrecked shafts, torn feathers, and glinting, twisted broadheads scattered over the churchyard. 'How the hell do these buggers find enough silver to be this wasteful with their arrows!'

Jed kept his response to himself. *They take it from fuckwits like us.*

§

A bow-shot's distance from the churchyard, across the field and within the cover of a stand of sycamores, David Horsman narrowed his eyes against the sunlight glinting from the church windows, and leaned on his yew longbow as if it was a staff.

He hadn't joined in with the attack; he'd spent too much time and effort painting his latest batch of arrows, with precise yellow spirals around the black shafts, to waste them on plainshooting. His bow was strung and ready, though, and he hefted it to the horizontal, ran his fingers over the horn nocks at both ends, ensuring the loops of the string were securely set into their carved grooves, before reaching down to his quiver and angling the arrows so they were ready to draw.

David knew he was pushing his luck raiding close to a village in broad daylight, and so was primed to make a move against his will. His talent and impatience had led him here, short-handed and lacking a credible plan. To make it worth the risk, he needed to mask his doubts, and concentrate on crafting the best possible outcome for his company.

A blink of light caught his eye as the polished silver broadhead of another Badbury arrow smashed on the perimeter wall. There was still no sign of the thieves; their nerve was holding. His was wearing thin.

David reached for the binoculars slung round his neck, brought them to his eyes, and adjusted the focus until he had a clear view of the one vehicle parked in the lane by the church.

'Helen, check out the Land Rover, it's got to be theirs. If they've left their bows behind, they might've left the stone too.'

The woman behind him exhaled, lowered her longbow, took a yellow-fletched arrow off the string and stabbed it into the ground. 'When can I aim again?' Helen moved up beside him, flicked a strand of hair from her face, and spoke in a deliberately dispassionate tone. 'This is boring.' She raised an eyebrow at David's untouched arrows. 'And expensive.'

He kept looking straight ahead. 'Soon.'

'Why don't we just storm them?'

He realised he didn't have a good reason not to. *Why am I dragging this out?* 'I want to see if they'll try to access the Wolfstone.'

She pulled a sceptical face. 'You're waiting for Catrin, aren't you?'

Helen had an unnerving habit of answering his internal questions, and he could never decide if it was because she was talented, or he was too open with her. He wasn't comfortable with either option. 'The quicker you get to the car, the quicker we can wrap this up.'

'Okay, okay.' She let out a resigned sigh. 'So, if the stone's inside and the doors are locked, do you want me to break in?'

'No, you might be seen. As soon as they surrender, I'll get the thief to fetch it for me. Then I'll shoot him.'

'Aimed?'

His frown levelled out to detachment. 'If I restore the stone, it'll be more valuable.'

Helen passed him her longbow, held his gaze for a moment, then headed into the open field. Pointedly she tugged her hair back up into a tight ponytail: her habit before taking aim. David got the message. She was expecting to be granted another chance at the mark she had missed at the start of the attack. He rested her bow against a tree, and watched as she picked her way through the half-grown grassy wheat, following and jumping the furrows by turns, until she reached the hedge lining the lane and ducked through a gap. David lowered the binoculars, rubbing his forehead; there would be a tedious amount of fallout to sort after today, not least between his companions.

Despite the promises made to Gareth and Alex to persuade them out here, he would have to make them wait for another raid, because there was no way he could deny Helen a chance to finish the one aimed shot he'd allowed. Disregarding the natural precedence of his Second and Third in favour of his Sixth would inevitably kick off a dispute, but they couldn't blame him for not knowing how small the thief's company was; he needed the information they would give up, whereas his companions didn't need the shots.

David suppressed the anger at his dwindling control. He took off the binoculars, dropped them, and pulled an arrow; sliding it across the bow above his fist and nocking it in one movement. He tested the tension of the bowstring but didn't draw.

Unless the insignificant little company created a readable connection by aiming, or accessing the

Wolfstone, they would remain unidentified, protected by their meekness.

David did have a vague sense that they were a Stone company: some trace of their essence resonated with the rocks in the walls and the church, with the writing on the graves – and with the Wolfstone itself.

Unable to satisfy his nicotine craving, David was overly aware of the tin in his pocket. He couldn't risk a smoke because a flame held that close might draw a mark: heat attracted heat. He tapped out a quiet rhythm on the tin. *Never take the third light from a match: a sniper sees the first, takes aim at the second, and shoots the third.* A bitter adage from the trenches whittled down to fit the fields of home.

Though the thief's company was proving to be disappointingly docile, David had a growing intuition that Silbury had risen to his provocation. The edge of his awareness was being chilled and abraded by the gritty shadow of a white hill. He smiled. It would play nicely into his hands if they had the stomach for a fight, although he knew from experience that negotiation was always Catrin's preferred tactic.

It was never his.

There was a whistle.

David scooped up the binoculars and trained them on the Land Rover. Helen was standing beside the car with one arm held up to attract his attention. He raised his own in answer, and then Helen made a fist and raised her thumb as if giving judgment in an arena: the Wolfstone was there.

This vindication still wasn't enough for him, something important about this other company was eluding him. Even though everything marked them out as lacking combat experience, he was aware that his own behaviour was being altered by ego and vengeance, and how those energies were simple, intoxicating, and blinding. What might be pushing them to take such risks?

Stepping back now, instead of wading in further, would be wiser but weaker. That notion just hardened his attitude. Some Firsts would have called off the attack at this point, acknowledging the helpless state of the targets, but he didn't feel obliged to make allowances for ignorance. He had learned the Lore the hard way, so must they.

He followed the line of another of Gareth or Alex's arrows, shot high so it would turn in the air and fall straight down beyond the churchyard wall. There were signs of scurrying movement in the graveyard, but not of a hit. His companions' clarity was a spur: they knew what they were doing and why.

This was the best outcome of a worst-case scenario, and as much control as David could hope for within his currently limited scope. Yet he found his unease fixing on the question of who had made the shot against the thief's company. It wasn't a sniper, that much was certain; he made it his business to keep track of that kind of activity and knew that nothing had been declared to a Sanctuary for weeks. Another arrow plummeted from the sky, tipping from a stall into terminal velocity, David heard the crack a second after it broke against the wall.

The state of play surrounding this talisman had already escalated once – granted, because of him – but there was enough to deal with without drawing fire from another company with a stake in the Wolfstone. He needed to find out who they were and what they knew, but resolved to delegate to his Second, since Gareth possessed a Stone-like talent for investigation – almost to the point that if loyalty hadn't figured so highly in his priorities, they might have ended up in rival Hallows.

He spotted Gareth, then Alex, moving out from the cover of a gnarled oak, halfway between the copse where David stood and the church. They were making no effort to stay hidden anymore. Gareth's red hair showed blatantly as he threw back the hood of his sweatshirt, and as they walked towards the graveyard, Alex stuck his arrows through his belt, where the sun made diamonds of the exposed silver heads. Having been plainshooting at almost point-blank range, deliberately shattering their arrows in explosions of splinters, and without any retaliation, they were nonchalant. They held their bows low, with arrows on their strings like they intended to finish the job, with or without his sanction.

David raised his hand and shouted, 'Hold!'

They stopped in their tracks. But they were not looking at him.

§

A fire-arrow arced overhead in a long graceful curve, trailing smoke and a sound like tearing cloth.

It fell into the centre of the field, flared and burned to a black stick.

Lawrence and Jed spotted it at its zenith, watched it smudge the clear sky, then dive out of their line of sight.

'Is that meant for us?'

'Can't be, lad, raiders don't tend to announce their intentions. Plus, it would be rather after the fact, don't you think?' Lawrence waited, then put a finger to his lips and pointed back at the field. 'Notice it's all quiet on the western front?'

'They've stopped?'

'If we're very lucky, the cavalry might have arrived.'

Jed rose warily to check over the wall, nothing seemed to have changed. Then he saw a woman: blonde hair, nice figure, no bow, cutting across the field from the direction of the lane. She broke into a run when she ran out of shelter, making for a stand of trees. No bow but definitely one of them. *Why can't I find someone like that to introduce to the company?*

'Anything happening?'

'No… Wait, there're some more people coming.'

'Outsiders?'

Five figures were approaching the church from across the fields, trekking quickly in single file, all armed with half-drawn loaded longbows held down to their sides.

'Lore.'

An answering fire-arrow streaked out from the copse he'd seen the woman enter. This one didn't arc high in the air, the line was low and straight, and it landed in a burst of blistering sparks at the feet of the challengers. They raised their bows and scattered, heading for shelter in the nearest overgrown hedgerow.

Jed dropped down beside Lawrence. 'I reckon we've got a chance if we make a break for it now.' He wiped the sweat from his forehead with the back of his arm, streaking dirt across his cheek, 'All their attention's on this new company.'

'There, I told you we weren't their intended target, we've just fallen foul of some opportunistic thugs.'

The hint of self-satisfaction riled Jed. 'Why wouldn't we be a target? We've got talismans, we can all aim.'

'You sound disappointed,' Lawrence observed with a wry smile. He clapped Jed on the back. 'Come on, lad, let's seize the moment!'

They heaved their First up from either side, supporting him under the shoulders, then broke from the shelter of the wall, towards the churchyard gate. Peter's head slumped forward and he gave out a weak cry; the toes of his boots scraping a noisy trail through the gravel, and their own footsteps crunching, but speed was more important than silence now they were fully exposed. They ran full tilt, skidding as they took the corner, and barged through the wooden lychgate, adrenaline lending them strength as well as a fatalistic courage.

When they made it all the way to the Land Rover without feeling the burning touch of a mark, they were far more surprised than elated. They clambered into the car, and Jed had it fired up and revving before Lawrence had finished bundling Peter into a stiff crouch against the bulkhead. Close to the stone again Peter reacted with a plaintive moan, his eyes widening into a coma stare. Lawrence put his arm protectively across his First's chest. *For pity's sake, don't start screaming again.*

The wheels spat grit and the engine threatened to stall as they jolted into the lane. The burst of noise hit the church and shattered its halo of jackdaws, but by the time the last bird had fled the tower they were through the village and out into the open countryside beyond. They had escaped, but there was no sense of celebration.

Lawrence reached for the stone. It lay where he had left it, tucked behind a plastic crate. The papers that remained around it had dried and peeled back, presenting the stone like the heart of a dead flower. As much as he wanted to, he couldn't dismiss Jed's conclusion that the attack was prompted by their possession of it.

He moved it to and fro at arm's length, not picking it up. Curious yet apprehensive.

It was the size of a large brick, dark grey, possibly granite and plain except for one side. Facing him was a relief-carving of a stylised wolf. It was portrayed crouched and tethered but the attitude suggested a pounce rather than an animal at bay. Its mouth was agape, spewing what appeared to be spiralling clouds that coiled around a blackened concave disc.

In the past Lawrence had encountered talismans that took a form completely unrelated to their alignment, and so he tried not to let the ominous imagery affect his attitude – though it was undeniable that ever since Peter had unearthed the stone, nothing good had come of it.

He pushed it back amongst the crumpled papers and wiped his hands free of the dirt and of its indefinable taint, and resolved to remain impartial until sensible explanations were forthcoming from his First.

But in his heart, all he wanted to do was grab the damn thing and throw it out of the window.

§

David Horsman heard the Land Rover's engine gunning, listened to it pulling away. He didn't turn to watch. The thieves weren't getting away; they were only postponing the inevitable.

Helen was less sanguine. 'For fuck's sake, David! If we hadn't wasted all that time plainshooting we'd have the Wolfstone back by now!' She raised her bow with an arrow pulled back to her elbow, ready to draw back fully, staring towards the dense row of elders and hawthorns bordering the field.

'It doesn't matter. We'll find them again, then we'll clean them out.' He pulled an arrow from his side quiver and examined the scalpel blade of the silver broadhead. 'If it makes you feel better, I'll let you shoot all three of them.'

'Forget them! You planned this, didn't you? You let Silbury catch up with us so you could have a go at Catrin!'

He half smiled. 'And you don't want a chance to shoot her?'

Helen turned away, closed herself down. She hated Silbury's First, resenting the shared status that bound Catrin to David and superseded her own influence over him; despised the jealousy that kindled in her gut when she saw the way he looked at Catrin sometimes. But she ignored his taunt, denying him a reaction.

David left the question hanging and went back to observing the closest edge of the hedgerow where Silbury had taken refuge. There was no sign of movement. It was a hasty and therefore poor choice for a hiding place, leaving no route out without having to cross open land. Silbury had effectively marooned themselves, which helped to offset his own company's disadvantages, but fed his restlessness – he didn't have the time for a siege, or the inclination to take responsibility and use up silver to raise a protection against outsiders.

He spoke as if talking to himself. 'If we plainshoot from here, they've got no real cover.'

Helen looked aghast. 'It's one thing to scare the shit out of a couple of unarmed thieves, but this a challenge from Silbury – it's serious! If you hit one of them we could lose everything!'

'Don't you trust me to miss?'

'Right now? No, I don't.' She lowered her arrow, and took her fingers off the string to make a grab for his longbow, but he stepped back out of reach.

'Remember your place, Helen.'

There was a feral glint in his eyes that went beyond the anticipation of combat, she felt a volatile passion envelop him like a sudden shadow, and withdrew her hand, disturbed, hurt and silenced.

David turned his glare back to the field and the hedge line, shifting his feet until he had a good contact with the ground. He raised his loaded bow in an unhurried, measured arc, and Helen was momentarily reassured by the look of deep concentration on his face – then in a single motion, he yanked the string back to his chin and loosed his arrow without any attempt to find a mark.

'David! No!'

The arrow cleared the field in three heartbeats and vanished into the thorn and elder trees of the hedge.

There was a faint cry.

He laughed mirthlessly as he fitted another arrow to his bow. 'This won't take long. We'll drive them out and she'll have to surrender.'

'It's too dangerous!'

He drew back an arrow, shot again, watched its flight into the trees, and then reloaded. 'I don't expect you to join in.' His shoulders tensed as he hauled back; forearm in line with the arrow, three fingers on the string, hooked either side of the nocked shaft. 'But if you do, I'll let you have all her silver.' He loosed.

Helen bit her tongue. He never missed a trick.

She looked towards the churchyard wall and saw David's attack being mirrored arrow-for-arrow by Gareth and Alex who had taken up position beside the yew, their shots too quick to have been aimed. *So you primed them, but not me. Thanks.*

Despite her misgivings she took a long breath and raised her own bow, not to shoot, but to prepare. If Catrin did show herself, Helen intended to be ready.

And her arrow would be aimed.

§

'Stay down!' Catrin held tight to her Second's wrist as she teased out a jagged length of arrow piercing the flesh of his palm. She gritted her teeth in sympathy as it came out snagging and pulling on the torn skin. 'Can you move your fingers?'

He flexed his hand gingerly, and winced when air forced in with the impact bubbled from the puncture, followed by a steady trickle of dark blood. 'I'm okay – really – just let me get my bow.'

It lay on the ground beside him, struck from his grip and spattered with blood, a long gouge led to a crumpled silver broadhead embedded in the wood; the rest of the arrow had shattered. The bow was too badly damaged to ever shoot again but unthinkingly he reached for it.

Catrin yanked him back. 'Patrick, leave it! They're plainshooting!'

'What?' He stared at her, dazed by shock, glasses askew.

'Did you feel a mark?'

He shook his head, mirroring her fearful expression and finally showed the presence of mind to lie low beside her, as two more yellow and black shafts whipped through the branches above them. 'Aren't those shots aimed at the others?'

'No.' Catrin squeezed his shoulder to get his full attention, then moved her fingers up to touch his throat. 'Your bow saved your life – your hand was level with your neck.' She watched as realisation replaced confusion in his eyes, and then pointed to a deep ditch running under the trees. 'We've got to get further in.'

They crawled rapidly through a mesh of dead branches for the shelter of the dry streambed, with Patrick holding his bleeding hand away from the ground, and Catrin sliding her bow ahead of her. Thorns snagged their clothes and skin as they tumbled over the stony sides of the ditch in their rush to get below its edge.

Catrin flinched as another arrow sliced through the leaves above them.

She had confronted aimed shots before: the somebody-walking-over-your-grave shiver of the initial touch, then the burn of a focussed mark; and had fallen three times before, with the agony of an aimed arrow in her chest. But this was a whole new level of fear: stark and primal, to be faced without the salvation of the Covenant.

'He's never broken the Lore like this before.' Catrin, out of breath, peered up and down their visible stretch of the curving ditch, hunting for a potential escape route. She wanted to call out to the rest of her scattered company, but didn't dare. 'Why is he doing it!' She shook her head and started fumbling through her pockets to find something to use as a bandage. 'What the hell makes him think he can get away with it?'

Patrick was cradling his hand and trying to slow his breathing. He raised an eyebrow at the question. 'Friends in high places?' He accepted a wad of crumpled tissues from Catrin with a nod of thanks, and cupped them around his wound where they instantly soaked to scarlet. 'If Badbury are getting their kicks from plainshooting now, it's just one more reason why we shouldn't be here.' He raised his injured hand, blood tracing a thick line down his forearm. 'I've certainly learned *my* lesson.'

'Meaning?'

'Let's just get out of here.' He reached up his good hand to touch her face. 'Nothing is worth this kind of danger.'

A Badbury arrow split a branch just above their heads, bringing down a rain of leaves then skewing into the ditch. It came to rest vertically, tip downwards, caught on a root. The fletchings were raven-black and the wooden shaft was dark grey, spiralled with yellow lines: identical markings to the one that had struck Patrick.

Catrin paled with anger. Seizing her longbow she rose to her feet, dodged her Second's awkward one-handed lunge to grab her and his desperate pleas for her to stay down, hauled herself up the slope of the ditch and ran. With a suicidal boldness she defied the oncoming arrows, shoving her way through a tangle of elders until she could see the field and the church, but still had cover.

As she had hoped, the lack of answering shots had emboldened them: David and Helen were clearly visible between the trees.

Catrin wiped her fringe back from her face, drew a blue and white arrow from her side quiver, nocked it to the string and raised her bow.

Patrick was still calling to Catrin as loudly as he dared, with his head just above the edge of the ditch, when he heard a shuffling of leaves and snapping twigs coming up behind him. He turned towards the sound, snatched an arrow from his quiver, gripped it in his good fist, and held it point-out like a knife – only to see his three other companions approaching at a crouching run along the ditch. The woman and two men held arrows on their awkwardly slanted bows, fingers hooked tight on the strings even though there was no chance to take aim. For a dreadful second Patrick wondered if they had been plainshooting in response, but one look at their full quivers and defeated expressions told him they had abandoned their hiding place out of fear, not revenge.

Patrick signalled them to stay behind him and keep down. He put his arrow away and kept his bloodied hand out of sight. 'What the hell are you doing here? You should've stayed where you were!'

The woman shuffled forward, she was out of breath more from fright than running. 'We saw the arrows – they're only shooting at you – so many – they're plainshot aren't they?' She looked around frowning. 'Where's Catrin?'

'She… she's moved up to where she can take a shot.'

'You've got to get her back!' Leah fought to keep her voice from quavering. 'Take the shield – use it – like an ordinary one!'

The man directly behind Leah, taking his cue from her, unfastened a small, round oak shield hanging from his quiver. There was an air of repressed reluctance about his movements as he passed it across, but he didn't say anything. The shield was bound with strips of bronze cut and tapered into the shape of a feathered wing, the wood was stained woad-blue, and the polished boss at its centre was indented with a spiral of hammered vees, like a distant flock of birds.

Patrick quickly slid his bloody hand through the leather grip on the inside of the buckler before Leah could notice his injury; there was no time for an argument. He glared at each of them in turn, 'Stay here! No matter what you hear – or feel… or whatever.' Then he turned to climb out of the ditch.

'Wait! Your bow!' James, the younger of the two men and at the rear of their small group, looked around for it, frowning.

'It…' Patrick stumbled over the explanation. 'It's broken.'

James fixed his eyes on Patrick, knowing there was more to that statement but also knowing to shut up. Wordlessly he presented his own bow.

With his good hand Patrick accepted it – they didn't need to know that he couldn't shoot. 'Do *not* follow me!' He looked at each of them in turn.

Simon, ward of the Wingshield, was unable to contain his frustration and muttered through gritted teeth, 'So we wait here like fucking rats in a hole?'

'Until Badbury run out of arrows. Yes.'

Patrick left it at that, brooking no more dispute. With a conscious effort he redirected his concern from the rest of the company towards his First, took a deep breath, raised the shield above the level of the ditch, and scrambled up within its meagre protection.

Almost at once an arrow hit the wood, kicking it back into his shoulder. Resisting the urge to drop down, he kept running, bent double, holding the borrowed longbow tight to his side. He swiped the shield against the branches in his way, snapping off the embedded Badbury shaft at its neck.

The instant he reached Catrin he realised he was too late. She was preparing to shoot, so any intervention now would be a dangerous distraction. Silently, Patrick dropped the bow, went down on one knee, as close beside her as he dared, then held the shield so that it faced the field, bracing himself to lift it if an arrow came her way.

He followed her stare.

Catrin had a perfect sight line to both figures at the edge of the copse, but there was no hesitation in her choice of target. Her mark was David Horsman.

The inevitability somehow made it easier, but she would still have to be quick and fluent when taking aim. He was one of the best dowsers in the Lore and would definitely feel her mark. Her only advantage was David's overconfidence, evident in his current behaviour – his guard was down.

Several Badbury arrows lay on the ground around her or protruded from tangled branches, their refined silver blades debased by being plainshot into brutal tools for slashing flesh and splintering bone, yet the danger and the desecration didn't reach her. She could sense Patrick readying himself to raise the Wingshield to protect her, felt his pain and the blood running down his arm, but even that didn't matter – his presence, the onslaught, couldn't distract her anymore.

Catrin could feel the connection, the perfect line that her arrow would take.

She drew a long steadying breath and pulled the bowstring back; the ash arrow shaft smoothed across the yew, her arms and shoulders locked into shape, the silver broadhead settled above her fist, the blue feathers against her cheek, the painted white sunburst below the nock held steady under her eye. For a heartbeat. For two. For three.

She unfurled her fingertips.

The arrow sliced into the air.

§

A second too late to react, David felt a point of heat flare in the middle of his chest. The intent read like a signature.

Disbelief, and Catrin's arrow, hit him simultaneously.

The impact threw him backwards, forcing the air from his lungs. He staggered trying to keep to his feet. His longbow slid through his fingers to the ground, the shaft nocked on the string twanging away uselessly into the grass.

He looked down in bewilderment at the arrow impaling his chest. The honed silver arrowhead cutting him away from life, suspending him between heartbeats, between breaths.

Between worlds.

He fell to his knees, retching blood.

A searing light blasted through him, scouring every cell in his body, burning out all trace of his mind until nothing existed except agony. And the arrow.

§

Catrin closed her eyes, held the line, revelling in its clarity.

Holding it taut, holding the lightning back to prolong David's suffering.

She smiled.

Then let it come.

The earthing coursed back along the connection created by her shot. She opened herself up and let its heat, the ripped-out shock of his life force, cascade through her body in brilliant splinters.

Catrin held the consummation for as long as she could, containing its fire until the rapture began to slide towards pain; her system scorched by the intensity.

She let it go.

And the living energy drained through her, flowing downwards, drawn into the ground, spreading away into the land, the bedrock, the hidden pulsing veins of aquifers, the packed clay and the crumbed earth, the webs of mycelium and into the deep delving roots of the yew trees.

All but the last dregs of it.

As Catrin came to her senses she bent down and grabbed the Wingshield from Patrick, held it tight and diverted the last of the power into it. Hunching down within its shelter, waving away Patrick's questioning touch, she shut her eyes and felt for the potency of the shield.

Found it.

Held it.

Drew out its strength and spread it like a wing, holding its protection over herself and over Patrick. Sweeping it wider to cover Leah, then Simon, then James where they cowered back at the ditch.

The defence was complete. Her company was safe.

Catrin breathed out.

§

Helen had reacted with a stifled cry, wrenched out of her own preparation as David was hit, to witness his stumbling collapse. Immediately on guard she had dropped to one knee, tipped her bow parallel with the ground, pulled it to full draw and sighted down her broadhead to where Silbury were hiding, but couldn't find a mark. The arrow in David's chest blazed into a line of blinding white light – then was gone, consumed by the energy it released.

He toppled forward, empty.

Helen loosed a plainshot arrow, recklessly low, towards the place in the trees where she knew Catrin must be – there was no response other than a muted impression of its flight being cut short. If it had been an aimed shot, she could have used the connection to determine if Silbury had accessed a talisman, but even the faint indication she had picked up was undeniable, she knew their major finds well enough: *the Wingshield – fucking bought with David's heat!* She looped her longbow over her shoulder, ran the few paces to David, rolled him onto his back and dragged him behind the cover of a tree. She jammed her back against the protection of the rough trunk, breathing fast, looking down at David's inert body.

Helen checked around desperately for any sign of Gareth or Alex. There was no movement or sound except a brief flurry of jackdaws scolding from the church tower. *Have they been felled, too?* Adrenaline stung her gut at the thought of shouldering the responsibility for all of them, even though she was within sight of a hollow yew. She took out her phone intending to call for help, but it had been too close to the earthing, and the screen was a mess of monochrome lines.

She knelt beside David, furious at his recklessness, at herself for feeling so vulnerable, at Catrin for everything else. She smoothed his chilling brow, pressed her fingers to the bloom of blood on his chest and the spatters around his lips, then bent down to kiss his forehead as if he were a forgiven child. *Why did you let this happen?*

His life was fading by fractions; each heartbeat slower, each breath more shallow than the last. David's body had been stripped of its vitality, leaving only the basic metabolic functions; a primal grip sustained by the Covenant but weakening with every passing minute. Helen looked behind her toward the potential redemption of the dark churchyard yew, sickened by the risk and the irony of needing to drag her unconscious First across open ground to safety, even with the knowledge that Silbury would never plainshoot.

Helen checked her phone again – it was still scrambled. Two companions frustratingly unreachable, and two missing: *Where are they?* Her gaze flicked from David to the yew to the last place she had seen Gareth and Alex. If they weren't already felled, if they were hiding by the yew or the churchyard wall, they might see her and come to her aid; create a diversion by lofting their last arrows against Silbury's defence. She looked down at David again – at what Catrin had left of him.

It was so long since anyone had successfully found a mark on her First that a sense of invulnerability had been pervading the company. Helen had her misgivings, but for the rest of Badbury it was a source of pride. Only a handful of individuals were capable of shooting David now, and though it was acknowledged that Catrin was probably one of them – a risk formerly neutralised by the truce – he had chosen to goad her into a fight.

The Forts of Maiden Castle, Brent Knoll and South Cadbury all vied for supremacy with the alleged justification that their Firsts could overpower an aim. David had been rising up those ranks, honing his reputation as well as his skill, and therefore this arrow from Catrin would continue to wound him long after the scar had faded to white.

If he survived.

With bloodstained fingers she stroked his hair and traced his lips. They were icy, faintly blue and his breath was so feeble she couldn't feel it even when she put her open mouth to his. Panic shivered through her.

Helen scanned the field, knowing she had to make a move or lose David. At this point she would have been grateful for the arrival of outsiders to curb the threat of more shots, but the landscape remained deceptively empty. She knew there was no reason for Silbury to linger because the Wolfstone was gone, and the plainshot silver was useless to them, but couldn't be sure they had left, because the influence of the shield lingered like a mist, masking their movement. If they had shot Gareth and Alex, they might well be waiting for her to show herself so they could make their victory complete. The thought of being at Catrin's mercy disgusted her, the fact that David had put her there, added a bitterness, but he was dying right in front of her, needing her – only her – and that deeper understanding outweighed her dread.

Helen unbuckled his quiver, took off her own and laid them alongside her bow – if they were spotted, being unarmed might play on Silbury's sense of honour. She wiped her palms dry on her jeans, grasped David's wrists as tight as she could, and then with a series of heaves began dragging him into the open field. She walked backwards, digging her heels into the soft turned earth, concentrating her thoughts on the sycamores they were leaving behind, tangling her identity into their roots. If anyone from Silbury was keeping track of her with something other than sight, that unmoving trace in the trees might buy a little time, perhaps enough to make it as far as the yew. Helen furtively reached out for the refuge of the great yew behind her, locating its position with the smallest edge of her mind, closing down everything but her objective – anticipating the touch of a mark with every step.

'Helen! They've gone!' Gareth's shout hit her like an arrow.

She twisted towards his voice, stooping protectively, but when she spotted him emerge along with Alex, slouched and dejected from the dark row of thorn trees by the church wall, with their quivers empty and bows unstrung, she straightened up. The wave of relief at no longer being alone overrode her frustration at their obvious defeat. She quickly closed that feeling down before they caught up with her.

Helen greeted them with a nervous smile but neither of them met her eyes as they roughly took David's arms from her grip, passed their bows to her, and then hoisted their First up between them, settling his weight ready to carry him over to the yew. Before Helen had the chance to recover her thoughts, her companions marched unevenly away without a word. She dashed back to gather up the bows and quivers and made to follow them.

Gareth, Second of Badbury Rings, turned back to her, his face unreadable. 'I surrendered to save you.'

His words emptied her.

'Go and clean up.'

Chapter Four

Glastonbury Tor loomed benignly, replete with dreams and stories, over the small town. It rose in a steep stepped cone from the Somerset Levels like the island it had once been; above the traffic and street noise, above the temporal world, crowned with its windswept medieval tower, and holding its magic bunched up in ridges around its grassy sides, like green silk skirts held up out of the mud.

The air smelled of incense and impending rain.

In a place already laden with the baggage of centuries of pilgrims, the Tor, the Holy Thorn and the Chalice Well served as repositories of belief, claimed by all and fulfilling every diverse calling without prejudice. Even the Bowlore had found a home here, although for the moment – to Ninestones' dismay – there was no sign of its presence.

'How much longer can we wait?' Jed sat hunched forwards on a bench, restlessly scuffing his trainers on the pavement. He nodded in the direction of the car park where the Land Rover was, with Peter still hidden under blankets inside.

Lawrence sat up straight, tension and back pain maintaining his posture. 'I wish I knew lad. More than anything.'

'What if nobody turns up? Do we have to go up the Tor or something? You can wait here and I'll go.'

'No, it's best if we stay together.'

'Why?'

'Because I think we should.'

'Can't we reach out to them? I could try dowsing for where they are.'

Lawrence looked along the street where every other shop window was brimming with crystals, wands, amulets and pendulums. 'You'd be drowned out by the interference, lad.' He held up a hand to stall Jed's response. 'As I said, we're supposed to present ourselves and they'll come to us. I'm afraid that's their official method of contact for companies with which they have no personal relationship. To put it basically, everything has to be on their terms.'

'That's bullshit.'

'In light of our present circumstances, I have to agree with you.'

'What if they know we're here, but they've decided not to help us?'

'Oh, I can't imagine that would ever happen.' Lawrence's flogged his optimism onwards. 'Still, belt and braces? Perhaps it wouldn't harm to devise some sort of contingency plan whilst we wait.'

Jed straightened up. 'Okay then, plan B: we go back in time and tell Pete not to screw everything up by claiming a talisman he can't fucking control!'

'That's enough, lad. You've made your point.'

They fell into an agitated silence.

The bench they sat on grew harder. The traffic lulled from its afternoon peak. Hunger vied with anxiety in the pits of their stomachs. Lawrence leaned forward, pinched the crease of his trousers straight, rubbed at a smudge of dried blood on the lapel of his jacket, and then patted the breast pocket containing his brandy flask. 'Fancy a snifter?'

Jed didn't respond.

When Lawrence looked to where he was staring, he understood why. A beautiful young woman was watching them from the pavement opposite.

She was initially indistinguishable from the usual Glastonbury crowd, with her long black hair and embroidered purple dress, except that her expression was hard and focussed, unlike the pacifists wandering by. She aimed her gaze as if it were an arrow.

'Ah.' Lawrence offered a tentative smile. 'They've sent us a pre-Raphaelite witch.'

Before they had a chance to decide on their next move, the woman, apparently motivated by finally being recognised, crossed the road and approached them.

She looked them up and down, ignoring Lawrence's proffered hand and Jed's emotional panic. 'I am Judith, Second of Glastonbury Tor.'

Lawrence fought hard against his preconceptions. *This young thing, Second of Glastonbury?* 'Lawrence, Second of Ninestones. Delighted to make your acquaintance.'

She didn't return his smile. 'Which Ninestones?'

Lawrence frowned, thrown by the question. Jed butted in. 'Winterbourne Abbas.'

She kept her eyes on Lawrence. 'You must specify. There is more than one Ninestones in the land.'

He wanted to point out that there was still only one in the Bowlore, but he stopped himself. Her attitude made him doubt this knowledge. She was from one of the most powerful and influential companies in the system, so it was quite likely that she had contact with sites he hadn't even heard of.

She turned to Jed.

He gazed into her pale blue eyes. Then remembered himself. 'Jed, Third of Ninestones... of Winterbourne Abbas.'

Judith raised an eyebrow. 'So you said.'

He felt his face redden.

'Come with me.'

Judith's imperious attitude had such an effect on them that they began to follow without question. Then Lawrence, with a surge of embarrassment, remembered Peter. 'Our First is in need of help – he's back in our car.'

'I know. My company is preparing a place for him. He'll be taken care of.' The ambiguity of the statement was accentuated by Judith's cold tone.

Lawrence hesitated, suddenly nervous. 'Won't you need me to unlock the car for you?'

She turned to them. 'In all this land there is only one lock that needs a key to open it.' For a second her gaze rested on Jed. Then she continued walking up the street, knowing they would follow.

Lawrence muttered, 'I assume that was a *no, thank you*.'

'Come on.' Jed was anxious, but not for Peter's sake. 'We'll lose her.'

As he watched the young man break into a trot to catch up, Lawrence felt for his hip flask, and with a knowing look raised it and silently toasted Jed before following on.

It began to rain gently. The air was warm and damp as a greenhouse, heavy with the breath of wet summer pavements and grass. By the time they reached Judith's home the drizzle had slicked her hair into black lines down her back, wrapped the dress more tightly to her body. She hadn't spoken or turned around. Jed had not taken his eyes from her. Lawrence was growing more concerned by the minute as they obediently trailed behind.

The house she brought them to was raised up from the road on a sloped driveway, surrounded by trees and built in an anonymous Seventies style that Lawrence found incongruous given its setting at the foot of the Tor. Gothic revival would have suited better.

They entered through a frosted-glass door left ajar for a collection of cats that were lolling like furry apostrophes on the tiled floor of the hallway. Judith greeted each one affectionately, smiling for the first time.

The softness left her face the moment she straightened up. 'Wait here.'

She left them alone, walking to the end of the corridor and shutting the door she passed through with a brusque snap. Before it closed they heard the murmur of conversation, caught a whiff of incense and cigarettes. They were left with the distinct impression that they were at best an inconvenience, and at worst a liability.

'What d'you reckon?' Jed whispered.

'Well, I like the cats.' They wound around Lawrence's legs as he bent to stroke them.

Jed was forced to commit. 'What do you think about Judith?'

'I think she's obviously a very capable young lady.' Lawrence concentrated on the cats, distributing an equal amount of attention to each animal.

'And nice-looking?'

'Undoubtedly.'

'But you don't like her.'

Lawrence looked up with surprise at Jed's candour. Saw a friend adrift and needing affirmation. 'I don't dislike the girl, I just find her manner a little off-putting that's all.' He smiled reassuringly.

Jed looked away, aggrieved. 'Just don't do anything to piss her off. Remember, she's your equal in the Lore and we need her help.'

'I beg your bloody pardon!' Lawrence's conciliatory mood flared into anger. 'Remember *your* place, lad, and don't presume to tell me what's important when it's perfectly obvious where your priorities lie – you didn't take your eyes off her backside the whole way here!'

Judith cleared her throat.

She stood in the doorway, lips pursed. The cats streamed to her, meowing and purring, stretching up on their hind legs to be stroked.

Lawrence opened his mouth to offer an apology but she interrupted. 'My cats seem to like you.' She smoothed back her damp hair and stared at both of them in turn. 'But then again, it's nearly time for their food and they're friendlier when they're hungry.' She allowed the awkward moment to linger before motioning them to approach. 'Come in and explain to us what happened to your First.'

Lawrence and Jed followed her sheepishly into the next room. Jed couldn't even bring himself to look up from the floor.

Inside were four people sitting on mismatched dining chairs, nursing mugs of tea, leaning towards each other and conversing in whispers: a woman with short turquoise hair, tapping her foot and smoking; a man writing in a leather-bound notebook and wearing a knitted hoodie, giving him a monkish cast; a willowy woman with stooped shoulders and pursed lips, and another, older woman with the bearing of a matriarch. They looked up neutrally at Jed and Lawrence as they entered.

The room was bright despite the dull weather, lit by a wide window overlooking the Tor. The bare plaster walls were hung with an array of paintings and photographs featuring the Tor: shrouded in mist, silhouetted against a sunset, haloed by a full moon, or tangled in spirals, stars or Celtic knotwork. All the pieces of wooden furniture were stripped of paint and varnish and stood on limewashed floorboards, adding to the weather-worn aesthetic. A thin haze hung in the air from the cigarette smoke and the bouquet of joss-sticks burning by the hearth.

The room's focal point appeared to be a collection of crystals and geodes, displayed like a petrified peacock's tail around a tall candle flickering on the mantelpiece. Above it, lying on a narrow shelf of polished yew wood, rouged by the candlelight, lay the most beautifully worked piece of silver that Lawrence had ever seen: an arrow, precise in every detail but rendered in solid metal. Unmistakably the work of the Smith.

The matriarch stood up to greet them. She was dressed in layers and shades of green, worn like a collection of heirlooms of dubious quality but great sentimental value. Her hair was long and slate-grey, held in a plait down her back. She stood stiffly as if overly formal or favouring an injury.

Her eyes, Jed noticed, were an identical blue to Judith's.

'Welcome. I am Megan Wright, First of Glastonbury.'

Lawrence inclined his head respectfully as he took her hand. Her grip was warm and firm.

'Lawrence, Second of the Ninestones of Winterbourne Abbas.' He glanced at Judith, raising an eyebrow. *Was that good enough for you?*

She looked away dismissively.

Megan reached out for Jed's hand as he mumbled his introduction, cupping it in both of her hands and holding it for longer than Lawrence judged necessary. Then with a nod, she had Judith guide him to a seat by the window.

Anticipating Lawrence's first enquiry, Megan spoke quickly but gently as she showed him to an empty chair next to her own. 'Your First is in some form of deep shock, *not* within the protection of the Covenant. I can't safely pull him out because there is something holding him down, something elusive and dark. The edges I can reach are cunning and very old, and feel the same as the talisman you brought with you. Do you have an explanation?'

Hearing their predicament summed up so bluntly left Lawrence momentarily dumb. *No. I haven't a bloody clue.* He shook his head. 'Peter… our First, went out alone and in secret to get that stone. I don't know why.'

For a second Megan and Judith exchanged a look. Lawrence pretended not to notice. He would tolerate their condescension for a while longer, as they were far more likely to let slip a useful piece of information if they continued to assume they were talking above a simple Stone company's head.

'Do you have *any* idea about the nature of this talisman?'

Lawrence inferred from Megan's tone that she was not going to divulge anything unless he displayed at least a modicum of understanding, so he was left with no choice but to recount the little he had discovered from Peter's notes.

She listened without interrupting. The attention of the whole room focussed on him.

He concluded: 'There really isn't any more I can tell you I'm afraid, other than my instincts tell me that the stone is a malign influence.' Lawrence noticed nods of agreement amongst the members of Glastonbury and took heart from the endorsement. *Right, then. Now it's your turn.*

Megan straightened in her chair. 'I agree. And the more I learn of it, the more certain I am of its link to the altered lie of the land.' She was addressing her company rather than Lawrence. 'We must interpret its influence as quickly as possible, and not allow our observations to be diverted by its dark nature. Do not judge it by its origins, instead divine its potential.' It sounded as if this wasn't the first time the subject had been discussed.

The man holding the notebook wrote something down in a deliberate hand. Lawrence assumed it wasn't just the minutes of the meeting.

Then the thin woman spoke: 'Can we handle the stone?'

Lawrence was about to answer when he realised that the request wasn't directed at him. The proprietorial attitude of the Glastonbury company was beginning to annoy him. 'If you don't mind, I'd rather the stone was kept under wraps, as it were, just for the moment.' *It's our bloody talisman, not yours.*

The atmosphere in the room chilled.

'You made contact with us, presumably in the hope that we can help you.' Megan admonished. 'And we have an obligation to try – but to do so requires a level of trust that you seem reluctant to give. Remember that all companies are one within the Bowlore, in helping you we help ourselves.'

'Not a particularly altruistic motto, is it?' Lawrence sensed Jed's rising discomfort and reined himself in a little. 'I'm sorry. My company are obviously very grateful for all you're doing for us, but I'd feel more comfortable leaving decisions about the stone until after Peter has woken up.'

'As you wish.'

Lawrence foundered in the awkward silence that followed. He wanted to leave the room and its unfriendly occupants. 'Would it be possible to see Peter now?'

'I have created an area of peace for him, a safe place for him to return to. Your presence would disturb him.'

'But he knows me, he trusts me. I'm his Second, for goodness sake!'

'He didn't trust you enough to tell you about the stone.' The comment cut Lawrence to the bone, as she intended it to. 'I'm simply maintaining the privacy he obviously desired. Since he is a First I must respect his wishes above yours.'

Lawrence leaned forwards on his chair, hands clasped in front of him in unconscious supplication. He spoke quietly, humbled by her words. 'Isn't there *anything* I can do for him?'

Megan shook her head. 'Not yet.' Then she sighed. 'Come with me, I have the feeling that you would find it easier to talk in private.' She led the way from the room in the now familiar manner. Lawrence glanced back at Jed, but Judith had spoken to him and he had eyes only for her.

He sighed. Everything moved in slow motion here, weighed down with significance.

He followed Megan to a small room overlooking the garden, its window was open to the light breeze and the air inside was fresher. She invited him to sit on one of the large Indian floor cushions in the middle of the room. If he hadn't been so tired he would have declined, but the ignominy of his descent onto them was worth it for the relief, and he felt less inhibited now they were alone.

When Lawrence looked up from arranging his legs so that they wouldn't cramp up too quickly, he found that Megan was staring at him.

'Judith is my daughter.'

Lawrence nodded, unsure of how he was expected to react.

'That is not the reason she is my Second.'

Apparently Megan could perceive his thoughts *and* his prejudices. Lawrence leaned back, disconcerted.

With hardly a pause she changed the subject. 'We need to examine your First's behaviour. If Peter is keeping something this important from you, it could mean he's answering to some other authority, one whose demands supersede his loyalty to his company. As a First, I cannot imagine any situation where I'd willingly choose such a path, and I've never come across it before in any other company. So it would seem he's been offered a reward, been threatened, or he's in thrall. Which do you think it is?'

Megan's method of offloading stark facts, and then – whilst the recipient was still reeling – demanding an explanation, again left Lawrence mute.

Eventually he mustered a reply. 'We're just a small company. Our only regular associates in the Lore are two other Stone companies with whom we have a truce.

There's no one who would do something like that to him, I'm sure.' Lawrence rubbed at his chin, bewildered. 'Peter spends his time studying, not making enemies.'

'He seems to have made enemies of Silbury Hill and Badbury Rings.

'What?' He was shocked. 'You must be mistaken.'

'David Horsman of Badbury Rings found the talisman and promised it to Catrin Fitzgerald of Silbury Hill. Already blood has been spilled and honed silver wasted.'

How does she know that! Lawrence tried to buy thinking time by smuggling a lie behind a truth. 'I honestly had no idea who was attacking us – or why. I'm not trying to keep anything from you.'

She gave him a look bearing the same intensity that Judith used to such effect. 'Glastonbury is one of the anchoring roots of the Bowlore, and it's our responsibility to divine, interpret and disseminate the will of the land. Since all the companies are a manifestation of its consciousness, nothing that happens within the system can remain hidden from us for long.' She paused as if about to correct herself, then continued. 'And of course, texting is quite useful too.'

Lawrence smiled nervously at her unexpected flash of self-deprecation. Megan returned his smile, but he still felt unsettled.

Ninestones' policy of seclusion evidently didn't give them any real protection – they had always kept their heads low, literally and figuratively, yet had still become a target, and their infrequent dealings with other companies meant news was scarce and unreliable, often hardly more than rumour. To Lawrence's discomfort, the insular nature of his particular branch of the Lore was being mercilessly exposed, along with his own failings. Of course Glastonbury would know what was happening, he'd been foolish to think otherwise; they had some level of contact, overt or otherwise, with all the companies, regardless of their affiliations. Megan already knew more about Ninestone's business than he did, and it offered some insight as to why Sanctuaries showed peripheral companies like his so little regard.

Lawrence shifted uncomfortably, wishing he could lean his back against a wall.

He wiped his tired eyes, too weary to play games. 'Can I be blunt and ask how much you actually know, and how much of your questioning has simply been to establish the extent of my ignorance?'

Megan ignored the implied criticism. 'Information concerning woken sites, major finds, raids and sniping, inevitably travels quickly, but something like this event, where the line of intent has been deliberately concealed, is much harder to delve.' She took a moment to compose her next words. 'We've been aware of this disturbance for some while now, but the specifics are still eluding us. It will take time to divine its source... time we may not have.

Because your company is an intrinsic part of its pattern, your help could make the difference between the system prevailing or being its prey.'

Her indefinite but chilling warning served only to make Lawrence feel as if his back was finally up against the wall that his muscles craved. 'I really don't believe that I have the capacity to help you. But if you allow me to help Peter – at least see him, try to reach him – then perhaps we'll *all* be the wiser as to what's going on.'

To Lawrence's surprise she nodded. Either the sense of his words or his resigned desperation had finally moved her.

He didn't care which.

§

The rain shower had moved on, and thin beams of sunshine were slanting through breaks in the cloud layer, tracking like spotlights over the Tor and the meadows and gardens below it; illuminating a tree here, a flowerbed there, in wet-paint colours, turning them to fleeting portraits before fading away. The warmth condensed the aromas from leaves, blossoms and earth until breathing felt more like drinking. Branches dripped rain and birdsong; petals cupped jewels that melted to quicksilver at Jed's touch, drawn into the labyrinth of his fingerprints; crystal beads threaded on the grass broke as he walked by, wicking into his trainers and the hems of his jeans.

Without speaking, Judith slipped her cool fingers into his hand and led him across the soft, saturated lawn, past statues of goddesses with amethyst-geode wombs, and carved driftwood with fae faces peering out from the knots and grain. Jed half-expected them to blink or speak as he passed.

If not for the nervous cramp in the pit of his stomach, he could have been walking through a dream.

They reached a stone bench set beside a small lily pond, where two young yew trees had been clipped and plaited into a sheltering bower. Their limbs were smooth and slim, their leaves hung like tresses, their roots coiled around the lion's-paw feet of the seat and trailed off to sip at the water's lip.

The damp stonework of the bench was patterned with lichen and the silvery, indecipherable italics left by snails. Judith folded the skirt of her dress behind her so that she could sit on its dry velvet, and brushed the place beside her free of leaves by way of an invitation for Jed to sit beside her. When he hesitated, she offered him a more palpable sign, reaching up for his hands and pulling him gently to her.

Jed was held fast by her eyes, her form, her scent, her heat. The need to have her deluged his senses in a wave that swept away her other aspects: her arrogance, her cold words – the way she was manipulating him.

Given his talents, he knew that he could push wide the doors she kept closed and understand her better than anyone – if he dared to try. But willingly captivated, as he had been from the first moment he set eyes on her, he surrendered to the passion she invoked, and bent down to take the kiss.

Chapter Five

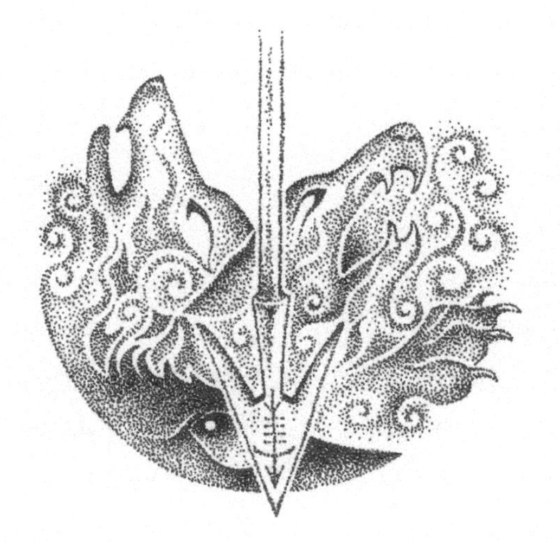

By the time Catrin's alarm clock dragged her from disturbing dreams and the twisted covers of her bed, a bank of cloud had already cast a dreary pall over the dawn, and she opened her curtains onto the disappointing reality of a grey and chilly morning.

She slumped down on the edge of her bed with a resigned sigh, and unplugged her phone from its charger on the bedside table. With her thumb poised over the screen she stared at the icons, mulling over her options, waiting for her anxiety and work-ethic guilt to subside enough for her to call in sick. It wasn't actually far from the truth, she was feeling shaky and hot, and the beginnings of a headache lurked at the base of her skull. Mercifully, it was still too early for Winifred to be awake, so she left a text message containing the appropriate level of regret and threat of infection. Having dealt with the intrusion of mundane life, Catrin switched off her mobile, placed it back on the table, face down, and allowed her Lore fears full rein.

No path she could envisage took her anywhere but further into trouble. There was no other First, or even Sanctuary, she felt able to confide in, because the root cause of the conflict was her fixation with wolf talismans, and though Catrin trusted her own judgement, others wouldn't. The guilt of having endangered her company burned in her gut, and deterred her from seeking her Second's advice: it would come, inescapably and relentlessly, soon enough, but right now she was just too tired to face it. She padded back over to the window and opened the casement wide, not caring for once that almost as much car exhaust as fresh air blew in from the road outside her flat. Catrin took a deep breath.

Procrastination in the form of taking a shower seemed to be the least damaging move she could make, so she turned up the radio to drown out her thoughts, and headed for the bathroom.

In the shower Catrin lifted her face to the spray, enjoying the sensation of surrogate tears. Without the time constraint of having to leave for work she allowed herself longer than usual, but instead of easing her tension it gave her too much time to reflect. Eventually she gave up, pulled on her dressing-gown, fixed a strong cafetière, and fetched her laptop. Settling cross-legged on the bed she went through her emails, steam wisping from the mug in her hand, her damp hair spotting the keyboard. Most of the messages were inconsequential – however one glared at her reproachfully from the screen until she deleted it, unopened, and snapped the computer shut.

Unseasonably winterish light from outside lent the room a sombre cast that matched her mood. The walls; chalk white and bare of pictures, appeared gloomy instead of the inspirational tabular rasa she had envisioned before moving in. The new furniture was personalised in a perfunctory way with cushions and throws, but her books and ornaments remained bubble-wrapped in a stack of plastic crates. Her flat was a necessity, not yet a home.

Catrin hunched over her coffee mug, keeping it close to her face, sipping without tasting, and staring unfocussed through the window towards the swaying crowns of a row of nearby trees. She could feel the vestiges of the high gained from her shot and Silbury Hill's victory, melting to nothing beneath the glare of her ignorance. As long as the whole story continued to elude her there was no hope of gaining any control. She was being tangled up and dragged behind something she couldn't see. Leaves flickered in her eye-line, vapour misted her view.

A song she liked came on the radio. She sighed and closed her eyes, allowing it to distract her.

The doorbell rang.

Catrin jumped at the intrusion, then made a grab for the radio to turn it off. She wrapped the dressing-gown tight across her body and up to her neck, cinched the belt, and went to the front door. Her hand touched the handle, then wavered before turning it – *it might not be him* – she closed herself down in a reflex reaction, not daring to reach out. 'Who is it?'

There was a pause as the visitor reacted to the sharpness in her voice. 'Me.'

Catrin exhaled, leaned her forehead against the cool wood of the door, eyes shut in exasperation. 'Bloody hell, Patrick, can't you take a hint?'

'Are you going to let me in?'

'No.'

The prolonged silence on the other side of the door almost fooled her into believing that he'd gone, until the letterbox was slowly pushed open. His voice came through, loud in the small tiled hall. 'We've got to talk. Not just us, the whole company.'

'Listen, Pat, I've got a shitty day at work ahead of me. I've... I've got to meet Winnie, the accounts need doing – I'm psyching myself up for that. I can't talk Lore right now.'

Patrick put his mouth closer to the opening. 'Don't try to fob me off – I know who you're really meeting with today.'

On the other side of the door Catrin flinched, biting her lip. She bobbed down so that they were eye to eye through the letterbox and pushed it wider. 'How the hell did you find out?'

He stared back at her. 'I didn't. It was an educated guess.'

She released the flap of the letterbox so that it snapped shut on his fingers. Patrick swore, then began hammering on the door.

'We can continue this conversation through your front door if you like, Catrin, but I'm not going away.' He carried on thumping.

Her shoulders slumped in resignation. She undid the lock, the clicks of the mechanism lost against the barrage, and walked towards her living-room.

The door gave suddenly under Patrick's fist, swinging wide to reveal the empty hallway. He leaned over the threshold keeping his bandaged hand on the doorframe. 'Catrin?' There was no answer. He stepped in, closing the door carefully behind him.

He found her sitting on the sofa, pouring coffee into a mug, her face a solemn mask. She didn't raise her eyes.

'Well, Pat, I'm all yours.' She clunked the cafetière down on the table beside her. 'What's it going to be? The full lecture, or just the usual passive-aggression?'

He settled in the chair opposite, his expression neutral. 'Tell me what'll work and I'll use it.'

'Shall I surprise you by saying nothing will?'

He drew a long breath and looked up to the ceiling. 'So, what has he promised you this time?'

Catrin shifted back on the sofa, abruptly angry. 'Don't patronise me, Patrick! I'm simply being realistic. We need to negotiate with him. Yes, chasing after Badbury was a mistake, I'm willing to admit that.' She ignored his raised eyebrows. 'But I'm not going to pass up a chance of getting hold of the find that goes with the Wolfstone.'

'What, by striking up another so-called alliance with that plainshooting Neanderthal? Brilliant idea.'

'There's not going to be another truce, I'm talking about a simple exchange that's all.'

'Exchange of what?'

'Talismans, claims, it hasn't been decided yet. That's why we need to meet.'

'Did he call you, or did you call him?'

She hesitated. 'I spoke to Helen. Horsman was still too cold.'

Patrick narrowed his eyes. 'And since when does a Sixth make those kinds of decisions?'

She thumped her mug down on the table. 'When she's the ward of the talisman I want!'

He nodded. 'Or maybe when she's the one sleeping with her company's First. I wonder if Gareth knows anything about this?'

Catrin shut her eyes, controlling herself, hunting for the right words. 'Pat, please… trust me in this. There has to be a reason I'm being drawn to the Wolfstone. I have to listen to my instincts.'

'And I have to tell you that no one in your company is willing to follow you on this path anymore.'

She opened her eyes, spoke with sad acceptance. 'Are you speaking as my friend or as my Second?'

'Both.'

'I understand.'

Silence settled on them.

Eventually Patrick broke it, in a studiously reasonable tone. 'We all appreciate that it's your responsibility to make the decisions, but you keep using it as an excuse to seal yourself away in some kind of ivory tower. Silbury's a company, Catrin. A family. We don't need this loneliness-of-command bollocks any more than you do.'

She glared at him. 'So, my style of leadership pisses you off as well?'

'That's not what I meant.'

'Hasn't it occurred to you that I take everything on because it's always left up to me? I don't see you coming up with any answers!'

Patrick felt his sympathy waning. 'They're not *answers*, Catrin! One sniff of a find that has anything to do with a wolf and you can't rest till you've claimed it. No matter what that does to the rest of us.' He raised his injured hand.

She didn't register the slight. 'They are worth the risk, every time. And as for the stone, no one could've anticipated it would cause this kind of trouble.'

'Except that getting involved with Badbury was practically asking for it!'

Catrin turned away. 'Oh, change the fucking record.'

He rubbed his chin. Waited to calm down before he tried again. 'Don't you see what you've done to us? Can't you stand back from yourself just long enough to see what Silbury has become?'

'What the hell is that supposed to mean?'

'Look at what you've reduced us to: when we're not picking up the pieces from needless battles, you've got us begging for scraps from a Fort with one of the worst reputations in the Lore. You're endangering and demeaning your company. It can't go on.'

'How dare you preach this crap to me straight after complaining that I don't share anything with you – this is the perfect example of why! You just look at short-term outcomes, jump to conclusions and then dump them on me! If I've got a complex it's because *you've* given it to me.' She blinked hard and shook her head as if trying to clear it, and then continued, dejected, almost to herself. 'Am I really the only one in Silbury who cares about our place in the system?'

Patrick balled his good fist and brought it down on the arm of his chair in exasperation. 'We're not a Fort company – you can't expect us to behave like one!'

She leaned forward and looked straight at him, conviction expressed in every quiet word. 'But that's precisely the problem, Pat. We don't know what we are. And unless I do these things, we never will.'

§

The sky was patterned like tide-swept sand. The rippling clouds spread until distance pressed their bands into a featureless layer along the horizon, the pearly light smudged and dulled into a faint grey smog.

A chilly breeze, peppered with dust and grit, set leaves and litter swirling into corners and scurrying along walls.

Bound up but restless, the wind tugged at its leash.

When Jed woke up he assumed that the curtains were still drawn shut, the room was so dark. He slid his hand across to where Judith should have been lying, but found her place empty and the sheets cold. He sat up, suddenly bereft. Her dress was gone from the end of the bed, teased from the tangle of clothes they had left the night before. Jed felt abandoned.

He looked at his watch; it was almost midday. *Shit!* He grabbed his jeans and shirt, dragging them on as he headed for the door. He knew his thoughts should have been with Lawrence and Peter and of what was happening to his company, but guiltily he found he could only worry about where Judith was, and if she was angry with him for some reason.

He clattered down the stairs into the hallway. All the doors to the rooms were shut and he felt too self-conscious to try them. Instead he waited quietly, hoping to hear a voice he knew behind one of them.

After a moment, to his delight, he heard Judith. Her voice was muted and he couldn't make out her words, but he reached out, ready to knock politely, a smile forming as he rehearsed in his head the appropriate greeting or apology. He would be able to tell what was needed from the look in her eyes, her beautiful, knowing eyes.

He hesitated with his knuckles an inch from the door. Megan was in there too, he could hear her steady voice.

'Call to him again.'

After a pause long enough to appear as if the request had been ignored, he heard Lawrence's tired, cracking voice. 'Peter… please. Come back to us.'

Jed's eyes widened and he stepped back – his First was being summoned. Now that he was aware, he could feel the faint heat of their concentration. *Why didn't they tell me?* Lawrence didn't have a fraction of the talent that he possessed, surely Judith and Megan could see that? But even as the jealousy flared in him it burned down to guilt at the sound of Lawrence calling quietly, relentlessly, as he must have been doing for hours.

He straightened his t-shirt and knocked softly on the stripped pine door. To his disappointment it was Megan who answered. 'Come in, Jed, your timing is perfect.'

Embarrassed, he stepped inside. Lawrence was seated on a reversed dining chair, using the backrest to support his folded arms. His eyes were puffy and dark-circled but he smiled up at him. Judith was standing in the far corner. She didn't smile.

Peter was lying on a white metal day-bed, covered by a patchwork quilt. He looked to be asleep rather than unconscious, something about his face had changed for the better. Jed was flooded with relief even though the toll on the rest of Peter's body was all too evident. His bare torso was visible above the turned down cover, and lines of dark purple bruises fanned out to his shoulders from the disturbingly recognisable rectangle in the centre of his chest.

'We think he did that to himself, trying to hold onto the stone. The bruising has been coming out all night.' Lawrence spoke softly. 'But he's so close to waking now, so near. Come here, lad. Talk to him.' Lawrence looked at Megan who nodded her approval.

Jed stepped up to the bedside and reached out his hand, placing it gently over his First's skinned knuckles and torn fingers: the stigmata left by the Wolfstone. Peter's hands were warm at last; life pulsing through them on its natural course, and his face, though dirty and stubbled, showed the grateful, wary exhaustion of someone free from pain but who anticipates its return at any moment. He lay as if just below the surface of clear water, visible yet isolated in another world.

Jed opened himself up, visualizing the privacy of a hooded cloak wrapped around his head and back, in a self-conscious protection against what he supposed was a judgemental audience. He slowed his breathing and reached out for Peter's mind.

Suddenly a black shape broke into Jed's vision, the spectral impression of a ragged, lunging monster. He yanked his hands away from Peter's, stifling a cry. Judith came up behind him, and the shock of her touch on his arm made him jump again.

'What did you see?'

'Something. I don't know… something black.' He shook his head and turned to her for reassurance, for guidance, to see her face. He wiped the back of his hand across his mouth. 'I can taste ash. And lead.'

There was the merest hint of respect in her voice as she leaned in close. 'Are you sure?'

Jed nodded. 'And – it's like I've bitten my tongue – like blood, or iron.'

Judith paled. That innocent comparison brought the most unguarded reaction from her that he had seen. Her eyes widened. She turned to her mother. 'I told you those red marks on the filter papers weren't from his cuts!' She pointed an accusing finger at Peter. 'He's the channel for the storm!'

'Enough, Judy!' Megan's words were spoken more to safeguard her company's privacy than from any consideration for Jed and Lawrence's feelings.

Lawrence, as tired as he was, straightened up, surprise and impatience in his voice. 'If my First is being accused of something, could you at least have the courtesy to explain what it is?'

'Peter is not being blamed for anything,' Megan replied, although Judith's expression indicated otherwise. 'The influence of the stone is flowing through him and Jed is sensitive enough to pick this up and articulate his impressions… vividly.' Her glance made Jed wish he really had bitten his tongue.

'I'm sorry.' He wanted to clear the taste from his mouth, to banish the after-image of whatever lurked in Peter. 'I was only trying to help.'

'Hang on, lad! I think you have,' Lawrence gripped Jed's arm. 'Look!'

Peter was frowning, not with pain but in concentration. He appeared to be trying to force himself to wake. Fluttering movements of his eyelids, lips and fingertips were the only indications of his immense effort; he was in the grip of a nightmare, and sleep-paralysis was weighing him down, smothering his attempts to speak or open his eyes.

Jed immediately feared a return of the screaming and shattered man they had found in the yew, but Lawrence stood up, energised by the change. 'He's fighting it at last!'

They gathered around Peter, watching his struggle but unable to help, knowing the battle was his to win, or lose, alone.

The wounds on his chest began to bleed again. Dried scabs beaded then oozed red, and to their horror, new welts appeared, drawn out in parallel stripes radiating from the bruise left by the stone.

Jed instinctively reached out to his First, despite his fear of what the touch might reveal, but Megan prevented him from making contact. 'No! They've seen you, they could use you as a place to hide.'

'*They*?' Lawrence placed a protective arm across Jed, pushing him back. 'Exactly *what* are you referring to?'

Before Megan could answer, a massive spasm clenched Peter's body, arching his back up from the bed and flinging off the covers as if something had charged up at him from below.

'Judy, get my arrow!'

Judith jumped at her mother's command, running from the room.

Peter's eyes showed only the whites, lids flickering as he strained to open them, his teeth gritted together in a jaw breaking grimace. But he wasn't the victim this time – Jed could see – something of the Peter he knew and respected was showing through the pain, his strength was coming back to him. And Jed knew he needed to join the fight, no matter what terrors he might see, no matter what the risk. He prepared himself, braced his mind for the anticipated onslaught. Reached out to touch Peter.

A cool, exquisitely sharp influence sliced between him and the savaged body on the bed. Something akin to a slow-motion line of intent from an aim; as fine as a silk thread but with the momentum of a tidal wave, sundered and dispersed his focus.

Megan held the silver arrow like a wand, pointing it towards Peter. She did not speak but her expression clarified as she found her mark; her eyes shining like the crystals over her fireplace, all facets, points and edges, leaving no place for compassion. And for the first time Jed and Lawrence were left in no doubt that she was as much of a warrior as anyone from a Fort.

At once a writhing tumble of images superimposed over Peter's prone form in a confusion of grey and black. These shadows raked their claws across his chest, scrabbling for purchase, desperate for escape.

Megan called out: 'Get back!'

And set them free.

§

Peter dreams.

He knows he is dreaming.

It is as if he has always lived between the worlds.

He knows this place well, the landscape. The Land. He has come to dream here two times before. Forced in on the point of a silver arrow.

He has listened to the hearts of stories. Watched the spiral patterns of time, form and break, form and break, form and break, like curling waves.

Flowed through the Land, from woken site, to tree, to woken site, remembering the paths, until his heartbeat lost its synchronicity with the yew, and he was drawn away.

This time is different.

A Blackness dogs him, drives him on, keeps him dreaming its dark thoughts.

He tries to pull away, but the agony of resistance exhausts his soul and he gives in, allowing the Pack to take him where it will.

He runs. Looking for an opening, for an unguarded space wide enough to let them all through.

The Voice summons him. He stumbles and the Pack streams by on either side, until he is pushed on again by the withering pain. On and on.

Then comes the Touch.

It passes through the thoughts of banked defences, of cold earth embraces, past the teeth and claws of his sentry. A familiar warmth. A shaft of sunlight cutting through round-bellied storm clouds.

Bringing remembrance and knowledge and guilt.

He reaches out to the proffered hand just as the Blackness picks up the scent and savages the line of recognition into dust – every mote a dagger scoring tears from his eyes.

The dust mantles his dark warder, and is breathed in. Savoured. Remembered.

Peter feels for the shattered warmth, fights to follow it back to its source. His sudden purpose confuses the Pack and he breaks away before they can entangle him. He sees daylight and runs towards it. Two trusted faces fill his vision as the Dreams give ground to waking.

He is quick, but not as swift as the grey tide pursuing him – it overtakes, breaks over him, rams him aside in the headlong race to escape.

Only the Blackness comprehends that Peter is the Doorway. It calls the Pack with the voice of stone and soil, the voice of the delved earth – and they turn back to hunt for their freedom through his guts and his heart and his screaming lungs.

The Arrow cuts, splitting him open, releasing the unbearable pressure. The Pack bursts forth, leaping out of him in a victorious, vicious birth.

Then peace...

And the Blackness hides so deep, so well, that even Peter does not know it is still there.

Chapter Six

David Horsman cupped his cigarette like a spiv, warming his hand, unwilling to waste its paltry heat in the short gaps between lungfuls, and with each inhalation he held the smoke until it was as cold as he was.

He sat on a bench in a Bristol square, hunched and brooding, his black trenchcoat buttoned to the neck, the collar turned up, and the cuffs pulled over his hands. He shifted against the backrest, adjusting his position so only his shoulders were touching the slats; grimaced at a snag of pain, stifled it, then glanced around for a diversion. Everything seemed to be drained: the faces and clothes of passers-by, the pathways, dark lampposts, and dull cars in the regimented Georgian streets beyond the trees. The monarch at its centre, on his bronze horse, ruled over a faded kingdom.

David slowly and carefully sat up straight, trying to slough the weight of the past. With his talent dulled from the shot, he wasn't able to screen out the cloying hubris and violence that lingered from when the Queen's Square fell to riots and fire. He did find a shallow resonance in its long-lost marshland, and drew it around himself with a kind of dismal satisfaction.

He finished his cigarette, burning it right up to his fingertips, then flicked the tiny stub away. Tentatively he slid a hand inside his coat and touched his fingertips to the place where the arrow had hit him. It was deeply painful, the scar tissue new and delicate. He felt as if he'd been gutted with a hook, and his mind was still full of disjointed echoes from the forgotten dreams, like sounds too low to hear, felt as vibrations through the bones of his skull. Tired of it all, David closed his eyes for a second –

glimpsed the ground from a dizzying height – and gasped, eyes wide.

Helen was gently nudging his shoulder from behind the bench, using the side of one of takeaway coffees she carried. 'Sorry, didn't mean to startle you.' She passed the cup to him. 'Careful, it's hot.'

He accepted it with a nod, discarded the lid and took a scalding mouthful. It tracked satisfyingly down his throat, but felt only lukewarm when it reached his stomach. He wanted to drink faster, gulp it down before the stinging heat could dissipate, but he controlled the urge. It was all too easy to get burned after being shot, trying to feed the craving for warmth.

In an ideal world he would still be in his bed beneath layers of blankets, or slumped in front of his woodburner, its door wide and a stack of logs to keep it furnace-hot. And maybe, now and again, taking some of the heat he needed from Helen. Instead, he was waiting for Catrin.

Again.

Helen sat down beside him, sipping her latte and squinting up at the blank slate of the sky. The light was too diffuse to tell the direction of the sun, yet the overall glare was strong enough to sting her eyes.

She had arranged this meeting, and was the ward of the talisman being used as the lure. The circumstances should have given her a sense of authority and a certain degree of power, but debilitated as he was, David retained control.

If she harboured any thoughts to the contrary, they were dispelled as he abruptly gulped the dregs of his coffee and straightened up, disguising the impulse to hold a hand over his scar – she noticed – by patting down his pockets for another cigarette. Helen frowned, the tension from David felt like squandered heat.

He nodded a curt acknowledgement to the couple approaching them along the straight path opposite.

When Catrin and Patrick drew level with the bench David eased himself to his feet. Helen remained seated, sipping her coffee, feeling outranked and peripheral.

'Nice shooting, Catrin.' David allowed the tension to build then added a small sarcastic smile, drawing them back onto familiar ground. He took out a cigarette and lighter; turned up the flame until it ribboned, and held it too near his face. 'Anyway, Patrick, have MI5 snapped you up yet?' He clicked the lighter shut. 'No, honestly.' He blew smoke. 'I hardly knew you were there when you were watching my company.'

'Fuck you, Horsman.'

Catrin quickly stepped between them to break their eye contact, and reached behind to lay a reassuring and controlling touch on Patrick's injured hand. 'Look, let's just cut to the chase for once.'

'What, no foreplay?' David made a fist over his scar. 'You're insatiable.'

Patrick let out a mirthless laugh of exasperation, pulled away from his First and turned to leave. 'I'm sorry, Catrin, I was wrong to come. I want to support you but I can't be a part of this... fiasco.' He took a few steps, hesitated and then turned to jab an accusing finger at David. 'He's just a plainshooting bastard who shouldn't even be in the Lore!'

David's grin dropped. 'Forts *are* the Lore – *bastards* like me are its lifeblood!'

Patrick levelled a pleading look at Catrin, but when she showed no sign of following him, he shook his head and marched away.

She watched him go. There was no point trying to call him back; it was a testament to his loyalty that he had come at all. As the space between them widened she became painfully conscious that he might have been walking away from more than just the meeting.

'Right then. Shall we get down to business?' David's attitude was abruptly sober. 'What are you offering?'

Catrin took a moment to orientate herself in the shifting mood, girding her emotions with a silent mantra: *Get this talisman for Silbury. Get this talisman and the path will be clear.* 'Show me the find, then I'll tell you what I think it's worth.'

She didn't notice Helen's smile.

'You didn't really think I was going to bring it with me, did you?' David raised an incredulous eyebrow. 'I wouldn't expect *you* to turn up with a grab-bag of Silbury finds for me to pick over. This is a preliminary talk, Catrin, that's all.'

'That isn't what you said!'

'Technically, it isn't what Helen said.' He shrugged apologetically. 'I can't be held responsible if you don't have the patience to wait for me to get warm before you make these arrangements.'

Her heart sank. He was playing her. *Patrick was right. I should have gone with him. He was right...* then something about that realisation sparked her resolve. *He was right... but so am I.* She stepped into David's personal space knowing he couldn't back away. She matched him in height and took full advantage of it, staring him straight in the eyes. His coffee-and-cigarette breath felt cold, his skin was ashen and his pupils abnormally dilated, causing him to squint against the pallid daylight as he raised his face to hers. He crossed his arms tightly over the raw scar from her arrow, unable to control his reflex to create a barrier against her closeness, and needing it more than the cigarette he had to discard.

Catrin felt for the remnants of her mark and teased out a small, jagged ghost of the agony she had inflicted on him.

David winced and shuddered, had to turn his head away.

She leaned in and put her mouth close to his ear, as close as a kiss. 'Give me the talisman.'

Helen scowled and put her cup down on the bench. 'David? What's happening – are you okay?' She hadn't heard Catrin's whispered command, but the look on his face was enough to tell her that somehow the power had shifted.

Her First slowly uncrossed his arms, and held out a hand towards her with the palm up. He didn't look at her, instead he locked his gaze on Catrin. 'Let me have the knife.'

'What? No!'

'Do as I say, Helen.'

She sprang up from the seat. 'You promised my dagger would only be bait!'

'I can't keep every promise I make.'

It was Catrin's turn to smile.

§

Patrick was observing the proceedings from an emotionally insulating distance, standing by the wall of a grand Georgian townhouse at the edge of the square. He pretended to scroll through his phone, hands trembling slightly, over which he glared at the three distant figures gathered by the bench. Almost immediately after storming away, his temper had been doused by a sense of duty that wouldn't allow him to abandon Catrin altogether, and after surreptitiously checking that they weren't looking, he had sidled into the shadow of the wall. Removing himself from the disorder and studying it was a compromise his anger could accommodate, plus he knew he needed to calm down before examining his choices, such as they were. Soon the effect of watching from a desensitising distance, surrounded by slow traffic and snatches of ordinary conversations, became blandly reassuring: evidence that the world was a safe, ordered and sociable place.

Sometimes he longed for his lost ability to enjoy everyday normality as a solid fact and not just a screen, beyond which were innumerable further curtains to pull back or peer behind – the thrill forever teetering on the brink of vertigo. Ignorance would be a blessing if it meant he could disregard the scene taking place a bow-shot from where he stood. But the fact that four years before, he had chosen to invest in an alternative reality, fated him to be constantly aware of the gulf between himself and the unknowing majority. It could be inspiring, right now it just made him feel lonely. The covert world to which he belonged bred a kind of contempt for anyone outside of it: an unavoidable aspect of human nature that he disliked – especially when he saw it in himself.

Patrick stroked his thumb across the screen without looking at the parade of images and text. His gaze moved up to the far statue on the plinth, to its brazen idolatry of sovereignty. He sighed. The Lore, inevitably, had its strongest grip on Firsts, as they were the anchoring roots of the system, but that status was intoxicating and could lead to trouble. He'd seen it too many times in Catrin. When Firsts got together they had a tendency to close ranks, regardless of Hallow. It was as if – even as they gathered companions for their sites – they envied the Smith his singular, unchallenged authority.

Patrick saw his role as a counterbalance to Catrin's impulsive behaviour; a left-brain to her right. The Bowlore had been dormant for so long that its new growth was wildly exuberant and needed to be managed, even if sometimes the bonds between companions were stretched to breaking point in the process. He took a sour solace from the distress Helen suddenly appeared to be in, with her arms outstretched in anger or supplication towards David. At least he wasn't the only one to get frustrated with their First.

But how many had made the sacrifices he had? How many had ruined a promising career by never accepting promotions in case it left no time for the Lore? And how many had neglected, lied to, and eventually abandoned the only person they had ever been in love with, because he could never become a part of that deeper reality?

Patrick scowled. It was common knowledge that the companies were littered with broken relationships and lost jobs. *Stop feeling sorry for yourself, St. Patrick, you're not the only martyr to the Lore.* He rested his bandaged and aching hand in the crook of his other elbow, and watched the miniature players silently acting out the script he would be expected to work from when he met up with Catrin again. *If...*

He could defect. Patrick knew she wouldn't hold him back if he asked to leave the company, but in doing so he would almost certainly precipitate the haemorrhaging of Silbury. Simon and James were already disillusioned and would follow suit if he left. *I can't do that to her.*

His phone had lowered without him realising, he lifted it but it stalled halfway to his eyeline. He leaned forward, as if reducing the distance by that tiny amount would clarify what he was seeing.

As he had expected, the meeting had broken up acrimoniously – that much was easy to tell, even at a distance, from their body language – and all three had walked off on separate paths, but heading directly towards him with head held high, was Catrin. *What the hell's happened now?*

Almost as if she had heard, Catrin looked straight at him. She smiled.

Patrick felt a wash of relief and hope – and then embarrassment as he realised that David's dig had been right. *I really am a shit spy.*

§

After Helen had put the length of two streets between herself and David, her angry momentum dissipated. She slowed to a halt on a steel bridge spanning the river, and leaned on the railings to stare at the boats moored on the slow brown water below. The metal drew the warmth from her hands: at first pleasantly cooling, then achingly cold. She gripped even harder onto the steel, using it as a distraction from her misery.

A couple, holding hands, broke from the thin flow of people walking past to add their padlock to the rows linked through the mesh of the rails, and she watched as they closed up their fragile promises in a rudimentary talisman of their own making. They smiled, kissed and let the key drop into the river.

Helen's heart burned down to ashes.

The dagger – *her* dagger – was gone.

The feel of it still pushed into her palm. Its essence, weight, and shape so real that each time Helen blinked away tears she expected it to swim back into focus in her hand – the reluctant, obedient hand that had pulled the knife from its leather wrap and to the teeth-gritted syllables of the word *willingly*, given it up to Catrin.

She had hunted David's expression for anything that would alleviate the betrayal, any hint of mutual conspiracy, some unspoken plot, but his stare was unrelenting and she had found nothing in it to comfort her.

Grief cut her voice.

And then Catrin had drawn the knife from her, as if from a sheath, leaving her hollow. The grey, pitted metal had gleamed sorrowfully in the scattered light from the clouds, disclosing its scored circle and cross symbol of Venus as a thin black script on the blade in the final moment before Catrin slipped it inside the edge of her coat.

Hate was too small a word for what Helen felt. And heartbroken was far too poetic.

Chapter Seven

Lawrence and Jed were sitting on either side of Peter, and whenever they shifted, the spindly frame of the bed complained in disconsolate, metallic squeaks, bowing under their combined weight. They did not speak. The childlike vulnerability in Peter's face when he had begged for promises that the stone was safe, and then his evident pain as he struggled to sit up and answer their fervent questions, had been too harrowing. Pity had silenced them. Lawrence rested his hand on Peter's forearm, patting it from time to time, and offering occasional tight-lipped smiles of reassurance. Jed compulsively traced the endless knotwork maze of his tattoo with one fingertip, without looking down at his forearm.

They had been left alone for some while, their nerves in shreds – ever since Megan and Judith had both rushed from the room, shouting afterthought orders for them to stay. Like loyal, cowering dogs, they had obeyed.

The small room appeared to be untouched: the side-table supported a jug of lilies, their curled white petals opening onto green throats, and their powdery yellow stamens pinched out. Leaning against the willow-pattern jug were two paperbacks of Plath and Hughes poems, bookmarked with blackbird feathers, and beside them a glass of water that had been brought for Peter, still full and unspilled. The faded Chinese rug under their feet was unruffled, its tassels tidy, and dust motes slowly swam and glittered in a shaft of sunlight from the window.

The peace was surreal, adding to their unease, and rendering the appalling image of the swarm of shadows that had erupted from Peter so out of place that, although they had only just witnessed it, their minds were already replacing the outlandish reality with denial.

How could something so brutal and ferocious leave no trace? The room should have been wrecked; it had been crammed full of massive grey forms, screaming, high-pitched howls, a choking stench of animal fear and foul mud. The chaos so terrifying that they had fallen to the floor, arms over their heads, helpless with panic.

How could Peter survive that? How did they?

And then Megan had brought the full force of her talent to bear and exorcised the apparitions, scouring away the horror and darkness with a flare of silver light so intense that even now, nearly an hour later, as they stared around at the bewildering serenity of the room, they kept involuntarily blinking away the diminishing fire of afterimages that had been left like bruises on their vision. Slashes of red, like eyes.

Baleful, mad with hunger, eyes.

Lawrence blinked hard and rubbed his temples. The eyes were undeniable – shrinking, becoming more peripheral, but there. He squeezed Peter's arm again, then let it go and felt for the brandy flask in his pocket.

'Pass it over.'

For a moment Lawrence couldn't move. Hope surged through him but he curbed his reaction and slipped the nearly empty flask into Peter's waiting hand; the metal looking pristine against the brown smudges of dried blood and dirt. Peter finished off the brandy in one mouthful, closing his eyes as he savoured its harsh warmth.

Jed and Lawrence watched, mindful of his fragility, leaving the instigation of any further exchange up to him.

He handed back the flask, wiping his mouth with the back of his trembling hand. He tried to smile, but his haunted eyes couldn't maintain the illusion and he let it fall. 'I'm... so very sorry.' He hugged the patchwork quilt around himself. 'I thought... No, I *was* doing the right thing. I never meant... for this...'

'It's alright.' Lawrence laid a pacifying hand over Peter's. 'We understand.'

Jed shook his head almost imperceptibly, muttering, '*I* don't.'

Lawrence glared a warning.

'No,' Peter sighed, 'he has every right to be angry. I lied to you both... I had no choice.' His rounded shoulders slumped further. 'And I have also been... misled.' He coughed, his voice hoarse from strain. 'But please, you must believe me, I only did it to protect you.'

'Well, it didn't fucking work.' Jed's defiance was growing, given licence by Peter's apparent recovery.

'For God's sake lad, pipe down!'

'Are you going to tell us what's so great about this stone? Why it's worth putting us through this fucking nightmare?'

'Jed!' Lawrence looked as if he was about to shove him off the bed and right out of the door, until Peter laid a restraining arm across him.

'Yes, I will tell you… of course. You deserve to know.' He frowned in concentration. 'And the stone is safe in a Sanctuary. So now, perhaps, my part in this is… over.' He paused, framing his thoughts, and then lowered his voice to a whisper, motioning them to lean in close. 'Everything I have gone through – everything you must have gone through – will all be worth it. The stone is not just a talisman.' His eyes were unnervingly intense, shining with emotion as he stared at both of them in turn. 'It is a *Treasure*.'

Lawrence, already doubting Peter's lucidity, felt obliged to take charge again. 'I really think you need to rest, let's talk about the stone when you're feeling stronger.'

For a second, there was a flash of such anger in Peter's face that Lawrence flinched. And then it was gone, replaced by acquiescence and a weary nod.

'Yes… you're right.' His reasonable tone sounded forced as he placed a spread hand over the blackening, rectangular bruise on his chest. 'Maybe I *am* rushing this… I can see you're not ready.' He rubbed his eyes as if trying to wake up. 'I must read the signs.' Although his brow furrowed he looked like he was about to laugh.

Jed was about to speak up again when Lawrence surreptitiously kicked at his shin. The younger man scowled but kept quiet.

Lawrence's expression was full of intimation. 'I'm sure Megan would want to know how Peter is – could you go and see if you can find her, lad?'

'I'll see if I can find Judith.' He stood up abruptly and the bed frame squeaked and rocked.

'Good-oh.' Lawrence stared past him.

The door had been left ajar, Jed went up to it, snatched at the handle and shut it hard behind him – though not as hard as he wanted to. On the other side he stopped, jammed his hands in his pockets and kicked the floor. Yesterday, when they'd first arrived, the tiles of the hallway had been scattered with lounging cats, but now it was empty, despite the enticing stripe of afternoon sun coming in through the glazed front door. He missed their soothing presence. After what had just happened to Peter, the cats were probably miles away by now, teetering on the topmost branches of trees. They were lucky: no one expected them to stay, or blamed them when they didn't.

He walked over to the door leading to the room with the chairs and crystals, where Megan's silver arrow was kept on the shelf over the fireplace, and where Glastonbury apparently held their meetings; it seemed the obvious place to start looking. He couldn't feel anyone's presence, but that didn't count for much when around Sanctuary talents. He listened, knocked, waited – heard nothing, and went in anyway.

The room felt stuffy even though the window was partially open. The fleeting sunlight lensed through the glass, warming the air and bringing out the faint ashtray-smell of a room used for smoking. Unconsciously, he chose the same chair that Judith had showed him to the day before, and turned it to face the looming Tor before slumping onto the frayed cane seat.

He put his feet up on another chair and gazed up at the hill beyond the garden and trees, watching its green flanks alternate between light and dark as they were stroked by shafts of sunshine. Before long he became aware that the pace was picking up. The wind rolled the tops of the bushes, blustering hard enough to snatch rooks from their nests in the spindly trees, and swirl them like black litter. It had also purged the tower of sheltering pilgrims, and only a few restless figures trudged the scarring paths or milled around the summit.

The ruined stone belfry maintained an amicable truce with the Tor. The church had risen from the inspiration of the hill, and fallen to earthquake and dissolution, but the steadfast tower had remained, proving its worth by completing the iconic silhouette of the hill. The Tor was a beacon and a promise of transcendence, but to Jed it appeared strangely two-dimensional, framed by the ragged sky, no more real than the paintings on the wall behind him.

And for a site that purportedly shared out knowledge and wisdom, it remained frustratingly mute and obsessed with its own journey.

No wonder Peter feels safe here.

Jed's disenchantment had been creeping up on him for months, yet he was taken aback at how abrupt and complete the break felt, as if the very last bastion holding it back had been his anxiety for Peter's life. Now that he appeared to be recovering, Jed's shock and disgust at the broken bonds of trust between them had finally ripped him free of his sense of obligation, and left him spinning in the exposed air like the tumbling rooks.

It was like falling out of love. He just didn't want to be with them – with Ninestones – anymore.

Or perhaps, there was only enough devotion in his heart for one cause at a time.

§

Judith sat on the carved stone bench by the pond, holding her loose hair back so that it wouldn't whip across her face. Her eyes were downcast.

Megan stood beside the wind-ruffled pool with her arms folded tightly; their exchange having slid – almost inevitably – from a discussion between a First and a Second, to that of a clash between mother and daughter.

'But if you allow yourself to be distracted you'll put everything we've worked for at risk.'

'It won't distract me!'

'Following two paths at the same time will split your attention, that alone will make you vulnerable. I can't sanction that.'

Judith looked up. 'Are you trying to protect me?' It was an accusation.

'Yes, I am!' Megan raised her hand for silence, stalling her daughter's response. 'Of *course* I am. Because set against unlocking the Treasure, this coming storm is nothing more than a diversion – one you will *not* waste yourself on.'

'But you will?'

'I'll do whatever has to be done.' Megan plucked a gold chain hanging below her throat, drawing up a small iron key. She reached behind her neck, undid the clasp on the necklace, unthreaded the key and held it out. 'And so will you.'

Judith stared at the key, her temper abruptly doused. A break in the clouds heightened the metal's modest shine. She was quiet for several heartbeats. 'Is it time then?'

Megan sighed, casting her gaze around the shivering garden, at ripped leaves and petals scattering the lawn, and then upwards to the broken blue and white of the disordered sky. 'I think it has to be.'

Reaching out slowly and respectfully, with her hair blowing into a dark halo around her head, Judith nodded, accepting the key into her cupped hands.

'So mote it be.'

Chapter Eight

David was agitated.

The mid-morning daylight was too dismal to paint by and he hated working by artificial light. His scar ached like a punch to his ribs, forcing him to sit bolt upright. Although his heating was on full, he couldn't get warm.

He was pathologically obsessed with what Catrin was up to, and Helen still hadn't answered any of his calls or messages.

He tried to focus on the dozen broadhead arrows fanned out on the table before him, but his concentration was being repeatedly broken by the irregular bangs and rattles coming from the loose sash-window beside him, as it was blown against its frame.

Fuck. He slammed the flat of his palm on the table and gave up, screwed the lid back on the tube of black acrylic paint and rinsed his brush clean in a glass jar. The stained water swirled into eddies around the wooden handle. He whisked it around again and then poised the brush over the whirlpool, letting it drip into the centre of the miniature maelstrom. David had always been inclined to dismiss sympathetic magic as being too obvious and simplistic: folk remedies and hexes for the ignorant who would read too much into any superficial similarity in a vain attempt to control their lives. Nothing more.

And yet.

Another gust shuddered the panes of glass in their frame, drawing his attention back to the turbid sky. Was there another hand somewhere, stirring up the rising wind?

He stood, walked over to the window and reached up with arms wide, to lean on the frame with his paint-smudged hands. He stared at the jostling cloudscape, scrutinising all its shades of melancholy, yearning and loss. There were no answers there, and watching the display brought no resolution, only a kind of emptiness.

A kind of hunger.

He gripped the edges of the window frame as if the walls had dissolved and he was left holding up a slab of sky.

An impulse began to rise in him.

He wanted to rush up into that boundless place and run yelling, screaming, through the dizzying, mutable ravines and mountains, catching glimpses of the shackled world as it rolled away far beneath him. Purpose promised itself to him up there, the stark cold grey swarmed with intent. There was a role for him amongst those torn clouds, a wind to lift him onto its many backs. A place in the hunt.

The knowledge hurtled into him, wild and uncontrollable, from a source outside his current sphere of influence. He couldn't pull it in the direction of his will, it flowed through him, tugging his senses in its wake and he found himself panting, mouth wide, his mind full of schemes and possibilities inspired by the gale, his face pressed against the invisible cold constriction of the glass, steaming it over with clouds of his own.

David had trained himself to control the climax of a shot and to guide the overwhelming rush of energy for his own ends, and he fully intended to learn how to channel this new sensation as well, because – despite his ego – he knew, with absolute certainty, that he would not be the only one in the Lore receptive to the revelation of the storm.

First come, first served.

He forced himself to calm down and allow his interpretation to crystallise. One facet shone out plainly, focussed through the lens of his Hallow – that whatever was coming would need to be faced with a full quiver, and therefore the most immediate practicalities had to be taken care of. With fresh eyes and renewed enthusiasm David inspected the sheaf of half-finished arrows fanned across the tabletop, but then passed them by and headed for the kitchen, needing something, anything, to satisfy his sudden gnawing pangs of hunger.

§

Catrin nestled cross-legged in the middle of her sofa. On a patted-flat cushion beside her was a plate covered with cake crumbs, on the other side was an open carrier bag full of leather offcuts, and balanced on her thighs were scissors, a reel of linen thread, and the remote.

The local news was showing on the small TV in the corner of the room, but she had it on mute, content with just its visual company. Normally Radio 4 was her choice when working with her hands, but the depressing quality of the daylight demanded colour, the brighter and more synthetic the better. She sat wrapped in an oversized cardigan with the sleeves rolled up, repeatedly flicking her fringe from her eyes as she bent over her project – at the balance point between the mundane and the miraculous.

The weather forecast filled the screen, she glanced up, then registered its implication and leaned forward to study the barometric hexes criss-crossing the map. Isobars tight as fingerprints overlaid the lands of Wessex, but she didn't bother to turn up the sound, the presenter couldn't tell her what she really needed to know. Catrin's reaction sprang from a deeper place, not their amber-warnings and serious expressions.

A slight movement at the edge of her vision broke her concentration. The living room window was firmly shut but a draught had sidled its way through the frame and was making the white muslin curtains billow; slow waves rising and falling in a gentle, eerie motion. Catrin dismissed the intrusion, changed channels to a property programme and turned her attention back to the leather sheath she was stitching. Practicality was the best insulation against fear.

Catrin examined the edges of the sheath where the tiny holes awled through the leather waited for her poised needle. She had never intended to go to any kind of trouble for the dagger because the talisman was merely a means to an end, and would be traded or spent as necessary – whatever it took to get the Wolfstone. But becoming its ward had changed her attitude. The knife was more than just an adjunct to the Wolfstone, it had its own story. Handling it had exposed it as a talisman that had run its own course through the intervening centuries since its creation. A twisting, tainted course.

It lay on the low table in front of her, on a spread square of black silk; a wrapping that had proved to be an insufficient barrier against the melancholy nature of the blade. Why Helen had been so wedded to the dagger was beyond her.

The short, pewter-grey blade lay pointing away from her, its pitted surface speaking not so much of age as hasty construction, with imperfections resulting from air bubbles and particles of grit. The knife had been cast as a whole, the tang extending through the battered, unpolished yew wood handle to the simple disc of the pommel. The edges looked as if they would crumble away at the first stroke of a whetstone, and yet the blade gave the impression of being both sharp and poisonous. If there was lead content in the metal making up the knife it would be toxic to some degree, and might indeed exacerbate any wound it caused, but Catrin sensed there was a deeper significance to that danger, something she didn't feel confident to delve into until more of its past was understood. It didn't look durable or practical enough to be a tool, it lacked the efficiency of a true weapon, and when she handled it the metal felt inert yet poised, Damocles-like. Catrin held onto the hope that she would be safely rid of the knife before that aspect of its core was exposed.

It was too precious to leave in her flat, and too tainting to hide at Silbury Hill. Her uneasy conclusion had been that it would have to be carried until it had served its purpose.

Catrin tugged hard on the final stitch and tied it off, trimmed the thread close to the leather and smoothed the sheath out, pleased with her handiwork. She picked up the dagger, fed it in and it fitted perfectly; gripped by the leather so that it wouldn't slide out by accident but loose enough that it could be easily drawn. Now that the blade was covered by something formed and imbued with intent she found it was no longer troubling – her thoughts could turn to plans rather than doubts. She nodded to herself, satisfied.

And then, on an impulse, Catrin picked up the long needle, held it like a pen and scribed a neat and accurate facsimile of the dagger's Venus symbol into the leather.

Another gust of wind breached the window frame with a faint, mournful shrill and the sky reached out to her with slow waving, white muslin arms.

§

The beech trees growing on the top ramparts of Badbury Rings hillfort repeatedly bowed then righted themselves as the inconsistent wind passed through their canopies. At the summit of the hill was a small clearing and at its centre, on the ground, sat Helen.

She was sheltering beside a table-sized stone plinth that bore a weathered steel map engraved with the compass points and noteworthy features of the surrounding countryside. David would sometimes stand on it, using it like a dais on occasions when the fort was empty of outsiders, and when enough of his company were present to make the performance worthwhile.

This time Helen was the sole representative of Badbury.

She had been on the hill since before the dawn, wandering the curved banks and ditches and threading her way through the trees. She had cried, composed herself and then cried again, seeking a reassurance that her site, for once, couldn't deliver. Her body felt hollow, her soul exhausted. It would have been less painful if David had turned his longbow on her.

Helen leaned back, resting on her arms and turned her face up to the sky to let the wind tug at her hair and soothe her sore eyes, welcoming its rough caress. She heaved a sobering sigh – and then narrowed her eyes to stare intently at the racing clouds, as if noticing them for the first time.

The wind parted her lips and blew into her mouth, she opened her throat and let it breathe for her. The gusts of the gale filled her lungs in pace with her body's need, the tidal rush of the wind through the treetops was the sound of the air moving in and out, and breath by heartbeat by breath by heartbeat, her sense of self – too often overwhelmed by David's – was restored. The hill beneath her felt like a friend, a companion. The sky? Perhaps... not yet.

She knew her shooting was faultless, second only to David for speed, and remembered how that talent had brought him within her sights. When she was still new to the company – and he was still married – they would vie for the most marks on a raid and afterwards celebrate their victories or commiserate their losses secretly and passionately, here within their Fort, still high from the shots they had made. Their complete detachment from the mundane world insulating them from guilt.

And back in the days when he still kept his promises, he had given her the dagger. They had taken it, on impulse, from a tiny museum of curios in the village of Hatiston, and he had permitted her to claim it because the blade was decorated with the Venus glyph, the sign of a woman. The sign of love.

She smiled at the memory.

There would be a time for reconciliation, there always would be. The love she had for him was, of necessity, preserved by a kind of selective amnesia. But roused by the storm, her focus was being drawn towards another target: one with whom she did not share any mitigating allegiance or history, one she would have to take down covertly. That factor wouldn't be the problem, Helen had faith in her ability as a sniper, but there would be repercussions from this act of revenge. She stood up, wiped her face, and smoothed her windblown hair back into a tight ponytail.

It would be worth it.

§

Patrick chewed pensively on the end of a fluorescent green highlighter, popping its lid on and off. Every so often he held the lid in his teeth to strike a neat line through a relevant word or passage in the scuffed booklet he was studying.

He pushed his glasses up the bridge of his nose, and reached for his mug which was acting as a makeshift paperweight for a pile of leaflets; some of which had been sorted to one side and marked with Post-it notes scrawled with comments, mostly in Catrin's handwriting. She had loaned him this assortment of small-press and self-published literature, everything she could find about the tiny parish of Hatiston, in the hope that Patrick's fresh and unbiased eye would spot something significant. Thus far he had nothing new to report. His eyes felt far from fresh now, he had a headache, his back was stiff, and to add to his discomfort, when he raised the mug to his lips he found he'd already finished his tea. He couldn't remember drinking it, which justified a break to make more. Sighing, he dropped the pen onto his desk in resignation and headed for the kitchen.

Whilst waiting for the kettle to boil he paced the floor, too agitated to remain still. Catrin's Wish Stone – her bloody *Wolf* stone – was starting to obsess him almost as much as it did her, and after extracting the stone's associated talisman from Badbury, there was clearly no way she was coming back from the edge. That miserable and ugly knife had killed the last hope of persuading Catrin to abandon her crusade.

At her request, and out of forbearance, he had taken on the responsibility of investigating the stone's folklore so that she would be free to concentrate on bonding with the dagger on a more intuitive level. The sheer, plodding difficulty he was experiencing in the task, convinced him that at least one Hallow could be eliminated from Silbury's options: he was definitely not a member of a Stone company.

None of the information he had gleaned so far gave him any comfort. He couldn't see why this talisman would be any more useful than the other wolf finds Catrin had been infatuated with. There was nothing about it online that wasn't already in the literature regarding the legend, resulting in his present repetitious, low-tech slog through the paper trail, and it was yet to yield anything other than the dry bones of a depressing, long dead tale. It was beyond him how Silbury's path could be revealed by something so morbid in nature. Their Hill should shine, blazing chalk-white across the land and the Lore. This bit of dismal, occult flotsam would only serve to stain it.

And mark it for the attention of darker forces.

Patrick finished making his fifth tea of the morning, took it back into his study, paused in front of his page-covered desk, took off his glasses, polished them on his sleeve, sighed – and then went back for a packet of Digestives.

The local history booklets, mostly decades old, and presumably written for lost tourists (he couldn't think why anyone other than a devoted genealogist would make an effort to visit the place) were concise to the point of uselessness. The tale of the death of the last wolf in England – just one amongst many dotted around the country – was Hatiston's most obvious claim to fame, but even that had been downgraded to a dry footnote, added beneath an exhaustive inventory of pew, rood screen and ceiling-boss carvings to be found in the church. Just one pamphlet; cheaply photocopied from hand-written text rather than printed, considered the story to be worthy of expansion. Below a tiny copy of a woodcut, grimly entitled *The Flaying*, was written the only description of the event that felt like a true link with the past. It gave a postulated account of the stone's history as a Viking relic, before it became invested with Hatiston's claim to the wolf extinction, and even mentioned the dagger. Catrin had heavily underlined a sentence that read: *'A crudely made pewter knife, reputed to have been used to skin the wolf, can be seen on display in the local museum.'* Patrick smiled bleakly, not since Badbury had paid it a visit.

Yesterday, after Catrin had returned triumphant with the dagger, and Patrick had doused her mood with realism, they had agreed to investigate the museum in the hope of gaining some insight into the link between knife and stone. And any hint of a connection that Catrin could use to draw the Wish Stone to her.

They had eventually found the place by luck, rather than GPS or by signage – both of which it lacked – tucked away in a cottage that had been the village shop back when Hatiston had been lively enough to support one. The original signboard above the door had been overpainted in green and gold capitals that began confidently, but bunched up to accommodate the final letters, until the last M of museum was half the width of the first. The amateurish and neglected look of the place raised their hopes, it was much more likely to yield the kind of information they wanted if it wasn't sterilised by organisation. The dusty bay window of the shop was haphazardly crammed with vernacular treasures: mad-eyed clockwork toys; gas masks and ration books; broken fossils; faded seashells; chipped commemorative plates; moth-eaten stuffed birds; unfathomable Victorian kitchen-implements; Roman coins; flattering miniatures in lockets; rusted farm implements; faded samplers expertly stitched by girls of eight; flint axe-heads; cavalry swords bleeding trails of braid and tassels; mourning jewellery crafted from jet and woven hair; glass animals, glass eyes, glass walking sticks; cigar boxes full of tarnished medals; sepia photographs of long dead families; and brass shell-cases pulled from the sides of trenches and hammered into love tokens. Dust and pathos rimed every surface.

A handwritten card hanging inside the window said 'open' but it looked like it was never changed. When they pushed on the door experimentally, it swung wide, jingling the cobwebbed shop-bell above, which to their surprise, actually brought the owner out from a back room. He held a half-eaten sandwich and an air of resentment, and made it plain as he spoke through slow, noisy mouthfuls, that he had no interest in history and couldn't tell them anything more about the exhibits than whatever was written on their yellowed paper labels. With a shrug, he explained that he'd inherited the results of his grandfather's hobby along with the house, and the building would soon be put up for auction, but the contents were to be displayed for as long as possible, then donated to other collections, according to his grandfather's wishes.

At this Patrick and Catrin had exchanged a sceptical glance. They surmised from his attitude that in a matter of weeks the entire museum would be on eBay or in a skip; all the irreplaceable social history destroyed, the stories gone, the strange timeless beauty destroyed. And from the viewpoint of the Bowlore, another idyllic hunting ground would be lost. The depressing inevitability added its taint to the musty air.

The owner looked them up and down, finished his sandwich, stifled a belch and then, after pointedly dusting off of the donations box with the back of his hand, grudgingly left them to browse.

As soon as the owner had closed the door behind him, they set to searching the crammed shelves, crates, tables and glass cabinets, knowing full well that their chances of finding any traces left by the dagger were slim to none. It had been missing for long enough that its space in the collection had probably been taken or concealed with drifting dust, and since the Wolfstone itself had dropped out of the records back when it was buried in the sixteenth century, its trail was fragmented and centuries cold, and there would be no residues from that narrative.

But then, unexpectedly, one exhibit had attracted their attention. In a corner, leaning against a wall, beneath the glassy glare of a fox's mask; propping up a witch's poppet bound in rough red wool, a bunch of swan and heron feathers, and a child's pair of hobnailed clogs, was a rectangular panel cut from a thick oaken door.

They both experienced the rush of recognition.

Catrin had lifted its attached tag to read: *'Circa 1300. Removed during restoration of St Agnes' church, Hatiston. 1913'.* Somewhat baffled by the strength of their reaction to something so relatively ordinary, she turned the label over to check the reverse: *'reputedly bearing the claw marks of a phantom dog'.* The tag dropped from Catrin's hand, and she traced her fingertips down towards a row of black gouges in the wood, but before they had a chance to properly examine the panel, the owner came back bearing a bunch of keys and the news that he was closing up – for the very last time, judging by his indifference. Feeling as if they had been bundled off on a tangent as well as out of the museum, they had ended up driving home in almost complete silence, lost in their own thoughts, with their reaction to the find of the panel more tormenting than productive.

Settling back at his desk, Patrick sipped his tea, stretched out his shoulders, and opened another booklet from the pile, keeping its brown cardboard cover open with the side of his injured right hand. He noticed that the bandage was grubby with cheap ink smudged off the pages, and for some reason that harmless contamination unsettled him. He needed to change the dressing but didn't want to be reminded of his vulnerability; of the cut through his hand and his broken bow. The wind shook the world outside his window – it felt like a bad time to be unarmed.

Patrick raised his hand out of harm's way and leaned his elbow awkwardly on the smeared page. He skim-read the stories of local witches, ghosts, boggarts and murderers, found nothing of interest, and tossed it aside. If there was a Black Dog linked with Hatiston he was damned if he could find it. None of the local history books mentioned it, and they were usually the best source of lost folklore. It was almost as if whatever had happened at the church had been deliberately expunged from the records. Had the door panel really needed to be replaced? It had appeared solid enough during their brief investigation, and although the three parallel gouges were deep, ingrained with dirt, old varnish and the patina of age, they didn't appear to have affected the integrity of the wood. The oak had felt like iron to the touch. Was it replaced because some zealous vicar of St Agnes' had taken it upon himself to drive out the devil-dog – to take out the Trash?

Patrick's ignorance about the spectre did not diminish its capacity to unnerve him; the absence of verifiable facts only left more room for his imagination. Now he was aware that its grim presence lurked behind both the stone and the dagger, it haunted him like the apprehension of mortality: it would not be denied, and with each day, each hour, each minute, it was drawing closer.

Chapter Nine

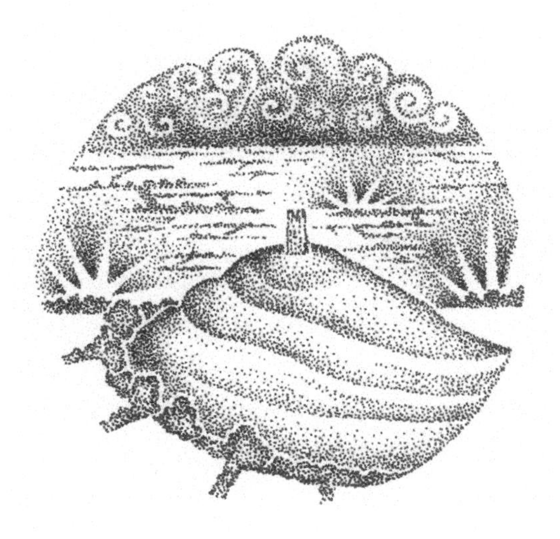

The sun faded to a pallid disc, and by early evening was lost behind thick clouds, ushering in a premature and disquieting dusk. The daylight crept away exhausted.

The wind's strength grew.

Judith held a ceramic bowl on her lap. It was half full of water, and a thin steam wafted from its surface carrying the warm and soothing medicine scent of tea-tree oil. She tore a fresh handful of cotton wool from the roll beside her, dipped it in, wrung it out over the bowl and continued to dab at the welts on Peter's chest and arms. A bedside lamp had been brought in as task lighting for the job, and it lit the growing pile of dirty and discarded wads that lay like stained snow on a spread tea-towel at her feet.

Every time Peter sucked in a breath or winced, she would pause and hold her closed hand over his chest, then slowly unfurl her fingers to channel away his pain until he relaxed again, whereupon she would continue her duty, efficiently but without any lasting empathy.

Jed was gazing at her from the side of the partially open doorway. He had positioned himself tight against the door jamb so that she was visible but the rest of the room was not. No one else in there concerned him anymore.

Judith knew that he was watching, and never looked up from her work.

She was simultaneously so distant and so intense an experience, Jed still felt as nervous in her presence as when he'd first laid eyes on her. The only warmth she gave out was that of the energy she used; he could sense it like a soft draught against his skin whenever she raised a hand to soothe Peter's hurt.

Jed closed his eyes and breathed it in.

Lawrence was trying not to give in to sleep, sitting as upright as he could on what he now considered his chair, having spent most of the previous night on it. Dutiful as he was, he wasn't looking forward to a repetition of that experience. His eyelids drooped, he blinked hard and opened them wide again.

He was very slightly – as much as he could manage towards someone he disliked – in awe of Judith's abilities, fully comprehending now that her arrogance was born out of knowledge. So, in deference to her need for concentration he remained quiet, the fact that this also gave him an excuse not to engage in conversation with the two companions from Glastonbury seated beside him, was just fortunate happenstance. He noticed them watching the proceedings hawkishly, as if they were searching for signs in Peter's reactions. Lawrence wasn't sure what augurs were to be found in the moans of a wounded and, although he hated to admit it, emotionally disturbed man, but they surely couldn't be positive.

He surreptitiously stretched his arms and legs, stifling a yawn.

Peter's attempts to communicate had stuttered to a halt after Jed had gone for help, and Lawrence was wracked with guilt, believing that his decision to calm Peter's disjointed confession had precipitated the breakdown. Of course he had done it for all the right reasons, but was left with the rueful thought that to have found out more from Peter in that rare moment of privacy, might actually have been worth the anguish.

And as for Jed, well, he was next to useless – away with the fairies. *Certainly one in particular anyway.* For all his forgivable, youthful failings, Jed had never disappointed him before now.

Lawrence was forced to accept that, to all intents and purposes, he was now the only functioning member of Ninestones. *What on Earth am I to do?* He shifted in his chair, twisting to rest one elbow across the backrest. He cupped his chin and sighed. His body was vacillating between adrenaline rushes and bone-deep weariness. *I'm too old for all this nonsense.*

And even though he was surrounded by people who would probably offer the best advice he could hope to get, he had absolutely no intention of asking them anything.

At last Judith was finished. Peter appeared to be sleeping; his breathing was slow, deep and regular. She dropped the swab she was using onto the tea-towel, picked up the corners and tied them tightly. She spoke without turning around. 'Take this outside and burn it.' She put it and the bowl aside, and stood up. 'Pour the water over the ashes, smash the bowl, salt the pieces and bury everything at a crossroads.' Then she left without even glancing at Lawrence, although for a second he thought she was instructing him, before Judith's companions; the man in the hoodie and the slight woman who had been watching from behind him, got up to collect the bowl and bundle. As the woman passed she smiled and touched Lawrence's shoulder. 'Are you alright?'

He smiled back. 'Fine, thank you.'

'I'll make you a cup of tea. With sugar?' He nodded his head, and then they were gone too.

For some reason that simple act of kindness cut through his composure, and though he tried hard to stop himself, his chest began to shake with silent sobs.

'Lawrence?'

He raised his head, wiped his eyes, and saw to his astonishment that Peter was sitting up. 'Oh, I...' He cleared his throat to steady his voice. 'I thought you were asleep.'

Peter shook his head. 'I've already been asleep for too long.' With some difficulty he swung his legs over the edge of the bed. 'Help me up.'

Lawrence hesitated, disturbed by the messianic glint in Peter's eyes. He had hoped that the healing from Judith would act as a balm to his mind as well as his body, but it seemed even her talent had its limitations.

Peter fixed his stare on the half open doorway. 'There's something that must be done... before any other decisions are made.' He tried to stand and Lawrence belatedly stood up to offer a supporting arm. 'Come in here, Jed.' He reached out to the door with his hand spread in invitation.

After a long pause, and with a reluctance almost as tangible as Judith's power, Jed shuffled into the room. His arms were crossed and his head down, but his jaw was set with a determination that reminded Lawrence of the days when he was still learning how to aim. He stood in silence before his First.

A windblown branch of wisteria growing around the window frame outside, scrabbled and squeaked against the glass.

Peter waited, and then prompted him. 'I can't say it for you.'

Jed raised his head, there were tears in his eyes. 'I'm sorry. Things have changed... *I've* changed. I can't be a part of the company anymore.' He took a deep breath, drew himself up straight and uncrossed his arms, 'I want to leave.' He corrected himself. 'I, Jed, Third of Ninestones, want to leave your company.'

All three of them felt the tearing wrench of the words.

Lawrence held his breath in anticipation of a protest, but none came.

'Of your own free will?'

Jed nodded. 'Yes.'

'Then, I Peter Oldfield, First of Ninestones, release you.'

Jed, struck dumb by emotion, backed towards the door as if he couldn't bring himself to turn away. Peter crumpled back onto the bed, diminished, once again having to fall back on his severely depleted reserves. He put his hands over his face, shutting out potential complications. 'Jed, you've made your decision… Just leave.'

But Lawrence couldn't contain himself any longer and he turned to Peter, 'I can't believe you're letting him do this!' His First didn't respond, so Lawrence made a grab for Jed's arm instead, almost shouting into his face. 'How can you possibly claim you're doing this of your own free will when that Judith girl has got you wrapped around her little finger! Did she tell you to do this?'

Jed tore his arm from Lawrence's grip. 'For fuck's sake – no she didn't! I've been wanting to leave for months but you just didn't fucking notice. What stopped me is that I didn't have anywhere to go before!'

'You're joining *Glastonbury*?' Lawrence let out an incredulous laugh. 'How can you expect me to take that seriously when all you ever do is complain that we don't shoot enough? The whole thing is utterly ridiculous lad!'

Jed stared at him, his eyes dark, his lips tight and pale with anger. 'You've *never* taken me seriously, have you?'

Lawrence's face fell as he realised his mistake.

'All this time. All this fucking time, you've treated me like a kid… and I've taken it because—' He swallowed back his tears. 'You found me. And you showed me… that there's *real* magic in the world.'

Lawrence's grief cut his strength away, he felt as if he was going to fall. In front of him stood a young man who had grown from the boy he had met at the stones, to a companion who eclipsed him in almost every regard, and the only superiority Lawrence retained; his life experience, had apparently taught him nothing but condescension.

Jed hugged himself to suppress the ache in his chest, his hands clenched into fists. He wiped his eyes on his sleeve. 'If anyone, *anyone* else had called me *lad*… I would have fucking decked them.'

It was all that needed to be said.

He turned away and walked out, quietly pulling the door closed behind him.

§

The wind harried the night until it was deserted. Some aspect of the weather, some indefinable primitive threat, managed to disturb even those insulated by the most rational, limited or dulled sensibilities; driving nearly everyone to ground behind bricks and mortar, locked doors, pulled curtains, and soothing screens.

For the few who remained, the storm cleared the land, and laid out a battlefield.

In a handful of the dark swathes lying between the glimmer of villages and the orange glow of towns, isolated flashes of sharp white light flared up then winked out like lobbed fireworks, but they were not followed by a shock of noise; the incandescence was released from life, not gunpowder.

Jed and Judith stood at the summit of Glastonbury Tor, huddled together in the lee of the tower. The gutted belfry howled and moaned as the wind tore through it; the two open doorways and roofless tower acting like a massive chimney, pulling in and accelerating the surge of air to such an extent that there was more shelter to be found on the exposed crown of the hill than within its thick stone walls.

The prevailing winds shifted, again and again, forcing them to circle the tower to remain within its protection. They accepted this shepherding with forbearance though, as from all four aspects they could observe the sporadic but unmistakable evidence of skirmishes taking place far out across the reclaimed floodplains of the Somerset Levels.

Distance stripped away the violence, reducing the clashes between companies to nothing more than a transient light show against the blackness. The shots were much less obvious than any of the lights from the cars, streets and houses, meaning that only those in the Bowlore would ever be able to read them for what they were.

As they watched, one battle died away with five shots one after the other, and then at the foot of the Mendip Hills another started up with three simultaneous flashes, almost certainly an ambush – a characteristic sign of the Forts.

Jed and Judith pressed against each other and the cold stone, their hands and bodies resonating with the deep vibrations emanating from the core of the tower as it sang with the gale.

Jed shouted over the roaring air. 'At least they're not plainshooting!' He was trying to follow Judith's example and remain impartial, but the sheer wildness of it all was intoxicating. He suppressed his misplaced feelings of empathy for the fighters, and the mutinous notion that he was still a freebow – that if he really wanted he could chose to join a Fort instead of Glastonbury.

Judith shook her head. 'They won't do that – they're shooting for the storm even though they think it's for themselves and for their own hunger.' She swept her hair to one side and tucked it down into the collar of her coat but it was soon pulling free again. 'Their bellies are as big as the sky, nothing will satisfy them.'

He watched another flash, then another. 'How will there be enough room in the yews?'

'There won't, the Covenant protects us from battles, not wars.'

He turned to her, wide eyed. 'What'll happen to them?'

'The Forts will use up restored talismans to keep their companions alive. Beautiful, vital, irreplaceable finds will crumble to dust. The soul of the land will be diminished.' She held his hand and stared into the night. 'But no one will die.'

'No one?'

'Not tonight.'

The implication of her words silenced him.

Jed went back to observing the snipers on the Mendips. There were two more flashes and then nothing. He scanned the landscape for another battle.

Abruptly the wind swung around the Tor again, as if pivoting on the castellations of the tower. It found them out, blowing full in their faces and tearing at their clothes and hair. They ran from it, hand in hand, into the refuge of the opposite side.

From their new vantage point they saw a clash, barely two miles away, sparkle to a climax and then vanish in a matter of seconds.

'Shit! That was close. They wouldn't raid a Sanctuary… would they?'

Judith nestled closer into him so that she didn't have to shout. 'They're hunting. Can't you feel it?' She took hold of his other hand to make a protective circle. 'No one is safe.'

Jed pulled her into a tight embrace. 'You will be.' He stroked her hair, as much to keep it out of his face as to comfort her. 'I promise.'

Her response was not what he expected: she pulled away in anger, her long coat, tattered skirt, and hair in wild streamers. 'Never make promises you can't keep!' She pointed at the sky, jabbing her arm upwards. 'Don't reveal your ignorance to this storm, it is your weakness and the weak will always fall before the hunt!'

He was in turmoil. Her reaction and words confused him but also left him in a backwash of heat that, fanned by the gale, felt too close to rage and too close to lust. He allowed her stare – visible even in the dim reflected street glow from the underbelly of the clouds – to cut through it and chill him. 'I *know* the Forts are using the wolf energy! I understand all that – I get it!'

For a moment it was a toss-up as to who was going to abandon who on the hill, but then Judith appeared to think better of her outburst, holding down her flapping clothes, folding back into herself as she stepped back within the relative calm of the buttressed wall. She looked up at him shaking her head. 'Your heart and your mind are full of the storm, you think you understand but you don't.'

He frowned.

This time, she put her arms around him.

'Jed, the Forts *are* the wolves.'

§

Lawrence fumbled the keys into the passenger door of his Land Rover, pulled it open and hustled Peter inside.

'Put your seatbelt on.'

Peter ignored the instruction in favour of arranging the Wolfstone on his lap, stroking its sides attentively. He picked and brushed away flecks of dried mud from the carved wolf as if he hadn't even heard.

Lawrence sighed, and slammed the door shut.

There were worse things to worry about tonight.

The practical reassurance of the car's engine rumbling into life on the first turn, was soon tempered by the limp needle on the petrol gauge. They would have to find a station and fill up on the way, a delay they could do without.

He grabbed a torch and a map from the scuffed dashboard licked his thumb and flicked through the pages, holding the torch awkwardly in the crook of his neck. 'Jed lad, could you get—' he stopped himself. He glanced across at Peter who seemed not to have registered the slip, and then reached behind the bulkhead for the bucket of maps himself.

He sighed and rubbed his tired eyes. *And then there were two.*

The wind buffeted the car, nosing at it, urging them to run.

Lawrence found the map showing the road he was after, memorised what he needed, tossed the torch onto the dash, locked his seatbelt with a smack of his hand and put his foot down so hard the Land Rover almost choked to a stall. Jed would have been proud.

Driving at top speed they reached a petrol station set in a floodlit oasis of concrete and illuminated adverts. Lawrence filled the thirsty car till its gullet spilled greasy lines down the khaki paintwork; he knew it might well be a long time and many unplanned miles before they'd have another chance to refuel. How long the engine would hold out was another matter. Lawrence patted the warm bonnet as he trotted by on his way to the kiosk. 'Keep it up old girl.'

Peter was jerked out of his absorption with the Wolfstone by a packet of crisps and a Mars bar landing in his lap.

'Sugar and salt – should keep us going for a bit. They didn't have any decent sandwiches left I'm afraid.' He hefted a bottle of Evian out of the flimsy carrier bag. 'Water?'

Peter shook his head.

'Pity,' Lawrence muttered, 'you wouldn't believe what they charge for Frog tap water these days.'

The smallest smile crept across Peter's lips.

'Of course, if you hadn't already finished my reserve, I could've offered you something a little more restorative.'

'It's okay, I'm not hungry, or thirsty.'

Or indeed any bloody use. 'Right then.' He gulped some water, took two large bites out of the chocolate bar and dropped the remainder beside the torch on the dashboard. *I should have waited for that cup of tea.* 'Let's get on shall we?'

He swung the car away from the neon illusion of safety, and back into the dark streets.

It took almost an hour of changing direction on twisting roads and lanes before Lawrence realised, with trepidation, that the wind had been at their backs the whole way from Glastonbury.

Chapter Ten

The ancient yew at Hatiston defied the dawn light. Its rocking, groaning branches clawed the night's shadows from the walls of the church, from the gravestones and the unkempt hedges, scooping them under its wide shielding limbs, and giving them a place to linger, cold and unassailable.

Catrin was caught unawares by the dreary atmosphere. She pushed through the creaking lychgate and stood in the high grass and nettles where the path used to be, wishing she had brought longer boots and a thicker coat, and perhaps even a torch.

The dagger felt like a lump of lead in her pocket.

If there was a reason for her to be here, it wasn't evident. It was akin to searching a room she knew to be empty, but her patience had run out and she was tired of justifying herself to her company. Although she had spent the previous night awake, going over and over the idea, it still felt like an action taken on the spur of the moment. And that, if nothing else, led her to trust her decision to investigate the churchyard.

She glanced up at the scattering of freshly broken tiles lying like ripped pages over the slope of the church roof and in its gutters. The gale was heaving one of the yew's enormous branches back and forth, sawing it through the ridgeline, and the underside of the limb showed red where its bark had been rubbed away. The church looked beleaguered, hunched and awaiting the next blow. The only vital sign remaining was its weathervane swinging and spinning with the wind, in a flicker of gold, out of reach of the tree.

Everything was moving frenetically, driven to exhaustion, torn and broken and at the mercy of the gale; all except for the gravestones and the darkness under the yew.

Where Catrin knew she had to be.

She waded through the billowing grass and weeds towards the tree, and as its gloom closed around her the air fell strangely still and became cold enough to turn her breath to vapour. Fleeting ghosts slid away from her direct stare; sourcing their shapes from the oldest parts of her mind and their voices from the whining wind. The rush of air through the canopy overhead provided a background white-noise for the unsettling pocket of calm in which she found herself.

Catrin became overly conscious of her heartbeat, her breathing, the heat of her blood; as if the pulse of life was an affront to all the quiet death beneath her. She tried to breathe more slowly and control her hammering heart, but it still contended with the gale as the loudest noise in her ears.

A step ahead of her, and a body's length from the trunk of the yew, lay an exposed span of thick root, crooked like the knuckle of a digging finger, and where it plunged back into the ground there were small indications of disturbed earth scattered with twigs and leaves.

The sight of it brought her to the edge of tears. That backfilled hollow should have been her sign, someone else should have been standing where she was, chasing after the dregs of echoes and cursing their luck.

Cursing the betrayal.

The dagger.

It blazed in her mind for a second, red hot from the crucible.

Red with blood.

With a gasp Catrin snatched her coat away from her thigh as if the knife was going to scorch through the fabric and burn her. In a hiatus of shock she stood poised for something else to happen, but its exposed heart seemed to have closed over once more. The unpredictable blade settled down by her side like an agitated wild animal, tense and ready to strike out at any provocation.

Slowly, nervously, she slid her hand into her pocket.

The sheath felt cold, the rough yew of the handle only as warm as any ordinary wood, and so she composed herself, curled her fingers around the knife and pulled it free.

Gunmetal grey as the skies, brutal as the job it was created for; it lay across her outstretched hands, the blade pointed away from her. And Catrin knew, as she studied the Venus glyph, that what filled those scratched lines was not tarnish or paint, but the black crusts of old blood.

She felt sick. How could such a repugnant thing bear the mark of love?

Possibilities welled up from the depths of Catrin's consciousness in a half-instinct, half-intellect uncertainty. She opened herself to the talisman lying across her palms. By shifting the blade to the fingers of her left hand she let it choose its balance-point. It wavered then settled and she brought it close to her face, concentrating on the pits and creases in its coarse surface, trying to establish a dialogue, *why were you made?* Catrin felt its essence slip away from her reach, and in truth she was too afraid to follow it further in, *deception, trap, death,* that aspect was clear enough to stop her leaving a place from which she could safely turn back. Working within those limited impressions meant using too much of her own perspective – musing rather than making a true connection – which would severely limit her conclusions, but when knowledge was so sparse it would be better than nothing. Held at eye-level the metal surface looked like a landscape in miniature, a grey desert, barren except for dried black riverbeds. It was a place untrodden; the Virgin mark on the blade a significant parody, there was nothing unsullied about its form. If Helen had delved into its history, she definitely hadn't walked this path: *kept away by the same fear?*

Framed by what she already knew, and what hints the dagger had let slip, Catrin's ideas resolved, and with a nauseating twist of her gut – of her womb – came a thought that the feminine mark had been used to contrive a ritual. A spontaneous, desperate attempt to ensure that any supernatural vengeance for the use of the knife would fall upon *an innocent woman... a wise-woman?* and spare the villagers. Catrin shook her head: innocent wasn't quite right, this woman had *willingly* flayed the struggling sacrifice of the wolf. The story drew her mind towards the dagger and changed its equilibrium, it tilted on her steady fingers and she had to shift its position so that the blade tipped up again. The moment she did, the teased-thin connection retreated and Catrin had to reach deeper than she wanted to. It was unsafe, treacherous ground, but her rationality kept her from venturing too far and unbalancing the blade again. The villagers had lived in a time when wolves were considered vermin, their eradication was a logical act, and therefore the Venus glyph might simply have been added to celebrate the fact that it was a she-wolf that had finally succumbed to the purge of its species. The shape incorporated a cross, and pragmatic rural folk always tended to hedge their bets – it all fitted. And yet why would they care enough to etch the shoddy blade with that specific commemoration, when everything else about it was executed with such disdain?

Without warning, the weight of the dagger bore her arm down and Catrin had to grab the hilt with both hands to stop it falling. The point was pulling towards the backfilled hole dug by the thief, and she immediately responded by holding the knife as if dowsing, allowing it to guide her until she stood directly above the vacant hollow and the broad, gnarled root that dived down into it.

Catrin knelt before the root, and the blade slanted forward, pivoting on its crosspiece as she fought to hold it off the ground. Evidently the knife had spent some part of its form or history lying in this small grave along with the Wolfstone. The bond between them was there, easier to perceive now that the atoms of the metal had been reminded of their previous alignment. *I was right to come here.* She allowed a small defiant smile to curve the corner of her mouth. If the dagger was this attracted to the fading residual energy that the stone had left in the ground, how much more potent would its response to a hotter trail be?

Her perseverance felt wholly justified. Now that she had tasted the gritty, acrid link between the talismans, there would be no place where the Wolfstone could remain hidden from her, and no one else's claim would survive the cut of her jagged blade.

Catrin stood up, closing down and reinstating her control over the dagger so that she could pull it to her body, turn it, and replace it in the sheath she had created – all the while intrinsically aware that her own claim upon it was the merest filament binding its skittish, deadly energy to her will.

A frown of concentration crossed her forehead. A small but significant connection niggled at her memory: the Fenris Wolf of Norse mythology had been bound by a fine thread – it had a name, one she couldn't quite recall.

Then the translation came back to her, with a slamming gust of wind that made the yew's topmost branches groan in sympathy.

Deceiver.

§

Helen woke up with a violent start.

She was lying along the two front seats of her car, huddled beneath her coat, where she had spent the long and shivering night, at war by turns, with cramp and numbness.

Condensation had fogged all the windows, so she wiped a weeping porthole on each one to check outside. The drab light showed nothing was amiss.

Nothing new anyway.

The gale continued to yell around Helen, its stretched, incomprehensible vowels only slightly deadened by the casing of sheet metal, glass and plastic. She drew back from the window, hunched disconsolately on the driver's seat and contemplated how exhausted and misguided she felt. The night had been so cold, disturbing and lonely, she was astonished that she'd managed to fall asleep at all. Resisting the temptation of the heater or the radio –

conserving the battery was more important than comfort – she pulled on her coat, turned up the collar and raised the hood until only her dishevelled hair and dark-circled eyes were showing.

Helen's mobile rang plaintively. With mild surprise she pulled it from her pocket; the reception had been erratic, dropping in and out without warning ever since she had parked up in the lane. She read the messages and missed-calls, and a brief grim smile touched her lips. The novelty of being chased was good for her ego, a small but pleasing victory. She'd never held out for so long before, and was revelling in the power that came with not caring. He could wait. No doubt there'd be hell to pay, but hell was already whirling invisibly all around her – the air was sick with it – what would a little more matter?

Helen reached back through the gap between the front seats to where her yew longbow and flame-yellow arrows lay, awaiting the grip of her fist and fingertips, and the touch of her face.

She stared through the misted smears on the windscreen, along the tapering lane to the swaying yew tree and the derelict church. The golden weathervane on the tower flashed bright against the dull clouds, strobing like a stalled animation, the hound on the arrow caught in mid-leap. She identified with its plight – they were being spun by the same wind.

And then, what she had been waiting for caught her eye: a low, thin edge of blue and chrome, showing at the furthest turn of the lane, revealed by the blustered branches.

Another parked car.

Helen sprang up, threw back her hood and frantically scrubbed at the windscreen.

Catrin's car.

Helen cursed the betrayal of her weak body. After enduring what had felt like the longest night of her life, she had apparently succumbed to sleep at the crucial moment. Reaching out as much as she dared, Helen still felt nothing. Catrin was guarding herself well – along with the dagger she undoubtedly carried. There was no hint of its proximity even though Helen, above anyone, was sensitised to the sharp, shimmering taste of it in her mind.

How it used to feel in her hand.

How it would again.

Catrin had her talents – so what? None of them would protect her from an aimed shot. In fact, the distraction of whatever mission she was on might make it easier to find a mark on her without being detected.

Helen drew an arrow from her quiver. Holding it in both hands she levelled the broadhead in front of her eyes until the golden dog of the weathervane blinked like a small star on its honed tip. The rune of the Bowlore struck into the white metal blurred with her condensed breath as she brought the blade to her mouth and kissed it, then her lips compressed into a thin line. The talented Catrin Fitzgerald, First of the great and pointless Silbury Hill, would fall before this arrow.

And if the shot wasn't declared – if Helen were to walk away with the dagger and not look back – Catrin would become just another body in the graveyard.

§

It was time to leave.

Catrin knelt down beside the shallow scrape and cupped loose earth into it before patting it firm and flat. To an outsider it was indistinguishable from the surrounding soil, but to her eyes even the negligible signs of disturbance were obvious and aggravating. She wanted to erase all indications of the theft, heal the violation, so she scattered dead leaves and fallen sticks over it, and to make sure that they wouldn't blow away and expose the scar, placed mossy shards from a crumbled gravestone on top.

The root that had dutifully held the Wolfstone looked like all the others tapering away from the trunk; like them, it buttressed the towering yew and delved into the strata of life and death. But this one felt as if it had lost its purpose; the tree slackening the flow of sap to shed the injured wood, and that perhaps on another visit, she would find the root soft with rot. Catrin wondered if it would have appeared so bereft if everything had gone according to plan, and she'd been able to claim the stone. *Or am I looking for justification?* Maybe it was a sign that the Wolfstone should actually have stayed where it was, safe in the embrace of the yew. Maybe she was responding to a predisposition to reinstate and preserve that long internment? She shivered. *Am I the First of a Barrow?* Catrin shook her head, dismissing the thought. Her white hill spoke to her of light and life and air; the womb of the earth reflecting the loving touch of the sun, nothing like the introverted and censorious aspect of the Barrows.

The coldness of the wind percolated through Catrin's defences. She felt suddenly vulnerable and her hand went to the knife, seeking reassurance where none was to be found. It lay quiet, layered inside the sheath and her pocket, tethered and unforthcoming.

She did not take its passivity as a good sign.

The typical signals of being observed or under threat: the sound of a snapping twig, the rustle of leaves, the alarm call of a bird, were being drowned out by the turmoil of the gale, and yet a primal, animal sensitivity was telling her she wasn't alone anymore. She fought down the instinct to bolt, and instead opened herself up just enough to reach out and feel for any focus of intent.

Her eyes were drawn to the road.

Then she realised her escape route had already been cut off.

Catrin ran towards the trunk of the yew, stumbling over roots as she fled for cover behind it. If she could keep its bulk between her and the sniper, she had a chance.

The prickle of aggression was strongest on her left side and moved steadily, indicating that the source was stalking her, sizing her up. Catrin was torn between closing herself down as much as possible to impede any attempts to find a mark, and actively seeking out the identity of the sniper. She shifted around the yew keeping her back pressed tight to the trunk, knowing that the current impasse couldn't last much longer.

Catrin fumbled for her phone and raised it to eye level, maintaining sight of her surroundings as she flicked a glance at the screen to see if – by a stroke of luck and good timing – the signal had improved. But the blackspot remained, and she shoved her phone, and any hope of help from her companions, away.

A pinprick of heat stung her chest.

Catrin bent double and dived further around the tree, sucking in a quick breath, brushing at the burn in a futile reflex.

The heat faded.

But like a brief foam crescent left on the sand by a receding wave, there lingered a small, usable resonance.

The line between her and the dagger tightened.

'Helen!' She kept moving as she shouted into the wind. 'I know it's you!'

The sensation of focus broke, and then intensified as the pretence of stealth was abandoned. Both of them knew that the escalation could increase their immediate danger – or offer a way out.

She attempted to split Helen's concentration again. 'Are you trying to get the knife back? Is that what this is all about?' She carefully circled the yew as she spoke. 'I know you're angry with me – but remember, it was David who made you give it up!'

Another touch. Hotter than the first.

She flung herself down and scrambled to the other side of the tree, gasping as the broken mark cooled. She took a gamble; an echo of the one played against her. 'You're wasting your time! I don't have it with me!' She waited. Sensed uncertainty. Pushed further. 'You didn't honestly think I would bring it with me did you?'

Catrin braced herself for another burning touch.

Nothing came.

'You stupid bitch! D'you think that's the only reason I want to shoot you?'

Catrin was shocked to hear the question coming from the cover of a hedge almost directly opposite, and silently admonished herself for underestimating Helen's abilities. She put the tree between them again. 'I know that you hate me... I don't know why!'

'You fucking know why!'

The heat that blazed in the centre of her chest was so intense that Catrin couldn't help crying out. She tried to run but she was pinned by the pain – held in place by Helen's perfect aim and primed for the arrow that would follow in the next heartbeat.

The blade in her pocket flared into life.

§

The arrow hit like a two-fisted blow, driving the breath from her.

Shock dilated time.

She watched the arrowhead slowly push out the fabric of her coat before the blade cut through it, the silver wiped clean of her blood. The shaft buried in her back whiplashed, expending the last of its force deeper into her body with each flex of the ash wood.

In absolute silence the graveyard tilted up, rushing towards her face.

And then the earthing tore into her, famished and ferocious, ripping Helen out of her body and throwing her to the storm.

§

The blackthorn hedge parted and Badbury Rings, carrying strung bows and sparse quivers, pushed their way through the thicket and into the churchyard.

At their head was David Horsman.

He grinned, eyes wild from the shot he had made, and bowed flamboyantly. 'You're welcome.'

Catrin stepped back and back, shaking her head in revulsion.

Chapter Eleven

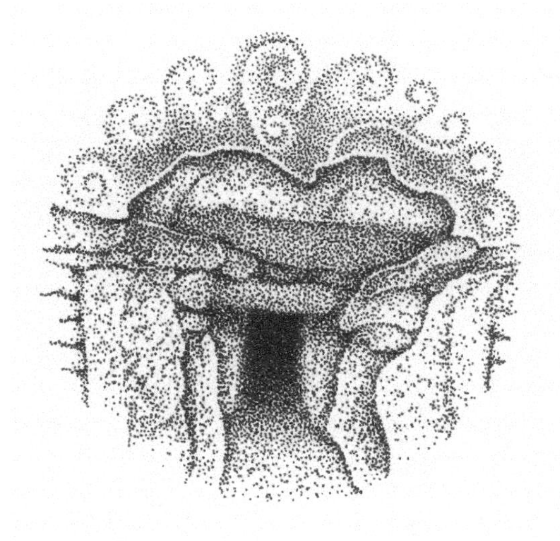

Lawrence trudged behind Peter, puffing and blowing from the pace set by his suddenly energised First. The rutted footpath up the slope to West Kennet long barrow led them into the wind, and Lawrence had to push against it to make headway. It was so strong he was almost tempted to lean into it for support, but he knew there was no relief to be found on this forced march, physical or otherwise.

On the previous night, their less than cordial welcome at the home of West Kennet's First had ended on a sour note, that even the fine wine and cheese on offer had not been able to take away.

Although their unannounced arrival had been met with apparently genuine surprise, Lawrence's instinct led him to suspect that subsequent reactions to the news of the Wolfstone and the encounter with the ghostly wolf pack were deeply disingenuous.

His misgivings were born out after they had been hustled into a large and comfortable room, and left to rest: when Lawrence tried the door he found they had been locked in. Apparently, Barrows practised much the same style of hospitality as Sanctuaries.

With their options vanishing and weariness overwhelming them, they had accepted their fate; almost as if they had inadvertently sealed it in the manner of a fairytale, by eating the proffered food. Too deep to drag themselves free, too tired to resist, they had slumped into the worn Chesterfield sofa, and shared the warmth of a thick woollen throw.

Tree branches scratched at the window panes, and blown leaves pressed against the glass like black paw prints. The wind had howled down the cold chimney, stirring ash in the grate and filling the room with the sweet bacon scent of old woodsmoke.

Paintings of noblemen and women of the manor stared down judgementally from the oak panelled walls, necks stiff with starched ruffs and righteousness. But Lawrence was beyond guilt or fear of condemnation, and with his crystal wine glass still in his hand, fell to snoring almost before his head sank back onto the soft leather.

Peter had spent a long time returning the glares of the God-fearing paragons while he finished the bottle, his eyes red with unshed tears, and the dawn had leached the comforting glow from the table lamp beside him before he had eventually fallen into a shallow, fitful sleep.

Now, Lawrence, walking up this apparently interminable hill, found he could barely distinguish between the events of hours or days ago, they all blended into one long and anxious drive. The lack of sleep and loss of control had induced a kind of insulating apathy, which – if Lawrence could only have spared the energy – he would have found just as annoying in himself as it was in Peter.

Lawrence tried to glean a little hope. Peter's behaviour was altering, showing signs that their roles might be reinstating. When they had parked up in the lay-by at the entrance to the footpath, and before the First of West Kennet had even opened the door of his Mercedes, Peter had leaped out of the Land Rover, hugging the stone in a tight embrace and striding ahead as if the visit had been his idea all along. Whether he could keep that advantage on rival territory would remain to be seen.

Whatever the original nature of the alliance between Peter and the Barrow's First it remained unmentionable – he closed down whenever Lawrence questioned him about it – and it appeared to be in flux. Even in his current state of detachment, Lawrence was able to read the appraising looks and guarded body language passing between them. It spoke of mutual suspicion, and a kind of awkwardness that comes from being in the presence of someone with whom you have a past, but no future.

The long barrow loomed above them, its pelt of tussocky grass swept flat by the gale, filling the crest of the rise like the huge hulk of an upturned barge, beached and abandoned to the elements. With the hope of finding shelter Lawrence redoubled his effort to keep pace with Peter. West Kennet's First brought up the rear, maintaining just enough of a distance so that no words could be exchanged.

The last stretch of the path, worn through to the chalk, led them up to the great table-sized stones flanking the entrance. Lawrence, feeling as if he were being worn away by the eroding wind, was dismayed to find no respite from the battering. The monoliths gathered the gale and threw it back into the sky in a sweep of rushing air that sucked their clothes and hair upwards, making them look like they had jumped down from the roof of the barrow and were still falling.

Giles Montford, First of West Kennet, walked between them to reach the entrance of his site. He ducked inside, disappearing for a few moments to check that the burial chambers were empty of outsiders. When he reappeared, framed by the stone slabs, with his black coat billowing, his lean pale face with its sculpted stubble and permanently aloof expression, it appeared to Lawrence that at least some of the gothic clichés he'd heard about Barrow companions were evidently true.

'Bring the stone inside.' Giles' clipped tone brought them to attention.

Peter hesitated for a second, and then walked into the dark earth. Lawrence followed on, looking forward to being out of the wind. If there was also a shelf of rock where he could have a seat, so much the better.

The tomb was lit by two lightwells set into concrete panels in the roof, and the subdued daylight was muted further by the narrowness of the shafts and dirt on the glass. There were signs that a more apt, but damaging, illumination was employed by other visitors: small blobs of wax or smudges of soot on ledges and in crevices where the stone walls could accommodate a candle.

Giles took his place at the furthest end of the barrow and Peter stood close to the entrance, waiting. Lawrence loathed the compliance implicit in his First's attitude, and his own incapacity to alter their course. Glowering, he leaned against the nearest wall, resigned to the role of observer.

Giles exuded superiority, enhanced further by being in the heart of his site. Sympathy or explanations were not on his agenda – no matter how much Peter might deserve them. The earth swallowed speech, turning his words to whispers. 'Give me the Wisht Stone, and I can create a safe place for it.' He pointed upwards and circled his finger as if stirring. 'Then, I can undo all the damage it has caused.'

Peter was abruptly and surprisingly defiant. His hands whitened on the Wolfstone. 'How do you expect me to believe anything you say when you sent me to my death?'

The only sounds were the muffled gale and Lawrence's choked breath.

Giles waited, controlling his response. He sighed at the subject change but went along with it. 'If that really had been my intention, you would not be here.'

'I was a means to release the wolves, wasn't I?'

'You credit yourself with such importance, Peter. I beg to differ. The Wisht Stone was ripe for the plucking, several companies were aware of its existence – it was merely a race to see who could get to it first.'

'And you made sure it was me.'

Giles looked up at the dull light and shook his head slowly, already tired of explaining himself. 'You knew what you were being asked to do, you agreed to the terms.'

'I agreed to save a Treasure from the Forts.'

Lawrence had to bite his lip to stay quiet.

'And so you did.' Giles inclined his head slightly in a sarcastic nod of thanks. 'Mission accomplished. Now hand over the stone.'

'It isn't mine to give.'

The next question hung unspoken between them.

Peter answered it anyway. 'I never claimed the Wolfstone, the Treasures belong to the land, not the Lore.'

There was a long pause while Giles assessed the extent of the mutiny, then he pointed at Lawrence. 'You – get out.'

'He's my Second. I want him to stay.'

Lawrence stood up. 'It's all right, you should resolve this in private. I'll wait outside.'

'No. I want you to hear everything... my confession – and his.' Peter held up the stone, his eyes fixed on Giles. 'I thought I was some kind of catalyst, that I was heralding the next level of the Bowlore's evolution. I was a fool. It was all lies.' His voice caught in his throat. 'I *wanted* to believe... I made it too easy for you.'

Lawrence gripped Peter's trembling arm, strained from holding out the stone, and tried to support some of its weight, worried that his First's faltering words presaged another breakdown.

Peter pulled away and raised the stone up high. 'This is not one of the Thirteen! It's just the marker from a grave I should never have disturbed!'

Giles sprang from his position and drew face to face with Peter, the stone wavering over both their heads. 'If you hadn't indulged that supercilious little distinction – if you had claimed the Wisht Stone as I instructed, the wolves would be tame now. *You* have created this hunt!'

The strength in Peter's arms suddenly drained.

Giles calmly stepped back as the stone thudded at his feet.

Lawrence made a grab for Peter as he staggered to the ground, just managing to catch him before his head cracked against the wall. 'Give me a hand, for God's sake!'

Giles dropped down on one knee beside them and turned his attention to the stone.

Lawrence was disgusted, but unsurprised. He braced Peter into a sitting position. 'Is that bloody thing all that anyone cares about anymore?'

Giles didn't look up as he responded. 'He bested the wolf pack, so I doubt that a brief lecture on the consequences of his actions is going to finish him off.' The stone had fallen so that the carved wolf was face up and he studied it intently.

Without touching it, Lawrence noted.

The open contempt being shown for his First served to drain Lawrence's spirits even further. Why, at every turn, were they faced with companies that cared only for their own selfish ends? This malaise spreading through the Bowlore appeared to run even deeper than the chaos of the loosed wolves. He looked at Peter's disconsolate expression and, with sorrow, knew him to be a spent force. Giles stood up and then stared closely at Peter. He seemed to be focussing somewhere within Peter's head, searching for something.

Lawrence was growing increasingly uncomfortable, his arms beginning to ache from supporting Peter. 'What's the matter now?' He was ignored, as he had expected to be.

'Listen to me, Peter.' Giles reached out his hand, long-fingered and elegant, more suited to the string of a violin than a longbow. He gripped Peter's shoulder. 'Claim the Wisht Stone now, put an end to this.'

'Now hold on there! An end to what?' Lawrence couldn't stop the edge of panic creeping into his voice. He pulled Peter closer to him.

A simmering anger abruptly filled the barrow, seeping up through the earth and stones, into the hollows between time and place to where the bones lay, generations deep, cluttering every alcove, crushing out the stagnant air until there was nothing left to breathe. Lawrence clawed at his throat choking on the stench of rotting flesh, of burnt skin and hair, crying out for air, for life. He scrambled towards the entrance and out into the hammering gale from which he had wished relief only minutes before. Hauling himself free of the grip of the ground, he took great gulps of the wind that blasted his heaving and shaking body.

Lawrence hated himself, cursed his cowardice, shouted pleas for forgiveness into the black mouth of the barrow. But he was unable to take even one step towards its hungry gape.

§

The Sanctuary of Glastonbury Tor gathered its combined talent and went to work.

Megan Wright set her companions to dowse for the errant Ninestones company; with crystals, pendulums of yew, and their shining arrows; any tool to concentrate thought. Yet despite this united effort of will, nothing more than vague impressions had been revealed. Megan recognised that this very lack of information was possibly their best clue as to the type of force they were pitted against, but without conclusive proof she couldn't justify adding to the havoc within the system by levelling accusations.

She held her own silver arrow close to her chest, point down, before her face, like the sword of a knight preparing for battle. The cool metal warmed against her skin.

Time was against them.

Her initial plan to allow Ninestones to escape and then track them, had ended in disaster; they had simply disappeared into the storm, their trace scattered like the wind-ripped leaves. Something about the ease with which it had happened disturbed her. If Ninestones was being reeled in, she would have to keep a safe distance so as not to snag herself and her company on the same hook.

Megan closed her eyes and reached out through the roots and branches of the Bowlore.

She knew that any intervention on her part – meticulously judged or otherwise – would have repercussions, but she had already made herself complicit by releasing the wolves from their fleshly prison. She wasn't seeking out a path, it was finding her.

There was nothing she would have done differently; preserving the system and saving the life of Ninestones' First had overruled all other concerns – and the wolves with their yearning, bitter hearts, had needed her just as much. So what else could she have done but attempt to honour the bloody debt incurred by her ancestors, by granting them the small compensation of freedom within the domain of the Lore?

The ongoing birth pangs shook the air as the gale fought against anything that resisted its will. Her house was holding out against the breath of the wolves, although the walls felt like they were made of straw. The pack owed her nothing, and she was in just as much danger as anyone else.

And there was something else.

Something hiding, cloaking itself in the rush; something older than the hunt.

It strayed unbound, intentionally freed from its accustomed bonds and byways, a law unto itself. An elemental entity, birthed at a pivotal shift lost in the deep past, when a friend was refined from a foe.

On the ancient knife edge between trust and terror…

Between dog and wolf.

Megan opened her eyes, and lowered her wand.

If a Yeth Hound was on the prowl her suspicions were confirmed. Only one Hallow could let slip that particular dog of war.

The Barrows.

Chapter Twelve

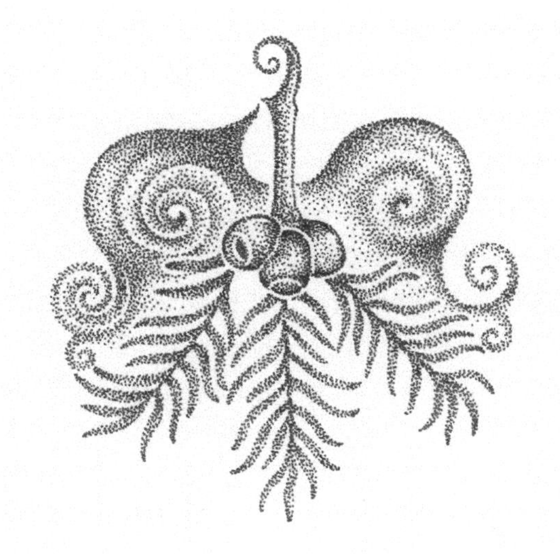

Jed listened patiently as Judith held forth on the subject of Forts. Against all his expectations she was extolling their virtues – and explaining their vulnerability.

He leaned back against the carved wooden headboard, watching her get dressed at the foot of the bed. He studied the curve of her back as she shrugged into her purple and black striped jumper; her sinuous movements captivating him. He wanted her again but knew she would not be persuaded.

'...Like attracts like, the wolves and the Forts are both predators, so it was inevitable that the pack would express itself through their Hallow.' Just for a moment she looked genuinely troubled. 'But this storm could overpower the bonds within the Lore. They could bring us all down.'

Jed abruptly tuned back in. 'What, you mean everything? The whole system?'

She nodded, walked around the bed to sit by him and stroked a finger down from his forehead, over his open mouth, the tip of his tongue, to his throat and then to his chest. She rested her hand over his heart. 'I know you're finding yourself drawn to the Forts – despite your promises. Can't you feel their confusion?'

Jed fought unsuccessfully against the blush that rose up from his neck. He thought he had closed down better than that.

'It's... I don't know. I feel like I'm being pulled in all four directions.' One more lie but what did it matter. 'I'm still trying to get my head round being a freebow.'

She smiled and stroked his cheek with the back of her curled fingers. He loved her touch and yet he was starting to find any non-sexual gestures patronising. He tried to control himself but knew – to his shame – that his principled acceptance of a place in Glastonbury was degenerating into a baser need just for its Second.

'It's okay.' She leaned in and kissed his eager mouth, then pulled away and put a finger on his lips. 'I won't tell my mother.' A bucketful of cold water couldn't have worked better.

He caught her wink but the damage was done. He half-smiled to conceal his irritation, pushed off the covers and stood up to pull on his jeans and shirt.

By the time he looked up again she was waiting by the door, but her mood had changed and her face was clouded with thought. Instead of walking out she closed the door with the softest click, leaning against the wood with her hands behind her as if they were tied.

'Jed, if the Bowlore is pulling you to the Hallow of the Fort… then that is where you should be.'

He blinked hard, as if trying to bring this latest version of her into focus, afraid that it was just a test.

'And I will give you all the help I can to find your new company.'

Hiding his reaction was impossible and pointless. He allowed the vigilantly dammed thrill of recognition to burst through the barriers he had raised, only just managing to suppress a grin that hooked at the corners of his mouth. 'I thought maybe it was just my reaction to the storm – I didn't want to let you down.'

'As long as you remain true to yourself,' she whispered, 'you will never let me down.'

Before she could turn her face away he caught sight of the glint of tears in her eyes, and this amazed him far more than the Fort revelation. He vaulted the bed to get to her. 'I'm sorry Judith, I'm really sorry, I don't *want* to leave you.' He held her closer and tighter than he had yet dared. He felt her nod.

'You must go where you're needed.'

She stayed in his embrace, making no attempt to break away, but there was an air of expectation as if she was creating a pause for him to fill with some further confession. He didn't know what to say. He had apologised, promises only annoyed her, and he couldn't say goodbye – not yet. With a grimace he wondered if he was transgressing yet another Lore or Sanctuary code of conduct that he was expected to know; it wasn't his fault he had been trained by backwater little Ninestones. *What does she want?*

The moment lingered, holding its breath. Her pressing, needful warmth and the exhilaration at his longed-for release, see-sawed on the balance of his priorities.

He had to say something.

'I love you.'

The world stopped.

All eyes watched, all ears listened; time stepped back a pace to make room for his words. And their answer.

Judith raised her head. Her sky blue eyes dazzled him, but beyond their shine something brighter than the glitter of emotion looked back at him. He tried to focus but she quickly slid her arms round his neck and kissed him – chaste and almost childlike – pressing her soft, closed lips to his. 'Thank you.'

Thank you? Jed's puzzlement was soon swept away by her smile; at last it seemed he'd said the right thing. He smiled back, more relieved than reassured and kissed her again, his tongue hunting for a passionate reply.

She cupped his face and drew away. 'We have to go.'

'Where?'

'To find your company.'

The desire that filled him felt like love. It had to be love. Judith and the Hallow of the Fort, equal and ideal. Everything he had been hoping for, knowingly or not, since he joined the Bowlore.

'Take this.' She held his hand and slipped something cool and metal into it. A key. 'It's a talisman, for the unlocking of something that needs to be found.' She closed his hand with both of hers. 'I give it to you willingly.'

Jed was overwhelmed. He could feel her influence like a tracery of heat through the iron, ready to be pulled back at his acceptance. The metal sang with significance, poised to unlock potential; exactly what he needed. 'Thank you.'

Judith waited, then gave him the look he knew all too well: *And...*

'I accept this talisman. Willingly.'

The kiss she gave him pushed every thought but her, out of his mind.

§

Patrick tapped the screen of his phone over and over. Each connection went straight through to Catrin's voicemail.

He felt like he was sending up flares over a lonely sea.

'Is she still not answering?' Leah kept her eyes on the road ahead as she spoke, driving her car the same way that she aimed; slow and steady.

'Yes. Look, are you sure you don't want me to take over?' he tried to keep the edge of impatience out of his voice.

Leah was quicker on the uptake. 'If I go any faster on these roads, in this wind, we're going to end up smeared all over a fallen tree.' Leaning forward on the steering wheel, she peered over the bonnet to negotiate a smashed branch scattered across the lane. 'Anyway, you need *both* hands for this kind of driving.'

Patrick didn't need or want to be reminded. He curled the fattening fingers of his plainshot hand, uncomfortably aware that the aching heat in the wound was starting to spread.

Oak trees lining the road lashed in the gale, their lower branches whipping the roof of the car as it passed, the straggling bushes and hazel saplings in the hedgerows appeared to whirl like green-man dervishes.

And Hatiston was still more than twelve miles away.

He tried the mobile again, without much expectation. There was the smallest pause before her voice came on and that subtle difference alerted him to the possibility of an actual pick-up. He almost dropped the phone in his haste to snatch it to his ear. 'Catrin?'

'…Yes'

'Are you okay? Where the hell are you?'

'Fine… We – I'm on the way to West Kennet.'

'What? Why?'

'Because that's where the Wolfstone is.'

'Oh my God, Catrin! What are you playing at?'

Leah tapped his leg, mouthing '*What's happened?*', but he waved her away and pointed for her to watch the road. She scowled and clenched the steering wheel.

'I'm not *playing*, Paddy.'

She never used that nickname. Suddenly the static on the line spoke volumes. 'What do you want me to do?'

'Meet me at West Kennet.'

His mouth went dry. 'The company? Or just me?'

'Isn't that one and he same thing now?' The strain in her voice melted into sadness.

'Leah's here. The others are... busy.'

'So, just my Second and Third.' The connection cut out – then it was back. 'Don't forget your bows.'

'But you know I can't...' *What the hell?* He was being dragged in the wake of her codes.

'How long before you get here?'

The hedges crawled by. *Forever at this rate.* 'I don't know, about an hour?' The line broke into an echoing hiss that sounded like he was listening to the storm broadcast over a radio, and then the signal indicator flatlined. 'Shit!'

'What?' Leah checked all around and then brought the car to a halt at the side of the road. 'What's going on?'

'I'm not sure. Catrin wants us to meet her at West Kennet.'

'Why *there* of all places? Is she okay?'

'No, I don't think she is. Someone else was with her, listening in.'

'Giles?'

He shook his head and pointed to his bandaged hand. 'She told me to bring my bow.'

Leah frowned, then her eyes widened. 'Oh God! Do you think she's with Badbury?'

'I'd stake my other hand on it.'

§

The hollow yew was huddled at the centre of a swaying thicket of elders growing beside a disused bridleway. What remained of its stunted limbs had grown straight up, thrusting half-starved leaves through the noose of its neighbours towards the light. Its other branches, from a time when it carried a flourishing canopy, had fallen, and were growing coats of emerald moss amongst the ferns and leaf litter.

Its mood was one of forbearance, yet there were signs of recovery in the feathery lime-green leaves that lit the tips of the branches or straggled, like randomly placed decorations, around the yawning trunk.

A year previously, Badbury Rings had discovered then quietly adopted the tree. All hollow yews, no matter how unpromising their circumstances, warranted reverence and attention, and any that could be kept secret and reserved even more so. They had respectfully trimmed back the surrounding elders, so that the abundant aphid-sticky foliage no longer stole all the light, and the slumbering yew had responded.

Evidently the tree had been cherished before. A rusted band – bolted on at the height of the Industrial Revolution, when the order of iron was applied to everything – encircled its girth to prevent the horseshoe-shaped bole from splitting in half. The flaking metal looked bitten where the bark bulged over its edges, as if the lips of the tree were slowly closing together over the brace. One day it would be gone, and only a crease would show where it had been swallowed up.

For now, the iron strap was just another obstacle between David and his objective. And his temper was already short.

'You'll be joining her if you don't get out of the fucking way!' He shoved Gareth, his Second, to one side so that he could see Helen's cold, prone form as it was being unceremoniously posted under the band. 'Hold her arms, not her legs! Just get her in so we can leave.'

Touching. Catrin watched the proceedings with a mixture of disgust and fascination. She had heard tell of, but never witnessed a laying-out by a Fort. The sheer lack of respect – a contempt presumably born of familiarity – shocked her. Or maybe it was yet another symptom of the feeding-frenzy that was ruling them. Neither alternative offered any reassurance.

Helen's body crumpled into the heart of the yew and after no more than the briefest of checks to ensure she could breathe, and that a sprig of yew was tucked into her limp hand, she was abandoned to the mercies of the Covenant.

David pushed himself upright using the metal brace, and brushed his hands clean, apparently assuaged. Until he caught Catrin's eye.

She took an involuntary step away, such was the intensity of his gaze, only to feel the point of an un-aimed arrow prick the small of her back. She moved forward again.

David stared at her. 'So, let me guess. We're not up to your exacting standards?'

She waited for the arrogant smile but it never came; for once she wanted it. 'No, it's not that, it's just… different… from how I'd do it.'

'Different good? Or different bad?' He moved in closer.

His concentration upon her, like the scent of blood, attracted the whole company. The arrow at her back pushed hard enough to sting.

Catrin unconsciously held her breath as she tried to calculate whether an answer or silence would cause the least aggravation.

'Good or bad?' David's impatience made the choice for her.

'I don't judge your Hallow. No one does.'

A burst of laughter, briefly rivalling the noise of the wind, filled the space around the yew. It broke the deadlock but did not lighten the mood.

'Are you fucking kidding me?'

'You're only doing what we all do – we all have our path to follow.'

He almost smiled. 'Go on.'

'The Lore needs us all.'

'Even plainshooting bastards like me?'

Lying was not an option. 'That's between you and the Barrows.'

'And you – the First without a Hallow, have the moral high ground?'

She blinked. He had hit his mark. 'I've *never* claimed that! I'm not above the system, I'm just as much a part of it as anyone else.'

'But you can be objective.' He touched a finger to his forehead, then to hers, and added in a whisper, 'So you alone can see into my soul.' Then abruptly, his attention was caught by his own mocking gesture. He brought his finger up to his face, nodding to himself, performing all the while. 'Tell you what, I'd hate any guest of mine to feel uncomfortable so I'll do a little something to make you feel at home.' He turned and went back to the tree, motioning her to follow.

She stepped away from the jab of her guard's arrow, dreading what she might be swapping it for.

'You like your little rituals don't you? Keeps everything under control.' He dug into the outside pocket of his quiver. 'Normally I'm not a big fan of control – as you know – but even I have one or two little customs of my own.' He brought out his hand, fingers pinched together. 'Take these.'

Catrin glanced at what he held, and her fear spiked at the sight of the pinkish-red berries. She didn't move. If he intended to poison her she wasn't going to help.

He made a sad face. 'You said you didn't judge me.'

Is this a test? Reluctantly she raised her hand, palm up. Test or not she had no choice. Badbury's collective sense of anticipation rose like a confining wall around her. As a last resort she scrutinised his body language for signs of his true intent but he gave nothing away; his talents were easily a match for hers and he was further screened by the tumult of the storm.

The three yew berries felt like hail dropping onto her skin. Cold and hard and unforgiving.

'Close your hand.'

Their chill seeped into her – her warmth fed them. And she knew that a fraction of her essence travelled with that exchange of heat, binding them to her. *He's covering his tracks!*

He might have read her, or simply seen the look in her eyes. 'No need to panic. I'm just allowing you to share in the experience.' He leaned against the yew. 'I think our relationship is ready for a new level of intimacy – don't you?' Tracking his scattershot appetites was keeping her off-balance. Exactly as he wanted.

He opened his arms in invitation, but his words were an order. 'Come here.'

Catrin felt as if the air was running out, as if the dismal sky; already ungenerous with its light, was being cinched tight shut over her head. The confinement David had taken off the hollow yew, he now imposed on her.

For the first time since she had joined the Bowlore her faith in it was faltering. The hold that the Covenant had over the Forts seemed tenuous at best; only their self-serving nature forced them to toe the line – they preserved it to save themselves.

But how far past rational decisions were they? If the glory of gratification had finally overtaken their fear of the consequences, everything would be lost.

She would be lost.

'Oh, and they're not for you, in case you were wondering.' He revelled in the power her obvious conclusion gave him, but lacked the restraint to prolong it.

Bastard. She bowed her head to hide her reaction.

'They're for this disloyal bitch.' He waved a thumb towards Helen's body.

Catrin looked up, her eyes glittering with distress. 'I'm not going to kill her for you!'

'Kill her?' David took a step closer, encircling her shoulders with his arm. He put his face close to hers. 'Why the fuck would I want to make you break the Covenant?'

A thousand reasons coursed through her mind. 'Two birds with one stone?'

There was a hesitation, his arm stiffened into a yoke across her back. Then another bark of laughter made her jump. 'You see? This is why I keep you around – you're so fucking entertaining!'

She pulled away, and he let her go.

For a heartbeat, she tasted a glimmer of doubt; a chink in David's armour. And then it was gone.

He was darkly sober again. 'Use the juice from the berries to mark her with the rune.'

Why?

'Draw it on her forehead.'

Where she can't see it.

So she won't wipe it off. 'You can reach her through here.' He pointed with his foot to a sagging gap below the iron band, through which Helen's pale face and part of her arm could be seen. 'You're the only reason she's in there. Think about it; the Wolfstone, the dagger,' he coughed, 'me.' The smile came back. 'Mostly the dagger.' He pulled it out from his belt and pretended to admire it. 'I can't see what all the fuss is about. Must be a girl thing.' He scratched at the Venus glyph. 'I have to confess I was really enjoying your little cat-fight. It was a shame to have to step in and put an end to it.'

'You arrogant—' She overcame her outrage and managed to censor herself. 'I didn't ask you to shoot her.'

'Yes, but it was so much more effective than just telling her to hold – she would have ignored my order anyway.' He kicked at the ground near the split so that a spray of debris spat through the gap and onto Helen's face. 'Wouldn't you!'

The pendulum of his mood was swinging back to anger.

Tell me the truth. 'Why do you need me to mark her?'

He glared at Catrin. 'To remind her she's just a Sixth. To make her think back to her initiation – the *only* fucking time a Badbury companion should have to raise a bow against one of their own!'

Another crack in his façade let through a jag of anguish. Maybe if they had been alone she could have used it, but surrounded by his company it was too much of a risk. Even so, impetuously, she took the chance. 'Why me?' The dagger; in David's possession yet so recently bound to her, gave her a minute leverage.

'So that you'll take responsibility for the shot.' He frowned at his candour, suspicious. 'Watch yourself, Catrin.' He gave a signal and the circle of Badbury drew tighter. 'Or I might lose interest in you.'

She backed down, cloaking herself in compliance.

Bending down on one knee, she opened her hand. The yew berries formed a bright trefoil in her palm, undiminished by the wan light. The plump, cup-shaped flesh cushioning the poisonous seeds that were clearly visible, as if pressed in from outside; their deadly cargo unrepentantly displayed.

She crushed them into pulp against her skin and fished out the seeds.

David took them from her, wrapped them in a fallen elder leaf picked from the ground at his feet, and put them back in his quiver.

Her fingers were already sticky with the juice, but she dabbed some more onto the tip of her ring-finger and reached through the split in the trunk. Helen's skin was white and deathly cold, a foil to the warm red lines that Catrin drew on her rival's troubled forehead.

Despite the care that Catrin took, the restricted space meant that the ogham rune smeared, one line into another. The vee of the arrowhead, the downstroke of the shaft, and the stylised fletchings were clear enough, but the four crosspieces of the Hallows formed a solid block beneath the curve of the bow.

The visible results didn't matter. The mark of the Bowlore had been made.

Whatever it was that had compelled David was apparently appeased, and there was a noticeable drop in the level of tension. Catrin looked up cautiously but the expression on his face spoke more of guilt than game plans, a state she had never witnessed in him before.

As if seeking absolution, he began explaining himself in a quiet voice that she could only just make out over the rush of the wind. He kept his eyes on the solid form of the yew as he spoke, and she wasn't even sure if he was addressing her or the tree.

'We mark the rune on the companion who teaches us to shoot, to honour their courage… and to pay respect to the yews.'

So, Badbury did have their rituals, all companies did to varying degrees, but Catrin was finding these glimpses of doubt more disconcerting than his outbursts of rage. *Does he really care what I think?*

'Nothing matters more than the Covenant.'

She glanced down at Helen. *Now that you're so close to breaking it.*

She almost made me break it. Another, stronger gust of wind blew his mind shut again, closing him away with his cravings and his anger. 'I also put it on Firsts I shoot. Be grateful it isn't you in there.'

Believe me, I am.

'Right – we've got an appointment with West Kennet. Let's not keep our tame Barrow-wights waiting!'

As his companions shouted their assent he leaned in and added an aside for Catrin's benefit. 'And let's not keep poor *Paddy* waiting either.'

§

It's an ill wind… The doom-laden proverb was repeating over and over in his head, as if his mental processes were stuck in a holding pattern. Patrick pulled forwards against the seatbelt to peer through the leaf-scattered windscreen. *...that blows nobody any good.*

Ambiguity annoyed him at the best of times; probably as a subliminal reaction to Silbury's indefinite state, so he found even the small dose of it within the saying aggravating, and yet it remained in his mind, playing like an irritating jingle. How ill would this wind have to be before David Horsman couldn't gain anything from it? Or Giles Montford? His kind had been reaping whirlwinds from the moment they'd stepped off the ships from Normandy.

There would always be some wounds that time couldn't heal, and always those who would hold them up as a badge of honour even as they fell. So here he was, running headlong into god-knows-what for the sake of Catrin, the one person he seemed to have an endless capacity to forgive. And if by some miracle, he made it through the rest of the day without paying the price of this loyalty, he would forgive her again. Such was the lot of a Second.

...it's an ill wind... I'm just Samwise bloody Gamgee...

His whole hand throbbed with a deep and disturbing ache. Animal instinct told him the pain was more than should be felt in a wound of its size, even the pressure of his blood when he held his hand too low, was enough to make him grit his teeth.

An ironic demise from a dose of lockjaw would be preferable to blood poisoning, but his tetanus inoculations were up to date, and the tight, hot skin of his thickening fingers told its own tale.

…that blows nobody any good…

Leah brought him out of his introspective loop. 'There!' she pointed to the flat-topped cone of Silbury Hill as it came into view. 'I told you I'd get us here in less than an hour.'

Her commendably positive attitude worried him. If she was assuming that being a Third would insulate her, she was seriously underestimating the danger they were in.

Beyond the warm and welcome sense of recognition their site inspired, there loomed, literally and metaphorically, the presence of West Kennet long barrow, their neighbour from Hel.

'Drop me off at the Hill.'

She was about to protest but then saw his expression. A wall of wind suddenly hit the car and she had to fight the steering wheel to bring them safely through it and into the small car park near the base of Silbury.

She took a moment to regain her composure, by which time he had clicked open his seatbelt and was reaching for his coat. 'And no, you're not coming with me.'

'Since I'm the only one of us who can still shoot, I think I should.' Leah's eminently practical nature often gave her licence to overstep her place, but for her sake Patrick had to pull rank.

'*I* will walk from here to the barrow, and *you* will drive – very carefully – back home.'

'No, I'm not leaving you.'

He put his good hand over both hers where they still clutched the wheel. 'Please do as I say, I'm flying blind here – I can't see anything for this bloody storm, and if I have to worry about what I'm dragging you into as well, I'll be even more useless to Catrin than I am already.'

'You're not dragging me, I want to help.'

'Leah, be realistic. If I end up needing help what could you do?'

'Silbury isn't just you and Catrin!' She faltered, instantly wishing she hadn't spoken. She took a breath and stared up in dismay at their great earthen mound, suddenly fearing that she had become a part of the Hill only to witness the physical degeneration of its chalk core being replicated in the collapse of its company. 'I'm sorry, Patrick.'

'Look, I know you want to protect me – and you know that I can't let you.' He squeezed her hand. 'But it's not the end.'

She blinked away tears. 'Then why does it feel like it is?'

'That's what I'm going to find out.'

He got out of the car, and then bent down so he could see her. She was like Catrin in many ways; younger, more straightforward, but with the same enduring spirit and high principles. If Silbury could draw in companions like her then surely there was hope for it. The shining hill was still calling to those who could hear.

This time of uncertainty and doubt would pass, the mound would be mended, the voids shored up and replenished, the white scars would heal to forgiving green – and the company would fill its own empty spaces.

'I *am* going to wait for you here.' Leah looked up at him. 'I hope you understand.'

'I do.'

This place was their home.

Patrick stalked across the fields with greater assertiveness than he had anticipated, he found he could ignore the wind as it tugged and tripped him. The brief communion with his site had replaced his loyal resignation with a sense of purpose, and even the stuck-needle words in his head had blown away. He was on a mission; though where it would lead him was yet to be revealed.

Judging by the increasing pain in his hand, he was heading in the right direction to find out.

§

Jed flipped the key from hand to hand, and waited.

The low tumulus beneath his feet seemed to be the only place not reverberating with the gale. If he reached down into the earth he could feel a tiny void of calm, where the ashes and possessions of a heart that had stopped beating more than three thousand years before, had been gently reclaimed by the land. He closed his eyes against a brief stab of empathic sorrow: *early summer; the waiting womb lined with purple and yellow meadow flowers. Birdsong and weeping carried on the wind. The crackle of flames and smell of woodsmoke and burning hair. Lying on the pyre in the clothes and jewellery she would have been married in. So loved. So beautiful. She*...he pulled away from the connection, letting the wind dry his sudden tears.

It wouldn't look good to meet the representative of a Fort with his eyes wet from crying.

Chapter Thirteen

Helen dreams her way through a forest of yew trees. They are young and straight, bright with berries, and everywhere she looks they stretch away to the horizon.

The sky is lit with the glow of fire, and burning arrows fall about her, igniting the trees. The berries burst into flame before the leaves, so that the red of ripeness is swapped for flames in the instant before the trees blaze into ash.

She runs with the Pack.

They howl and bite at the rain of arrows, snatching the brands from the air and running with them in their jaws.

The trailing flames catch their coats on fire, and Helen can feel her own hair burning, smell the stink of it, but as long as she runs fast enough, the heat cannot reach her skin.

Then she is hit from behind and falls to her knees.

She staggers back up, netted in flames, needing a knife to cut away her scorching hair, but her dagger is gone.

White light slices her free.

§

On her cold forehead was the smear of a yew berry, the red lines reminiscent of the rune. If it was for protection, it hadn't worked. If it was there as a sign for him, it was unnecessary.

The Lore was in flux; the behaviour of many companies consequentially erratic. It was better to ignore the mark than read too much into it.

Her breathing was long-spaced, shallow, only a step from death, her life slowed to the point where it could fall in step with the yew. Communion had been reached and her eyelids fluttered with the dreams.

Perfect timing.

He brought out a bracelet. Its shining gold twists were roped into spirals, the centre of both finials set with polished garnets, red as the yew berry juice. After warming the heavy gold between his palms, he eased open the ends just wide enough to slide them either side of her exposed wrist.

The yew sprig fell from her cold fingers.

He cupped the bracelet in both his hands, holding up her arm, and reached into the core of the soft metal for its sterner, unrelenting heart. Then he closed the finials until they touched, completing the circle.

At once there was a change in Helen.

With a reactive gasp she jolted away from the touch of the bracelet, weak shock on her unconscious face, then, as the increasing depth of each breath quickened the pulse beating defiantly against the gold clamped around her wrist, her eyes flickered open.

He examined her sightless stare. She still looked through the tree, through him, through their fragment of time, and on into the land. He smiled.

Some elements of the Covenant would not be rushed or circumvented. He liked that fact.

Gradually, her unfocussed innocence was blinked away and replaced by a confused frown. She saw him now: a stranger, and became aware of the nauseating burden of constraint. Only her physical weakness kept her from kicking out.

He allowed the bracelet to slide through his grasp, and Helen's arm fell back to her side with the weight of the gold. He made himself comfortable against the split in the yew, half sitting on the iron strap that bound it, knowing that the comparative brightness of the sky would silhouette him and prevent her from seeing his face clearly. Disorientation was often as useful as magic.

'I am Blake Chowdhry, First of Avebury.'

He waited patiently.

'Helen... Sixth... of Badbury Rings. She whispered in a reflex response, reaching for the constricting heat at her wrist.

'Well, Helen, I have a favour to ask.' His tone cleared her head, chilled her. 'I need someone shot.'

'...What?'

'I've done you a favour.' He nodded at the bracelet. 'By waking you early I've probably saved you more than a day, and time is a very valuable commodity, especially at the moment. I'm now inviting you to repay the debt.'

Helen stared at the beautifully worked Celtic gold, felt how deeply its roots spread into her. She sat up with a scowl, feeling as if she had woken from a dream of falling and was about to hit the ground awake. Then as her head cleared, the initial confusion flashed through fear into anger. 'Fuck your favour – and fuck you!'

He sighed. 'Alright, if you prefer I can *call* it in.'

The threat brought her up short. 'No! ...no, wait.' She was powerless and no amount of rage would change that fact, but at least it was only a Sanctuary she was at the mercy of. She rubbed her free hand across her eyes, resigning herself to yet another shift in her fate. 'If I do it... will that be it? No small print?'

'None. It'll just be a straightforward transaction. I'll borrow your talent, then you can go.'

Helen controlled the pointless and impossible urge to run. 'Okay, I'll do it... I don't have any choice.'

'That's true. You don't.'

Refusing the offer of his outstretched hand, Helen pulled herself unsteadily out of the yew and stood up. Her disorientation seemed to drain away into the ground like a lost earthing, and to her surprise she felt strong enough to walk, yet there was a superficial feel to the healing that had been imposed upon her, as if she was being supported by a framework of aerial roots.

'I found your bow and quiver,' he pointed to where they had been hidden; tucked into the rangy branches of the yew, 'but you were left unguarded.' He shook his head, the judgement left unspoken.

She didn't respond, lacking the energy to justify the actions of her Hallow. Her spirit too weighed down by the bondage of the bracelet.

'I'll fetch them down for you – with your permission.'

My permission? She couldn't detect any facetiousness in his tone; codes of conduct meant more to Sanctuaries. She nodded, not trusting her strength to hold out for a climb.

Blake briefly laid his spread hands on the yew before scaling its trunk to reach the stashed weapons. Though it was awkward not to, he didn't throw them to the ground and climb down after them, he kept them close, untangling them, and himself, at every step before jumping the last drop. He didn't offer them back. 'Right, let's go.'

Helen followed. Hating him.

He was considerate enough to walk slowly as he led the way back to his car. The talisman had replaced her lost heat and she wasn't even shivering, but the energy was woven from the thread of a mind and a motive that had nothing to do with true healing or the will of the land.

Helen was warm within her torn and bloodied coat, and there was no pain.

Small mercies were all she could hope for.

When they reached his car Blake unlocked it, placed her bow and quiver across the back seats, then held open the passenger door. Helen slumped in and yanked the seatbelt down, stabbing at the buckle beside her until it clicked in.

Blake shut the door, walked round to his side and got in without looking at her. He reached for the ignition. 'You're behaving like a child.'

Helen raised the middle finger of the hand bound by the bracelet.

'Please don't try my patience.' He reached across, touched the gold for a second, and Helen experienced a choking weight as if the air around her had solidified. Then it was lifted.

She looked away in submission.

Blake pushed her wrist down and turned back to the wheel. 'I'm not taking you far. As long as you cooperate, you'll be rid of me soon enough.'

Helen kept as far away from Blake as possible, hunched against the car door, with her face to the window. The moment of the arrow's impact replayed through her nerves every time they hit a bump on the road; she flinched away from the backrest when they drove over small shattered branches, and rubbed restlessly at the circle of dried blood on her coat.

The battered countryside blurred past her.

Then, through her desolation and the veil of the thrall she was under, Helen became aware that the crowns of the trees were no longer being flattened by the gale, and that the flying debris of leaves and twigs had stopped pattering against the windscreen. Although the clouds still tore overhead, the wind at ground level was dropping.

She had little knowledge of meteorology, and whether it was even possible for an isolated calm to form beneath a stormy sky, but all her instincts – even blunted as they were – warned her that it wasn't just some atmospheric fluke.

The power was shifting again.

Leaving her behind.

The streaks and strata of the clouds appeared to converge somewhere beyond the horizon, racing away without her. As if the gold on her arm made her too heavy for the wind to carry anymore.

They turned onto a rutted farm track leading to a fallow field, coming to a halt as soon as the car could no longer be seen from the road. She remained unmoving and preoccupied, but when Blake reached behind their seats for her bow and quiver, she ventured a glance at him. His composure was not as perfect as it had first seemed; he made small fidgeting movements with his fingers as if figuring a tally, and his face was lined with a frown. She derived a splinter of consolation from his agitation.

Outside of the car again, they could appreciate how much the wind had calmed, but the physical respite was shallow, the storm still surged far above, untamed and unpredictable, and the air held the dry static-charge of suspense.

They walked along the length of a tall blackthorn hedge that underlined the heavy sky with its hushing leaves and hidden spines. They reached a gap: a shadowed, unwelcoming gateway marked by a broken fencepost and a coil of rusted barbed wire.

Blake stopped and pointed for her to go on ahead. 'Through here.' The bracelet stung against her skin, reminding her that there were no requests now, only orders.

She walked into the darkness.

On the other side was a copse of tall alders. The ground was spongy with old, damp leaves and tiny cones, and the trees crowded around a wide ditch and wrapped their roots over its edge. There was hardly more than a meandering trickle of water at the bottom, but the exposed roots and scoured banks showed where the winterbourne stream cut its teeth every year.

Blake pointed ahead. 'Your mark is in the middle of this next field.'

She peered through the branches but saw no one.

'I'll find a place for you to shoot from. Ready yourself.'

'If you want me to prepare, you'll have to let me hold my bow.'

Without hesitation or apparent concern he passed it to her, along with a single arrow selected from her quiver; implying there was less significance in him carrying her weapons than she had supposed. 'You trust me, then?'

'I don't trust anyone from a Fort company.' His tone was matter-of-fact. 'But you can't harm me, with or without your bow.'

We'll see, you sanctimonious cunt. Helen swept her hand up to where the loose string was wound around her longbow and began to unfurl it.

As Blake made his way through the copse with her quiver over his shoulder, the yellow fletchings of her arrows flashed like a target on his back, and she harnessed the aggression it invoked.

He vanished into cover.

Before calming her mind for the shot, Helen invested this last spark of anger – and it burned through her before she quickly closed it down. To plot revenge on a Sanctuary companion was practically heretical; they were considered unassailable – above the bow, not prey to it – even though there was nothing overtly codified into the system that protected them from attack. Sanctuaries were left alone, like nests of hornets, but Helen felt she might muster the defiance to stir this one up.

She composed herself, put on her leather shooting glove, stuck the arrow in the ground at her feet, braced her longbow against the back of her thigh, and bent the limbs just enough to slide the loop of the string into the crescent groove carved in the horn nock. Ensuring it was safely set and holding the power of the yew wood ready, she closed her eyes, ran her palm back down to the centre of the bow, gripped hard, raised it to shoulder height and opened her eyes.

Blake was standing right in front of her.

'Follow me.'

Startled – impressed despite herself – she did.

The figure in the field stood exactly within range, on the centre of a grassy tumulus that over the centuries had been ploughed over and eroded to a shallow mound. He was making no effort to hide his presence.

Helen was unnerved, it was too easy. She suspected that Blake was being trapped, but this was Sanctuary business not hers. She had no inclination to stretch for whatever was being held out of reach: having no personal investment in the confrontation gave her a layer of emotional defence. *Don't analyse, just shoot.* The quicker this was over with the better. She willed herself to disregard the encumbrance of the bracelet, and settled into her stance.

He had found her an ideal place with a clear sight-line, no overhanging branches to foul the shot, and sufficient cover not to be seen. *Not bad for a no-bow.*

Blake studied her as she fitted the arrow to her bowstring. Every movement was fluid, strong, perfected. He felt a pang of envy.

It was years since he had chosen the Sanctuary path; years of healing, progression and refinement, and so the reluctance he'd felt when he handed back her longbow had caught him by surprise. It had felt right to carry a bow and a full quiver, to hear the rustle of stiff feathers, to feel the balance and weight of the yew in his palm. He managed to suppress the longing, but it had set up disturbing echoes.

He remembered how it felt to shoot.

And why he had given it up.

Helen pulled back to full draw, breathing in slowly and deeply. Her face set.

Blake moved in closer.

Her fingers opened letting the string whip.

He watched the arrow accelerate away and could almost see the line of intent guiding it to its mark. She was fast and well practiced; her target only now – and too late – showing that he felt the aim.

Blake pulled a fist-sized lump of rusty metal from his pocket.

The arrow hit the mark: a perfect chest shot, taking the figure down without a cry. … He drew his silver arrow from under his coat, touched the point lightly to Helen's back, and held the corroded metal to the silver fletchings. Waiting.

The next heartbeat brought the reciprocal impact of the earthing. Helen rocked backwards a step, holding her bow in both fists as if saving herself from a fall. Blake took her weight and pushed up hard against her with his shoulder so that his arrow wouldn't pierce her. Before she could react to what was happening he drew away all of the shot, ripping the flow out of her before it could course into the ground, diverting all of it into the ball of metal.

He held Helen. Held the metal, furnace-hot, between them. Felt rather than heard her screaming. Kept the lightning prisoner in the atoms until all of its energy was devoured and the blazing pain subsided.

Rejoiced at the sensation of crust and grit crumbling away between his fingers until his stinging palm pressed against cool, flawless iron.

Helen crumpled to her knees, gasping, still holding her bow. Blake let her and his arrow fall, engrossed in rubbing away the last of the rust from his prize.

It was a padlock, shining up dully under his polishing thumbs, shaped like a simple lily flower, and keyless. The metal of the face was decorated with engraved lines and tiny hammered dots depicting curlicues of leaves wound around the keyhole. It had a pre-wars air about it; from a time when function and beauty were integral, and handcrafted technology was unapologetically pretty.

Blake held it up to the light, smiled sadly, then put it away.

He turned his attention back to Helen, who was struggling to her feet. She hit his hand away as he reached down to help her.

'What the fucking hell was that!' She was furious, shaking. 'What did you do to me?'

'Only what I had to.' He picked up his arrow, and then offered his hand again. 'If you give me your arm I can release you.'

'Don't touch me! Not after that!' She backed away. 'I thought Sanctuaries were supposed to be trustworthy! Supposed to be civilised!'

Blake's expression darkened. 'I could have made a slave of you.' He pointed his silver wand at the bracelet. 'Instead, I gave you a choice. I think that's *civilised* enough for you.'

Helen shook her head in outrage. 'So, Sanctuaries are so far above the rest of us, so fucking *evolved*, that now you can force others to do your dirty work and steal shots instead?'

'You have absolutely no idea what you're talking about.' Blake spoke with quiet contempt as he turned away. 'You need to see to your victim now.'

'*My* victim?' Thrown by the subject change she was left staring at his back as he retraced his steps to the track. '*You* made me shoot him!'

'Righteous indignation doesn't sit well with someone from a plainshooting company.' He continued walking. 'When you decide you want to be released, let me know.'

'Wait.' Despising the way she was having to back down again, Helen clutched her bow and ran to catch up, even though the exertion threatened to bring her to her knees again. 'Take it off me.' She held out her arm, fist clenched. 'Then you can explain how the fuck I'm supposed to get him to a yew on my own.'

'You and your companions have more experience than me – give them a call.' He took hold of her outstretched wrist, opened out the gold bracelet and slipped it off.

'Is… that it?' She stared at the place where it had been, her skin marked with a faint red welt as if it had been grabbed and twisted.

'I willingly release you – is that better?' He handed back her quiver and turned to go. 'You'd better wipe that mark off your forehead or you might find yourself fielding awkward questions from outsiders – it looks like blood.'

Helen shouldered her arrows, reached up quizzically, touched her skin, and felt the sticky residue of yew berries. Froze.

David? She dropped her bow and folded as if shot again. Had her First and her whole company turned against her? With the removal of the baffle created by the bracelet, her intuition was returning: filtered through pain.

She laid her palm over the raw scar on her chest, torn between needing, and not wanting, to know. The faint remains of intent were heavily overlaid with the hunger of the pack, so she couldn't be sure who had shot her. But when Helen looked at the stain on her fingertips, she knew beyond doubt that Catrin had made that mark.

The treacherous possibilities threatened to fell her, and she fought back tears, scrubbing at the rune with her sleeves.

For the first time, Blake felt concern for her. Her obvious anguish was not caused by his actions this time. And that allowed him to care.

Hesitantly he crouched down next to her. He could see she was trying to control herself, but her breath escaped in stifled sobs. This unexpected show of vulnerability disarmed him completely. 'Look, I won't ask what this is about, but I will help you if I can.' She didn't respond. 'I'll take your— the victim, to a yew for you.'

She nodded. 'Afterwards… please… just take me home.'

A simple request, but in her tired whisper was a despair that Blake recognised.

The Bowlore, for all its aspirations, contained the potential to degenerate into savagery, driven as it was by a primal imperative that harnessed human desires for its own ends. Sometimes the risks appeared less important than the rewards, and stakes were raised without any real concept of the depth of the possible loss.

When that happened, he knew – from bitter experience – how the mundane world could seem like the only bolthole.

He put a hand on her shoulder.

Helen shrugged it away, wiped her eyes and picked up her bow. 'Let's get this over with.'

When they reached the tumulus, they found the target already profoundly cold and hardly breathing. He had been thrown forwards onto his face by the impact, his hands trapped beneath him where they had grabbed the arrow punching through his ribs. Blake gently turned him over. Helen stood back, unwilling to touch the chill body, to acknowledge the tainted exchange. And something else was disturbing her. The target somehow felt familiar; there was a resonance in the tiny part of him that lingered, suspended by the Covenant.

'Where is he from?' She ventured the question to fill the silence, unaccountably nervous of the answer.

'He's a freebow.'

Helen frowned. It didn't fit, Badbury had never been in conflict with anyone like that. Was he someone she had picked off in a raid?

Then she realised.

Blake studied the face turned towards him; it was frozen in pain, deathly pale and smeared with chalky soil. With difficulty he opened the young man's clenched fist, and found the token he was expecting.

The key.

Blake always prepared himself for alterations in the plan; it was in the nature of the Bowlore for it to respond and evolve, the trick was to recognise the signs and allow them to guide you. The trick of a trust-fall from a precipice.

He could see that Helen had been pushing her limits, behaving as he would expect anyone from a Fort company would; entangled in the storm and the reckless spirit of their Hallow. But she was deserving of more respect than he'd been prepared to give. Helen's path had led her to the yew for a reason, for more than just a convenient adjunct to his plan. Her involvement might well be vital and her ignorance no longer served any purpose. It would be much safer to offer her a haven – betrayed, he suspected, not just by him – safer to have her as an ally than to discard her, as he had initially planned.

'I owe you an explanation.'

Helen was so adrift in the situation now that she almost didn't care anymore. 'If you like.'

'Help me carry him. We'll talk in the car.'

by ivy. It gave the room a claustrophobic, underwater feel, and Helen had to overcome the urge to hold her breath.

The room was small, low-ceilinged, carpeted and wallpapered with patterns of pink and red roses. The blousy blooms stared like inflamed angry faces from every uneven wall. Although Helen realised she must be reacting to a protection that Blake had placed over the room, the knowledge couldn't dissipate the overwhelming sense of being in a place where she should not be – somewhere she was hated.

Blake took her arm and guided her to the table at the centre draped with a pristine linen tablecloth. A long wooden box was placed upon it, decorated with painted lilies in Art-Nouveau whiplashes; slightly chipped at the corners but unmarked at the meeting of lid and hasp. The flowers took on the meagre light from the window and reflected it gently but perfectly white.

Blake placed his hands on the lid, slowly and reverently, and took a long moment before he applied pressure enough to lift it. Helen leaned closer, purged of vengeful thoughts. Entranced.

A waft of perfume released from the box filled the air, as if the essence of spring had somehow been closed within it. All the exuberant life. All the promise.

Helen stifled a gasp, breathing in air as shockingly cold and clean as meltwater. Blake stood firm and solemn, but all the care was gone from his face. He moved to one side as he opened it fully, allowing her an unrestricted view of the contents.

There, nestled on a padding of white silk, lay a slim spiral horn. It filled the full length of the box, longer than an arrow, its thickest end not cut but rounded like a shed antler, its ivory point as sharp as a dagger.

Helen recognised it instantly: a narwhal tusk. An interesting and probably powerful talisman, but surely not what Blake wanted it to be. To her surprise, she felt an almost painful stab of disappointment.

'Wait.' Blake whispered. 'Watch.'

He took the iron padlock – the metal lily – still warm from his pocket, and closed the box, tightly confining the air of springtime so that the stuffiness of the room clamped back over their mouths like a dusty hand. Then he hooked the lock through the silver hasp, and pressed it shut with faint click, sealing it.

There was a change. Helen could feel it: the unmistakable, vertiginous lurch of the land realigning itself.

In a swift, silent earthquake, it settled into a new pattern – reforming the invisible web of energies into a framework that encompassed the Treasure she stood before.

Helen sensed the spiralling exultation, knew beyond doubt that it heralded one of the Thirteen.

And that she had absolutely no desire to take it.

Silence and dust.

Green light and red roses.

A place quietly slipped from the grip of time, and preserved unnoticed, in an amber cottage.

They stood, unwilling, unable to break from the suspension of the event. They too were held above the rush, and it was so peaceful, the tranquillity so absolute, that it seemed an offence to breathe, to allow their hearts to beat.

With great effort, Blake broke the dream-paralysis, shaking his head and gulping in air like a diver surfacing. He grabbed Helen, dragging her away from the box to the edge of the room, where the static energy was less intense – and she could fight against him.

'Open the box.' Helen forced out her voice. 'I need to see!'

'You saw it open.'

'I saw it open.' She stared intently at him. 'Now show it to me unlocked.'

The understanding Blake saw in her expression unnerved him. He realised he was still underestimating Helen, assuming the moment he'd allowed her to witness would be enough to pacify her, and be more than enough to win her over. Instead it was drawing her further in.

Helen's involvement was becoming too intimate, and it was all his fault. *Trust her part in this.*

The protective aura of the room had been magnified to such a degree that even Blake found it hard to step back into its influence. The Thirteen had defences of their own, he was pleased to discover – they would not be the passive commodities that many in the Lore would prefer them to be. They would be safer, but wilder.

He had tried to anticipate his own reaction to this fearful responsibility, tried to imagine the weight of taking on the burden of this, and later perhaps, other Treasures. Thought about having to express a devotion to duty, that could eventually conceal a need for the sovereignty they would inevitably bestow. Fearing that he might slip back on the path he had chosen, until he was no better than the avaricious woman glaring at him from the doorway.

He almost laughed out loud at his naivety. No company could possibly hold more than a single Treasure at a time, he felt sure of that now. Plans would have to be adjusted accordingly. *The Barrows will not be pleased.*

With effort, Blake stepped up before the box. This time he tried not to resist the pressure but allowed it in, hoping that equilibrium would reduce the discomfort. Acclimatising properly would take much more practice: his body was rigid, his breathing laboured, every small inhalation was a conscious effort.

His mind was racing.

This act would be pivotal.

Even though it hadn't yet been organised, the opening was intended to be an occasion worthy of gathering all the First's from the elite companies. Nothing was to be done in haste, and what had happened today was supposed to be just another step along the path. However, here he was, poised to steal the moment as it was unfolding; following his instincts instead of the plan, and witnessed by a nonentity from a company that even the most charitable in the Bowlore would describe as unsuitable. *But it feels right.*

He searched in his pocket and brought out the key, closing his hand over its preceding story, then reached out to caress the arched lid of the box with its white lilies, their fresh, dewy petals shining on the living wood.

His fingertips followed the tracery of tendrils, moved down over the lock to the keyhole. With delicacy, he inserted the key and turned it, coaxing it to open. Hoping that its surrender would be his vindication.

Praying.

The Lily Lock slipped open. Its weight moved from the hasp into his palm. He unhooked it and laid it aside. *Thank you.*

He turned to beckon Helen, but found she was already making her way over; forcing herself through the pressure, her eyes fixed on the box.

For the first time in days Helen felt something close to happiness. All the betrayal, the disappointment, the loneliness, that had hit her like a series of punches, faded in the presence of this strange, wonderful, secret object.

All she wanted was to see it, breathe its essence again.

Touch it.

Blake watched his hands on the lid as if they were not his. They moved slowly to the line where the box would part; hesitating, shaking.

He found himself becoming impatient at their slow progress, yet was unable to make them move any faster.

Then the lid was held. And lifted.

Light streamed from the opening. Filling the room, filling them. It cast no shadows, emitted no heat. It was as if solid matter offered no hindrance, instead it took it in. Welcomed it.

Everything in the room shone, appeared to glow from within with a brilliance that made Blake and Helen shield their eyes. They perceived it as light, but they stood embraced within purity. A distillation of the silver-white shaft held in the box.

Too bright to look upon, too virtuous to touch. Immaculate.

The Alicorn.

Chapter Fourteen

On the crest of the hill, near the megaliths marking the entrance to West Kennet, Patrick spotted three members of Badbury with bows, and – to his shock – an old man being held at arrow-point. He prayed that their prisoner was not some luckless outsider, because if their violence was spilling over into the mundane world, then the Bowlore's days were numbered.

He presumed that the core of the gathering was sheltered in the depths of the barrow. *How the bloody fucking hell am I going to pull this off?* He had no bow, no companions, no talismans, and stood facing Mount Doom. *Where's a ring of invisibility when you need one?* He managed a brief sardonic smile at the fact that he moved in a world where one might actually turn up.

If Catrin was holding out against Badbury and refusing to give up the dagger, then he could at least try to be the voice of reason – if he could get through to her. But there was no telling what David was capable of bribing – or threatening – her with, if he was now collaborating with West Kennet.

Whatever lay ahead, there was nothing left to learn by skulking under cover. *Time to go.*

The winds howled in chorus.

§

The silver arrowheads were tipped out into a clinking pile at Giles' feet. Some were bent and crumpled, others undamaged or just smeared with mud and grass; all had been broken from their shafts and gathered in the leather duffle bag that David now upended.

'My my, even by your standards, Mr Horsman, this is quite a profligate use of the Smith's fine workmanship.'

'I hear he likes to be kept busy, Mr Montford.' This was as close to facetious as he dared to get. Giles possessed a level of authority that even David had to respect.

'And yet, you appear to be going out of your way to deny him his raw material.'

The plainshot silver gleamed on the earthen floor under the skylight, unusable.

'Perhaps I need to remind you that if you take my company for granted – treat it like some kind of esoteric landfill – then the pact will be rescinded.'

David knew that as First of the premier Barrow company, Giles' rank was unassailable, and if he decided to shun Badbury's plainshot leavings, no one else from that Hallow would be willing to offer their own site as a substitute.

The message was clear: the dagger – David's bargaining chip – was forfeit.

He struggled to control his anger, knowing that it would only increase his vulnerability. *It's just a knife... Helen's knife.* He was suddenly pinned by regret, though not enough to stop him, because above all else his company needed indemnity: here was where he paid the price for living on the edge of the Lore.

He took out the dagger, and turned it on the flat of his palm so that the handle faced towards Giles. For a split second his attention was drawn to the glyph on its blade, but he hurriedly closed down the faint feeling of recognition, he was already giving too much away. If there was an extra element to the knife, Giles would have to figure it out for himself.

'I, David Horsman, First of Badbury Rings, willingly give you this talisman.'

'Very nicely done. Who'd have thought you would remember all the words, in your current state?' He took the knife by its rough yew handle and lifted it up to the light to examine it. 'I, Giles Montford, First of West Kennet long barrow, willingly accept this talisman.' He spoke in a throwaway tone, more to dismiss David than out of familiarity with the evolving codes.

David waited. There was always a caveat with Giles.

'However, as we both know, another element of this equation is still missing.' He flipped the knife, caught it deftly and laid it on top of the Wolfstone. Then his hand lingered over the blade and he frowned. 'You've left me with a considerable amount of work to do before these can be interred,' he focussed his displeasure on David. 'Unlike the Smith, I don't relish that prospect.'

'The only loose end I'm aware of will be arriving here any moment.'

Catrin froze. Hoping against hope that Patrick had understood her warning, knowing full well that even if he had, it still wouldn't stop him.

Giles looked unimpressed. 'A show of confidence from one so mired in the storm is hardly going to win me over.'

'I took care of my Sixth.'

'And you want kudos for your act of betrayal?'

That hit home, and David couldn't help biting. 'I did what I had to do – I reined her in, I drew all the influence of that fucking dagger out of her!'

'Remember where you are, Mr Horsman.'

David ignored the reprimand. 'I've delivered everything you wanted!' He pointed at Catrin. 'And more!'

And the wolves, as well as the dogs, fetch for me now.

'But I didn't ask for Catrin, did I? Throughout this entire affair, each time my specific instructions have been ignored, chaos has ensued… Wouldn't you agree, Peter?' He turned to where Ninestones' First was hunched and humbled in a corner of the barrow, the stub of a black candle burning in a niche above him.

Peter didn't lift his head or even show that he was listening.

Giles continued, unmoved. 'The Wisht Stone can mar the judgement of those who fall under its influence.' He paused while his audience took in the sobering wreckage of Ninestones' First. 'In my battle to maintain an unblighted line of intent, I've found it necessary to recruit, how shall I put it? Some *disparate* individuals to my cause.'

David scowled.

Catrin was growing increasingly suspicious of the confessional slant that Giles was introducing. He had to be up to something, his Hallow wasn't noted for its openness.

'You are a guest here, Catrin, nothing more or less. You may leave at any time.' Giles offered this freedom with the certainty that she would never walk away from the stone. Each time he glanced at her she was staring at it, fixated. Without having to lift a finger he had secured Catrin's – albeit unwilling – allegiance, and he silently congratulated himself on having successfully deflected the anarchy brought in by the windblown Fort.

'Your various talents, under my direction, have delivered the Wisht Stone to a place where the threat it represents can be contained, thereby preserving the stability of the Bowlore.'

How very fucking noble. 'So, what do I get for helping to fetch one of the Thirteen for you?' David, realising that all routes to a negotiated gain were cut off, opted for the kind of brazen honesty that might expose Giles's divide-and-conquer strategy. A rash move, but the storm still raged above and within him.

Giles eyed him, debating how to respond.

He could disregard Peter and pull David to heel with the pact, but Catrin's focus was suddenly fully on him; he could feel the heat of her stare, and so he had no choice but to continue the charade. 'Your reward is to live through this disaster. Your reward is to continue your antics and still be protected by the Covenant. Your *fucking* reward, Mr Horsman, is to redeem yourself by helping to bury the very talisman that would have buried all of us!'

'Talisman… or Treasure?' Catrin's voice was low, but it cut through the guts of the barrow like a knife.

Giles had to shut down quickly to cover his mistake. He silently cursed his lapse of concentration. 'The Wisht Stone is a law unto itself, a thing apart. I sometimes find it hard to refer to it as a Treasure when it's put the system in such danger.'

She knew he was lying and a strange calm filled her. She felt so close to the truth, so entitled to it, that the mere fact that Giles was ward of the Wolfstone no longer mattered. Her claim was stronger because the stone, and its dagger, were rightfully hers.

There was a noisy scuffle at the entrance to the barrow; swearing and protests blown away on the wind. Then Badbury's Second ducked inside. 'Someone to see you, David.'

Despite the namecheck, Giles was the one who straightened up and nodded his permission, glad of the well-timed distraction.

Dishevelled, with a cut lip and cradling his injured hand, Patrick was pushed inside on the point of an arrow. He stumbled against David who shoved him away.

'You're late Paddy.' But resisted the temptation to add a jibe about his plainshot hand, even though the signs of Giles' discomfort had bolstered his confidence. He wanted to hedge his bets with Catrin, so reined himself back and addressed the Barrow's First: 'One loose end, as promised.'

Catrin broke away from the lure of the Wolfstone to rush over to Patrick, cupping his face in both hands to examine the red weal across his cheek. 'For fuck's sake, Pat! Why did you come here? You can't help me.'

Patrick was dazed from a punch to his jaw, his hand felt like it was being held over a flame, and the dynamic within the barrow was vastly different from what he'd been prepared to find. He tried to orientate himself but pain and dizziness closed over him, cutting him off.

And Giles was aware that as fast as he was tying up the other wayward threads, his control over Catrin was unravelling; and that her strands would be harder, perhaps impossible to rebind.

He couldn't let that happen – there was too much at stake.

...As if the ground had been suddenly jerked from beneath their feet, they all braced themselves, grabbing for the solidity of the barrow's walls. A shock-wave pulsed through them and they stared at each other; levelled and united in their mutual confusion.

§

...Megan shuddered. She dropped to her knees and spread her hands wide on the ground, working her fingers through the grass, into the soft earth, reaching further down and deeper with her mind. She let out a long breath, as if she had been holding it all her life.

Her frown softened to a smile. 'So... it is done.'

Behind her, Judith nodded and held her silver arrow to her heart, tears spilling from her closed eyes.

§

The Smith ran his fingers through the small pile of assorted silverware left on the capstone: spoons, brooches, a dented Edwardian sugar bowl, chains, charms and a machine-cut rectangle prised out of an electrical switch. He stirred the scavenged collection, there was nothing of particular interest. He would choose his cut from the hallmarked jewellery; whichever pieces could be easily exchanged for cash, but the rest would undergo a more profound and subtle transformation within his crucible and upon his anvil.

The beech trees encircling Wayland's Smithy danced with the gale that tore across the Ridgeway, filtering the violence from the air, so that within the solid shelter of the long barrow's threshold, with its four great facing stones, he would be able to work.

He scooped up his payment and stepped down from the broad slope of the barrow's crest into the relative calm between the megaliths.

The influence of the storm had abruptly increased his workload, and brought down the quality of the hastily garnered silver. All the various companies needing arrows abided by an unspoken code of conduct, out of respect for the sanctity and neutrality of his site; hanging back along the roads and tracks when they recognised that someone from the Bowlore was ahead of them in the clandestine queue. However, as much as this pacing maintained the peace, it had also resulted in him having to live in his van at his site for the past two days and nights. He needed a shower, he craved a meal that wasn't spooned straight out of a blackened can heated in the embers of his forge, and he desperately wanted some kind of reassurance that the Sanctuaries had the situation under control. Their ominous silence was leading him to the conclusion that his gut feeling was right, and that nothing would be resolved without his direct intervention.

Do I have to do everyone else's job as well as mine?

The sun was nowhere near to setting, and yet so much of its light had been cut out by the racing clouds that the evening was already gloomy and perfect for forging, the glow of the radiant silver would guide his hammer as he drew out, spread and folded the toffee-soft metal.

He hooked his arms under the cross of his anvil and rocked it on its yew wood stump, over to the calmest corner. He shovelled charcoal into the tray of his lit forge, sending up spirals of black dust, white smoke, and snapping sparks. He picked up his hammer.

...And then dropped it clanking against the anvil, as a jolt went through the ground beneath him.

The land was shifting: flexing and curling itself like a serpentine root around a vibrant new anchoring energy.

The thunder of its movement resounded through the atoms of the Whetstone of Tudwal Tudclyd, veiled in the deepest chamber of the barrow; striking up a chord from an almost forgotten harmony.

Filling one of the voids left by the old, lost Thirteen Treasures of Britain.

In triumph, the Smith punched his fist up to the darkening sky, then opened the three fingers of the bowstring in salutation.

The Bowlore had found its mark.

Chapter Fifteen

Burrow Mump.

Megan smiled as she gazed up at it. Here was another ridged cone of a hill, another ruined church dedicated to the dragon-slayer St Michael, another captivating beacon to rule over the Levels. A quieter Tor.

It served her well as a substitute for Glastonbury on mornings when the solstices and equinoxes brought out revelling congregations of seekers, dreamers, wanderers and the lost. Megan preferred to watch the ruby sunrises from here, far from the clamour, chanting and drumming of her home site.

But its relative lack of fame did not denote insignificance.

It was not part of the Bowlore, and owed as much of its identity to the rebellions and battles fought around it, as to the symbol of peace on its crown, yet it was an intrinsic part of a greater geomantic pattern; an expression of the bond between the land and those who lived upon it.

River, road, field and hill sketched the outline of a great dog onto the landscape. Five miles long from the nose where Megan stood, to its tail at the hamlet of Wagg, it guarded the Glastonbury Zodiac – the most liminal sacred structure – where those who believed and those who decried shared an equal standing.

Judith followed her mother up the slopes of the mound and into the teeth of the gale. The wind chafed tears from their eyes, sucked the breath from their lungs and snatched their words away. She took hold of Megan's arm to support her as they slipped and stumbled up to the shelter of the chapel.

More of this building remained than of its equivalent on the Tor. It lacked a roof, but was essentially whole.

From where they approached, the follied Gothic arch of the empty east window, framed their view of the belfry.

For centuries the chapel had tried and failed to maintain a foothold. Eventually the puritan wrecking crew of the New Model Army gutted it after torching the orchards at Wagg, and every impassioned attempt to rebuild it since had been in vain; as if the harm, like grit, was ingrained in its russet and dove-grey stones.

Caught up in another kind of civil war, Megan knew that if she couldn't determine the source of the storm, then it would take far more than wassailing burnt apple trees, to heal the Gurt Dog of Langport, and restore everything that he – and she – protected.

Megan and Judith pressed into the shelter of a wall, took out their arrows and settled themselves to work. They focussed down through the layers of abandonment, of construction, of pious anger, of siege, of rebellion, oppression, resistance, retreat, peace...

A sudden, sideways tug... and they were watching a cavalier soldier pull a lead musket ball from his neck and hurl it at the skies, as he walked out through the chapel doorway into the light...

Judith refined her aim so her energy wouldn't be borrowed again.

Megan held the line of intent. Smiled.

...Bedrock.

Here rested the loyal hunting hound of the demoted and diminishing god who bided his eternity beneath the Tor.

Here was Dormarth.

§

Spiralling scents of the Land are pulled in and savoured. Some are rejected on a stalled breath: the stink of burning, metal and acid, soured earth bleeding into bitter water.

Hedge-hackles bristle in the gale.

A Hand from Home smoothes them down.

A Voice from Home calls.

Dormarth!

Moor-ear pricks up.

Who Runs?

Pack!

Who Hunts?

Pack!

Who leaves the pathways?

?

Who roams?

?

Who Seeks?

Dog!

Who set the Dog free?

?

Who holds the Collar?

Hand! Dig! Bone!

More.

Hand! Dig! Bone! Hand! Stone! Sharp!

The Voice offers scents from Home. He sniffs them in greedily.

Good Dormarth.

§

Peter, crushed beneath the weight of a misplaced sense of responsibility, shivered as if someone had walked over his grave.

If his grave was to be here, shared with so many others – if he sank down and gave in to the shrouding blackness – he knew he would never rest in peace, but would spend whatever afterlife he was granted, endlessly shivering under the tread of all the outsiders and all the Lore who would be bound to come here. *No more than I deserve.*

He shuddered again.

Was this another earth tremor? He peered up at the animated expressions on the faces of the others, their voices a continuous, muffled gabble. They showed no shock. He let his head droop back down.

A tearing jolt.

He gasped and sat bolt upright.

For an instant his vision was filled with a swarming mass of black, looped in a vast frenzied ouroboros. He retched violently, curling over his fisted hands, drooling spit, his body reacting to his psyche's need to rid itself of the nightmare.

...peter!

He tried to listen.

...wrong...runs?

'Please – help me!'

...can't...hunts?

'Pac-lease!'

...you need to...ways?

'What?'

...you home?

'What?'

...too weak...seeks?

Suddenly he knew. 'Dog!'

...you set...him free?

'Me?' It was loose before he had started to dig out the stone.

...who holds the collar?

'West Kennet!'

...more.

'Giles!'

The sickness left him. Words left him.

All he wanted was to sleep. And never dream again.

§

The Smith, his face livid with sweat and the glow from the forge, pounded the bellows feeding air into the bed of charcoal. Pink and orange flames flared and crackled, polishing the ashy coals into diamonds, and swarms of tiny white sparks stung the bare skin of his arms, above the protection of his leather wrist guards.

The rich tang of metal and burning, the clink and chime of the striking tools, the warm flickering light, lent an almost cosy ambience to the solemn forecourt of the barrow.

He only worked when no outsiders were visiting his site; when there was no one marvelling, exploring, sheltering, taking photographs, bringing candles or leaving tokens. He took any offerings left by the superstitious and the hopeful: the coins, charms and jewellery; and measured their value by the intent they had absorbed. Those he deemed worthy were placed behind the row of kerbstones around the sides of the Smithy, so that their line of contact would be preserved by his curation – he owed that much. Any fearful or perfunctory payments were tossed into the roadside ditches.

He had no time for the flowers and pretty pebbles – unless they were left by children – he was the Smith, not a bloody fairy.

The silver rods, still hot from the polished stone moulds, lay like runnels of static mercury on the ground around the tripod legs of his forge. He picked one up in his bare hand, and turned it to admire the quality.

The batches of silver left by the Barrows were consistently good: Stirling or above, always old. Their payments were outnumbered in frequency five to one by the Forts, but never outclassed.

The Stone companies left the least, but they would always offer something personal with every hoard; some treasured possession. He enjoyed working with that energy, appreciating the sacrifice it represented, and the arrowheads he made for them were consequently finely tuned and easier to aim. He hardly ever got back a damaged miss-shot arrow from their Hallow to melt down, whereas some of the Forts would have him reworking his material every time.

Six rods of silver at his feet, a seventh in his hand.

Two for South Cadbury, two for Brent Knoll, one each for Scorhill Stones and Stanton Drew, and the one he held – the purest – for West Kennet.

As he studied it he realised that it wasn't just the calibre of the metal that had attracted him. There was an intent rising off it, a signal that rippled the air around it as surely as the heat-shimmer.

The specifics were lost in the colliding atoms, so he quenched the rod in the wooden bucket beside him; stirring it in the cold water to still the background noise, before holding it close.

Giles' talent for covering his tracks knew no equal, but it would seem that even his abilities had been affected by the havoc. Here in his hand was an overlooked path that ran right overhead, and into the heart of West Kennet long barrow.

The source of the storm.

The Smith watched the dark spiralling clouds breathed out by the wolves. Listened to them crying out against the hunger sawing at their guts.

The headlong rush was not an expression of liberation, it was the panicked stampede of a wild force leaping at the walls of its prison.

And there was a faint trace of a darker influence as well. It tasted elemental. Older and more ambiguous.

Giles Montford held it.

But his grip was slipping.

§

There was a rupture in the veil. The whipcrack of a breaking collar.

Peter's garbled responses were cut short and clarified all at once.

An apparition rose up, unfolding out of itself, filling the furthest chamber of the barrow; gaunt, massive, black as despair.

Catrin cried out an incoherent sound of terror, grabbed Patrick by a fistful of his coat and dragged him with her, only just resisting the urge to use him as a shield, as they scrambled backwards, round-eyed with horror.

David, closer to the entrance, had already fled and was outside with his back to the huge stone slabs of the forecourt wall, lit in the failing dusk by the torch-beams from his company. *What the fuck!* He jabbed a finger at the doorway. 'All arrows at the door! No aiming – loose on my word!'

Badbury reacted immediately, training their arrows in a bristle of yellow and black on the opening to the mound. Then Catrin and Patrick stumbled backwards, gasping, into the ring of silver points, and for a second it felt as if David would lose control. His Second immediately aimed at Catrin, but David shoved Gareth's bow-arm away from her and back towards the entrance.

No one moved.

A faint and tired voice filtered between the stone slabs behind them. 'What the bloody hell is going on now?'

It was ignored.

The faint yellow glow emanating from the mouth of the barrow flickered and broke, as something within moved between the doorway and the flame of the single candle Giles had deigned to burn.

The twilight drained away, outlines replaced detail. In vigilant silence, with bows almost at full draw, Badbury formed a silhouette around the facing stones, their dropped torches creating a latticework of white lines on the ground.

A deeper shadow cut the candlelight. The doorway went black.

Badbury, as one, pulled the fletchings of their arrows close to their cheeks, fighting against the buffeting wind to keep their mark.

Movement.

Giles stepped out into the sweep of the deflected wind, his long coat flapping like the wings of a carrion bird.

Only two of Badbury lowered their bows.

He glared at the arrows still levelled at him. 'Mr Horsman! Control your company!'

With glances toward David as they sought his sanction, they let down their bows, but kept their arrows nocked.

Giles stood firm. 'Badbury Rings! You have outstayed your welcome at my site. If this is a challenge I *will* accept it!'

That sobering proposition brought David to his senses. 'Everyone hold! Move back!' He straightened up and stepped forward to face the First of West Kennet – even though being closer to the lair of the monstrous thing Giles had bound to the barrow, filled him with dread and drew his eyes compulsively to the doorway.

Giles moved in closer, brooking no distraction, his voice too low for anyone else to hear over the wind. 'If you ever overreach yourself again, I will make it my personal mission to sever Badbury Rings from the Covenant.'

And he could. The damning evidence against the Fort lay in a glittering, sharp-edged pile on the floor of the barrow.

David's anger was struck up and stamped down in a second. He had to yield. He studied Giles' trenchant expression, saw there was no way out, and shook his head in bitter disgust at his own lack of foresight. After checking the barrow door for signs of movement he turned to his company. 'We're leaving!'

Gareth was incensed. He held his bow tilted, arrow on the string, ready to pull it again. 'Not without the Wolfstone!'

The wind masked any murmurs, but nods of agreement rippled plainly through the company.

David drew level with him, grabbed a fistful of his shirt at the neck and pushed him back hard. 'Do as I fucking say or you'll be following Helen into the yew!' Then he pulled him up close and added quietly by his ear, 'And if we take Giles on now you would die in there.' An understanding passed between them, and his Second backed down.

He let go of Gareth and opened his arms wide as if to console his company with an embrace. 'The Wolfstone is out of the game,' he held out his palms to stay any protest, 'beyond *any* Fort's reach. But there are still eleven other Treasures out there!' Gareth raised his bow above his head to lead a salute but the response from his companions was half-hearted. David read the mood. 'And remember that Cadbury, Uley, Brent and Maiden are burning up their talismans and filling yews because of *us!*'

Heartfelt yells followed that declaration.

Catrin kept her arm locked around Patrick's waist, as they surreptitiously stepped back and back, taking advantage of the commotion. His right arm was draped across her shoulders, and even with the wind blowing past them she could feel the fever-heat coming off his poisoned hand. If he collapsed now they were done for.

She heard David's rousing speech; felt him skilfully steer his company away from potential mutiny.

But she watched Giles.

He had folded his arms and taken up a solid stance in front of the door to his barrow. Not to impress or to defend, but to contain.

The elemental he had loosed was fighting against him. She could feel the waves of pacing pent-up hatred and defiance emanating from the barrow along with the sepia light.

Giles' guard dog was turning on him.

Catrin wondered how far away they would need to get from West Kennet to be safe when it did break out. How far she could force Patrick to run before he collapsed; how to keep him hidden and safe when she had to leave him, and return to claim the unguarded Wolfstone from the depths of the barrow.

§

Lawrence had not been able to follow any of the wind-snatched words and noises from his place in the scant shelter of the facing stones. Hunched down and exhausted he had allowed this exclusion to cut him away from responsibility. Nevertheless, the unmistakable turn of mood from anger to fear had pierced his isolation. Cursing his stiff joints, he heaved himself up from the ground and, suppressing a limp, began to walk towards Giles. Insignificance made him invisible: no one tried to stop him.

He appreciated that in the long and noble history of grand gestures, his was probably going to be amongst the smallest, soonest forgotten, and almost certainly most pointless ones.

But it was all he had left in him.

Chapter Sixteen

Giles raised barricade after barricade, drawing up the energy from the ground, from the rocks, the packed earth, and the chalk bones of his domain.

To no avail.

The elemental force manifesting within his barrow nosed at the walls he built up, scratched and worried at the flesh of them. The deepest aspects of his Hallow and the Black Dog were so alike that it merely pulled in his desperate attempts at containment and fed ravenously upon them, growing more solid and more real with every bite.

Giles, used to obedience, had never believed that the very resonance which allowed him to summon the Dogs might also render him vulnerable to them.

The one he had called years before, had come to heel and paced beside him, its saucer-eyes fixed on his face, awaiting his command.

This one had lived too long in the company of wolves.

§

...Lawrence cleared his throat to try again. He looked up at Giles, who was a head taller than him, thirty years younger and a force to be reckoned with in and out of the Lore. His Byronic features were lit by sporadic torch-sweeps from Badbury as they departed, momentarily turning beads of sweat on his forehead to frost, his eyes to dark sockets in a pale skull.

'Excuse me... I said I'm willing to take Peter's place.' Lawrence waited, marvelling that his own manners were so hard-wired that even under these dire circumstances he felt obliged to be polite.

Giles didn't respond, his face falling back into shadow as the last Fort companion left his site to join the flickers and silhouettes on the track leading down to the road.

Lawrence was just debating whether to throw caution to the real and metaphorical wind, and venture past West Kennet's First to look for Peter in the chambers, when a blast of freezing air, like the shearing edge of an oncoming blizzard, slammed into them.

It wasn't part of the wolfstorm – it stank of death, not desperation.

And it blew from the maw of the barrow.

§

Megan's mobile rang.

She placed her mug of tea on the kitchen table, between two purring tortoiseshell cats lying on a pad of drawing paper, obscuring abandoned sketches of themselves. She checked the caller's name and sighed, letting the ringtone play itself out, while she took off her coat and draped it over a chair.

The cats, with their legs tucked under, looked like fur tea-cosies. Megan hoped they possessed similar qualities because it was likely to be a long call.

She sat down wearily, then answered without preamble. 'Listen,' – she heard the glottal catch of an interrupted word. 'Before you start, just take it as read, that I know at least as much as you do about this matter – therefore I *will* know if you're holding anything back from me.'

There was a pause as the caller composed himself. 'I need to tell you about West Kennet.'

'I'm aware of what Giles is doing.'

'About him keeping a Black Dog in thrall?'

'Yes.'

'And about the Treasure?'

That stopped Megan in her tracks. The upper-hand was swapped. 'Go on.'

'He's claimed the Wolfstone – Wisht Stone – whatever the hell it's called, and he's going to inter it.'

Her mind raced, connected, clarified. She smiled to herself as the upper-hand was returned to its rightful place. 'Ah, I see. Giles has beaten you and the rest of the Forts to the stone, so you've come to tell tales on him.'

'For fu— God's sake Megan!' There was another muffled pause like the phone had been briefly pressed against clothing. 'I just thought you ought to know what he intends to do – surely he shouldn't be allowed to inter one of the Thirteen?'

'If it *was* one of the Thirteen, he wouldn't be.'

'What?'

'Did you feel the land accept it?'

'Yes, we all did!'

'And Giles told you it was for the stone?' In the silence that followed she could almost hear cogs whirling. 'I've learned not to judge a man by the company he keeps – as you well know. But you need to remember that there are no trustworthy truces or alliances to be made with a Barrow.'

'That lying bastard! The second Treasure is still out there? That shock-wave was... what? An earthquake?'

'Did it feel like it was just a three-point-nothing seismic jolt?'

'No.'

'Your quarry went to ground – you could say found sanctuary – at that moment.'

'Wait! So *you've* got it?'

Megan had to pull the phone away from her ear. 'I do not have one of the Treasures, and I am not about to tell you who does... I think, considering your state of mind at the moment, we should end this call now. I've already said far too much.'

'No wait! At least tell me what it is!'

She sighed. He would find out soon enough anyway. 'It's an alicorn, the horn of a unicorn.'

'What the *fuck* kind of fairytale crap is tha—' She tapped the screen and cut him off. One cat opened one eye, she stroked its head and reached for her mug of tea. It was still warm.

Megan could tell by his voice how exhausted he was, physically and mentally, and how badly torn by the havoc. What he really needed, more than anything else, was sleep.

Regrettably, the days when she could have sent David to bed, were long gone.

§

Catrin and Patrick edged their way around West Kennet – expecting the sounds of pursuit at every step – until they had the humped bulk of the long barrow between the Dog, the retreating Badbury companions, and themselves. Then they scanned around for their next point of cover.

Silbury Hill rose tantalisingly close, but acres of open fields surrounded West Kennet, and the track currently being used by the Fort overlooked all the approaches. Though Badbury appeared to have lost interest in them, it wasn't worth the risk of drawing their attention by making straight for the hill: predators would always react to the sight of fleeing, injured prey.

The only option was to make a run for the nearest hedgerow, and follow the snakes-and-ladders route of field boundaries, back down to the protection of their site.

Patrick's voice was hoarse as he strained to be heard over the storm. 'I came here to save *you*!'

'Keep trying, maybe one day you will!' She gave him a quick kiss. 'For luck!' *We're going to need it.*

They ran.

The ruts in the ploughed soil, invisible in the darkness, hampered Patrick's already unsteady gait. He tripped, throwing them both off balance as Catrin hurried him along.

The feeling of being exposed was intense. She started to shake, tried to convince herself it was just from the chill of the wind.

Knew it was not.

Patrick was trying his best but he was weakening, as if the monster was drawing on the poisonous connection leading to his hand. She hated herself for missing such a critical part of the pattern, yet why would anyone think of looking for a line of intent from a plainshot arrow? With hindsight it was pivotal – the first arrow loosed in the name of the Wolfstone, to find its mark.

Catrin couldn't bring herself to check behind, dreading what she might see; instead she committed them both to achieving the illusory shelter of the hedgerow. If they could be well hidden by the time it came after them, then… then what? Would a few scant bushes and trees foil a Black Dog? With the desperate reasoning of a child she felt that if they could hide; if they couldn't see it, the monster might pass them by.

In folklore, to see the Dog meant death. Sometimes, in the fickle way of elementals, protection. But Catrin had seen the immense shadowy form shake itself free of Peter, as it finally sloughed off its sheep-disguise, and that glimpse told her that this incarnation did not escort lonely travellers.

She made them run faster, dragging Patrick by his good arm, the weight of his sickness countered by the strength of her panic.

The mounting pressure formed an image in her mind's eye, of an unstoppable burning cloud blasting down the slope, of an excruciating death that would engulf and petrify them in their agony.

Of the pitiless lava-red eyes of Black Shuck, scorching her body and soul to ashes.

§

Another phone call.

Megan downed the remains of her tea and answered at the first notes.

Chapter Seventeen

Peter lay pinned by gravity. He trusted it was so; his back was pressed into a cold and gritty surface, it could have been a wall or the floor – no way was up – and only a smothering darkness reached his eyes, opened or shut, as physical and unyielding as the rock pushing against his palms. He felt emptied of pain, emptied of life.

His body took a breath. Bitterly cold.

Let it go, losing precious heat. Giving himself away.

Took another. Held it.

Let it go. Slowly, fearfully.

...Nothing.

His tears obeyed the pull of the ground, pooling in the hollows of his eye sockets and tracing chill lines to his ears and neck.

Then he understood that he must be lying on his back.

And that the Black Dog had let him live.

§

The Land is webbed with lines. Light and dark. Some of sinuous water, some of jagged fire, some of bruising footsteps, layered with memories.

These Trodden Ways – paths of the Ones who have chosen to leave the Pack and fall in step with the Shapers – are calling, grieving. Pacing a lament.

From prey – to jealousy – to tolerance – to trust – to love.

To betrayal – to hate.

Stone marks the line.

Blocks the Way.

Tricks and traps.

The Hand that holds Stone is Prey.

§

Giles was flung forward by a wall of icy air as solid as the howling black form erupting in its wake.

Even though all his contrived fetters were sundered and useless, he still had the presence of mind to twist as he fell, so that he could face the enraged Dog. It landed with both huge front paws on his shoulders, bearing him down with the weight of its undeniable physical presence; the crushing density of collective terror, the pressure of mounded and pounded earth and the tonnage of boulders.

Giles craned his head back and stared straight into the hot blood of its eyes.

§

The connection to Megan's mobile crackled, phasing in and out with the hills and the turns of the road as he drove.

'It's loose.'

'I know. But it may still answer to you.'

The Smith paused. '…Or to my silver.'

§

Lawrence staggered back, almost thrown by a wind so fetid and laden with death that it could have been the first exhalation of a robbed tomb.

He lowered his arms from his face. Then wished he hadn't.

Looming over him and blotting out the mouth of the barrow, framed by the dim stain of light from distant towns and the miserable slate of the storm clouds, was an immense Black Dog.

Lawrence was rooted to the ground by a primitive terror exceeding anything he had experienced before. Even the bombs of his earliest childhood; the drone then the awful breath-held silence before windows turned to daggers and walls to landslides, had never provoked such dread in him.

The Dog's shaggy pelt was rippled into long spines by the wind. Its shoulders, level with Lawrence's horrified face, hunched as its head swiped down, jaws agape and lips snarled back from jagged teeth. Its eyes were stretched so obscenely wide it looked like the creature's skin was peeling back from its flesh; as if the glut of energy had swelled the elemental beyond the capacity of its adopted shape.

He watched its muzzle sweep over Giles as it feasted on his scent, on the last of the broken bondage, forcing the Barrow First to share its panting breath while rags of saliva, like the seepage from a corpse, dripped across his face.

Giles did not flinch. Did not struggle or beg.

The Dog licked back strings of drool. It cocked its head, ears pricked.

Listened.

Slowly, it swung its head round to focus its hellish glare on Lawrence. Then bared its teeth in a savage, sentient grin.

Lawrence was petrified in the red light of the Dog's eyes. The world around them blackened to an abyss, and he was engulfed by the reality, the stripped and raw certainty, of his own death.

The inevitability drained him of hope, yet still he dragged in a breath, pulling against the vacuum of mortality.

Pulled again.

Used the remnants of his will to strike a spark of life from the flint of his heart. Struck again. Struck another. Each one instantly smothered by the void that waited for him.

Witnessed all his possible deaths replayed. The close-calls and distant threats that would have – should have – killed him.

The reproachful stares of those who had not been spared, judged him from the eyes of the Dog. Jostling for their turn to plead for explanations, demand recompense, shout their jealousy and their hate in voices that rose and fell with the wind... *made me climb up but I couldn't hold on as long as you... were too young to be called up you lucky little... by little you pushed me away so I walked home alone that night... raid when you ran out of the bloody shelter... from the storm, you said it was where... is my family? where are my grandchildren? my line... wasn't where you said and I had nowhere to run... all your cars into the ground, but you couldn't even... stevens, you promised! and now we're never going to... be the one that died instead... of all my loved ones crying... out for help and yet you still... and so cold... water on my ideas! it would have saved... the best till last... breath I took... everything from me but you're still there... is no justice! it was your time... to pay for all you have...* Yes... *all the luck... ran out when you left me... me, me! thank god I died before I realised what a selfish bastard you...* Yes... *should be dead...* Yes... *just like...* Yes... *us...*

Yes.

Peter plunged the dagger with such force, such venom, into the Dog's matted hide that only the crosspiece stopped his hand from following the blade down into its flesh.

§

An unearthly scream of agony scythed through the gale.

The skies startled to a momentary halt, seeming to draw in a shocked breath. The wind swirled in confusion, snagging spiral eddies and whiplashes from the underside of the cloud layer before regaining momentum and streaming into a curve. The leading edge closed on its own tail until the whole sky was moving in a great widdershins circle.

Patrick was felled by the dreadful scream as surely as if he had taken an arrow. Catrin bent double beside him, covering her ears, tears running from her squeezed shut eyes.

The keening was filled with outrage and torment, kindling a kind of revolted pity even as it terrified. The wail rose in pitch and volume until their bodies, the ground and the sky were resonating with anguish.

Then it stopped.

The howling of the wolfstorm was welcome by comparison.

Catrin didn't move. She couldn't, fear had locked her limbs. Her mind, betrayed by a body that would not flee, sought safety in the deepest recesses of her consciousness.

Patrick opened his eyes to the whirling, dizzying sky.

No protective yew cradled him, no Covenant saved him from the burning in his hand, no companion could lift the venomous burden, or even share its weight. He turned his face away from the nauseating carousel of clouds and vomited, heaving over and over, until there was nothing left in his body but the poison.

It's coming.

Get up.

Catrin heard her own voice echo in her head. Level and calm and insistent.

Run for Silbury.

It broke the thrall of her panic.

She wiped her eyes and looked down at Patrick who still lay gasping and convulsing, obviously beyond any hope of continuing. *I can't leave him!*

Run.

'Pat! Get up!' Nothing in this or any other world could have got her to look back along the rise to the source of the scream, but she knew that the Dog was closing in on them. 'Get up! Get up!'

Run.

Patrick turned his face to her. In the darkness his mouth nose and eyes were just black holes. He grabbed her arm and pulled her down to his death's-head face, the stench of sickness on his breath. '... Run.'

She shook her head, but her muscles cramped from straining against her will. Death behind her, death before her. *Tell me again!*

'Don't let Silbury... die.'

He always knew how to get past her rejection.

She held in a sob, kissed his hand.

And ran.

Her legs were heavy with the lead of nightmares. Four strides and she was out of breath, five and she tripped, six, seven, *faster,* eight, nine, she found her stride, *faster,* her long legs ramming into the soil, her arms pumping like an athlete's, *faster,* the Dog still behind, life and Silbury Hill before her. A dream of running, a dream of flying, her body carried without conscious effort, almost without sensation, through the wild darkness. Branches lashed, gravel sprayed up, her feet hit tarmac. All she saw was her hill. Her home. *Home... A car, wheel-spinning into the road. Leah's fearful eyes reflected in a rear-view mirror... replaced by running figures with raised bows, red from the car lights, falling back into shadow and shrinking with distance.* Catrin took heart, escape was possible. Escape from the wolves.

Escape from the Black Dog.

A fence, tangled grass, a breath for every pace, *faster,* the hollow, the rise, *don't look back.* She flung wide her arms to embrace Silbury, threw herself upon its motherly slopes, ripping fistfuls of grass as she hauled herself up and up to the safety of its level crown.

From her vantage point, her eyrie, she gained the courage to look down.

The gale dragged her back but she drew in its feral energy with her deep, exhausted gasping, no longer afraid of its taint. This was her place. She was unassailable.

There was nothing waiting below, no haunting black on blackness pacing hungrily around the hill, no red eyes sweeping its flanks. *Where is it?* For an awful moment she thought it must be behind her, silently mocking her faith in Silbury as it poised to strike. She spun around, arms half raised, ready to run again.

Nothing.

Then she knew.

The whole hill seemed to ring hollowly, sharing her despair as her screaming calls to Patrick were eaten up by the storm.

§

Lost in delirium, Patrick almost laughed. *Which one is Mount Doom? Kennet or Silbury?* Had he bought Catrin enough time to run but sent her to the wrong place? He coughed and spat, the acrid taste of bile on his dry tongue, bitter failure in his gut. *What can I do?*

The eyes staring down into his told him.

Die.

He slowly raised his swollen hand, the pain so much a part of him that it hardly registered.

He would keep the monster occupied for as long as possible. Catrin must be safe by now but he couldn't be sure; the world was spinning, the rushing hiss in his head was louder than the storm, he didn't trust his perception of time. If all he could do was ensure that she survived this night then his job was done. He could at least be the loyal lieutenant, the faithful hound. He hawked up a weak laugh, his vision filled by the scabrous head of a dog bound only to its hunger.

I will hold the line.

The Black Dog sniffed at the hand held out to him.

Something about the gesture appeared to stall the creature, as if it was confused by the implication of trust. Patrick gently laid his crabbed fingers on its muzzle. The chill of the coarse fur was like a balm to the aching heat of his infected wound.

The Dog cocked its head. The ferocity of its glare softened to curiosity.

Its mouth gaped, and it licked Patrick's hand with a curled tongue as slimed and cold as something drowned.

Hold the line.

Though the rest of his body shook, Patrick kept his hand steady.

The line.

The Dog's eyes suddenly lit up like the heart of a forge, the bellows of betrayal fanning them to a fearsome brightness. Patrick squinted into their unforgiving depths and locked his arm straight.

There was a tug, and a pain less than the poison. But his fogged mind could only lock onto the impossibility of his stump, as his severed hand was gulped down.

Chapter Eighteen

The Smith stared past his reflection in the cottage window and on into the whipped night. The megaliths of Avebury could be made out as pale smudges, like chalky thumbprints on the dark glass.

He rubbed his tired eyes. The drive through the storm had drained him more than he realised, and his overworked muscles, cosseted in the warmth of Blake's home, were relaxing into a fatigue that threatened to drag his mind down with it. He took a couple of paracetamols, crunching them to speed their effect before swallowing them down with a pint of iced water. He wiped his mouth and turned back to the room.

Megan watched him, concern on her face. She took the glass from him. 'Are you hungry?'

'Yes, but it doesn't matter and there's no time – let's get on.'

'Let me make you a sandwich.'

Overtly maternal gestures were always her classic tell. 'Megan, I'm fine. You, apparently, are not.'

She half smiled, but still headed for the cluttered, stoop-backed kitchen.

After she left, Blake leaned forward from his chintz armchair to whisper. 'She hasn't heard from Judy.'

'Ah.' He knew that Judith's wilfulness, rather than the possibility of her being in danger, was the Achilles heel of Glastonbury. He had warned Megan against appointing her daughter as Second; perhaps if she hadn't set up such an obvious test of allegiance, David wouldn't have turned to the Forts. It was fully accepted that the dynamics of friendship would influence the Lore, but families had been its bane from the beginning. Would there be a storm now if David had tuned his talents to a different Hallow? If he hadn't, on some level, been driven to represent his father?

His thoughts were sidelined by Megan sliding a plate of cheese sandwiches, dripping mustard, onto the coffee table in front of him. He gave in and started to eat, each mouthful bigger than the last, as he discovered how hungry he was. He offered one to Blake but it was declined.

The creak of footsteps on old floorboards overhead stopped the Smith mid-chew. He pointed upwards. 'She's awake.'

'It's alright, Helen understands. She won't be coming down.'

'But will she try to listen in?' The Smith was blunt, not wanting the irritation of conducting the rest of the meeting in whispers.

Blake, aggrieved at having to defend his decision again, shook his head emphatically. 'Her loyalty to the Lore is absolute.'

Megan folded her arms. 'Her loyalty is always to David.'

'Not any more.'

'She's not a freebow until he has released her.' Her tone indicated she thought that outcome unlikely.

'I trust her, and we're within my site. Please respect that.' Despite his assurances he knew Helen was listening.

He felt her surprise and gratitude at his defence, and also a faint, but deeper, recognition. He quickly closed down his own reactions to that intimation.

The Smith finished his last mouthful and flicked the crumbs from his beard and chest. 'If she does defect, make sure she's running to you for the right reasons.' He reached out to touch Blake on the arm, a small reassurance to stop his words being misconstrued. 'And make sure you're taking her in for the right reasons too.'

The line was almost overstepped. Blake nodded curtly and noncommittally at the advice.

Megan settled herself on a Winsor chair by the fire. 'I really don't think it's a good time to discuss this.'

'No.' The Smith took the hint. There was a pause as equilibrium was restored. 'So, are we agreed that there's a link between resolving this storm and the Alicorn?'

Blake looked up. 'If you're trying to convince me to access it, you're wasting your breath.'

'I'm not asking you to wield it like a talisman. Just follow the line, see if it might lead to an answer of some kind.'

'It's not like the Whetstone, I'm not its ward.' He ran his fingers through his hair, anxious and frustrated that he couldn't better articulate his feelings. 'Its purpose – its spirit – reaches beyond the needs of the system.'

'I understand, but that doesn't mean it can't be used by us. If it wasn't for the Lore it would still be just a length of old ivory in a box.'

'If it wasn't for my family, it wouldn't even be that!'

A gust of wind battered the window, the small panes shook in their frame.

Megan looked at them both. 'Perhaps this is the Treasure's first test.'

The Smith stroked his chin pensively, his hand still grimy from the forge. 'Or ours.'

§

Catrin suddenly became aware of a connection: a line pulled singingly taut, as if she had taken aim but hadn't yet loosed. The sensation brought her up short, silencing her screams and her tears for Patrick.

Something struggled at the other end. A clot of darkness fighting desperately against the invisibly fine thread, throttling itself with rage.

She felt along the line, slowly, cautiously, like an angler readying a rod for a strike. She crouched down to make contact with the earth of her hill, feeling through the layers of chalk, to the ghost of the oak totem; past the jarring metal ribs that propped the abandoned tunnels of thwarted robber-archaeologists; the seeping, backfilled voids where her heart plummeted. To the place where Silbury Hill touched the land.

As the gale circled her, pulling her hair and clothes, trying to haul her upwards and away from the centre of her site, she knew her instinct to go back for the Wolfstone had been right. From the place where her intellect and her hill met, she drew inspiration and became aware – with the shock of being jerked awake – that all the images of wolves she had found, bargained and fought over, were just a scattershot expression of her need for this one talisman. It must be claimed and sealed into her hill. Nothing else mattered. And if she was the last one left of her company, then she would simply go on alone.

Catrin stood up in defiance of the storm, keeping a firm but imperceptible grip on the connection, playing the Dog with increasing skill as she learned the feel of the line. She silently blessed Patrick's wisdom – and his sacrifice – but held back her emotions. There would be no room for mistakes, no second chance, no help.

The eyes of the Dog blazed into her mind.

And no mercy.

§

Giles picked up the Wisht Stone – committing himself to an alliance he could no longer avoid, and lighting himself up like beacon for all in the Bowlore to see. He felt as exposed as the poor bastard he'd thrown to the elemental: a necessary distraction unexpectedly but usefully magnified by Ninestones' First. How Peter had remained alive, let alone found strength enough to stab the Dog, beggared belief. There was a dimension of resilience in the Stone companies that needed to be taken into account; evidently their Hallow was more than just a home for antiquarians and archivists.

But they were still no match for the Barrows.

He reached into the talisman, tracing his finger over the carved wolf, more by feel than by the flickering light of the candle. West Kennet embraced him, its spirit inhabiting the slow swell and currents of the earth.

As he searched for the line, rubbing the stone wolf's tether like a rosary, he could sense the awareness of the high talents in the Lore responding to his touch.

The game was up.

This part anyway.

§

Catrin followed the line down Silbury Hill, placing each foot as carefully as possible so that the wind wouldn't dislodge her. In her mind she preserved the tension, as if threading it hand over hand, neither pulling nor slackening the connection that ran from her hill to the Black Dog.

She crossed the leaf-scattered road, heading for the track to West Kennet, unsurprised to find that she was drawn in that direction. The creature was probably going to ground at the place where it felt most protected; a whipped cur seeking its master's forgiveness. The thought repulsed her.

If she came upon Patrick… if he was dead. If she could bring herself to look at what might be left, no force in the Lore or land would stop her from seeking revenge. Her footsteps became heavy with anger, she had to remind herself to keep a light touch, but the desire to yank the noose tighter and tighter until any strained yelps and whines were choked into silence, almost overwhelmed her. *Stay calm. Get the stone.*

The Wolfstone.

It flashed into her mind, conducted along the connection, and its afterimage flared gold against the night, burned onto her retinas as if it had been real. She gasped and stumbled to a halt, rubbed her eyes, unable to see anything in front of her but a fading neon block and the crouching wolf. Then she detected a taint on the quartz flecks of the stone. *Giles!*

Catrin could feel him reaching into the stone for its black heart, for the Dog's, and then for hers. If anything tested her resolve not to lose control it was this. She cursed her gullibility, diverting her guilt and sorrow over Patrick into a hatred for West Kennet's First. Preoccupied with her own needs and the threat of the Forts, she had been blind to the machinations of her company's most obvious rival, but now that he had given himself away his influence could be seen at every turn.

Hold the line.

For all that she'd suspected and found collusion in the barrow, it was still a shock to have evidence that Giles hadn't only been receiving stolen goods – and inflicting collateral damage – but was deliberately responsible for her decline. That belittling lack of respect for her site stabbed deeply; Giles had never before dared to show such disdain. Was Patrick right? Had her obsession brought Silbury to its knees? Igniting a self-protective anger, Catrin pushed on, panting through the storm and up the track until the long barrow stood out on the ridge like a static cut-out shape, a sham hill propped up against the motion of the sky. She stopped to search the landscape, her night-sight recovering, but saw nothing. The Dog still battled; if it had been anywhere nearby the movement would have given it away even in the darkness. It could only be beyond or within the barrow.

The line yanked as if shaken.

She scanned the field, wondering how her route had bypassed Patrick; if he still lay where she'd left him. *Left him.* She blinked away the sting of tears, snatching herself back from an emotional drop she couldn't yet face.

Where are you? Then Catrin realised that she was following a path that any lost Dog would take: an old track, steeped in memories, ripe for haunting. Ripped away from its own trail, the elemental would surely seek out the comfort it offered. An unexpected empathy eclipsed her hate – a kindred spirit flailed at the end of her leash. They both suffered because of Giles.

Fury ate up the last of her fear. 'Show yourself, you bastard!'

The line slid through her imaginary fingers, she concentrated a friction to slow it. She took another breath to yell again, but let it go unspoken as a figure stepped out from the facing stones; her demand carried through the storm by a medium more intimate than air.

Catrin could only see the outline of his form, but she knew that Giles held the Wolfstone.

He lifted one hand awkwardly, shifting its weight as he approached. 'Truce, Catrin! The Wisht Stone is yours. I, Giles Montford, First of West Kennet, give it to you willingly!'

The Dog pulled, and too astonished to react she let it run – then snatched at the line too hard, too quickly, and the fine thread of it burned her. She damped down her hate, fought her desire for the stone. A clear mind was the only thing that could save her now. 'You expect me to trust you? After all that you've done?'

He walked towards her in measured strides, and came to a stop just out of arms-reach. 'Oh, I don't expect anything from you, Catrin. I never have.'

She stepped up and swung her fist into his face.

Giles turned with the blow to absorb its momentum, then straightened up. 'I've found that a woman will only strike a man if they know he's too much of a gentleman to retaliate.'

The amusement in his voice enraged her. 'I'll just rely on you being a coward.'

He ignored her retort. 'The Wisht Stone – what's your decision?'

It was too dark to read his expression, and the stone was so close the sense of recognition was overwhelming. She bought time with another question. 'After all the pain and damage you've caused to get it – you suddenly don't want it anymore?'

'The elemental's of no use to me, and the wolves are wild.' His tone held no regret or shame. 'The stone is a liability now that everyone knows about it. A peace offering is all it's good for.'

Catrin couldn't detect any duplicity. *He must know I have the Dog.*

'I'm cutting my losses, Catrin.' His voice dropped to a whisper, she had to lean in to hear. 'When you inter the Wisht Stone in Silbury, you'll understand why I'm choosing to concede.'

The line went slack, then tugged like a message. Catrin allowed it to pull, her mind spinning. The candid speech from Giles showed he knew her plans, and that the connections set up by the Wolfstone were fanning out like a web. *Who else is caught in it?*

They paused, assessing the repercussions of continuing with the most honest exchange they were ever likely to have.

'If I accept the stone, will that give you power over me or my company?'

'Quite the opposite.'

'You said *inter* the stone… is Silbury a Barrow?'

The atmosphere between them changed subtly. A tiny disturbing flicker of eagerness was quickly smothered.

'I offer you my guidance, as well as the talisman.'

'A Barrow more powerful than West Kennet?' She knew the question would penetrate his defences.

'You overestimate your importance, Catrin.'

'And you will always be Second to the Smith.' She felt him close over the Wolfstone and pull it back in an angry reflex, and the fear of losing it quietened her. There was nothing more to be learned. It was time to trust to her instincts, to let the Bowlore guide her.

Hold the line.

Accept the Wolfstone.

Cut to the chase.

'I, Catrin Fitzgerald, First of Silbury Hill, willingly accept the *Wolfstone*.' She added the emphasis, not caring whether he noticed. *I will choose the wrapping for this gift, Giles.* There was plenty in a name.

She felt the break. Then the thrill of a new connection sending its roots into her soul. Giles deliberately let the talisman drop from his hands before she had a chance to reach for it, forcing her to lunge forward and catch it.

The Wolfstone hit her palms like a living thing, its chill superficial, like cold air on the fur of an animal called in from the night. Underneath was a warm heart that was faithful to her, trusting and trusted.

Then it bared its teeth.

Catrin saw the jagged path of blood and betrayal stretching back and back and back, the vertigo of awareness making her sway. She fell to her knees and curled around the stone, hugging it, determined to pass the test she felt Giles hadn't taken – to pay the price he hadn't deigned to pay.

As in a fairytale, where the heroine must hold tight to a shapeshifting monster until, exhausted by her perseverance, it reveals its true form, she endured.

Hold the line.

Its essence would be hers.

Its power would be hers.

The Pack fills the sky, tumbling over itself, plaiting the clouds, tightening the circle around the White Hill.

Wild ghosts, oblivious to ownership, running as they ran when clothed in flesh instead of air. Below them the lost One struggles for breath, and they howl for their leader, their rival, their betrayer.

They smell blood.

The noose spasms, then falls so loose that the long tooth of the blade buried deep in its back screams louder than the throttling line. The lost One circles, seeking the pain, licking at the thick blood running cold claws down its back.

The thread cuts in again.

Down!

The Black Dog grovels, lidding its mad eyes. Fear and love amalgamate, solidify and set in place.

It submits to Hand that Holds Stone. Offers its throat.

And is forgiven.

Chapter Nineteen

Lawrence's head was still full of voices. They were not mere recollections filtered through the lens of guilt and justification, these were the echoes of spirits over which he had no control, against which he had no defence. The miserable chasm that Peter had slammed shut with the dagger had not swallowed him, but it had left him hollow; a sounding chamber for lost souls.

Peter held onto him as they placed one blind footstep in front of the other, tracing the most direct route away from West Kennet and back to the car. They were both in ruins, but thirty years less wear and tear counted in Peter's favour; his muscles could still be forced into action. Lawrence no longer had the physical reserves, and he couldn't muster the will to defy his frailty.

They were broken, useless, and now that the game had left them in its wake they had been summarily dismissed to make way for Giles' next move. The king of the Barrow and the queen of the Hill would continue the battle without a thought or care for them. At any other time, Catrin Fitzgerald might have offered a refuge, but her obsession with the Wolfstone had consumed her thoughts, radiating from her in a heat Peter recognised. He kept that sensation to his right, using it to orientate away from the barrow as they descended the slope; humble pawns swept off the board by the wind.

Peter watched the skies turning on the rallying point of Silbury Hill. If he focussed hard enough he could make out the forms of the wolves in the clouds. The more he concentrated the more they seemed like a flock of birds, wheeling to dazzle a hunting falcon.

His time with the Pack, and then with the Dog, had sensitised him to the scale of the suffering represented by the vast spiral of grey and black. His empathy caught him off guard, bringing him to the verge of tears – but it was now the only thing that could move him.

He stopped to steady his nerves, and to allow Lawrence to rest for a moment.

Confronting his mortality had left him emotionally dead. Even when he had mustered the rage to save Lawrence from the Dog, a part of him had stood by, indifferent to his own and Lawrence's torment. A lifetime of insulating denial had been torn away, exposing his sense of self as nothing more than a reaction to existential fear. With that acceptance had come a bleak peace – and the end to hope.

Peter knew he must adapt to this pared down version of himself, even as he mourned his lost humanity, because of the irrefutable fact that everything he believed, thought, or did was simply a means to keep his body alive; even the apparently selfless act of rescuing Lawrence served his own wellbeing. True altruism was a conceit, and morality a veneer – survival at any cost was the whole of the law.

The abyss had stared into him.

Yet the fate of the pack still touched his social-animal heart and intellect, a response that was evolving into a sense of guilt that could only be human.

England's slaughtered wolves demanded recompense. And he – a reluctant emissary into their world – wanted and needed their forgiveness.

'Peter?' Lawrence's slurred voice was overloud as he fought to concentrate through, and talk over, the crowd in his head. 'I'm alright now... let's keep going.' He pulled on his First's sleeve like a child wanting to hurry.

Peter didn't move. A lifeline within him reached out for another, stronger thread that was straining taut back at the long barrow. The filigree touched, and in a lightning second he understood. *Catrin has tamed the Dog!*

Another line, another flash: Silbury's Second lay in the field just ahead of them, *bleeding, dying... no... fighting* – he could feel a weak but defiant tug on the line.

He'd never known his talents so clear and true, it was exhilarating, like another sense had been granted to him. Gone was the cautious interpretation of instinct; knowledge was coursing back from each contact with the intensity of an earthing.

A pattern built up in his mind's eye. A web with the Wish Stone at its hub.

Catrin's line grew brighter as the one leading to Giles was sapped of energy. Hope prevailed. 'This way!'

Lawrence was pulled, bemused but willing, at a tangent to their course, but as long as they were heading for the car and away from the barrow, it was alright by him. Then they halted again and Peter let go, leaving him stranded in the whirlwind that blew inside and outside his head. 'Peter? Where are you?... Peter!'

'It's alright! Stay there!'

Before him lay the shape of a man. A step to the side and he would have been invisible against the dark ground, but Peter perceived him with his new sensitivity, and a fine thread linked them both. Another – the strongest – ran from the stump of the man's wrist, up the slope, through Catrin, and into the Dog.

The ragged wound was bleeding life as well as energy, and Peter pulled his awareness back to the physical to deal with the emergency. He knelt down and gently raised the man's forearm with hands still clammy from the Black Dog's blood.

...And from them comes a great poison...

Recognition shivered through Peter. Here was part of the story he had originally uncovered, affirming his choice to research the obscure alchemical path. But he could see that an older myth had bitten the contamination away, in a replay of courage and treachery that no one could have predicted. And so the web stretched out, catching innocents, making them pay the debts incurred by those higher up the strata of the Lore. Peter's brief exhilaration ebbed away. If he followed the other deceptively shining threads, how many other ruined lives would he find? Did the Covenant save them from one death so that they could be sacrificed in other subtler ways?

Peter felt the wolves clambering through his guts. The crushing prison of the Shuck.

A firm hand gripped his shoulder, pressing through the distance of his private pain. He turned to find Lawrence holding out a folded white handkerchief.

'I should have tied it to a stick and waved it… earlier… saved us all a lot of… trouble.' He bent down to push it into Peter's hand. 'Put it on his wound… it's clean. I may have another… somewhere.' He slowly patted his jacket pockets.

That small slice of practicality, the hint of Lawrence's character showing through, and his display of faith despite everything that had happened to them, pulled Peter back to himself. He shook the square open, draped and folded it over the man's stump and cupped it close to the pulped flesh and splintered bone. The cold arm flinched in reflex but held firm.

'Tighter.' Patrick hissed through gritted teeth. 'Hold it… as tight as you can.'

§

The woman cradles the Stone, wraps and protects it with her body. She is the matrix of cooling granite, growing crystal facets like salamander scales. Chisels of frost chip open her quartz eyes and they spark with the light from a lost sky. She feels the tattoo of iron gnawing trails and spirals into her upturned face but she cannot blink and cannot turn away.

She learns to love the pain.

Accept the scars.

When the lava of molten metal runs into the lines, she holds the searing pattern, bright as birth, in a web over the Land. Traces its course and all the connected paths. Sees her White Hill drown in blood, then fill with purifying fire.

The earth turns.

Moon to sun.

Silver to gold.

Chapter Twenty

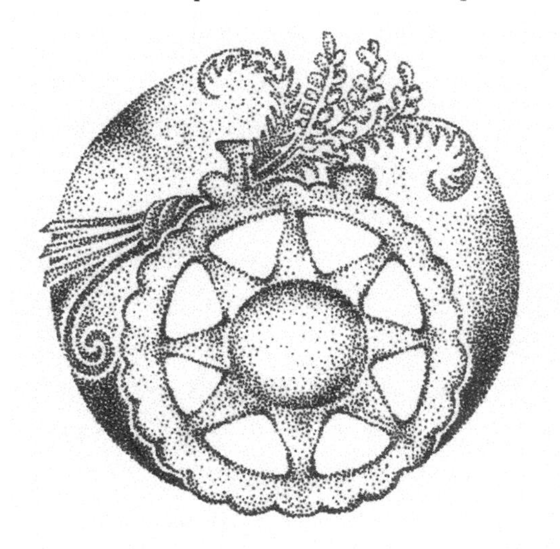

'I'm *not* responsible for Giles!' The Smith smacked his hand down on the stone sill. He didn't turn around when Megan came up beside him.

She addressed his reflection in the glass. 'That isn't what I was implying, but you must admit that your affiliation is seen as their Hallow's weakness, the chink in their armour. If they were truly confident of their impenetrability they wouldn't be so guarded.'

This was well worn ground and he answered flatly. 'The Sanctuaries have more influence over them than I do.'

'Only by default. Everything we try just drives them deeper.' Regret tinged her voice. 'I know Giles is at the root of this, but my connection isn't strong enough to break through his defences.'

He sighed, looked down at her and put his arm around her shoulders. 'Listen, you've been concentrating – quite rightly – on the Treasure. We'll deal with Giles after we've dealt with the wolves.'

'That could be too late. He's covered his tracks with Ninestones' First, with the Dog, the stone, and now this storm. I can only see where he's been, never where he's going. My greatest fear is that every decision I've made so far has been manipulated by him.' She paused for a second then looked up. 'I do know he's still at his site… perhaps, if you talked to him? …pulled rank?'

The Smith took his arm away. 'Don't ask me to compromise my neutrality. It's bad enough I've been drawn in this far.'

Blake nodded from where he stood by the fireplace, one hand zipping up his leather jacket, the other holding his silver arrow. 'It isn't good to be asked to do something that goes against your instincts is it?'

The Smith turned to him. 'This isn't the same as you accessing the Alicorn. Whether you're going to acknowledge it or not you *are* its ward – I am *not* part of the Barrows.'

'But you know you're the justification for their sense of superiority.'

'I've never given them grounds to think that!' The Smith chopped his hand through the air, wanting to cut the subject off. 'At least make up your minds if I'm their weakness or their strength. You can't have it both ways.' He grabbed his coat from the back of a chair, adding a declaration as he jabbed his arms into the sleeves. 'I'll never try to control their Hallow.'

'Why not?' Blake lowered his voice to counter the audacity of his words, surprised at himself. 'Is it because you might find out that you're just the First of Wayland's Smithy?'

The silence that fell between them was charged with anger.

Megan intervened, pushing them apart. 'That's enough! If I needed any further proof of the malicious energy in this storm, I have it now.' Although her eyes glittered with what could have been tears, her firm voice belied any such weakness. 'Questions have been asked and answers given – leave it at that.' Both men nodded, but she waited for Blake's fingers to relax on his arrow and for the Smith's fists to unclench before she stepped back.

Blake drew in a steadying breath. 'And we're expecting the *Forts* to control themselves?'

Megan spoke quietly, governing the atmosphere in the room. 'I believe we should help them to.'

The Smith gave a cynical smile. 'There's no hope of that – they're enjoying the ride.'

'Yes, but they value their freedom,' she persisted. 'If we use that as an incentive it might be possible to direct them.'

'Only if they're still capable of being rational.' Blake shook his head. 'And I really think they're beyond that now.'

'They're strong but we can't expect their Hallow to take the brunt of the wolfstorm for us. If we abandon them it could eventually tear its way through the whole system!'

'I'm not saying we should abandon them Megan, but we do have to accept that they're part of the problem, not its solution, we have to be realistic—'

The Smith's interrupted him. 'Exactly! Let's be realistic and use *everything* at our disposal to save the Lore.'

'I'm not going to bring the Alicorn. It needs to be kept safe.'

'And how safe will it be if the entire fucking system is destroyed?'

'Just as safe as it was before the system evolved!'

Megan held up a hand, trying to slow the dangerous momentum. 'I want the opportunity to try to reason with David before we make any decisions.'

The Smith was silent for a moment as he composed himself, allowing Blake to do the same. 'With all due respect, we don't have the time.' He was sympathetic, but the truth of his statement was borne on the gale that tore at the roof and threw itself against the windows and doors before running on towards Silbury. 'We can't risk everything for the slim chance of making a connection with Badbury. We've got to concentrate all our strength on the one aspect we can control.'

The euphemistic statement served to stifle the debate. An uneasy consensus of complicity, trust and resignation spared them from having to voice their plan, but the mood darkened.

'What I've learned from the Alicorn,' Blake's voice sounded as if it would break with emotion, 'is that control is less important than trust.'

Megan clasped her hands together. 'Yes, we must always remain open to the guidance of the land – so please trust *me* when I tell you that we have to protect the Forts or we'll lose the driving force in the quest for the Thirteen.'

Megan's conviction that the aggression of the Forts could evolve into a spiritual force, was an ongoing dispute.

The Smith looked away from her and towards the smouldering, ashy fire. 'Well, whatever the signs, they'll never get the chance to make the transition from blade to feather unless they survive this.'

Blake nodded but felt drawn to support Megan. 'Perhaps we should take advantage of this lull in the fighting to track the Forts down?'

'And do what? They've only stopped challenging each other because the storm's pulling them to Silbury. Their hunger's kept them from plainshooting so far, but if they suspect any intervention from us they'll react badly – it could make them lethal.' The Smith wiped his face pensively, allowing his words to settle. 'It comes down to the fact that we can't risk the sanctity of the Covenant for a handful of punch-drunk Forts.' He looked at Megan. 'Even one led by your son.' … She let his criticism slide, offering an alternative. 'We could use the Barghest.'

'What – to control them?'

'No, as a connection we could exploit, between us and the wolves.'

'Maybe… we could use the link to subvert the storm.'

'Wait, you mean use the Dog like Giles did?' Blake was unconvinced by the idea of employing one violent energy to curb another. 'I thought we were trying to avoid any

Barrow connections? Anyway, Catrin will need to be persuaded to cooperate, and we don't know where she is.'

The Smith detected a deeper reluctance under the stated practicalities, and took it as thinly-veiled disapproval. 'Locating her isn't going to be a problem, all the activity is closing in on her site.' He buttoned his coat, then added, 'If you have trouble spotting her, she'll be the one holding a fucking massive supernatural dog on the end of an invisible lead.'

Megan stepped in again. 'So, we're going to Silbury instead of West Kennet?'

The Smith focussed on her, understood, and took her hand gratefully. 'You must have known you were never going to persuade me to go there.'

'Yes. But I had to try.'

He leaned in and whispered. 'How do you keep so calm?'

She squeezed his hand. 'Practice, Neil. Lots of practice.'

Then her weary smile faded and she addressed both men with an air of matriarchal authority. 'Are we willing to follow whatever path is shown to us? To preserve the heartwood of the Bowlore at *any* cost?'

They answered together and unequivocally.

'Willingly. At any cost.'

Blake unhooked his car-keys from a forged iron hook hammered into the beam over the fireplace. A row of dusty horse brasses featuring sunbursts and crescent moons hung along the length of the woodwormed oak, and behind the largest was tucked a sprig of dried heather tied with red wool.

Megan shrugged into her coat. 'What are we going to do with Helen?'

Blake's answer brooked no argument. 'She's coming with us.

§

Helen had been pacing like a caged animal, as silently as she could on the old, creaking floorboards. She had learned where the noisy ones were and stepped over them, counting her footsteps, trying not to listen to the conversations murmuring up through the gaps between the boards. She was still on the edge of things, in a space all her own; privy to wonders, plans and conflicts.

Within the influence of the Alicorn it was hard to conjure up the anger she needed to protect herself, and reaching out to the storm just filled her with regret. Too removed from her Hallow to gain any invigorating aggression, she was left with a loneliness that stripped her of power. Far from making her want to shoot, the turmoil made her shrink away from the thought of battle; she had experienced peace in this cluttered haven, and wanted it again.

Footsteps thumped up the narrow wooden staircase.

'Helen?'

She was hiding in the gloom of the landing, the only light coming from under the shut door of the room where she'd slept, and so when Blake appeared at the top of the stairs, silhouetted against the glow coming up from the living-room, her heart missed a beat at the sight; a flashback shape of the thief who had ripped her out of the belly of the yew.

Then the memory bled away like an earthing she couldn't hold, and in its wake came a recognition that went beyond their shared bond within the Lore. She shivered, distraught at her inability to control her own fate.

Aware of her reaction, Blake halted, silenced and stung by guilt. Nervous of overcompensating in an attempt to salve his conscience.

He knew full well that the hurt he had experienced at the Smith's words of warning, arose out of provoked denial; it had prised at doors he had slammed shut years ago, ones he never wanted to open again. The Smith was right, there was a real danger of construing their shared rapture at the revelation of the Treasure as something more intimate.

He normally placed his trust in meticulous planning, and structured his company and its dealings in the same vein, but Helen and the Alicorn were now inextricably linked with a release from that constraint. Its power and her awe, framed the event.

It was a freedom Blake hadn't asked for, but which had brought about an experience and a reward he never could have dreamed of back in the early, shattered days after the loss of his wife. Codes and structure had been his salvation then.

Perhaps it was time to let them go.

Let go.

He offered his hand.

Helen stood firm, and concentrated on her own needs for once, placing herself ahead of every concern she could summon up. She relived the invasive, devouring anguish of Blake's imperious act of theft, aware that she ought to strike his hand away again – be true to her company and true to her Hallow – find her bow, nock an arrow and tear his soul out.

But here was the man who had stepped out of his role and placed all his faith in her. The man who, despite her lowly rank and her hatred, had shown her the purest magic in the land.

This time the gesture was not a gold-heavy command, it was an invitation.

So, trusting what it might bring, she accepted it.

§

Megan and the Smith waited in his van.

She sat squashed to one side of the passenger seat, whilst he corralled as many sandwich wrappers, empty cans, juice cartons, scrawled notes, lists of orders, bulging envelopes and zip-lock bags crammed with hacksilver, as he could, to create enough space for her to sit comfortably.

'If I'd known that we'd all be taking my van, I would have cleared it out.' There was more irritation in his tone than apology.

Megan untangled her coat from a bundle of silver wire stacked in the door pocket, and scuffed and scrunched a gap for her legs in the footwell. 'It's best that we travel together.'

She glanced over her shoulder at the rubbish that had been tossed onto the back seats, which was immediately joined by another hastily-tied carrier bag; it gave a muffled clink as it hit. 'I think there was some silver in that one.'

'It doesn't matter – I'll sort it out later.'

Megan found comfort in the Smith's sullen promise; in his implied confidence that there would be a calmer future in which to take stock and tidy up.

She closed her eyes, held her wand, and thought of Judith. But by concentrating on one child she inadvertently drew in a perception of the other; her sensitivity moulded by motherhood and her indivisible love for them.

There was a moment of brief, telling clarity: *a hollow yew caught in the gale and strobed by torchlight. Remorse. Waiting and watching in the cold.* A touch: *leave me! Leave me alone!* And then, in a replay of childhood rivalry, Judith was drowned out by her brother, her trace lost against David's storm-amplified ranting. Megan had to shut them both out.

At least they were alive.

The Smith waited until Megan lowered her wand and opened her eyes. He didn't ask anything; her face was set with restrained worry, and prying wouldn't help. Instead he pointed to Blake's parked car. 'What the hell is he playing at?'

Blake was reaching into the back seats to pull out Helen's bow. She already hugged her quiver, cupping her hand around the fletchings to stroke the ruffled tines back into shape.

'He's displaying his trust.'

'To her or to us?'

'Probably both. But don't be so quick to dismiss his methods, this entanglement with Helen has attracted David's attention – for good or ill.' She waited a moment.

'Either way, it might give us a way of reaching out to Badbury.'

The Smith raised an eyebrow. 'So, she could be a decoy instead of a loose cannon?'

Megan shrugged. 'Time will tell.'

If we have enough of it left.

Blake tugged the side door of the van, sliding it open on its noisy metal runners. The sudden wind sucked out a flurry of rubbish, lost into the night before he could snatch it back. 'Shit! Sorry.'

The Smith turned around. 'Just get in quickly – and put the bow and quiver behind your seats.'

The significance of the instruction wasn't lost on Blake, who wordlessly displayed the un-strung state of the longbow before laying it down.

Without meeting anyone's eyes Helen climbed in, laid her quiver on top of her bow and pulled the door shut behind her. If there had been a protection placed on the van she couldn't have felt more unwelcome. She sat beside Blake and stared out of the side window at the cloudscape. There was more of a place for her up there in the fury and fear, than where she was, even with the sanction of Avebury's First.

The number of words she'd exchanged with Megan over the years could be counted on the fingers of one hand; they shared no common ground other than the Lore and David – who maintained a kind of Hallow apartheid when it came to Sanctuaries, especially Glastonbury. On the rare occasions when they did encounter each other, she felt that Megan expressed a polite but definite disapproval of her.

As for the Smith, she had only ever seen him from a distance, and only if she happened to be with David when he went to pick up his arrows. Firsts warranted face-to-face handovers – provided it was convenient for the Smith – but anyone less than a favoured Second collected their finished silver from Wayland's capstone with only the rooks and the Ridgeway winds for company.

Sitting so close to him was disconcerting, and emphasised her displacement. Protocol within the system was often adapted to suit circumstances, especially within Hallows; but the walls of respect around the Smith were never breached. Without him there would be no Bowlore.

Helen concentrated on closing herself down. Even though she was invited she felt like a gatecrasher. And as the van pulled away she wished herself invisible, not to hide, but so that she would cause the least offence.

Then Blake leaned over and whispered. 'Without you the second Treasure wouldn't have been unlocked – you've earned your place here.'

The words warmed her like unexpected sunshine, and she held her breath to stop the threat of tears. Nodding mute thanks, she pressed her forehead against the cool of the window. Her breath hazed the black glass, and she stared through her hollow silhouette as it was projected onto the surreal, rolling backdrop of the storm.

Chapter Twenty one

David was fuelled by caffeine, nicotine, adrenaline, and the dread that if he gave in to sleep, other companies from his driven Hallow – likely fresher and with more arrows – would find his company skulking in the refuge of his house and rip the guts out of Badbury. For the first time since the beginning, he feared death.

He drowned the end of his cigarette in a ring of spilt black coffee on the low table, and then used it like a pen to slowly draw the liquid into a series of linked spirals, like the patterns on the arrows he was aching to loose.

His Second and Third shifted restlessly in their armchairs, scrolling through distractions on their phones, exchanging glances that related how thin their patience was wearing. Stifled yawns were caught and passed around in the heavy exhaustion that kept them all in their seats. Empty cups and plates lay on the floor or balanced on the arms of chairs. On the TV above the cold fireplace, detectorists searched a sunlit field, their dialogue lost in the wind moaning down the chimney. They unearthed forgotten treasures, perceived with a hint of mysticism that everyone in the Lore found relatable. When the screen filled with the image of a magpie stealing coins to hoard in its nest, the lyrics from the scene sang in David's mind as if the sound had been turned up: *...five's for silver, six for gold, seven's for a secret never told. Devil devil I defy thee...*

The hellish storm hammered at the windowpanes, constantly provoking them with its uproar and the Fort's empathic hunger. Reminding them that their Hallow was at the mercy of an ancient power beyond the reach of their talents and talismans. *I defy thee...*

His Fourth, Mathew, after a vicious argument, had left them half an hour previously, torn from his duty towards the company by persistent, worried phone calls from his family. His anger and frustration at being pulled back to the mundane, didn't fully mask his relief at being rescued from the disorder. David had extracted a promise that he would return, but didn't expect to see him again this side of dawn. His Fourth had failed a critical test of devotion, and it wouldn't be forgotten.

Lissa, his Fifth, had not disguised her disappointment in Mathew, and blanked his goodbye. She sat sullenly on the edge of her chair, gripping her longbow as if it was still growing from a yew and she was saving herself from being blown away. David never doubted her.

The three who remained were staying out of loyalty, storm-driven compulsion, and a fearful, perverse curiosity. If their world was coming to an end, they wanted to be there to witness it.

Even as the storm tore at him, David's resolve to never ask for help, held firm. It came from the solid conviction that they would never be abandoned. Beneath all the rivalries and hostilities, the bond between the Hallows was unassailable: they were the four strikes across the arrow of the rune, protected by the curve of the Covenant bow, and they all grew from the same deep-delving roots. And on a personal level, he knew Megan would not leave him to suffer; that he could rely on her despite their fundamental differences. He had sensed her reaching out to him earlier, and kicked against the contact, driving her away, furious at the implicit disapproval and mistrust; yet was still consoled by her attention. While the elite guarded the integrity of the system, he was free to indulge his instincts, and to allow the storm to carry him. But he was conflicted: Megan's strength was a reassurance that undermined his independence, and in some ways he felt as infantilized by her status as when he was still in Glastonbury.

He switched off the TV turning it into another darkened window, and reached across the table to pick up a small polished bronze figurine of a horse; its proud neck curved, its limbs held straight, its flanks decorated with crossed solar circles outlined with trails of knotwork. It breathed out the brightness of Salisbury Plain, where the smooth pale hills show the way up to the sky. This was the talisman he favoured when introspection disrupted his awareness. He stroked the surface of the metal. It was accessible, limpid as a chalk-stream, and the intervening centuries flowed away from his touch, exposing its heart like a gem on a riverbed. The creator of this elegant talisman had not been waylaid by any secondary concerns, this was the work of a resolute mind for whom only the end result had mattered. A mind that knew how to encapsulate a need, and find the route to its satisfaction.

Clarity. That was what he wanted and needed most – a way through the tangle of urges. 'Gareth? Do we face this or run?'

His Second looked at him over the black and yellow-barred fletchings of the arrow he was fidgeting with, and answered in a voice husky with fatigue. 'If we run now we'll waste our advantage, maybe miss out on whatever's left to divvy up when this is over... But d'you really want to know what I think, or are you just after a dose of bullshit and blind faith?'

A spark of interest reanimated the room. Decisions could lead to action, action to shooting. The wolfish desires still ruled them.

'Try both.'

Gareth slipped the arrow back into his quiver and took a moment to consider. 'Before we do anything else, you need to decide what you're going to do with Helen.'

'For fuck's sake!' David rubbed the soothing metal of the talisman against his forehead as if he could force its influence through the confusion of his judgement.

'You owe it to her.'

'Owe her? I'm not going to make her a freebow if that's what you mean.'

'Then what are we doing sitting here? We need to get her back.'

'No. She's coming back to *me*.'

Gareth raised an eyebrow. Evidently more information had come through the brief contact with Megan, than David had revealed to him. He couldn't tell how the dynamic had changed, but knew better than to ask. The storm was ripping apart every relationship within the company. 'Can we trust her?' *After what you've done?*

David stood the horse talisman on the table, turning it to face him. 'I can feel her reaching out for me.'

'Trying to get a mark on you more like.'

'Only if she beats Catrin to it,' Alex added, and uneasy laughter rose in stilted bursts, giving sufficient confidence to prompt another, quieter comment.

Lissa, dark eyes squinting with tiredness, spoke up. 'I really wouldn't take the piss if I were you.' Everyone turned to her, hushed by her remonstration. Her insight was respected – as Fifth, she had introduced Helen to Badbury. 'She's loyal, too loyal for her own good. But if you take her for granted you won't just alienate her, you'll make an enemy of her.' She kept her eyes down, wanting to mitigate any friction but needing to speak out. 'I've never taken a harder shot than hers.' Lissa took one hand from her bow and touched her chest. 'You should keep a talent like that on-side.'

David leaned back in his chair, ending the exchange. He held the fire-bright bronze horse, stroking its proud curved neck, its straight back and flared tail – then stopped abruptly. The tingle in his fingers felt like a warning.

Lissa's reproach had forced him to confront the idea of Helen as a potential defector. Whether he liked it or not, the reality was that he did owe her.

Everyone knew that Helen had complicated their relationship, indulged her jealousies, and made herself a liability by becoming obsessed with the knife. But it was also true that he'd gambled her devotion against his ambition, and lost – driving her into the arms of one of the major players in the Lore, and presenting her with a choice that he'd never intended her to have. What counted in his favour was that with her Badbury credentials and known relationship with him, no established company would dare take her on for fear of treachery. She'd probably end up in some companion-hungry sapling Fort. Hardly the threat Lissa was implying.

He clenched the horse and stamped it down on the table, hard enough for its hooves to dent the wood – angry at himself, at Helen, at the storm, and at every single decision he had made since discovering the Wolfstone.

The mood of wary dissension was deepening: quick glances being traded, fingers and feet tapping.

Alex was careful to criticise only himself. 'I should've stayed to guard her.'

There were nods.

David glared around the room. 'Not one of you had a problem when I shot her.'

Gareth decided to take the brunt of the brewing dispute. 'That was when we were high from the raid and believed we were hunting a Treasure. This is now.'

'We needed that dagger!'

Gareth kept his voice low. 'And you wanted to punish Helen.'

Pain surfaced at the thought of his betrayal. He dismissed it. Turned the facts like he'd turned the knife before handing it over to Giles. 'I used that fucking dagger to save *all* of you at Kennet!' The expressions he saw on their faces then, acknowledged the statement – Gareth had obviously told the company how close they had come to disaster. He fought to keep calm; his Second was with him, the others just needed reining in. There was no real challenge to his authority.

'I don't need to justify anything I've done. This is Badbury's path – take it or leave it.'

Stark and to the point. He knew when to play the allegiance card – it was incontestable. Their site and their Hallow held them.

There was a pensive silence, broken only by the rush and lament of the gale, then with a brisk nod of respect, Gareth moved them all on. 'So, what's our next move?'

David valued how effectively his Second was keeping the balance, but worried that Gareth's reasoning might be as compromised as his own – Seconds could lack objectivity – so he looked to his Third, and Alex covertly held up three fingers in the signal for a challenge. That was validation enough.

He stood. Met the eager stare of each of his companions by turn. 'We head for the eye of the storm.'

The room seemed to shiver at David's words. But the speed with which his company seized their bows and quivers told him that – this time – he had made the right choice.

§

The Land remembers all its children.

The mighty, the ephemeral, the favoured and the damned. All recorded and cherished in patterns of rings, or pressed between layers of sediment. These writings quicken to an empathic touch; baring souls long buried, crying out for a second chance, in a tongue understood only by those wistful and devoted enough to learn the language of the lost.

The Wolves keen.

The Yew stretches wide its arms to snag memories from the tops of the Hills.

Branches that touch the ground, hung and heavy with hollow carved Bone, give a voice to the rooted depths where the breath of air is banished.

The permanence of Stone takes on the scars of Life and Death, carrying their lessons and marking the Ways.

The Wolves run.

All they have left is what they were. There is strength in numbers, so they seek each other. They call out for more – and the Pack is swelled with hungry bellies and silver teeth.

But its Prey has fled and it can only feed upon itself. As Above So Below.

§

The night was loosening its grip on the sky, and a faint smear of red revealed the seam between air and earth, but the wolfstorm had allied itself with the darkness and began sinking over the hint of light, as if it wanted to eat the dawn and lick away its stain from the horizon.

A dread shivered through those in the Bowlore like the mark of an aim. It found them out, slipped past the gatekeepers of rationality and knowledge, and left them wondering how much of their blood would need to be spilled to ensure the end of night and the rising of the sun.

Silbury Hill was being watched from seven different directions. Each aspect presented the same huge, silhouetted cone, its inverted shape in the form of the funnel of the storm, centred above it.

Nothing more.

It was closed down and sealed against the Forts. But no level of protection would be proof against its ruin. If they had to dash themselves to pieces against its slopes to destroy it, they would, in wave after wave of hatred.

Chapter Twenty two

Viewed from the heights of Silbury Hill, the surrounding dark fields appeared empty, but Catrin knew it was an illusion. Every now and then, a stray spark winked in the pre-dawn gloom, the small tinder-flashes from groundshot arrows: sacrifices to secrecy, ensuring that outsiders would be kept away by more than the hostile wind and weather, and creating a means of concealment in a wide landscape with little cover and many watchful eyes.

Those random, negligible lights told her she was surrounded.

She considered raising a protection around the slopes of the mound, but feared inadvertently drawing upon the disorder that pervaded everything other than the chalk of her hill. Closing herself down and holding on was all she felt sure of doing, even here, where the latent strength of Silbury held her. There was no way to tell how dangerous the storm would become, or how savage the oncoming attack would be, so it was crucial, and bleakly practical, to conserve her energy for a last stand.

Abruptly, her phone buzzed back to life and missed calls piled onto the screen as if they'd been pushing at a wall that had given way. She had the means to call for help, yet the wish to use it evaporated even as it lay in her palm. Though the Bowlore used technology with impunity, this night was too drastically altered, too rooted in the otherworld, and it urged her away from conventional options.

Above all, she knew for certain that nothing in the mundane world could save Patrick.

She hurriedly scrolled down the list of names anyway – then stopped, her attention snagged by one she wasn't

forelegs and aligning itself to her feet. When she moved, it adjusted its position like a needle drawn to true north.

Catrin's natural reserve was eroding under the all this scouring focus; even the pale newborn day was breaking over her hill and nowhere else. She allowed herself to explore this unaccustomed self-confidence – aware that it could not last – and turned her talents inwards, daring to believe that the answer was within her. *As above so below.* The desperate pursuit of identity and purpose was drawing to its conclusion and her mark was finally in sight. Catrin drew on this concept as she would a shot, unashamedly pulling all she could from the singularity of her position; elevated above guilt and beyond consequence.

'Catrin!'

A growl from the Black Dog rumbled through the chalk mound.

'The Smith is here!'

Peter's shout snapped her out of her dream state, but she was held back from an appropriate response by her shock. Behind the Smith followed Megan, Blake and *Helen?* A plainshooting Fort's Sixth accompanying the elite of the Lore? Confusion stalled her further. *Have I lost a whole day?* Vacillating between realities made her doubt her perception of time, but no one could possibly be restored that quickly. The rescue party before her suddenly seemed more like an inquisition calling her to task over her part in Helen's shooting, and the familiar fear of breaking rules shattered the newly-spun glass of her ego. *Have I failed some kind of test?*

The hackles on the Dog rose and its growling grew into a low, huffing bark. It kept its head down but curled its lips into a snarl, exposing long bone-yellow teeth.

The Smith squared his stance and folded his arms. Catrin started out of her daze – whatever other accusations might be levelled at her, disrespect would not be amongst them. 'Quiet, Shuck!'

The barking hushed to a whimper.

'You've given it a name?'

Her conviction lessened with every halting word. 'The faithful aspect… the part that responds to me, needs a name… I have to meet the hound halfway to tame it.'

The Smith nodded slowly. Then straightened his arm, formed three fingers into the same shape they would make on a taut bowstring and pointed them at the Dog. It immediately fell silent, rolled over as far as the buried knife would allow, and offered its throat.

Catrin channelled her resentment into admiration; unwilling to compound her perceived sins. Surreptitiously she felt for the line – it was unbroken, the usurping of her authority had not involved any theft.

The Smith stood over the prone Dog. 'What's your plan, Catrin?'

Her eyes widened. 'For… the Dog?'

The Smith circled a finger at the sky and then at the ground. 'For everything.' He left her to scrabble for an answer as he bent down, grabbed a fistful of the elemental's rough neck and shook it hard, wrenching its unresisting head from side to side. With his superiority established over both the Dog and his audience, he stepped back. 'Well?'

Well? Catrin's memory overlaid the scene before her with a grimy café, and her intolerance of David's disguised but genuine ignorance. The parallels shamed her. 'I just want what's best for my company, and for the Wolfstone... and what's best for everyone in the Bowlore.'

The Smith wasn't impressed and spoke with a weary sarcasm. 'You forgot to mention world peace. Try again.'

What does he want from me? Inspiration struck. 'I'm going to inter the Wolfstone, here, in Silbury Hill.'

'That's Giles talking.'

The Dog grumbled quietly, righting itself and shuffling over to Catrin. She stopped it with a look.

'Come *on,* Catrin! I can't do this for you!'

His abrupt, frustrated anger caught her off-guard, and she took an involuntary step back. This simple reflex expanded beyond the confines of her body into the web of connections, carried by the power she currently possessed. She grabbed the shimmering lifelines and held tight for support.

The Dog slobbers and gags for breath, fresh blood oozing from its wound; the Stone is pulled down into the skin of the Hill.

Every mind concentrating on her was wrenched.

As if viewing from the storm's eye, she saw the Smith grab his head in pain. For a heartbeat – for two – for three – for a circuit of blood around her body, she knew the names of every individual watching her: their needs, their loves, their losses, their hate. The pantheon of desires and fears that made up the whole of the Bowlore, scintillating like an earthbound constellation laid out for her wonderment.

For her judgement.

Then.

Doors, portcullises, shutters, barricades and barriers of every kind, from the personally contrived to the archetypal, came slamming down as Catrin's momentary advantage lapsed. Distinct in the cacophony were the high talents on her hill closing themselves down with more tolerance than shock – but the one leading back to West Kennet shook with anger before cooling to the comparatively neutral trail left by the Wolfstone.

The last few threads snapped.

But one did not want to break away. Trusting her touch, Patrick faced her scrutiny unafraid. *I have done this for you – I would do it all again.*

§

Although David couldn't see her from where he was hiding, he now knew where Catrin stood, physically and metaphorically. Her brief yet intense display of power confirmed everything he had suspected: Silbury Hill was about to find its place in the Lore.

If he chose to acknowledge Catrin's impending status, made the effort to cultivate their strained and strange relationship, it might bear fruit. But truces and debts formed in a time of relative peace would mean nothing if this event stirred up a power struggle between the Hallows. If this path ultimately led to civil war, he would follow it anyway, scavenge anything worth taking, and stake Badbury's claim in whatever was to come.

David gave up fighting the cascade of random thoughts, he let himself be swept along by them, knowing he was relinquishing control and not caring. Freedom or falling; they both felt the same to him now.

But his deep, exhilarated breaths were stifled in his throat as he focussed on Silbury Hill. Like a resented, burnt-out love, it provoked and obsessed him. Even his own site exerted less of a draw, and that fact alone made him want to obliterate every last grain of chalk and blade of grass. He wanted to dig it away with his bare hands, kick it apart and level it, open its heart to the wolf-ridden skies and let the winds scatter its white dust, until there was nothing but a fading scar left on the landscape. His fist went to the place on his chest where he had taken Catrin's arrow. Only shooting would clear his head and fill him up, ground him back in his sense of self and his place in the Lore – it remained the single reliable constant in a world reduced to windblown splinters.

David watched the channelled dawn illuminate the mound of Silbury. Under the tapered storm it looked like the lower bulb of an hourglass filled with pale green sand. *Time's up.* He felt for an arrow.

Catrin's sudden assault had acted like a battlefield flare, revealing every hidden knot of watchers encircling the hill. No groundshot arrow or talisman tuned to shielding or deception, had withstood the pulse of disclosure radiating from the summit of the hill. In that instant David's awareness had been swamped with a useless din of information, but he had borne the pain and maintained his connection while others clamped theirs shut; gritting his teeth until the noise dissipated and split into a handful of distinct traces. There had been a second, maybe two, of identifiable resonance, but it was enough. The gathering offered no surprises; he recognised the presence of Maiden Castle, Cadbury Castle, Hambledon Hill and Brent Knoll, the major Forts along with his own, that had survived the wild hunt for the supposed Treasure. Like him, they had mustered their remaining companions and made their way to Silbury Hill, seeking answers and revenge.

And the elite had come to stand with Catrin, against the Forts. One way or another, the storm had forced everyone to reveal their hand. *So much for neutrality.* But in that stark knowledge was power.

No matter how many Sanctuary Firsts she called upon – even if the Smith himself stood with her – Catrin would never get the chance to assert her new ascendancy, and wield the Wolfstone to control the Hallow of the Fort.

Not while he had breath and arrows left.

Chapter Twenty three

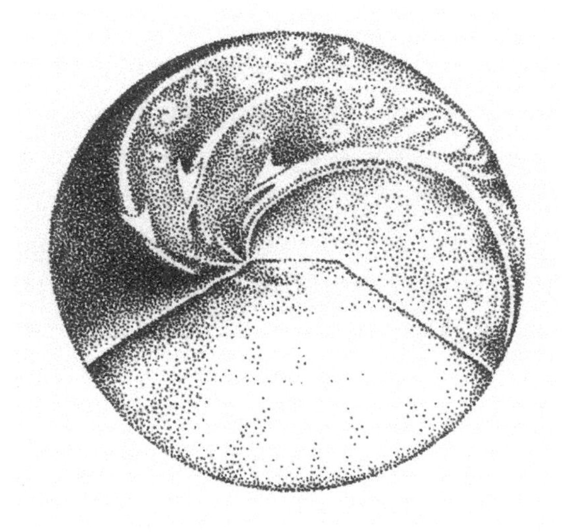

Peter was once again wrapped in agony, as if giant jaws had clamped around his head. His perception of pain had been moulded and set in shape by the Black Dog, and he now experienced any kind of distress as an attack by claws and teeth. When the tearing stopped he touched his face, expecting blood, but his trembling hand came away clean. Despite the brutality he knew at once that the harm was accidental; even from the other side of the hill he could see Catrin's expression was of exultation not anger. The Smith held her shoulders, supporting and calming her while she responded to his fervent interrogation; he couldn't hear what was being said, the white noise of the storm deadened any words that weren't shouted.

Peter slouched, exhausted and unable to rest, weary of suffering, yearning for the oblivion of sleep yet fearing the dreams it might bring. If the heartwood of a yew couldn't protect him from visions of the Dog, nothing would. His hard-won epiphany, inconstant as the stormy skies, wasn't enough compensation for the peace he had sacrificed. His former state of ignorance had acted as an emotional barrier between himself and those who had reduced him to bait and thrown him to the wolves, but there was no way back to it.

The lines threading the night were dimmed by the dawn, although he still felt their stresses and attachments. The one that ran through the stone and the knife, the Black Dog and Catrin, and into him, spooled his guts as it reeled him back in. The small distance he had managed to put between himself and the monster was reducing to a fraction of what he needed to maintain his composure. He found himself toppling towards the opposite side of the hill and had to take a step. Then another. And another. The bruised gouges the wolf pack had left across his chest, neck and arms, blazed with pain as if they were half-healed burns brought too close to a fire. *No more!* But Peter's belaboured instincts held true, dashing any hope that his part might be over and done with. He felt no resentment; such an energetic reaction was beyond him. His reluctant, heavy footsteps trailed lines through the grass; and he left the insect-buzz of questions from Lawrence unanswered.

And then Megan fell in step beside him. Peter couldn't voice his gratitude but there was no need. She stroked his arm and then linked hers through his, supporting some of the weight of his body and his mind. 'Remember your Hallow.'

He looked up from his stooped shambling. Found her calm face.

'Draw on the strength of Stone to endure, and have faith in your talent.' She smiled. 'I do.'

Those words confirmed his belief that the only reason he had survived was because he was First of a Stone company; that the attributes of his beloved Ninestones had preserved him. But the warmth of pride was rapidly chilled by the unbidden, unwanted clarity that told him those generous words were just a praise-wrapped request for more effort. *Can't you see I have nothing more to give?*

'We need you to interpret the connections between the talismans, the wolf storm and the Black Dog.'

'The *elemental.*' He deliberately stressed his preferred definition, grasping for the faint control it gave him. All its other names were rising up from his subconscious in a scavenging pack ready to devour his frail sanity, so he held them at bay with the plainest label; a smooth term, least likely to snag the scraps of folklore into a dangerous mass.

'Yes, the elemental.' Megan understood. She kept her silver arrow tight to her side and point down, channelling away his rising anxiety.

With each dragging step the Black Dog was becoming more aware of Peter. Recognition shivered along the line that bound them. Its leash was looser while Catrin's concentration was on the Smith, and it took full advantage. Cunning enough not to pull and draw attention to itself, it maintained a docile pose while slowly turning its head to fix Peter with a demonic, knowing stare.

The cool, grassy summit singed to ash, Peter was slipping down the rim of a crater towards twin chasms that opened into hell. The heat was blistering his skin, scorching his eyes, his hair was burning, the stench choking him— *oh God no... no! No!*

'No!' The Smith kicked the Dog. It yelped and fawned at his feet, then sought comfort from Catrin, inching up to her and nuzzling her hand. She took her cue from the Smith though, and resisted the urge to stroke it.

Megan positioned herself between Peter and the Dog, with the briefest warning glance at Catrin: *concentrate!*

Catrin wound the thought of the leash as tight as she could. The Black Dog gasped and lay still. Blood shone in tarry tracks through its fur, the rough yew hilt of the dagger was varnished crimson by it.

The Smith offered a handshake to Peter. Out of social habit he responded and allowed his limp hand and forearm to be clasped in a firm, soot-stained greeting.

'You're usually so careful to keep Ninestones out of trouble – I hardly ever see you.'

Peter met the Smith's eyes. 'It hasn't paid off.'

'No.' The Smith paused to consider his words. 'You know you're the only one who can save us now. I wouldn't be asking you otherwise.'

He nodded, accepting his fate. Whatever knowledge he contained would be given up; a burden carried for too long and bought at too high a price. The Lore was welcome to it. They could drain him of secrets, trace every link and empty him. His talent was unendurable; if they scoured it away then maybe he could rest.

Megan leaned in, lowering her voice so that it was barely audible against the moaning storm circling Silbury. 'You must speak.'

Must! Was no part of this nightmare to be under his control? He sighed. 'I offer… I Peter, First of Ninestones… willingly offer… to help you in any way

I can.' That was it. Any vestige of autonomy gone. From catalyst to puppet in a handful of words.

'Thank you.'

If they expected a response they were going to be disappointed. Anything more would be at their behest. Peter spread his arms wide and turned his face up to the whirlwind's heart. The patterns on the walls of cloud looked so much like the dark trails of metal salts wicking up a cone of filter paper, that he laughed aloud. It summoned a vision of Hatiston churchyard and his cherished notes lit by a dying day; one more connection for the elite to tease out. He hoped it would serve them better than it had him.

§

From across the crown of Silbury, Lawrence watched the shambling form of Peter straighten, then throw his arms wide, head back, and laugh at the twisting sky. But the apparent reanimation of his friend and First gave him no pleasure; the pose was too ridged, the laughter too desperate for it to be the sign of anything positive.

The Voices mocked his crumbling denial, as he fought the impression that Peter looked much more like a man surrendering than one being saved.

§

David kept his back to the hill and motioned his company to follow. A surge of increased intent to their left, had just alerted him to imminent attack. He swore under his breath. He wanted to get a clear mark on Catrin, anything else was just a distraction. 'Who the hell is it?'

Gareth scowled. 'If it's Brent Knoll, I'm up for it.'

David reached out towards the disturbance, spreading his fingers as if feeling for a heat source. 'No, not Brent... it's Maiden again.' He leaned back into the shadows at the base of the hill and scanned the dark fields, keeping his bow at a slant as he checked his arrow and put more tension on the string.

'*Fuck!* Matilda's after your breath for putting her Second in a yew.' Gareth matched his vigilant stance and drew his own arrow up to his chest. 'You won't get a mark on her – we have to move.'

'Wait. Over there.' David pointed out a patch of low windswept scrub.

There was almost no natural cover to be found this close to Silbury, and so other more subtle methods of concealment had to be employed. Talismans tuned to overlooking and disguise were being accessed; and around the hill, more than a dozen groundshot arrows stood up like thin leafless flowers, their small earthing held and wrapped around the shooter like an obscuring cloak.

David knew that the battles on the Levels had only been the first test; he was pitting himself against some of the highest Fort talents, and sight alone could not be trusted to detect their presence. Even after the intense shock, when Catrin had torn away those protections and camouflages, they had swept back almost immediately.

The uneven, whipping motion of the leaves and grass appeared to be as natural as anything could be in the grip of the storm, but his instincts were alerting him to rare, more surreptitious shifts. 'Over there.' A spike that could have been the limb of a raised bow broke the outline of the scrub.

Gareth turned towards the movement, let down his bowstring – but kept the arrow nocked – and reached into his pocket. He brought out a small gold disc, covered with a glass lens, and with a fine chain hanging from its edge. Superficially like a fob-watch, the ivory face of the device was blank, and the only moving part within the sealed chamber was a single bead of mercury. He brought it close to his mouth and whispered, then held it flat on his palm and studied the shuddering dot of liquid metal. This talisman had kept his great-grandfather alive in the trenches and shell-holes of Ypres, and he trusted it like no other.

The mercury rolled to the edge facing the hiding place and broke into three droplets; two spread out but stayed close, the other trailed around the rim until it settled opposite. 'She's sent a sniper round the back of the hill.'

'Fuck this!' David raised his bow. 'Cover me.'

'Cover you? Where the fuck are you going?' He, Alex and Lissa, had to dodge back out of the way as David shouldered past them, bow drawn. The Mercury Compass was knocked from Gareth's grip and swung on its chain like a gaudy, stage-hypnotist's prop.

Suddenly it was shot away – its chain lashing like an angry snake – pinioned on the head of an arrow.

'They're plainshooting! Get down!'

David heard the warning shout but didn't stop or turn back. His Second was more than capable of rallying his companions, and it would only take the time needed to draw their bows before Badbury would be fighting back. He couldn't have planned a better diversion.

He climbed, keeping as low as he could on his elbows and knees, closing himself down, careful not to break the silhouette of the hill, and sliding his bow ahead to part the long grass into a furrow that obscured his limbs. He had no doubt that the gathering on the summit would be aware of his approach soon, whatever precautions he took – there was no way he could stay under their radar. But he had no intention of falling to an arrow, plain or aimed, before he had the chance to shoot Catrin.

Chapter Twenty four

Blake and Helen stood apart from the others, at the eastern edge of Silbury's crown. They didn't talk, and their hunched shoulders and folded arms expressed a mutual apprehension.

Blake was keeping his distance from Megan and the Smith's workings, determined to play a non-partisan role, even though he had effectively allied himself to Helen's cause. His thoughts strayed again and again to the Alicorn. When he shut his eyes, the shaded dawn was turned to silver by the memory, and it took a conscious effort to ground himself in the present. Guarding one of the Thirteen Treasures was demanding more of him than he had expected. The spiritual aspect was overwhelming the practical responsibilities and imposing its own set of strictures.

Although he had known and cherished the slumbering form of the narwhale horn since childhood, its new incarnation had widened the way to a realm that was not only home to the beauty and purity he had witnessed, but also to the kind of terrifying, monstrous forces swirling above him. The dangers were real, and if he didn't cultivate a Janus-like ability to keep watch on both sides of the doorway, this level of volatility would be the rule, not the exception.

Blake tried to rationalise that his fears were simply cowardice, but he held his silver arrow as a shield, tucked into the crook of his folded arms; the shining fletchings by his cheek and the shaft crossed diagonally over his chest.

Helen had her arms crossed for a different reason; she was tensed against the need to shiver, and was trying to keep herself closed down and undetectable. Never had she felt so unprotected, a state exacerbated by being made to leave her bow and quiver behind in the van. Site protocol was the excuse; she couldn't bear arms uninvited, but discrimination against her and her Hallow felt more accurate.

The accelerated healing forced upon her by Blake wasn't as thorough as it had first seemed – or the effect was wearing off. Nauseous and drained, she yearned for heat, but the constricted dawn barely gave out light let alone warmth. They stood upon the only place not pummelled by the gale, yet it was still as much as she could manage not to lose her footing as the oppressive influence of the storm repeatedly pushed her off balance.

A shout went up – the words made unintelligible by the noise of the wind. The tone was familiar though, and with a start she realised it was Gareth's voice coming from somewhere below and beyond the curve of the hill.

Is David here? A pang of love and anger stabbed through her. To determine his whereabouts she'd have to drop her guard, and although distraught at not knowing, she couldn't justify the risk. Doubtless he would make his presence known soon enough if he was here with Badbury. Helen ventured a glance at Blake. *Should I warn him?* A test of her allegiance was the last thing she needed. A steaming bath, hot drinks, a stoked fire, sleep: these were what she wanted. Not this place. Not these people.

Another yell rang out, closer this time, and both Helen and Blake crouched down so they could peer over the edge of the hill.

A handful of armed figures were running near the base of the mound, those ahead darting randomly to foil a mark. There was a sudden scream of pain and one of the lead runners fell. A shouted name, almost lost against the storm, pinioned Helen: *Lissa?* Frustratingly, she couldn't discern faces from the height and angle of her vantage point. The storm's false night reached right up to the slopes of Silbury, and the figures were keeping to the shadows; but as she watched, two of them turned, raised their bows and loosed. Despite the swiftness of the shots, the arrows were aimed, and simultaneous flashes lit the field – even through her defences she could feel the faint trace of their earthing. Then they stooped to haul up what had to be Lissa's prone form, and ran into the gloom beyond the curve of the hill.

It took Helen a moment to process the event: only three of her companions left. *Have the others been plainshot?* She sucked in a breath. *Are they dying?* She made to follow their progress, reduced to the level of desperate bystander.

Blake grabbed her arm as she pushed by. 'Don't get involved!'

'For fuck's sake! How can I *not* be involved!'

'I don't want you to get hurt.'

Helen squared up to him. 'Then you're too late.' She ran to the other side of the summit and reluctantly Blake followed, his arrow held in a tight fist.

§

... is all your fault. 'No. I tried to stop him.' *you didn't try to stop me.* 'I did try, I did – I'm not a liar!' *then you're a thief, you stole my life.* 'It's not true!' *nothing you say is true.* 'Leave me alone!' *just as you left me alone... and left peter.* 'I couldn't follow!'

'Lawrence.'

'I couldn't follow him.'

'Lawrence!' Patrick raised his cracked voice as loud as he was able – then added under his breath, knowing it wouldn't be registered. 'Give it a rest, Sméagol.'

'I... I'm sorry.' Lawrence wiped his hands over his face. 'It's that... bloody dog, and Peter... being so close to it.' He grimaced with the effort of fortifying his mind against the voices.

'It's alright. I understand.' Patrick offered sympathy, even though his own mind was full to overflowing. His own turmoil didn't have a voice, but under these circumstances it was a very small slip from uncertainty to insanity, and witnessing that fall in an obviously good-natured man like Lawrence was hard to bear.

The blood from Patrick's stump had soaked up the sleeve of his shirt and seeped into the fabric on his shoulder and chest. Cold and clammy, as if his own numb skin had been flayed off then wrapped back over him.

He didn't have the strength to move from his prone position, but at least the wave of connective energy from Catrin had wiped away his pain – a relief tempered by his recollection of survival stories that described the state of tranquil well-being preceding death. Patrick consoled himself that the monster just a few steps away, paid him no regard, because if he really was about to die surely a psychopomp would take a passing interest in him?

The one thing threatening to tip his fragile equilibrium was the thought of the skin, muscle and bones of his hand boiling away to scum in its guts. He wondered if the poisoned blood within it would affect the creature, but knew if anything could thrive on venom, it was the Black Dog.

Another commotion in the surrounding fields below brought Helen and Blake around to Patrick's side of the summit. Without acknowledging him or Lawrence, they crouched briefly to watch over the edge, ready to move as the action circled the mound.

Just as Patrick was mustering the strength to ask them what was happening, a stark and undesirable answer appeared in the form of a flaming arrow. Shot from a distance it sheared low over their heads, the flickering yellow pennant of fire leaving a trail of smoke that followed the curve of the hill. He altered the question, and with effort forced it out. 'Who was that for?'

Blake shouted over his shoulder. 'Silbury!'

What was left of Patrick's blood ran cold. 'From which company?'

'Maiden Castle!'

Another burning arrow crested the mound and Blake and Helen's upraised faces were momentarily illuminated by the gold of the flame as they followed its flight.

Blake's expression was almost apologetic as he preempted Patrick's next question. 'Cadbury Castle!'

Two more fire-arrows crossed over Silbury, trailing smoke and cinders. Everyone on the summit watched their arcing descent and Blake's roll call continued, this time loud enough for everyone on the hill to hear. 'Brent Knoll! Hambledon Hill!'

Patrick felt as if his heart would break. This was it – his sacrifice would count for nothing. Silbury Hill would fall before it had even found its feet, as the wolf pack surrounded its wounded quarry, and worked together to bring it down.

A final arrow shot upwards. Higher than the others it seemed to be aimed at the eye of the storm and for a second it was whipped into a spiral of sparks before it succumbed to gravity and the stronger force of the will that had loosed it. It struck the centre of the summit just as its fletchings caught fire, turning the black feathers to stinking ash.

David stood up from the edge of the hilltop, his bow levelled at Catrin, an aimed arrow pulled up to full draw.

'Badbury Rings.'

Chapter Twenty five

Catrin gave the tell-tale shiver of the first touch of a mark, but riveted by the sight of challenging arrows soaring over her hill, she barely noticed. The Black Dog leaped to its feet, yanking its leash so hard that they both suffered.

It let out a sonorous warning bark before cringing back down.

A magnifying-glass pinpoint of concentrated thought began to burn.

She became conscious of what was happening.

As if no one else was on Silbury, as if there was no other call on her mind, her life, her duty; the calm between breaths and heartbeats stretched out to give her space to think. Catrin seized hold of the knot of heat and teased out the intent, removing the envisioned silver broadhead before the idea drew the actuality. The contact broke, and the aim cooled and evaporated to nothing more dangerous than a surge of impotent anger.

David reeled backwards, struggling to let down the string of his bow as the mental and physical tension of his mark was destroyed. *She killed my aim!*

I killed his aim.

Catrin revelled in the ease with which she had saved herself. Never having come close to breaking a mark before – despite months of practice with Patrick – she had eventually given up trying, believing that if it was beyond her ability in a controlled situation, it would be impossible to achieve in the heat of combat.

Yet she had done it. She had proved herself invulnerable. And David knew it.

Catrin shivered again – this time with the satisfaction of dominance.

Her self-indulgent lapse of concentration was all David needed. His next mark was obvious, effectively helpless, and would ultimately gain him even more leverage.

He swerved his bow around, aimed, let his arrow slip, and Patrick crumpled to the ground. Without looking away from his target he shouted to Catrin. 'Never forget – you're only ever as good as your Second!' Then brutally ripped out the shot.

Catrin experienced an intense, shocking empathy, as if the aim she had killed had flared back to life.

'*Patrick!*' For the second time she screamed his name from the top of Silbury Hill, but this time there was no uncertainty about his fate, no sliver of hope that he might have escaped – and most painfully – no doubt at all that she was the cause of his suffering.

The line between them flared and died.

The Black Dog licked its lips.

§

The meagre high gained from Patrick's essence wasn't worth the effort of holding; David let it bleed into the ground. But as he took another shaft from his side-quiver and fitted it to the string, he felt the ice sharp intent from a silver arrow slide over his back. He disguised a shudder and turned with his bow at full draw. 'Stay out of this Blake. I haven't challenged Avebury.'

Blake kept a firm stance, his wand held at the balance point and pointed at David's chest. 'I don't expect protocol to keep me safe from snipers and plainshooters.'

David fought the impetuosity of the storm. 'Rules are rules, Blake, you should know. Challenge me or fuck off.'

'I don't need to issue a challenge to protect the innocent.' He pointed at Lawrence hunched miserably over Patrick's cold body. 'You're nothing but a scavenger, picking off the weak and injured. I'll stop you in any way I see fit.' His arrow and his stare were unwavering.

David's expression changed, he shook his head slowly, frowned and blinked as if coming awake: Blake's measured, earnest warning had shamed him, and finally broken the hold of the wolfstorm. 'You're right… I understand.' He lowered his bow and took the arrow off the string.

Suppressing his elation at the breakthrough, Blake dispelled his mark.

Instantly, the burn and impact of an aimed arrow slammed into his back.

David nodded his thanks to Gareth who, immersed in the rush from his shot, couldn't acknowledge him. Behind stood the remnants of his company: injured, bloody, out of breath, almost out of arrows, but ready to fight. A surge of pride filled him. Badbury Rings had made it to the summit first.

Then his eyes met Helen's.

Though he gave no outward indication, the look she gave him – as she struggled against the grip of her companions – truly shamed him.

I understand.

§

The Smith held Catrin's face in his hands, turning her to meet his stare. 'Look at me! Only *this* matters. Listen to Peter!'

The Black Dog watched in her stead, its eyes glowing and its ragged ears pricked.

Megan and Peter stood facing each other. She was holding his bruised hands, gently but firmly on the shaft of her silver arrow, maintaining a physical contact that could be used to draw him back if he strayed too far. He wandered the unmarked land, and every means to keep him by her side had to be employed. If Peter was lost, they were all lost.

He mumbled to himself; a dream-logic monologue, nebulous and mostly too personal to be of use. Megan had to listen out for key words and fire off questions in the hope of capturing a connection.

'… The wolf is known to… see? See? It was never that colour before the conjunction… red as rust…'

'Peter – which conjunction?'

'Red. Red moon, red planet. And rings, beautiful rings… grey as dust, grey and rust, grey and one will fall upon the other…'

'Who is fighting?'

'The wolf of metals. And the Dog.' He began to retch and Megan had to blend healing in with her questions to keep him from being wrenched out of his shamanic state by the physicality of his response. He calmed down again but his face shone and his hands were slick with cold sweat. 'Trash! Skriker! Churchyard Grim! Guytrash! Barghest! Mauthe Dhoog! Scucca! Gurt Dog! Capelthwaite! Black Shuck!' He spewed the names out instead, and the elemental at Catrin's feet whimpered as if whipped by each one.

'Tell me more about the wolf.'

'Yes… yes. The child of Saturn. They killed every last one. Every last…' His eyes filled with tears. 'The breathless body of the king is thrown to the wolf… not to the end… not to the end that the wolf should wholly consume… The answer is carved in stone. Every answer you will ever need.'

'You *are* our stone Peter. *You* must give us those answers.'

'Ever need, ever and annihilate the king, but that by his own death. His own death. His own… the wolf should restore strength and life to him.' For a moment his expression softened, became wistful. 'There is a green hill… far...'

'Is the king Sil?'

'Sil. Los. Fisher. Gold. Nothing without stone… fury, rage and madness.'

'Catrin, do you understand any of it? We're running out of time!' The Smith kept her facing towards Peter, she resisted but to little effect. Despair was robbing her of strength and she lagged behind the meandering discourse. 'Concentrate!'

Concentrate! 'He means, I think he means…' *Breathless body. Could it be?* 'Patrick?' She didn't want to commit herself – what if it was the wrong answer?

'You must take responsibility for the interpretation. Peter's only the conduit.'

I'm responsible for everything. Everything! She needed guidance, a method to dowse a way through the labyrinth, a tool. A talisman.

The Black Dog yelped in pain.

Catrin focussed on the dagger. The brittle metal sheathed in the Dog's flesh.

Peter staggered forward but was braced and held by Megan's strength and silver arrow, then he spoke in a voice which, though flowing and trance-like, embodied more of his true self than Catrin had yet seen. The line between them sang with energy. 'As above, so below… betrayal, pain, anger and from them comes a great poison… I pulled them apart to find their stories… when they are restored they are shown to be the great and precious medicine… the last wolf and the first dog. If you heal them – you can stop this.'

Heal. That simple word had more of an effect on Catrin than all the other demands and admonishments put together. It alone made sense. She had been forcing every option into a framework of conflict for too long; pitting herself and her company against obstacles and individuals in the quest for identity. Catrin opened up to let the rush of clarity flow through her; a cold, clean earthing of water instead of fire. With it came a surge of stories gleaned by Peter; intense impressions, startling and momentary, but living on in the shot-flash afterimage they burned into her mind's eye.

A red-barked sapling grows up like a stretched hand to dip its fingers into the sky. It stands alone beneath a ruby moon.

The form of a wolf runs with molten metal, she touched her face, remembering the pain, *then quenched with gore and given into in the safe-keeping of the yew.*

Hate is placated. And the blood in the moon's face drains until it is white as bone again.

New voices drive Old Shuck from the crossroads and bait the stone with blood. The betrayal is swallowed. Dug up, scraped out, melted, cast and wielded; and a hot, heavy wolf skin wraps the buried stone. The Black Dog whimpered, the storm wolves keened. *The yew receives the killers' guilt, and the sorrow of a woman. The roots hold and cherish it.*

Recognition wrenched her free of the vision.

Catrin was abruptly thrown back into the turmoil, and found that the few seconds of dream-like, relative peace were being paid for by those around her.

The Smith had built up a shield. He stood between her and the aimed arrows, gutting them of intent and using their energy to form a defence. He blocked every mark, and the spent shafts dropped to the ground as if stalled by a headwind.

Megan and Peter were at her back, sharing the protection but they, like her, couldn't help flinching at the angry heat the Fort arrows left before they were deflected.

Peter continued to speak, his face brightening like the circle of sky above him, the marks stinging lucidity into his words. He pointed at the whirlwind. 'Antimony! The knife betrayed them – it's made from the wolf of metals!'

Catrin looked at him and shook her head, unable to appreciate his meaning, their connection faltering under the strain. She trusted in the Smith's talent to keep her safe but couldn't override the instinct to crouch down. Ideas came at her like the arrows, painful and useless. She took shelter from the Dog; its deep chest and bristled shoulders were a wall between her and the attack.

The storm was closing in, the violence tightening like a noose. Megan joined the Smith in fending off the shots, leaving Catrin and Peter in the shrinking calm at its centre.

Peter turned to face her, his tone adamant. 'You must pull out the dagger.'

Catrin was horrified, remembering the Dog's howls of agony. 'I can't!'

He straightened up from his cowed pose. The subtle increase in confidence altered his demeanour. Brought centre stage by accident and design, and now freed of his shackles, he was coming into his own.

For the first time since they had met, Catrin felt she was in the presence of an equal. The injuries he bore no longer defined him as a victim, but as the survivor of a mortal test few could have endured. She didn't question this abrupt change; her own experience was teaching her not to judge conversions brought about by the unmapped, perilous space into which they had been cast.

He shook his head. 'Don't waste your pity on the elemental. Look above you – thousands of slaughtered wolves are waiting for you to release them. You're the only one who can give them the peace they deserve.'

Catrin raised her eyes, and the sight that met them tore a sob from her throat. Sharing Peter's perception, she was able to see past her mind's need for reason, to a vast pack of wolves that swarmed overhead in a tight, frantic circle, mad with fear and hunger.

Peter spoke with confidence, though his expression was sorrowful. 'I think I understand my role now. I kept fighting it because I wanted to be in control but I've learned...' He glanced down at the Dog as he traced the hidden bruise on his chest. 'I've learned – the hard way – that there are always more layers than we think. There's always a bigger picture.' He gave a small, rueful laugh. 'I was fixated on the past, I thought all the answers were there. If I'd looked up from my books I would have realised what was happening. I really believed... was led to believe, that I was some kind of catalyst for the second Treasure, but I was being used.'

Catrin wanted confirmation. 'By Giles?'

He looked towards the long barrow on the nearby ridge and nodded. Then he knelt down so they were on a level. 'But he was able to manipulate me because it really *is* my destiny to reveal a truth.'

Catrin winced inwardly. Maybe Peter's mind was too damaged; the messianic delusions too deep.

'I'm the catalyst for Silbury Hill.'

His fervent stare held hers, and she too wanted to believe, like Peter – like anyone – that the path she trod had some higher purpose and led to a central, pivotal role. He saw her doubt. 'It's alright, I was confused before... but here with you – it's all clear to me.'

Trust him.

'Trust me. I can guide you.'

Catrin knew she had to take the chance. And what better place for a leap of faith than the top of a hill?

The Black Dog no longer had a hold over Peter, and it kept its head down and its ghastly eyes averted in deference.

It sidled closer to the Wolfstone set into the turf at Catrin's feet.

'*...inter the Wisht Stone.*' Giles's words returned unbidden to her, stripped of ulterior motive. A salute to what Silbury might have been. The centre of her hill: her damaged, dug out heart, would be filled – fulfilled by the Wolfstone, just as her intuition had insisted from the very beginning. She held her breath and wiped away the sting of tears.

The hot-poker touches from the marks cooled and were not replaced. Whether the battle still raged or whether it was over and won, she had no way of telling. Her focus was entirely taken up with the man before her, with his knowledge and the insight of his Hallow.

Peter's skinned and scabbed fingers took hold of her cold, trembling ones to steer them onto the hilt of the knife.

Without looking down she allowed him to fold her hand around the yew handle. It felt like a stick growing out of the ground, the surrounding coarse hair like scraggy grass against her fingers. In her mind she let the Dog revert to its basic substance; its skeleton becoming flint, its flesh leaf mould, its blood rainwater. She took back its name so that it was just an inanimate ridge of chalky soil.

Peter let go of her hand.

And she pulled.

For one blessed second it was like uprooting a dead branch; the dagger lodged in earth instead of raw flesh. Then a shudder ran through its form as the pain transcended the layer of substance acquired from Catrin, down to a permanent stratum built up over centuries of incarnation. The elemental lurched, twisting the knife, splitting open a fresh wound in its redefined skin. Blood welled out over her hand as she clutched the rough, unfinished wood through the slippery coating.

The Black Dog screamed: a human-sounding howl of anguish that tested Catrin's resolve to the limits. *Shuck, I'm sorry! I'm so sorry!*

'Don't let go of the knife.' Peter's steady tone cut through the noise.

Catrin held fast to the line between them, tethered it to the rock Peter had become; reached for the gossamer-thin thread leading to Patrick and drove away her empathy for the howling Dog with thoughts of how her Second had suffered. She made a noose of the leash, cinched it so tight that the Dog's cries were throttled. Closed her eyes, brought both hands together and heaved.

The dagger slipped out of the wound, birthed into her waiting fists, cauled with gore and slime.

A woman's hands hold the blade. The ash-white metal, still warm from the casting, shines through the blood and brightens it to rosy pink. The drips running down the uneven edges and over her fingers are the dark ruby of heart's blood.

The clamour and goading around her fades away, silenced by the sacrifice. Only one voice continues, intoning words of banishment and revenge in a language that even the speaker does not understand.

Hate by rote.

The soft pelt splits wide, parting at the lightest touch of the blade; the skin repulsed by the poisonous metal until it is spread like a red, wet blanket around the naked flesh of the Wolf.

The woman speaks her own words in her own tongue, in defiance of the crowd. She begs forgiveness from the twitching, diminished body, promises her strength for its journey, praises the beauty she herself has ripped away. Punishing blows rain upon her back and she does not resist. But the Wolf does not acknowledge her.

It lies curled and pitiful as a stillborn pup. Lidless eyes blind to her tears. Gashed ears deaf to her pleas. Lipless jaws silent. She scoops the slithering skin back around the chilling body.

There will be no forgiveness.

She mourns then. For what she has been made to steal, in this place where rules and memories fight. The blame is hers, as intended.

She too is a sacrifice.

But she will not die in their name.

A silver pin – from her hair, into her hand, onto the red blade. With her knowledge, with her will, she marks the dagger, taking it from them forever.

Honouring the Wolf and remembering herself in one symbol.

Then she drives it into her own heart.

Catrin sucked in a deep desperate breath. Her first – her last.

The knife, blade down, drooled blood in coagulating strings onto the elemental's back.

Shuck. Her hound – slumped, mouth agape, his fiery eyes dim.

Peter was speaking to her but she didn't recognise the language. Was it Latin? Was he lost in his learning and reverting to disjointed quotes again? She watched his lips curve, contain and expel air to form words with measured precision, could see from his expression that they must be important, but still couldn't comprehend the exaggerated moans and growls.

She looked around for help. The Smith and Megan stood with their backs to her, arms upraised, Megan's silver arrow held mid-shaft and side on as if it were the handle of the invisible shield she created. They were both locked in concentration, almost motionless, and Catrin did not dare call out to them.

The storm wind couldn't touch her, but the roar from the wolves beat against her ears in waves and swells of melancholy pain. The shrill notes were gone, replaced by a slow siren ululation that penetrated her whole body and forced her to time her breathing with its rolling warning.

The edges of her vision contracted and darkened; breathing so slowly was starving her of oxygen. A loud hissing blocked out Peter's strange drone, even the storm was hushed by the pervading white-noise of her failing consciousness.

Catrin gave in to the pull of the ground.

Soft grass cushioned her, she was aware of the individual leaves curling and crumpling under her weight, dew wetting her neck and creeping into her hair.

She stared up at the eye of the storm in child-like wonder, as filaments of dim purple light grew and forked like tree roots to fill the tunnel, spreading out until every wolf was caught in the mesh. The hypnotic carousel revolved; the bounding wolves held on their course as surely as if they had been carved from wood and spitted upon painted barley-twist poles.

Catrin's vision darkened and closed down just as another faint streamer of violet began to finger upwards from the dagger.

Chapter Twenty six

Helen kept low to the ground, trying to minimise her presence, blending with the anonymity of the grass. She had been left ostensibly under the guard of Lissa, who crouched nearby, her bow now a crutch, her wounded thigh bound with blood-soaked strips torn from a shirt.

Lissa's expression was strained by pain, and by guilt for the hurt she had been complicit in inflicting upon Helen. No words or looks passed between them. They were backed up to the edge of the summit behind the last of Badbury – shoulder to shoulder with the remnants of Maiden, Brent, Hambledon and Cadbury, as the Forts spent their remaining arrows in a futile attempt to penetrate Catrin's defences.

Frustration claimed their senses, and locked their marks on a target they could not hit. Their arrows flew and fell, flew and fell, like beleaguered birds beaten from cover towards the waiting guns.

An unspoken truce had formed as they battled to the top of the hill where, united by a common purpose, they had stopped wasting arrows on each other. Their rivalries were eclipsed by the threat from the burgeoning power of Silbury Hill. Catrin Fitzgerald drew their fire, their anger and their dread. The fact that they knew they were being manipulated; twisted like keys in a lock, only served to fuel their rage, stoking an easily accessible energy that gave a transient satisfaction as they spat it back out in blazing marks. The successful shots made on the way up had drained away before they could be channelled, as if the hill itself was thirsty for the essence of life, and would take anything it could to fill its vast, bloated belly. But they fought on, confined to the most basic expression of their

Hallow – shooting because every other choice had been robbed from them.

Helen watched her company lose autonomy to whatever plan had been devised by the Smith and the Sanctuaries; saw faces she knew from the other Forts wearing the same mask of desperation as those of her own companions. The much-vaunted neutrality of the Smith was a ruse then, a means of covering his tracks as he threw his lot in with the Hallow best suited to form an impenetrable bastion between himself and possible demotion. The Smith and the Sanctuaries would conquer the Forts with the Wolfstone, find and hold all the Thirteen Treasures – and reign supreme.

Some of the felled from the initial skirmish, lay scattered below the rim and on the sides of the hill: a few carefully positioned with the broken or crumbled remains of talismans that had been used to buy their survival; others left lying where they had rolled, their awkward, pathetic forms entrusted to the limited compassion of the Covenant; while their companions, lured on by the storm, wasted precious time and courted their death.

Helen's attention was caught by David. With his back to her he drew arrows from his quiver, nocked them, aimed and loosed.

In all the time she had known him, he had never left himself defenceless, and yet now he was down to three arrows and showed no signs of stopping. *Why are you letting her do this to you? Why does she mean so much to you?* The precarious framework of Helen's confidence was collapsing. *You would never risk this much for me.* She wanted to close her eyes and block her ears against the undermining poison of betrayal. All her defiance, cooperation, submission, detachment – none of it had saved her, and she was left cowering, sick and tired; forced into the role of spectator at the gutting of her own company.

Then the inevitable happened. Like the trailing edge of a cloudburst, the rain of arrows thinned, stuttered, and ceased. No one moved in the aftermath; hostage to the belief that such an investment of will and energy should amount to something more than a disjointed trellis of wood and feathers strewn across the ground.

When Catrin's demon Dog screamed out, Helen clutched her hands around thin air, momentarily convinced that her Venus knife was back in her grip.

§

David disregarded the nerve-sawing howl and reached down to his side for another arrow. *Fuck!* His stomach lurched and he patted down the empty quiver, needing to be convinced that his arrows were really gone. His insulated state of mind was punctured by the shock of his vulnerability, as if he'd woken to find that he had sleepwalked to the edge of a cliff.

Instinct kicked in, and David opened himself up to the influences webbing the hill in the hope of rearming himself with knowledge, but what he detected was a veiled, overwhelming panic. The end of the attack had sown a levelling insecurity, and every broken mark had left a psychological ache where the roots of intent had been repeatedly ripped out. No one held sway: not Megan, not even the Smith, and Catrin was a vortex of disturbance that David couldn't read; a static hiss that hurt to focus on. Although bows were being lowered all around him there was no mood of surrender, and the hunt remained in full cry. The storm wolves were now so much a part of him that he found his vision involuntarily overlaid with a view of Silbury seen from the skies. It revolved below his loping feet as a raised amphitheatre, upon which four central players faced a hostile crowd. Vertigo gripped him and he closed down again, putting his faith in gravity, and holding tight to the smooth yew of his longbow.

Abruptly the hair on the back of his hands and the top of his head felt like it was being stroked by warm fingers; the air was thick with electricity and the clean, metallic tang of ozone. Faint purple filaments jagged into life, linking him with the other Fort Firsts – by his next breath all of his Hallow was caught in a mesh of dim, preternatural lightning.

§

The elemental loses its shape. Fur, skin, flesh and bone subside, crumbling into scree. Its eyes darken and it withdraws to the remembrance of a trackway lying beneath a pelt of leaves, sewn with the stitches of fallen branches.

The Path is worn smooth again.

The Hand offers meat, warm and dripping with life. With a snatch and a gulp, truce becomes pact. They fall into step, matching pace and need. Soon quiet words and soft touch drown out the calling of the Pack, and yellow eyes are gentled to the brown of devotion.

Peter reaches down to touch Stone.

The alliance elevates them both to a place beyond their natural reach. But soon trust breeds contempt, and the best and worst of what they see puts down roots in both their minds, and they become each other's gods and nightmares.

Elementals watch the loyal companion fall from hound to cur, scavenging, skulking, biting the Hand that feeds, until the uncertainty creates a shape in which they can travel, enrobed in a form that suits their fickle nature. The Devil Dog or the Guide.

Death or deliverance.

When the Shepherds come into the Land to gather new flocks, they only find their hate reflected back at them: defiant, untameable, beyond slavery or salvation, so they set a trap baited with an ancient legend – despising the story as if it were a rotten carcass, but using it all the same.

The Hand offers meat. A stone is swallowed. And a truce is broken.

Nothing.

And then.

Peter offers his hand.

Words drift and curl like mist. '*…tale of a local hero who rid the village of a demon in the shape of an enormous black dog, by disguising the Wish (or Wolf/Wulf) Stone inside a lump of meat which was then fed to the creature. Weighed down by the stone it sank into the ground and became entangled in the roots of the churchyard yew.*' The Dog tests his scent. '*…would be buried alive at the site of a newly built church to create a guardian spirit known as a church grim.*' Finds and opens the fading memory of its jaws. '*…believed that if a gift of food was brought it would grant a wish. This later addition to the legend was probably extrapolated from the corruption of the Anglo Saxon 'wisht' meaning uncanny, and from folk-memories of heathen rituals involving blood sacrifice.*' Tastes his fingers with a stone-cold tongue. '*…shrine to Hati, the moon-eating wolf from Norse mythology and reputed to be the place where the last wolf in England was killed. The* *flayed skin of the wolf was wrapped around the stone and buried in the churchyard.'* Recognises him. '*...built on an ancient crossroads, and by observing this superstition the villagers may have been seeking to protect themselves from the animal's potentially vengeful spirit.'*

Peter keeps his hand outstretched. Keeps track of the Dog in the places where it is overstepped by the Wolf. Trusts his way past fear and revulsion to reach towards the loyal heart of an old friend.

§

Lawrence balled his fists against his eyes and rubbed at his haunted head. The new reality pervading his mind had virtually destroyed his personality. The refinements he had built upon the foundations of family and experience; all the subtle, private tuning and retuning that had gone into his making, was no match for his guilt. It had been given the run of his mind, and now it was dominating him with a cajoling, mocking chorus.

He stumbled back through all the crossroads of his life, tripped and snagged by the unconsecrated graves of every selfish or stupid decision he had ever made.

Apparently love had not survived the journey from life to death, only recrimination.

The Second of Silbury Hill lay beside him, his pale face lit by a paler dawn. Lawrence cupped his hands over the badly wrapped, bitten stump of Patrick's forearm, applying pressure to stem the flow of blood. Concentrating on the suffering of another was helping him to keep a semblance of himself alive. It was the one selfless act he was capable of performing in his condition, and he gripped onto it as tightly as he did the wound. There was no place for guilt, no reason for the voices to harangue him, he couldn't have stopped the shot... *why didn't you have your bow? why did you make yourself a victim?* Offering his body heat and protection was a good thing... *why didn't you stand and fight?* A blameless thing to do.

Patrick's drained body lost its residual warmth to the chill morning and to the ground, and Lawrence wasn't capable of noticing that the blood no longer dripped between his stiff fingers.

A voice.

Another voice joins the chorus. But this one possesses an honesty that abruptly throws the yells, murmurs and wheedling into a perspective that takes away their power. This new voice is real, it comes from outside his head, and the comparison is a bright beacon – the flare of a shot.

Like a fever breaking, consensus-reality shatters the hallucinations. He recognises the other voices as facets of his subconscious, and in that instant the ghosts hush and fade away.

And he misses them.

Lawrence! The voice seemed to be shouting from the other side of the hill, and the parameters of his awareness duly expanded to register it. He was being drawn out of himself, but he found the silence within and the loaded, storm conditions outside disorientating – he didn't want to face them alone. He couldn't.

The voice called out again. *Lawrence! Can you see the Dog?*

Why ask that? Why? The bloody hell-hound was at the edges of his vision and behind every blink – had been from the moment it had turned on him.

Let it guide you!

And then, rough fur slid beneath his palms, nosing him away from the body on the ground, raising him until he was standing and steadying himself against the muscled flanks of a huge animal that he couldn't bring himself to look upon.

It was warm.

He could feel the strength and the intelligence, the offer of friendship as it nuzzled under his arm so that the limp and reluctant weight of his limb slid around its neck like a collar. Its massive head lifted to rest upon his shoulder, and Lawrence squeezed his eyes shut and held his breath against the sight and stench; but his heart was beating too fast for his body to tolerate such abstinence, and he sucked in air in a reluctant hiss between clenched teeth.

It smelt of musky hay, of sweet clean fur. Of childhood.

Lawrence opened his eyes.

And every dog he had ever loved and trusted looked back at him.

§

Catrin holds three things: the Dagger, the Wolfstone and Shuck. They are wrapped in her life but that is becoming flimsy, even the faintest light penetrates her skin, loosening her from her bonds. The handle of the knife sticks to her palm with the glue of clotted blood. It is more real than she is, in this place between breaths, and it bleeds its power upwards to the wolves, with its crusted, bitten-edged blade aimed at the skies.

Free the Dog.

Shuck leaps exuberantly into the ground, diving below the surface and blending with the chalk. He comes back up covered in white, with ears stained red from a summons sent through the earth from West Kennet. When the sun stands still that obligation will be fulfilled, but here and now Shuck accepts the compulsion of his name and the pull of Catrin's leash, and shakes off the powder till his coat is black as the heart of a barrow. He pants and whines with anticipation.

Let Shuck go.

She feels for the line. It's time to let it go.

§

Lawrence's thoughts clarified. He tightened his arm about the Dog's neck and buried his fingers in its deep pelt. He wasn't alone anymore. Here was the one creature in existence able to accompany him and lend him the courage to set out on his journey. As his mind and body reverted to what he remembered as normal, he drew himself up, buoyed by a renewed purpose.

The physical deficiencies brought on by age were amply compensated by the presence of the Dog – no one would dare to obstruct or dismiss him now – and thus armed, he would be able to release Peter from his geas.

It was so obvious, so perfectly straightforward. He would allow the Dog to show him the way from life to death, whatever debt his First had incurred in the otherworld would be settled, and the destruction of the system would be averted. He was ready to let go and join the ghosts from his past, even if he too was to become nothing more than an echo in someone else's mind, a caricature quickened only by memories.

The hackles of the Dog rose, prickling Lawrence's palm, and he could feel his own thin hair tingling in response. This had to be it.

He raised his right foot in readiness, needing to make some kind of gesture, whether symbolic or practical, before he took his first step on the last road. Perhaps he should say something? Surely it was the duty of those privileged with advance notice of their demise, to leave a verbal legacy of wit and wisdom or even shameless sentimentality, but what was there to say? What words could possibly be more memorable than the sight of him leaving life with this legendary beast walking by his side?

It was already too late for such conceits. The air thickened, humming with energy and he drew in a deep, final breath. The sharp smell of seaside air and the presence of the Dog pulled him back to a place he thought he had lost. A place of sky and water and loose-limbed freedom. A beach. A beach of smooth, flat pebbles, every one a skimmer – fiver or sixer at least – and Jack, who'd chase anything, dodging through the coils of barbed wire to reach the sea and fetch him back a prize from the lines of shells and driftwood.

Sunshine warmed Jack's coat, the patch of black across his shoulders hottest to the touch as Lawrence grinned and ruffled the dog's scruff. The sparkles on the waves were so bright they hurt his eyes.

So he closed them.

Chapter Twenty seven

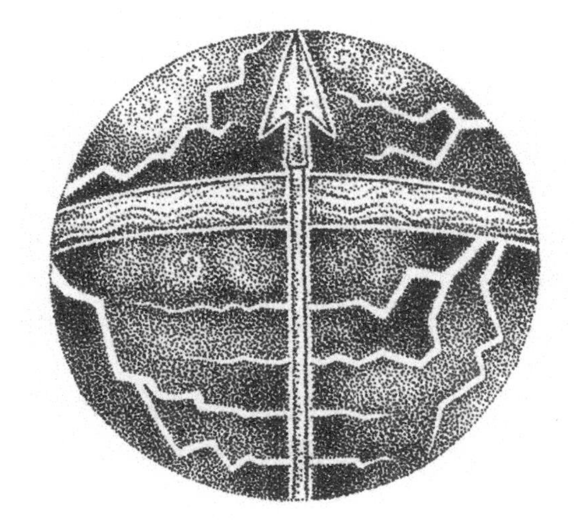

Go!

Catrin raised a hand wreathed in shimmering violet, stroked Shuck, and let slip his leash.

For one faltering heartbeat, one stayed breath, Shuck remained at her side, the enforced connection between them momentarily survived by a willing bond of friendship passed down the generations.

And then with a snarl, the hellhound of Hatiston, eyes ablaze, jaws slavering and teeth bared, turned away from her, ungrateful and indifferent.

§

Peter fell to his knees.

Lawrence his Second, his mentor, his best friend, was dead, and the stone-heavy reality pulled him down. *Why! Why?* Lawrence had defied him, all odds and every expectation, to make this last heroic sacrifice, but by doing so he had stolen Peter's place. 'It should've been me! It was *meant* to be me!'

Megan laid a steadying hand on his shoulder. 'Your Second took your place willingly – don't waste his bravery and his love. Finish your task.'

In desperation he grabbed for her hand, needing comfort and the promise of safety even if it was hollow. Spared the death to which he had resigned, he was suddenly mortally afraid again as the compulsion to live was restored. 'What do I do now? For God's sake tell me what to do!'

'Don't let anyone else die.'

Megan's words were a slap in the face. Guilt, remorse and ego evaporated. Her look commanded him and Peter obeyed.

Catrin lay where she had fallen, an ethereal glow haloing the bloody knife in her fist. She appeared to be holding her breath, waiting for his words – or waiting to die. The Black Dog's influence polluted the hill, making it too easy to contemplate death, making it needful, even desirable; but Peter knew the ends of all the tales, and redemption ran through them like a clear, pure stream.

Catrin's Second had also suffered terribly, and taken a blow meant for her, and so Peter empathised, completely understanding the culpability they shared. He knew what she wanted.

Absolution.

Gently he moved her hands up, and angled the knife so that the incised mark was in her eye-line, but she didn't even register that her view of the skies had been blocked. He leaned in and spoke in her ear. 'It's for you both – for you and the wolves. See?'

The Venus glyph on the grey blade glimmered in the light channelled down through the storm's eye; a binding mark as strong as any aim. To the woman – the wielder – looking at it from the grip, it was a sign of her potential. To the wolf faced by the blade, it was an acknowledgement of its power as the agent of revelation. Venus' mirror inverted to make a circle crowned with a cross, signifying antimony, the wolf of metals.

'Earth it into the Wisht Stone.'

'The... *Wolfstone.*'

Even though Catrin's voice was hardly more than a whisper, Peter caught the deliberate emphasis, and hope flashed through him. He hurried on. 'Tether the wolves to the stone.'

She frowned. 'No.'

Her rejection brought him up short and he looked to Megan for support, but she spoke straight to Catrin instead. 'Offer them a way back into the land.'

Overhearing her intervention, the Smith – with arms still raised in the act of maintaining their protection – shouted over his shoulder. 'Megan! Don't!'

She fought to keep the catch of emotion from her voice. 'I was the one who let the wolves through. I *must* help!'

He shook his head angrily. 'Peter has to be the catalyst!'

Peter's own anger rose like a stifled scream in his throat. He felt an almost irresistible urge to rush for the nearest bow, snatch up a fallen arrow and – even if it meant allying himself with the heretical Forts – take aim at the Smith.

Then with that violent impulse, recognition surged through Peter.

The suppressed electricity crackled, passing through air and flesh, seeking release.

He knew that the Forts had been unable to liberate themselves because, enraged and confused, they had chosen the wrong marks. He now realised that when they had turned on each other it wasn't an aspect of the chaos, but a sign pointing towards its resolution.

Peter grabbed Catrin's shoulders and almost shook her in his exhilaration.

'Listen to me! The Forts must shoot the wolves!'

The Smith lowered his head to conceal a smile.

§

Clouds and wind filled David's thoughts and blew away his concentration. His vision and body were crisscrossed with violet strands that teased out into fine veins spanning his fingers. If he raised his hand the filaments fled upwards, extending his reach to the curved walls of the storm; when he brought it down again the lines forked into the earth like greedy roots.

His longbow glowed like a ship's mast drawing down St Elmo's fire, and he was hypnotized by the beauty of it. He moved his hands through the enveloping aura, testing and exploring the visible bonds that tied him to his weapon, his fingers attracting restless twigs of purple light so that the yew wood seemed to grow once more; a sapling stretching its forked branches up to the sky.

There was nothing in life more important than the yew wood he caressed, nothing to want or need that couldn't be fulfilled by the dark heartwood and the pale sapwood; the seam where they met undulating like slow stirred blood and milk – the line, the cross and the curve, of his arm, the silver-tipped arrow, and the bent bow.

He raised his longbow to the tumult above him. Almost understanding.

Helen backed away from what she saw in the faces of her companions: the Smith had trapped and disarmed them. There could be no protection from her Hallow since every Fort on the hill was now caught in the flickering web that he had conjured from the storm; she was alone in her anguish. The lightning did not wrap her or illuminate her skin with its fey light, though she felt its teasing proximity like the tingle of a lover's touch over her skin and hair. From her singular state Helen observed the captivity of her Hallow with a kind of jealousy; it was the clearest sign that her company – and by definition David – had rejected her. She struggled to control herself, determined to bear the pain and preserve her last scrap of dignity.

In this limbo, where even the reduced standing of freebow was denied her, Helen was pared down to nothing, defined only by the negative space left by everything that had been stolen from her. So when Catrin's demon passed by, with back hunched and savage head swinging low as it tested the air for impending death, Helen almost couldn't stop herself from reaching out just to have it turn on her and make her important enough to kill.

But it moved on to take another life instead, and she had watched the delirious old man from the Stone company stand up to greet his oncoming death, and then fall as if there had been nothing inside his skin and his tweed suit but an abruptly exhaled breath of air.

Tears blurred her eyes, and her surroundings shimmered with colours that ran together and became beautiful under a circle of pearlescent sky; a watery lens of faerie-sight bought at the cost of everything she loved.

And yet.

The sensation of the knife lingered in her clenched fist.

'Helen!'

She turned towards the woman's call with a reflexive fury, but her response died on her lips when she saw what Catrin – crouched and supported by Peter – was holding out.

It was the Venus knife, black with blood, and gripped by the blade so that its handle was offered towards her.

Catrin's quiet voice carried across the top of Silbury Hill, as intimate as a whisper. 'The dagger is yours.'

Helen almost collapsed when the meaning of the words penetrated her defensiveness, but what coursed through her felt more like an earthing shot than elation

– this was nothing more than restitution; if Catrin was expecting a display of fawning gratitude she would be disappointed. A backwash of self-preserving cynicism drowned Helen's hope: it couldn't be a gesture to buy favour, there was nothing in her power to grant, and she was certainly no threat needing to be bought off. Suspicions of further betrayal were stifling Helen's yearning to shout out her acceptance of the knife, but in the end those harsh facts prompted her.

She had nothing left to lose.

Helen set her feet firmly in a shooting stance, and although she wanted to run to the knife and twist it from Catrin's thieving hand, she remained still and straight. Whether or not the noose around the Forts allowed them the awareness to understand, she was going to conduct this exchange for all to witness, in retaliation for the sordid and furtive way it had been taken from her.

'Say *all* the words Catrin!' A protocol had been set in motion that could not be revoked, freeing her from the need to be deferential.

She saw Megan bend to speak to Catrin, who nodded, and then the haggard First of the Stone company added his own whispered comment. Helen didn't care what they thought of her pedantry, the codes were her only insurance.

Helen was fully aware that she had invested too much of herself in the dagger, but she wanted to believe that somehow the crystals within the metal were aligned with a time when she and David were happy. Trying in vain to recapture that affinity, then losing the knife, had followed on inexorably, and yet it remained an icon of hope.

Catrin raised her voice again, without being reproached; speaking as loudly as her dry and strained throat would allow. 'I, Catrin Fitzgerald, First of Silbury Hill, willingly give you, Helen, Sixth of Badbury Rings… this talisman.'

Helen recalled having to force out a version of those same words from her own mouth, and she took pleasure in Catrin's distress before answering. 'I, Helen, Sixth—' and then fell silent. Was she still the Sixth of Badbury Rings? Was this a trick that would cheat her out of the dagger again? She was taken aback by the awful and humbling thought that perhaps Catrin had actually been trying to help her, and instead of gloating, she should have simply walked over and accepted the dagger.

An impatient, shouted order from the Smith broke through her paralysing indecision. 'Go to Catrin, say whatever you want – just take the fucking thing!'

His words goaded her into a trot before she even realised she was moving. She halted in front of Megan – avoiding eye contact and ignoring the Stone's First – then crouched down level with Catrin, who held the dagger at head height between them. Now that it was so close, Helen could see a fine line of purple lightning connecting the blade to the skies. *What am I being given?* Yet her reply came tumbling out, prompted by a fear that didn't have a single root but sprang from as many sources as the filaments of light. 'I willingly accept this talisman.'

And it was done. The dagger was passed over. There was a shift, an infinitesimal fraction of what she had experienced in the room with the Alicorn, and the Venus knife was hers once more.

Helen cradled the talisman in her cupped hands. Then through her requited love surfaced a revulsion for the way the sour-smelling blood of the Dog was fouling her knife. Suddenly the only thing that mattered was to cleanse it of the taint left by all those who had seized the dagger and used it for their own ends: loading the blade with so much corruption that it appeared to be knapped from obsidian instead of cast in brittle white metal. Helen rubbed it through the turf, turning it over and over, wiping this way and that, until the blood darkened the crushed grass in a broad curve around her. But still it wouldn't come clean. She polished it on her clothes, the rough edges snagging threads and ripping holes. She could sense how the venom had seeped between the atoms of the blade and altered the wood of the handle; each pore in the yew wood filled to overflowing, not just with the gore of the Dog, but with the essence of lives long since gone. In frustration she tried scratching and rubbing away the dirt with her nails and fingertips, and only succeeded in adding her own warm contamination to the stain.

The brightening air crackled with electricity. The line of fading violet that reached down from the storm was coiled, caduceus-like, along the length of her dagger, and this tight pulsing spiral drew her concentration away from the filth. Helen brought it close to her face to study its perfection, raising the point towards the sky, and the beauty of the pattern transported her back to a small room lined with roses and filled with the essence of spring. With a smile she opened herself up to its purity.

§

Catrin allowed herself to sink back into Peter's supporting arms. She could feel the fevered trembling of his overworked muscles as he held her up – a disturbingly intimate sensation to share with someone barely more than a stranger – but the strain had at least left him capable of affecting the physical world. If the winds circling her hill tightened any more; narrowing and twisting into a black ribbon, she felt as if there would not be enough substance left in her body for gravity to cling to. She would be snatched up by the wolfstorm and torn to shreds.

Peter was muttering under his breath, the sound vibrating through his chest and into her back. Catrin found the cadence almost comforting, and it flowed over her as if she were a small child listening to the melody of a conversation without understanding the meaning.

Then she watched Helen raise the dagger, and his words resolved.

'...take the grey wolf, the child of Saturn...' Peter spoke as if reciting a charm, placing emphasis seemingly at random through the broken text. '...throw him the body of the King. And when it has swallowed him, build a great fire...'

Catrin gazed around her at the piled arrow shafts, heaped like kindling awaiting a spark.

'...and cast the wolf into the flames.'

'Yes.'

§

Yes.

I understand.

David blinked, liberated from the prison of introspection. The purple glow, dwindling against the morning light, drew his gaze upwards to where the wolves kept manic pace with the gale. He saw them for what they were; kindred spirits in the grip of a power that was older and harder than they were, and trapped within story after story as they were passed from one narrative to the next. Their needs were empathically his, and as he rode the uplifting urge to release them, it was instantly transmuted into a craving to shoot. The instinct pressed down from the skies and forced its way up from the land to meet within him, and the deepening pressure of it made him gasp for air. The wolves and the Forts were one and the same, caught in the same trap, their shared strengths and weaknesses exploited, their essence blending together in the lightning. Every cell in his body hungered to earth this mutual energy.

His Hallow was the closest to the visceral workings of the Covenant and the manifestation of the land's starvation; the first horizontal stroke beneath the bent bow of the rune – it would be an act of devotion to make the ghosts of the wolves his companions. He would summon them to safety, beyond the grasp of the Sanctuaries and the Smith.

David's hand clenched on his longbow; without taking his gaze from the storm he crouched down and felt around for a fallen arrow. The factions within his Hallow were of no consequence at this moment, any arrow would count as his, but he deliberately stayed the impulse to check the branding of the arrow that he picked up, so that conditioning wouldn't break his meditation. David had not experienced such a profound sense of communion with his Hallow since the day he had discovered it, and the exhilaration made him want to join his voice with the banshee scream of the wind – but an even stronger fealty to his talent held him back, keeping his head clear for the task of aiming.

Grey shades upon grey, upon black, upon white, ash and cloud and mist and shadow merged and blended until they offered the mind of the watcher whatever it was willing to see. To David every wolf was a meticulous study in ink engraved onto the blur of the whirling storm wall. He could make out males, proud, thick-tailed and shaggy-necked whose physical strength had been broken by iron, rope and poison; lean she-wolves carrying or trailing the scrabbling pups they had not been able to protect in life; the old and the lame being jostled and overtaken by those in their prime, abandoned again and again each time they were lapped in the headlong rush. All the minute details of fur, claw, needle sharp or yellowed nub teeth; their lolling tongues, pursed and howling lips, drooling jaws and the white-rimmed despair in their eyes. And the blood on their pelts – for each bore a wound, the stigmata of their death. The gore soaked their necks or legs or flanks, shifting from red to violet as it spread through their fur then fled their bodies in a tangle of light.

With his eyes on the storm David laid the arrow on his bow, slid his fingers up the shaft, over the feathers, pinched the nock and then turned it once, key-like, so it bit onto the bowstring.

As if this was the signal they had been waiting for, his company followed suit. And then, in a widening ripple of bending and straightening up, every able companion from the bound Forts picked up a random arrow from the scattered remains of their Hallow's failed attack.

The combined tapping and rustling of so many arrows drawn across yew wood, restored the sigh of trees to a place that hadn't felt the shelter of branches for five thousand years.

David scanned the tumult for a single mark but his senses were quickly overwhelmed by the spinning mass of bodies; as soon as he fixed upon one leaping form another would eclipse it. It was like trying to follow the flight of a single bird inside a panicked, wheeling flock. Still, he raised his bow and bound his mind to the increasing pressure of the string denting his fingertips, keeping faith with the instincts that told him he was right.

The violet strands were now almost invisible, outcompeted by the approaching sunrise. Though the land beneath the cloud cover remained as dark as early dawn, the clear eye above them was brightening to azure, bleaching out the static lightning. And yet David could feel its undiminished electric charge with the smallest motion of his company, his Hallow and the wolves; the tension sliding through his body as if his nerves were threaded with taut metal wire. He closed down, concentrating on his longbow, seeking another dreamlike epiphany, but the superb fury of the purple lightning had waned to a shimmer. He shut his eyes, reaching deeper into the layered veins of energy, attempting to scry an answer from the pattern.

The transfiguration blazed into his mind.

Silver.

The perfect conductivity of their silver-tipped arrows.

It was the singularity he needed.

At once he recognised that there was no need to hunt for an individual mark where there were no meaningful distinctions. The convergence of electrical energy at the point of his arrow was the line of intent already laid out – all he had to do was loose.

The fletchings of the arrow slowly combed along his cheek as he settled his muscles into the shape that came most naturally to him. He locked at full draw and leaned back, aligning his longbow with the sky, the silver arrowhead reflecting the blue so that it seemed as if he were about to launch a lost fragment of the heavens back to itself.

§

Helen's dagger, held like a crosshair over the eye of the storm, was suddenly framed by flying arrows. They hissed past her, the bowstrings that launched them whipping and twanging all around. She could feel the air tearing as they passed, and sensed the heat trails of concentration from the aims. As if she was directing this earthly answering storm, the flight of shafts converged upon the very centre of the whirlwind marked by her blade. The Venus glyph caught the light, and in that moment the simple scratched symbol embodied the one thing left worth preserving: her faith. Helen stretched up her arms, borrowing energy from the skyward rush of arrows to lift the knife as high as she could, extending it in line with her forehead as if it grew from her.

All over the crowded hilltop, figures were stooping to snatch up arrows, nock, draw, aim, loose – the air was filled with intent and fierce elation; yew longbows curving back into crescents then whipping straight; the power of muscle, bone, wood and will combined.

Third arrows were snicked onto bowstrings as the first volley hit its mark.

Agony filled the air, the wailing of the wolves sheared into a multi-faceted scream, but it was a cry of release. The last push, the final breath, the sweet sting of the blinding, ending light.

The second volley streamed through the mass of grey bodies. The ghost forms pierced and tumbled; every arrow of the multitude threading dozens of wolves on its path up into the clear dawn.

The third volley struck.

§

The Smith experienced the strain and release of each shot, breathed thick, electrified air sliced into hissing tatters by arrowheads that his hands had wrought and his Whetstone had consecrated. Here was the ancient bond with the yews given flight by wood and wing; the resurrected lore that gave the means to steal life or to save it, to connect the world they knew with the land they dreamed of. This was the honed skill and perception that bound the past, present and future with the immortality of knowledge.

He clenched his fists tight, holding on, holding back – fulfilled and frustrated by the intimacy with a power that could never exist without him, but which he was forbidden to wield.

The patterns of heat and light that he knew from his craft were written through the air and over the earth and on the rapt faces all around him. Poised on the point of his silver, waiting for his signal. *I gave you magic.*

Now you want alchemy.

He unlocked his fingers, spread them like roots, like branches. He sank to his knees, twisting one hand into the grass and reaching upwards with the other.

§

The last wolf.

Running.

Ragged legs buckle and curl around the cold pain of deliverance, and she bites at the arrow piercing her heart, stripping the black feathers and spiral markings as it passes through the shadow of her body.

She falls.

Home.

The lines of intent flared into life.

Pure white lightning blazed to earth, flashing in jagged pulses along thousands of coruscating paths. And the swirling tunnel of clouds and the crown of Silbury Hill endured an instant upon the furnace face of the sun.

§

Giles raised his arms to shield his eyes against the splendour of the piercing light.

Then the shock of sound, from a thousand thunderbolts striking at once, convulsed the air and shook the ground; slamming shut on him from above and below as if West Kennet had been caught between vast snapping jaws.

He kept his feet and his nerve; allowed the muffled hiss in his ears to subside, and the neon afterimage to fade from his vision, before cautiously focusing on his closest rival.

This was an event that deserved to be savoured.

The Black Dog stood firm at Giles's side, watching him; impervious to the blast.

Chapter Twenty eight

The sun rose.

Like molten gold, it swelled to a dome and dripped up from the horizon, leaving a momentary dab of itself on the earth. It rounded then slowly ascended the sky, its fire at first humble, then swiftly intensifying until its glory could not be looked upon.

The king reborn.

The shreds of the gutted storm burned away under its gaze, the banks of red and purple and turquoise clouds dispersed to a mist that melted into a boundless sky of honey and amber. The wind had wilted to a breeze. By the time the mundane world was awake again, and early morning traffic had normalised the road that curved past Silbury Hill, only the superficial damage from the storm remained as inconvenient tidelines of hedge and tree debris, that scratched paintwork or snapped and popped beneath cautious wheels.

The hill was at peace.

Harebell, rampion, pimpernel, speedwell and modest English orchids adorned the millefleur tapestry that wrapped the chalk; their delicate shapes and colours only revealed if the observer will bow to within kissing distance of the ground; where the air is sweetened by the breath of plants, the rich earth, and the small jewels of creeping life. Where the presence of the land seeps up through the layers of time.

The deep earthen belly of Silbury, round and content. Sated by the sky.

On the summit the trampled grass was being ruffled back upright by the tousling breeze. Almost all other signs had been picked clean, according to duty.

Only three remained.

A brick-shaped hollow in the centre, the depression surrounded with singed and blackened grass, as if a fire had been ignited then instantly extinguished – where an alter stone dedicated to the wolf god Hati, had been driven into the heart of the hill by a hammer of lightning.

At the base of the mound, nestled within the surrounding shallow ditch, thin splinters of watch-glass, and a bead of mercury sitting like a silver dewdrop on the chequered petal of a snakeshead fritillary.

And blood, in small unnoticed smears, being gathered by the ordinary talent of the insects, to be woven back into the pattern of the land.

§

The hollow yew adopted by Badbury Rings, snared the brilliant morning in the mesh of its branches, the pale green of its soft new leaves turning to gold in the beams of the low sun. The encircling elder trees scented the clearing with their rich, herby musk; the warming air was threaded with birdsong, and in the distance hung the single-note tolling of crows.

The mottled light filtering down to the base of the tree burnished raven lines through Judith's hair. She sat, head bowed, leaning against the curved trunk with her eyes closed, apparently sleeping. Balanced across her lap was her silver arrow, curtained by her loose hair. One hand rested on the wand, the other reached through the yew's iron-bound entrance, holding tight to Jed's cold hand.

A sigh came from within the tree. The limp fingers in her grasp twitched, then flexed, animated by something more conscious than the dreams.

She slid her hand from his, carefully so that he wouldn't notice, and stood up.

Jed rose through layers of sleep, the depths now far below and already forgotten. Each breath he drew came a fraction sooner than the last, each heartbeat pushed a drop more blood. But his mind still drifted, and even when he opened his eyes, the dark red heartwood so close to his face was nothing more than another eyelid shielding him from the glare of daybreak. He stared through it unfocussed, unquestioning; engrossed in the conversations of the dwindling dawn chorus. A robin was singing up in the yew's canopy, and the pure notes felt like rain on the bare skin of his face and arms.

Jed?

'Jed?'

The voice was quieter than the birds, hardly more than a whisper, but it brought him fully awake in an instant. He drew in a shocked breath and tried to sit up.

Searing pain in his chest felled him again.

'Don't move. Not yet.'

Judith's gentle touch, so warm in comparison to his chilled skin that it was like sunlight, soothed the scar left by Helen's arrow.

Distress shunted his memories forwards. They piled into him, out of sequence, undeniable, unwanted. He scrubbed at his face and neck with trembling hands as if he could rub them away. *No!* That kind of treachery was unthinkable – beyond the pale. Lawrence's lowest conceivable benchmark sprang to mind *'Even the basest of the Forts'* but Judith was Second of a Sanctuary, surely she wouldn't betray someone in the Lore like that? *Not Judith… not my Judy…*

'Jed.' She leaned close, her heat nourishing his depleted body, a gift she knew he couldn't help but accept. 'You are not in love with me.'

Her words felt like silver: cold, sharp. Accurate.

When he looked up out of the cowl of his hands, she had her arrow raised between them. And with one small cutting motion, he was free.

§

Peter allowed the tears to track down his face unwiped, and dry on his hollow, stubbled cheeks. Every time he thought he had overcome his grief, another wave would crash and leave him floundering. He had managed to control himself previously because he had been so immersed in the compulsion to follow his path and serve the needs of the Lore and the land. The collateral damage was to be dealt within the aftermath – himself included.

When the connections between the stories had finally been revealed, he'd been enraptured, and they had overtaken all other considerations. Because he had been so close to death, he hadn't fully recognised its workings on the summit of Silbury Hill.

Now his focus had opened out again he saw everything with a painful clarity. This awareness revealed every part of him – an explicit and merciless exposure. He found himself craving darkness, and tried to find it at Ninestones. But by the time he'd arrived, the cover of night had already been torn into long shadows by the trees growing around his stone circle, and was repeatedly sliced by the metal of traffic on the road that passed by his site. He felt an empathy with the dregs of the stream separating his stones from the road: once running glass-clear over pebbles, with vivid pennants of weed waving in the current, it was now hardly more than a wet ditch. For the first time since he had bonded with his site, Ninestones held no solace.

All the immediate practicalities of Lawrence's death had been taken care of. Peter's input had been that of a mediator, nothing more. Glastonbury had quietly stepped in, overseeing all the extra protection and misdirection needed for when the Bowlore crossed into the mundane world. It was not a caring gesture on their part, it was to ensure that in his weakened state and dazed by sorrow, he didn't make any mistakes.

Peter had no illusions as to the nature of the Sanctuary wing being held over him, but he was grateful for it nonetheless.

And so it was that Lawrence had apparently died of a heart-attack during the night; his face so untroubled he looked to be only asleep when Peter had called on him first thing in the morning.

The standard procedures were set in motion: doctor, relatives, funeral directors, solicitors, wills – all the secular rituals put in place before Peter excused himself away from the artificiality, and from having to witness a good and brave man – his best friend – being comprehensively reduced to everything that he had cared nothing for.

Lawrence was gone – lost beyond the redemption of the Covenant.

Peter cupped the ashes of Lawrence's longbow and scattered them in pinches of grey upon each standing stone. He shook the last wisps of dust into the air at the centre of the ring, where they danced for a moment before slipping away into the trees.

At the base of the stone embraced by the stump of the felled beech tree, he scoured a hollow into the earth with his bare fingers. When it was deep enough, he took out Lawrence's silver hip flask, and laid it in the ground so that the engraving of three arrows bound by a branch of yew, faced into the dead roots and against the stone.

He pushed the soil back over it, pressed it down, and then disguised the disturbed earth with twigs and leaves.

With nothing left behind to show that he had ever been there, Peter turned and walked away.

§

Megan gazed from her garden up towards Glastonbury Tor. The shape of it always gave her comfort: the coned hill with its rectangular tower, as simple as a child's drawing of a castle on a mount, offering an accessible path into a complex and depthless truth. It was a gateway to the otherworld, to the inner realms – it always had been, and always would be. Its calming permanence was a salve to what she was feeling.

'Ninestones is gone.'

The Smith nodded. 'What do you want to do?' He was lying on his back on the lawn, enjoying the sunshine, his head pillowed on his rolled-up coat. His face was relaxed and his eyes closed, but his hands, with fingers linked together over his chest, were a livid red, and his nails engrained with soot and earth.

'We need to let this run its course – I don't think we should interfere.'

The Smith yawned and shrugged himself deeper into the soft grass. 'That's fine by me.'

Chapter Twenty nine

Helen shivered.

Something like a cross between recognition and a mark swept through her. She closed down her reactions. The pavement seat of a busy side-street café was not the best place to act irrationally.

David arrived, walking with head high and hands in pockets like nothing mattered. He nodded a greeting through the open door, but gave no acknowledgement to Helen before slumping down onto a chair beside her and scraping it up to the table. Without looking at her he took out his tin and proceeded to roll a cigarette. 'Want one?'

'No.'

Too much had happened between them – because of them – almost all of it beyond their control, and it was impossible to interact normally. Their shared experience had marooned them in a place where ordinary life had burned away and couldn't be restored or even feigned. This was the second day and the fifth time that Helen had tried to arrange a meeting – and the first one that David had actually turned up for.

'I need an answer.' Helen stared straight ahead. She sensed rather than saw his fingers falter. He dumped the paper back down and pushed the tin away, then stood up. For a second she thought he was leaving, but instead he went into the cafe.

Helen leaned back and stared up at the cloudless sky, watching the tiny paper-darts of gulls riding a thermal far above. Their slow spiralling added to her unease.

He came back holding two mugs brimming with dark brown tea, still eddying from being stirred, and set them down on the table. The steam rose in twin plumes that twined together before evaporating.

'David, it's alright, I forgive you for... everything.' As she spoke the words, she found to her surprise that they were true.

'What makes you think I want your forgiveness?'

Helen allowed her emotions to settle. 'Please, let's not do it this way, I've come here as a... as your friend.'

David raised his eyebrows, but didn't look up from fidgeting with his tin.

They both reached for their mugs, and spent long minutes sipping and staring ahead.

With a sigh Helen put her tea down first. 'Make me a freebow.'

'No.'

'I don't want to defect from Badbury – it would be wrong. The wrong path for me, *and* you. I need your blessing.'

'I'm not prepared to give it.'

'Why?'

David finished rolling his cigarette, lit it and then shook his head as if dissatisfied with the taste. He stubbed it out on the edge of the table. 'I need to unite the company, it's the only way to get through this.'

She understood his reaction. Long before this upheaval, the savage resurgence of the Bowlore had left its mark on him.

He slipped his tin into his pocket and shifted back from the table. 'You're too much of a risk.'

His worries flattered her. The power she had found on Silbury Hill had seen her through the fires of hell, kept her holding the Venus knife as the yew handle burned and its antimony blade melted, dripping though her fingers and back into the carved storm clouds, the full moon and Hati, on the face of the Wolfstone.

Now it insulated her against her greatest vulnerability.

'Let me go, David.'

He turned to her, and for a second his eyes held the openness she remembered wanting. It wasn't enough. He leaned in, stroked the curve of her face, but she pulled away.

'If you love me – make me a freebow.' A despicable move in any other situation, with any other person. The words he had never said: could she wrest them from him, could she win?

David closed down. And she felt him smother the warmth he had allowed to show. He moved his chair back, drained his mug of tea and set it in the centre of the table, then nodded almost imperceptibly.

'You're a freebow.'

She smiled.

A draw.

§

Blake stood at the front door of the cottage that his grandmother had left him, and let the sun warm his back. The scar from Gareth's arrow ached when he stretched, but he didn't let it stop him from tending the white roses growing around the porch.

As if responding to a second spring they were sending out more shoots and buds than he had ever seen. Even in his childhood visits, when all the roses seemed huge and thorny enough to hide a fairytale castle, he couldn't remember such abundance. Peacock, red-admiral and small blue butterflies basked on the warm stone of the cottage walls, opening and closing the books of their wings, and bumblebees hummed their frustration at the windows, tapping the glass as if wanting to be let in.

The simple pleasure of being surrounded by burgeoning life almost made him happy. If he had possessed the power to choose a form for that life, then he truly would have been content, but there was a void in his heart that nothing would ever fill. And then an image of Helen's face at the moment she set eyes on the cottage came back to him: her brief unguarded delight, so much like his wife's that he had needed to look away. He allowed the sting of that thought to subside and be assimilated, like the catch of pain from his new scar.

He was yet to decide whether being at the centre of a quest to replace the Thirteen Treasures was a solace or irony, when what he truly cherished was irreplaceably lost.

Blake became aware of a hopeful stare at his back, using the extra sense developed by anyone owning an old and pretty house in the village of Avebury.

The visitor raised her camera by way of asking permission, Blake nodded with a smile and then retreated inside.

As he closed the heavy door he wondered how the woman might react if she knew that the quaint English cottage she was photographing sheltered a unicorn's horn.

§

Giles allowed the elemental to nuzzle at his neck: a gesture copied from ordinary dogs, but coming from this beast, far more threatening. A lick or a bite – either could follow. He tightened his control. It sat down and its head remained level with his own, its breath panting in sulphurous gusts. He praised it with a cautious pat: the dried blood had made knives of its hair.

Saint Agnes' church appeared calm in the sunlight, the shadows from the great yew a gentle green dappling over the walls and roof. The centuries of oppressive secrets had been blown away, and it was just a humble and forgotten chapel, lost in the English countryside.

But it had the misfortune to be the only place in the land where Giles could tether the Black Dog.

The hefty iron ring handle that lifted the latch had rusted solid, and there was no feasible way of breaking through the seasoned oak of the door. Giles studied it closely, tracing his forefinger along the grain of the wood around the lock, following the lines into the tight spiral of a knot. The Dog stood up again as Giles' concentration shifted, its bulk filling the small porch of the chapel and blocking the daylight. He glared at it until it backed away a step and dropped its gaze.

Then he reached into the inside pocket of his coat and, after a moment, pulled out a long silver hairpin. The Dog pricked its ragged ears and let out a low whine, but kept its head down. Giles ignored it.

He disregarded the obvious option of using the pin to pick the lock, in favour of accessing the more oblique nature of the talisman. Holding it like a pen, Giles scratched the handle with the ogham rune of the Bowlore. Drawn into his realm, the door was his to open.

He held the cold iron ring, turned it. The latch lifted with a click.

He pushed, and the broad door swung wide. It was unlocked, not to a scene that the structure of the building had been made to receive: the Sunday faithful, a wedding party, a christening or funeral procession, but to an old and unforgiving native of the land over which the church was built.

It walked through the doorway – then paused to mark the threshold in the way of all dogs, real or supernatural – before loping up to the rain-filled font and lapping noisily at the green water.

Giles braced himself. This part would not be easy, even with his talent.

Most Black Dogs could be summoned and then sent back to their tracks and pathways, but this one was imbued with more than its inherent nature. Too many minds had touched and influenced it – minds capable of using the elemental as a route back to him.

The Dog would have to be dispersed.

Subtly, slowly, so that the Dog wouldn't notice, Giles reached down through the patterned floor tiles, through the mortar, the clay, the lead-cased skeletons, and the stone foundations of the church; to the original level of the ancient trackway. Then deeper still to the bedrock – the bones of the land. There, in his element, within the essence of his Hallow, he found a tiny fault line and teased it open.

The Dog stopped drinking and swung its massive head around, jowls dripping, head cocked quizzically.

Giles firmed his grip on the unseen edges below him.

The Dog's eyes blazed with fury. With a roar that echoed off the suppurating walls, it launched itself at him, claws scrabbling for purchase on the slimy, leaf-strewn floor.

Giles tore the fault open.

A shockwave heaved the ground, windows splintered, beams cracked, loose stones and slates crumbled and fell. The great yew tree shuddered and its topmost branches whiplashed, raining leaves over the church and graveyard.

The Dog made a last desperate leap, but Giles heaved the door with both hands and all of his strength, slamming it shut in the elemental's demonic, gaping face.

The wood shuddered under the impact, the crash thundering around the church. Giles stepped back, the echoes died, and there was silence. Then came a furious scratching that threatened to wrench the door off its massive iron hinges: the snarling, yelping frenzy of a trapped animal. He could hear long gouges being stripped from the oak by teeth and claws, the screech of iron bolts being torn out and creak of metal straps being ripped off.

The door wouldn't hold for long.

Giles pushed the trackway into the fault. It plunged snaking into the void.

The Dog fell quiet.

The bulging door settled back in its frame. A single loosened bolt dropped to the floor of the church, rolled, and was still.

A bright blue light suddenly pierced through the cracks around the door and beamed through the keyhole. Giles bent down to look through it and into the church, keeping his eye as far from the hole as possible.

He saw a sphere of light drifting above the nave. It radiated long, pivoting shadows that rendered the carved pews and statues ghastly, and made the stretched lips of the green-man faces, peering down from the beams, look like they were mouthing fearful warnings.

The ball-lightning drifted slowly, wavering from side to side as if confused or searching. It reached the altar and floated motionless, hypnotic and beautiful, illuminating the gothic arches, the wet stonework, and the jagged jewels of the broken windows. Then it sank down, little by little, to gently touch the dais.

The explosion sent Giles reeling backwards. A concussion of scorching air and stone shrapnel blasted wide the heavy oak door.

The Black Dog of Hatiston was vanquished.

Chapter Thirty

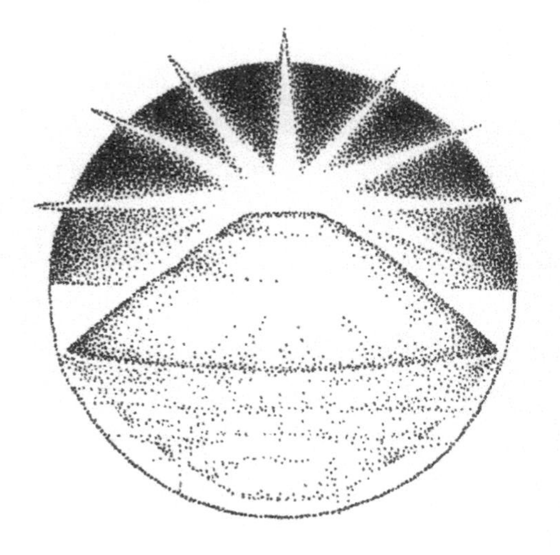

Gold.

The unfound riches hammered by forging minds into the shape of King Sil, bound to the Land by the strong limbs of his horse.

It rears up and sidesteps thieving thrusts into the Hill and bears the King into the quiet places, where the only sound is the deep echo of antler picks and the tumble of white rocks. The gold of its hide slides through the polishing chalk and its animal strength shields the King.

The spirit of the Hill.

Patrick falls screaming through layers of agony, drawn down by an arrow, conducted by the piercing oak tree that steered the raising of the Hill – through grass and earth, stone and chalk, burning in the white fire that follows him down.

Warm metal, shaped and fitted, catches his memory, holds and protects him, carries him away from the Blade of lightning and the binding Stone.

When enough of his mind is gathered, Patrick sees the Stone, an incandescent diamond, planted within the belly of his Hill, watches the Pack falling into the welcoming womb, then birthing back into the Land.

And as he is watching, the finest grains of white chalk filter the poison from him, they sift and purify.

Turn him to Gold.

§

Catrin climbed Silbury Hill. She chose the side furthest from the road, and kept low so as not to attract the attention of outsiders. It was early afternoon, not a time she would normally choose for a visit, but her hill was calling; and like a lover caught in the first mad infatuation of a relationship, she couldn't stay away.

Catrin stroked her hands through the feathery tussocks of grass as she pushed upwards. The sunshine on her back and the exertion made her sweat, and she was grateful for the breeze blowing across Salisbury Plain. The gentle wind carried the normal scents of wheat fields and woodland, and the sporadic, underlying taint of traffic. But with these came something else: a synaesthetic perception, manifesting somewhere between smell and taste and touch – as if her mind was still trying to select a sense through which to experience the information.

She caught the dark musk of dug ground, the mineral flavour of rock, the pressure of a lurking power fortified and preserved: West Kennet. But it was mingled with a lighter taste, a stony variation of her own site, and recognition thrilled through her body. This was the presence of Avebury, the closest site in her Hallow – no longer the haughty blank it used to be, but open and responsive.

A skylark poured its song into the air.

It was hard to filter all the other influences surrounding her. What she had previously taken for dowsing was nothing to the awareness she now possessed.

Catrin had been warned that this unbridled flow would be a disadvantage, perhaps even a danger, until it was properly harnessed.

Long conversations with Megan had armed her with the knowledge she needed to take her through this vulnerable waking stage; this second, fine-tuning of her site. '*Watch and wait.*' Megan had been insistent. '*Put down roots.*' The path would show itself in due time.

Catrin reached the summit. She stood with arms wide as the breeze snatched at her clothes and hair, letting the wind carry away the darker imagery lingering on Silbury. The memories kept encroaching on her consciousness – in blinks – *whirling skies* – she shut her eyes fleetingly against the glare of the sun – *screaming for Patrick* – raised a hand to flick a strand of fringe away from her face – *flaming arrows – lightning* – and was suddenly knocked to the ground by a bounding rush of energy.

Catrin had a momentary, vivid impression of a massive dog, transported with joy, leaping around her.

Then it was gone.

Two figures crested the hilltop and came running over. 'What the hell happened! Are you alright?' With each one gripping an arm they hauled her to her feet.

'Yes, I'm fine.' Catrin shook her head, dazed. 'I… I think it was Shuck.'

Leah's face blanched. 'I thought we were safe up here.'

Patrick smiled.

'We are.'